THE STA...
SOMETHI...

Unless you ...
at the trial, ... idea
what Hannan Liebling looks like.
And it's unlikely that you were among
the spectators. Because of the prominence
of the individuals involved, it would have
been easy enough to have turned that
trial into a national sensation.

But let's go back to last January.
Before all the trouble.
Before the trial . . .

*The Wrong Kind
of Money*

STEPHEN BIRMINGHAM

The Wrong Kind of Money

AN ONYX BOOK

ONYX
Published by the Penguin Group
Penguin Putnam Inc., 375 Hudson Street,
New York, New York 10014, U.S.A.
Penguin Books Ltd, 27 Wrights Lane,
London W8 5TZ, England
Penguin Books Australia Ltd, Ringwood,
Victoria, Australia
Penguin Books Canada Ltd, 10 Alcorn Avenue,
Toronto, Ontario, Canada M4V 3B2
Penguin Books (N.Z.) Ltd, 182–190 Wairau Road,
Auckland 10, New Zealand

Penguin Books Ltd, Registered Offices:
Harmondsworth, Middlesex, England

Published by Onyx, an imprint of Dutton Signet,
a member of Penguin Putnam Inc.
Previously published in a Dutton edition.

First Onyx Printing, May, 1998
10 9 8 7 6 5 4 3 2 1

REGISTERED TRADEMARK—MARCA REGISTRADA

Printed in the United States of America

PUBLISHER'S NOTE
This is a work of fiction. Names, characters, places, and incidents either are
the product of the author's imagination or are used fictitiously, and any resem-
blance to actual persons, living or dead, events, or locales is entirely
coincidental.

BOOKS ARE AVAILABLE AT QUANTITY DISCOUNTS WHEN USED TO PROMOTE
PRODUCTS OR SERVICES. FOR INFORMATION PLEASE WRITE TO PREMIUM MAR-
KETING DIVISION, PENGUIN PUTNAM INC., 375 HUDSON STREET, NEW YORK, NEW
YORK 10014.

For Caitlin

PART ONE

River House, 1994

1

Nine Lives

Unless you happened to be a spectator at the trial, you probably have no idea what Hannah Liebling looks like. And it's unlikely that you were among the spectators. Because of the prominence of the individuals involved, it would have been easy enough to have turned that trial into a national sensation. But, thanks to the shrewd public-relations work of Miss Bathy Sachs—of whom you'll hear more later—the more sensational aspects of the case were played down, and spectators were kept to an absolute minimum. It was no coincidence that Judge Ida Kaminsky, who heard the case, was assigned the smallest courtroom in New York County, with very limited seating. The right to a jury trial was waived because, as Bathy correctly put it, "When you've got a defendant who might be guilty, you want a jury. But when you have a defendant you know is innocent, it's better to let a judge decide." And it was no coincidence that, throughout the proceedings, the matter was referred to as a homicide and not a murder. As Bathy said, "All murders are homicides. But not all homicides are murders." Was it a coincidence that the judge assigned to the case was a woman? You decide.

Television or other cameras were not allowed in Judge Kaminsky's courtroom. Of course, the press and public could not be completely excluded, and courtroom sketch artists were able to capture Hannah Liebling's bulk, but not much else. They were not able to capture the fiery iciness in her blue eyes. They were not able to capture her commanding presence, though the few reporters who managed to find seating space tried to describe it for their readers. They were not able to capture what can only be called Hannah's heroic *poise*, her sense of self.

When the county prosecutor produced, for a second

time, the lethal weapon, she did not flinch. When he showed—*again!*—the photographs of the bloodied corpse blown up, in color, on the screen, many people averted their eyes. Not Hannah. She gazed expressionlessly at the screen, her face a mask. Has she no heart? people asked. Is she a woman devoid of human feelings?

Judge Kaminsky kindly set aside a small room adjacent to her courtroom for the use of family members during some of the more troubling parts of the testimony, and some members of the family repaired to this room from time to time. But Hannah—never. She was there day after day, calmly, collectedly, sitting in the seat that had been assigned to her, taking in every word, occasionally scribbling short notes to herself on a pad of paper. She had made a point, in the trial, of not being represented by any legal counsel. And when it came to her turn to testify she strode, almost regally, to the witness box, in her hat, her gloves, in her long mink coat, with her reticule slung over her left arm. She removed her right glove to be sworn in, and repeated her oath in a clear, strong voice. And when she began to testify, she did so in an accent that immediately caused the prosecutor to appear deferential, even shy, in her presence. He addressed her as "ma'am."

"In whose name is this weapon licensed, ma'am?" he asked her.

"Mine."

"And who gave this weapon to the defendant, ma'am?"

"I did."

No sketch artist could ever replicate that voice.

"*May-huhn.*"

Mrs. Hannah Liebling speaks with the kind of Old New York accent that has almost disappeared from the Manhattan scene. It is an accent that is a product both of Hannah's generation and social class, and as a result, it is spoken nowadays mostly by dowagers and grandes dames, both of which she is qualified to label herself, though she never would. ("Well, I *have* been called a doyenne," she once told a reporter.)

This accent, peculiar to New York City, where it evolved after the Civil War, involves a flattening and protracting of certain vowel sounds, turning short vowels into diphthongs. Take the word *bird*, or the word *word*. These become *buh-uhd* and *wuh-uhd*. There is a perceptible hint of what we call Brooklynese here, and also an echo of the Old South, as well as something that might have been borrowed from the German in that invisible umlaut. Hannah, it might be added, comes by all these influences naturally. Her great-grandfather, the first Marcus Sachs, emigrated to these shores from the Rhenish Palatinate and settled in Montgomery, Alabama, where he became a cotton broker before moving his family north after the war. The first Marcus Sachs actually kept slaves—not many, but three or four—and, following the principles of Deuteronomy, these were always manumitted after seven years of servitude, as Hannah Liebling is always careful to point out whenever the subject comes up, though it rarely does. As for Brooklyn, Hannah was born in one of those fine old houses on Prospect Park, a neighborhood that is now almost entirely black. But let's go back to last January, before all the trouble, before the trial.

Hannah Liebling is sitting now in the backseat of her Lincoln Town Car as it moves slowly down Park Avenue in heavy traffic. The rainy street ahead of them is a glittery sea of red brake lights refracted by the Lincoln's wiper blades. "Perhaps, Mr. Nelson," she says to her chauffeur, "it would have been better if we'd gone down Third." *Thuh-uhd.*

"Perhaps, Mrs. Liebling," he agrees. He does not point out to her that Third Avenue is, and has been for many years, a one-way uptown thoroughfare. After all, Hannah Liebling can remember when all the avenues in New York were two-way. The other two passengers in the Lincoln's backseat do not point this out to her, either.

These are Hannah Liebling's older son, Cyril—pronounced "Kyril"—and her granddaughter, Anne, who is just eighteen. Anne is the daughter of Hannah's younger son, Noah. Hannah often calls Anne her Little Bird. *Littuhl buh-uhd.* It is an accent that surely, in another generation's time, will have disappeared altogether.

"Sit up straight, Cyril dear," Hannah Liebling says

now, tapping him sharply on the knee with a white-gloved fingertip. "Don't slouch. Good posture is so important. It keeps the internal organs in alignment, and it's so easy to do. All it requires is practice."

Cyril straightens up, just slightly. His slouch is deliberate because he knows it irritates his mother. Though, at six feet four, Cyril instinctively ducks his head before passing through most doorways, he affects a scholarly stoop when in his mother's presence. "And straighten your necktie, dear," his mother says, reaching out to do this for him. Actually, Cyril is a fastidious dresser, but just before being picked up by his mother's car this evening, he had deliberately skewed his tie, confident that his mother would notice this and take him to task for it.

"And tie your left shoelace, dear."

She caught this, too. In the dark backseat of the car, Cyril smiles to himself.

"Appearances are so important," Hannah says. "We are judged by how we appear to other people. Actually, bad posture runs in my family. My father—your great-grandfather, Little Bird—had terrible posture. I actually think it shortened his life. When he died, the doctors said his internal organs were out of alignment. I also think bad posture may have killed my sister Settie. Settie had a tendency to slouch."

"Why would a slouch have killed your sister, Nana Hannah?" Anne asks her.

"Haven't I told you the peculiar way your great-aunt Settie died? It was most peculiar."

"No," says Anne. "What was so peculiar about it?"

With the back of his hand Cyril suppresses a faint yawn. His mother catches this and gives him a sharp look. But, after all, he has often heard how his aunt Settie died. From the front seat, Mr. Nelson looks straight ahead as the traffic inches forward. He, too, knows how Settie Kahn died, just as he knows many other of this family's secrets, but his job is to drive and not listen, though he is perfectly capable of doing both things at the same time.

"Was there a scandal, Nana Hannah?" Anne asks her grandmother eagerly.

"No, there wasn't any scandal," her grandmother says. "But it was a tragedy, a terrible tragedy, and I still believe that if it hadn't been for that slouch of hers, she'd be here with us today."

Cyril Liebling, who has resumed his own slouch in the backseat, sniffs audibly, and his mother gives him another sharp look.

"Tell me about her, Nana."

"You see, my sister Settie had everything—beauty, brains, a perfect husband, a perfect marriage, two beautiful homes, all the money in the world—"

"She was a vain, stupid, money-grubbing bitch," Cyril says.

"Hush, Cyril. She was *not*! She was beautiful from her soul outward. She had a beautiful, swanlike grace, and it was like watching a dancer to watch her move."

"When she walked into a room, she was like a star stepping out for a curtain call."

Cyril's mother ignores this. "But Settie had one flaw, or imagined she did. She thought—imagined, really—that her, well, that her *fronts* were too big. She grew up, you see, in the flapper era, when it was fashionable for women to have very flat fronts. Women taped themselves to make their fronts appear flatter. There was an artist named John Held, who always drew women with very flat fronts, and every woman wanted to look like a John Held drawing. Fortunately, I was three years younger than Settie, and so I escaped all that. But Settie, who thought her fronts were too big, used to scrunch her shoulders together to make her—fronts—seem less prominent. That accounted for the slouch. Actually, her fronts were a perfectly normal size." She touches her own ample bosom in demonstration.

"Anyway, her best feature was her long, swanlike neck, and, just by coincidence, there was a finial at the end of the stair rail in her apartment at fourteen East Seventieth that was in the shape of a swan's head, carved out of ivory. The staircase curved between the two floors of the apartment, and I always admired that lovely swan's head at the top of the banister it had blue jade eyes and a rather wistful expression on its face. Settie's eyes were also blue, and she also had a kind of wistful expression sometimes—for which I can hardly blame her, considering what she had to put up with from Leo Kahn! Anyway, she had a lovely silver satin pelisse trimmed with chinchilla that she often wore at home in the afternoons. And one afternoon, in December of 1937, she was wearing that pelisse, and she started down the stairs. . . . I have a mental picture of her, her shoulders scrunched together, with that little slouch of hers. The sleeve of her pelisse must have caught in the ivory swan's head, and it pulled her off her balance. She fell, caught by the stair rail, and she was instantly killed. Instantly killed, the doctors said. The ivory swan's neck also broke off in the fall. So there was my beautiful, blue-eyed swan, destroyed by another beautiful, blue-eyed swan. Rabbi Magnus spoke of this in his eulogy at her services." Hannah Liebling dabs her eyes.

In the backseat, Cyril Liebling draws an imaginary bow across his crooked arm as though stroking a violin.

"What a sad story, Nana Hannah," Anne says softly. "I wish I could have known her."

"Yes," she says. "Yes, it was. Very sad."

"What happened to Uncle Leo?"

"He married again. Much too soon, of course. I never saw him after Settie's funeral. Later, I read he died. If Leo hadn't been in Seattle when it happened, I would have sworn he had something to do with it. He was a dreadful man. But the only person in the house with her when she died was Celestine, her French maid."

"Actually, I suppose he did have something to do with it," Cyril says, slumping deeper in his seat. "He was always making remarks about her big boobs. And he bought her that dressing gown—or pelisse, as you call it. With those big, dangerous sleeves."

"But I thought you said she had a perfect marriage, Nana," Anne says. "I thought you said he was a perfect husband."

"Well, he was the right *kind* of husband, was what I meant. After all, he was a Kahn. Otto Kahn was a cousin. But he wasn't very nice to poor Settie."

"Screwed every showgirl in New York," Cyril says matter-of-factly. "Other than that, I found him quite a jolly old chap."

"Now, Cyril, we don't have any proof of that," his mother says. "And don't use vulgar language in front of the child."

"Otto did the same. All the Kahn men did. It was a Kahn family trait."

"And I'm not a child, Nana," Anne says.

"My point is, it's important to choose a husband from one's own world," Hannah says. "Settie did that. In fact, Settie married up. Of course, I had to be the rebel. I married down."

"But I thought Grandpa had pots and pots of money, Nana."

"Oh, it has nothing to do with *money*," Hannah says. "It has to do with one's being of the right *sort.* I was a Sachs, you see. We were of the right sort. Sachs, Saks, Seixas, Saxe-Coburg-Gotha—we're all connected. You have royal relatives, Little Bird, on my side of the family. They say the best Jews come from Frankfurt, where the Sachses came from—not from Odessa, or wherever my husband's people came from."

"Daddy says we're only secular Jews, so it doesn't matter," Anne says.

"Well, my husband used to say that once a man has ten million dollars he's no longer thought of as being Jewish. He's merely thought of as being rich."

"Of course, they were both wrong," Cyril says. "Both my brother and my father. If it's the wrong kind of money, and you're the wrong kind of Jew, it makes all the difference in the world."

Hannah says nothing, merely stares straight ahead. She knows the sort of thing to which Cyril is alluding. There have been episodes, episodes from the past, that would be better off forgotten. There was the time, for instance, when Jules and Hannah Liebling were buying the apartment at 1000 Park Avenue, on the northwest corner of Eighty-fourth Street. One thousand Park is a massive brown brick box, one of the great Park Avenue buildings put up before the First World War. Flanking the entrance are two Gothic figures, one a medieval warrior and the other a builder, replete with Masonic symbolism. More terra cotta figures, executed in a baroque manner, depict the builders of medieval cathedrals and Greek temples. The apartment itself was large—fourteen rooms and seven baths. The front rooms had views of the East River and, in the back, even the servants' rooms had views of Central Park and the reservoir. The apart-

ment was being sold by Richard McCurdy, the pharmaceuticals tycoon. The price was $200,000, which was a
lot of money in the 1940s. Today, apartments like Hannah's are priced in the millions.

In those days there were certain New York buildings
that were known not to want Jewish tenants. But, it was
thought, north of Seventy-sixth Street, attitudes were
more forbearing.

Mr. Truxton Van Degan III, of the building's board,
contacted Jules Liebling. "I'm sorry, Mr. Liebling," he
said, "but your application has been rejected by the
board."

"May I ask why?" Jules Liebling asked him.

"The board of a cooperative may reject any applicant
without stating any reason," Mr. Van Degan said.

"Surely it's not financial," Jules said. He had submitted documents to the board indicating a net financial
worth of at least $10,000,000, which he assumed would
be quite sufficient. "If necessary, I can produce evidence
of additional assets," he said.

"The building is not required to tell you why you were
rejected," Mr. Van Degan said again.

"Mr. Solomon Brinckmann, the investment banker,
owns an apartment in your building. He is a Jew. So I
assume that the reason is not because I am Jewish,"
Jules said.

"I'm sorry, but I can tell you nothing more," Mr. Van
Degan said.

"In fact, Mr. Brinckmann is on your board, is he not?"

"That is correct, Mr. Liebling."

"May I ask how Mr. Brinckmann voted?"

"I am not required to tell you how any board member
voted," Mr. Van Degan said. "But I can tell you that
Mr. Brinckmann voted with the majority."

"I see," said Jules.

"I believe there was a general feeling that one family
of your sort in the building was enough," Mr. Van
Degan said. "That another family might start a trend.
Of the wrong sort, as Mr. Brinckmann put it."

"I see," Jules said again.

"I'm sorry, Mr. Liebling."

"Let me ask you one question," Jules said. "I understand the building badly needs a new roof. Your board

wants to assess the tenants twenty-five dollars per square foot of floor space to pay for this. The tenants on the lower floors, who are not affected by the leaks, feel this is unfair. They feel the costs should be borne by the upper-floor tenants only. There have been many angry tenants' meetings about this. Am I correct?"

"That is correct, Mr. Liebling."

"And of course the longer the tenants fight about this, the worse the roof will get, and the more expensive it's going to be to repair it. Correct?"

"Sadly, sir. Yes."

"Suppose you were to tell your board that if they will reconsider my application, I will be personally willing to pay for the new roof?"

There was a pause on the other end of the line. Then Mr. Van Degan said, "I'm sorry, but you cannot bribe your way into a building like ours. It's been tried before, Mr. Liebling."

"Bribe? An act of generosity is a bribe? Let me ask you one more question. Mr. Stuyvesant Miller, of Miller Publications, is president of your board. Correct?"

"Yes. Correct."

"That magazine he just bought—*City Lights,* I believe it's called. It's not doing as well as Mr. Miller hoped. That new editor he brought in from England. She hasn't been able to turn the magazine around the way he hoped she would. Advertising revenues are down. The bottom line looks very bad. You might mention to Mr. Miller that I may be forced to cancel my advertising because of this situation."

"What situation, Mr. Liebling?"

"The situation I have just outlined to you."

"You would cancel your advertising in *City Lights*?"

"No. I would cancel in all Miller publications. There are seven of these, actually, in which my company advertises."

"I see," Mr. Van Degan said carefully.

"Mention that to Mr. Miller, won't you?"

There was another, longer pause. Then he said, "Very well."

"You do that," Jules said.

A few days later, there was another call from Truxton

Van Degan. "The board has accepted your application," he said in a pained voice.

"I see," Jules said.

"And your generous offer to pay for the new roof."

"Sorry, but that offer has been withdrawn," Jules said. "But I will be happy to purchase the McCurdy apartment for a hundred and fifty thousand dollars."

"Sir! The price of the McCurdy unit is two hundred thousand!"

"It just went down," Jules said. "I happen to know that Richard McCurdy is seven months delinquent in his maintenance payments. He's scrambling for money to pay off his wife in what could become a very messy divorce suit. He's also a vice president of Miller Publications, and Stuyvie Miller won't be very pleased to see some of McCurdy's wife's accusations if they hit the newspapers. I also know that your fancy building isn't very happy with the—shall I say, caliber?—of the young men Mr. McCurdy has been—shall I say, entertaining? shall I say shacking up with?—since his wife moved out on him. I happen to know that your building would do anything to be rid of McCurdy and his friends. Am I correct?"

"What—?" Truxton Van Degan sputtered. "What—what do you call this, Mr. Liebling? What do you call what you're trying to do to us?"

"What do I call it?" Jules said. "It's called doing business."

As it happened, the Lieblings' new apartment and the Solomon Brinckmanns' were on the same elevator stem at 1000 Park. Solomon Brinckmann died in 1976, and his wife sold the apartment and moved to Arizona a year later. Through the years when they shared the elevator, the Brinckmanns and the Lieblings did not encounter each other much. But whenever they did, they nodded and smiled at each other politely.

"Good morning, Mrs. Brinckmann."

"Good morning, Mrs. Liebling."

Only once had Hermina Brinckmann attempted something that might have been termed an intimacy in the elevator. "Someone told me that the great Mr. Al Capone himself offered to be your son's godfather," she said. "How exciting!"

"We Jews don't have godfathers," Hannah Liebling said.

"Oh, how I envy you your traditions," said Hermina Brinckmann.

"You have a few traditions of your own, if you cared to observe them," Hannah said.

After that exchange relations between the Brinckmanns and the Lieblings were somewhat frostier. The Brinckmanns often gave large parties. So did the Lieblings. In her ballroom Hannah could comfortably accommodate a seated dinner for sixty. But the two families never entertained each other. About a year after Jules and Hannah Liebling moved in, however, they received an invitation from Mr. and Mrs. Stuyvesant Miller.

"What shall we do about this?" Hannah asked her husband. "It's for a Christmas tree-trimming party. But they're not people we visit. We hardly know them."

"We do this with it," Jules said. He took the invitation and tore it in half, then in quarters, then in eighths.

"But it says R.S.V.P. on it," she said.

"They need us more than we need them," he said.

This is one of several episodes that are never talked about in the family. It is not a family secret, exactly. The Liebling family secrets are quite another matter. But the episode is a painful reminder that Jules Liebling's money was not made in one of the more fashionable ways. In fact, there are some who hint that his money was made illegally. The connection with people like Al Capone is the circumstance most often cited.

Ahead of the Lincoln now, the traffic on Park Avenue has come to a complete standstill. There seems to be an almost newsworthy case of urban gridlock at the corner of Fifty-seventh Street. Nothing moves. Police whistles sound shrilly. Arms in orange slickers gesticulate furiously in the air, to no avail. Park Avenue has become a parking lot. "I suppose it's the rain that's causing this," Hannah says to no one in particular.

"Anyway," Anne says, "I think it's silly to talk about how important it is to get *married,* and to marry the right *sort.* It's so old-fashioned, Nana. Nowadays a woman doesn't have to get married at all to have a successful life. In fact, I don't think I'll get married at all.

I'll just have a lo-o-o-o-ng series of lovers. Like your sister Settie's husband, I'll just screw around." She lies back against the seat and stretches her arms above her head, touching the car's ceiling with her fingertips, and smiles.

"Knees together, young lady," her grandmother says. "Gracious, if I'd talked that way in front of my grandmother, I'd have had my mouth washed out with Fels Naphtha soap! If you're saying things like that to try to shock me, you haven't succeeded. I refuse to let you try to shock me, Anne."

"Were you ever in love, Nana Hannah? Deeply, madly, passionately in love?"

"What a question! Of course I was."

"But I bet it wasn't with Grandpa, was it?"

"What a thing to say!"

"Look! I can tell by the expression on your face that it wasn't. I knew it! Who was he? Who was your one true, deep, passionate love, Nana?"

"I do not wish to pursue this line of conversation," her grandmother says.

It is another characteristic of Hannah Liebling, *geboren* Sachs: whenever the conversation gets vaguely interesting, she changes the subject.

"And look at your sister Settie. She didn't marry for love, either, did she? You say she married the right sort of man. But you also say he made her miserable."

"I don't want to talk about Settie. It makes me too sad."

"But it was you who brought the subject up, *Maman,*" Cyril says.

"No. It was you. You, with your slouching. *Sit up straight,* Cyril!" She raises the sleeve of her mink jacket and consults her gold watch. "We're going to be late," she says. Outside, the traffic lights go from red to green, then to red again, and then to green, but nothing moves. Horns are blowing loudly from all directions. Anne says nothing. She knows just how far she can push her grandmother, and she has pushed her just far enough.

Now, in front of the Lincoln, a small band—perhaps six or seven—of black youths jaywalks, or rather jay-runs, across the middle of the street. Some wear dreadlocks. Others have haircuts in extravagant topiary designs. They

run zigzagging between the bumpers, leapfrogging the
fenders of the unmoving automobiles, and one of the
boys slaps the Lincoln's hood sharply as he passes. Mr.
Nelson presses the button that locks all four of the car
doors and, simultaneously, taps the car's horn twice.

"Um-fuh-wuh," one of the boys shouts.

Another boy makes a leering face at the invisible passengers behind the tinted glass in the backseat of the
limousine, while another makes a vulgar gesture with his
fist. Then the first boy break-dances back across the
street toward them and slaps the big Lincoln's hood
again, harder. Mr. Nelson sounds his horn again, louder.

"Muh-fuh!"

"Goodness, right here on Park Avenue," Hannah
Liebling whispers as the boys, shouting and jeering, skip
and hop away and disappear into the traffic. "I didn't
know they came out when it rained." She leans across
the back of the front seat. "I have my can of Mace in
my purse, Mr. Nelson," she says. "Do you have yours?"

"Definitely, Mrs. Liebling. Right here in the glove
box."

"Do you really carry a can of Mace, Nana?" Anne
asks her.

"Absolutely. I wouldn't step outside my house without it. This isn't the same city I grew up in, when I
could walk to school and go skating in the park without my nanny. I also carry a gun." She pats her purse
authoritatively.

"Really, Nana? Can I see it?"

Her grandmother hesitates. "I'll let you look at it,"
she says, "but you mustn't touch it. It's fully loaded."
She reaches into her reticule and withdraws a small
Smith & Wesson .38-caliber automatic pistol with a bone
handle, and places it across her lap. "I know how to use
it, too," she says. "I've had fourteen hours of target
practice."

"Pistol-packin' grandma," Cyril says drily.

Outside, the noise in the street is deafening, as all the
motorists in the street, having nothing better to do, sit
on their horns. Had Hannah Liebling fired off her pistol
now, no one would have heard it. "I knew he should
have gone down Third Avenue," Hannah Liebling says.
"It's a wider street, and the lights are synchronized."

"He didn't take Third Avenue because Third Avenue is a one-way street going *uptown*, you stupid old fool!" Cyril says.

There is silence in the backseat of the Lincoln now, following this outburst. Anne, embarrassed, stares at her folded hands in her lap. Hannah gazes out the window. Finally she says, "Cyril, your nerves are bad tonight, I can tell. You need one of your pills. Take one of the little yellow ones. Besides, Third Avenue runs downtown. I am quite positive of that."

That is another thing to remember about Hannah Liebling: You can be right. But she *cannot* be wrong.

"Now do sit up straight, Cyril," she says.

And so there you have Hannah Sachs Liebling at eighty-two, a despotic old harridan with a will of iron and a heart of stone, who has managed to break the spirit of all three of her children, one after the other, and who is now, all sails flying and loaded with money to the Plimsoll line, determined to perform the same feat on the next generation, charging ahead at full speed, leaving devastation in her wake, taking no prisoners, two hundred forty pounds of pure hell. Why do some love her so? Perhaps because she has managed to keep two terrible and linked secrets locked in her hard but still evergreen heart. Once you tell a secret to another person, it's no secret anymore. Spill the beans to another, and you might as well tell the world.

Her husband was not a nice man, from all reports, though it wasn't easy to know him really well. Few did, in fact. Some women claimed to find him sexy. But then, money itself is sexy. He was certainly not handsome. He was a small man, but his head seemed too large for his body. By contrast, his hands were tiny, almost dainty. His manicurist always applied clear polish to his nails, and the sparkly fingernails only served to emphasize the daintiness of those hands.

They say all rich men make enemies, but Jules Liebling seems to have made more than his share. There are other stories along the line of the one about how he bought the big apartment at 1000 Park. There is the story of how he built Grandmont, the huge, extravagant house in Westchester, in Tarrytown, on the Hudson

River, overlooking the Tappan Zee. Again, this was in the early 1950s, and the contractor's price was $500,000. Again, this was considered a huge price in those days, though today, to replace Grandmont—it is gone now—it would cost many times that figure. The grounds contained a pool with a wave-making machine, two tennis courts, industrial-sized playground equipment for the children, and a sandbox for Cyril's baby brother, Noah, that was as big as a squash court. When the house was finished, Jules Liebling presented the builder with a check for $400,000.

"But, Mr. Liebling, our contract price was five hundred thousand."

"I'm paying you four. Take it or leave it."

"Mr. Liebling, I have a contract. I can sue."

"Go right ahead. Your lawsuit will cost at least a hundred thousand in legal fees. And until you get a judgment, you won't get a penny from me."

"Mr. Liebling, you are robbing me of my contractor's profit."

"Your profit is the boost your reputation will get from having built a house for me," Jules Liebling said.

There are other stories like this, not all of them involving real estate.

When he died, twenty years ago, it was decided that his funeral would be small and very private. "Only members of the immediate family, and certain Liebling employees, are invited to attend," the obituary notice said.

Jules Liebling had many influential acquaintances. The Duke and Duchess of Windsor were frequent house guests at Grandmont. The duchess traveled with her own especially cushioned toilet seat. There is a photograph of Cyril, as a little boy, seated on the lap of Queen Marie of Romania. Bernard Baruch nearly choked to death at Grandmont on a piece of shell in his Maryland crab cake. Ike and Mamie Eisenhower made a point of requesting separate bedrooms there because, as the first lady explained in her note, Ike snored. And speaking of bedrooms, the whole household was awakened one night when Frank Sinatra tried to get into Lana Turner's bed. Lily Damita was already in that bed, for what reason no one was ever quite sure. Hedy Lamarr was suspected of pinching silverware during her visit. John Huston once got drunk and fell head-first into the fireplace in the Great Hall, and had to be treated for third-degree burns.

But when Jules Liebling died, it was decided to keep the services small and private. Hannah Liebling was afraid that if she tried to stage a large public funeral at Temple Emanu-El, nobody would come.

In the eyes of some people, Jules Liebling's will treated all three of his children unfairly. Here is what *Business Week* had to say about it at the time:

> It is not uncommon, when a rich man dies, to discover that he has punished one or more "bad" children through disinheritance. But when a mogul's Last Will and Testament seemingly rewards two errant offspring and overlooks a loyal son, that is news.
>
> And that, on the surface of it, is what Jules Liebling did in arranging for the distribution of his estate, esti-mated to be in excess of $800,000,000 upon his death.
>
> Jules Liebling's widow, Hannah Sachs Liebling, was bequeathed 52% of her late husband's Ingraham Cor-poration stock, effectively putting her in control of the family-owned companies, with the specific wish that Mrs. Liebling assume, at least temporarily, her late husband's role as president and CEO of Ingraham. The older of the Lieblings' two sons, Cyril Liebling, 40, is a Manhattan public relations man. Though he has never been considered much more than a play-boy—and a sometime Peck's Bad Boy—he was left 24% of Ingraham stock in a lifetime trust, from which he is to derive the income. In 1969, Cyril Liebling was briefly jailed on charges of child molestation. The charges were later dropped when the alleged victim admitted that the charges were a publicity-getting hoax, and the name of the plaintiff, a minor, was never revealed.
>
> Jules Liebling's daughter, the oft-married Ruth Liebling Hower, 35, was left an additional 24% of the company in an identical trust. In 1956, when Ruth Liebling was just 18, she eloped with Brazilian copper heir Antonio Fernandez-Just, a man 39 years her se-nior. That marriage lasted barely three months and was terminated by divorce. There followed a three-

year career in Hollywood, during which Miss Liebling, using the name Ruth Radcliffe, appeared in several mostly forgettable motion pictures. But her film career ended in 1960, when she walked off the set of a picture she was making on location in Italy to marry Count Giulio di Pascanelli of Rome. Columbia Pictures sued her, but the lawsuit was settled, and the scenes of the movie in which she appeared, *The Archbishop's Wife,* were reshot without her.

Soon afterward, her second marriage was annulled when it was discovered that Count di Pascanelli had a living wife in St. Moritz. But a year later she was able to marry the count again, since he had by then shed himself of his previous marital entanglement. However, that marriage lasted only seven weeks before the couple divorced, with the count demanding alimony. This matter resolved itself with the count's suicide.

In 1965, Ruth Liebling married William Hower, who had been her personal physical fitness trainer. The Howers have since separated, and Ruth Liebling has reassumed the title Countess di Pascanelli, a title that she claims is papal, though the Vatican will not confirm this.

These marriages, and her abortive film career, are said to have caused her late father extreme distress, and are presumed to have cost him considerable sums of money.

Meanwhile, Jules Liebling's "good" son, Noah Liebling, 27, was left no Ingraham stock at all in his father's will. Noah Liebling has worked in his father's companies in various capacities since his cum laude graduation from Nevada State six years ago. In the industry, it was widely assumed that the younger Mr. Liebling was being groomed to head Ingrahams. But this is not to be, at least not for a while. For the time being, Noah Liebling is essentially just one of his mother's employees.

Jules Liebling's will does, however, offer Noah a window of hope for the future, if he plays his cards right. The will stipulates that 25% of Hannah Liebling's shares in the company—that is, 13% of the shares outstanding—are hers to do with as she wishes.

Mrs. Liebling could, presumably, make a public offering of these shares. The remainder of her shares are earmarked as "discretionary holdings." At such time as she feels is "fitting," the will stipulates, the remaining 75% of her voting shares are to be turned over to Noah, giving him a majority voting position in the company. That time will come, the will states, "when my dear wife feels that my son is fully ready to assume the reins of my company." That time could come next week, next year, or many years from now. Until that time Noah Liebling remains effectively tied to his mother's apron strings and could remain so until her death, at which point his mother's discretionary shares go to him without restrictions.

If Jules Liebling's will seems grossly unfair to Noah by some industry insiders, Noah himself—a highly popular figure in the industry—does not see it that way at all. Speaking to *Business Week*'s reporter without a trace of bitterness, Noah Liebling said, "My father was a very kind and loving man, and a very fair man. His will is a very human, and very humane, instrument, it seems to me. My older brother, Cyril, has his own business, and has never had any interest in running the company. My sister is an extremely talented and artistic woman who, by her own admission, let her heart rule her head several years ago when she turned her back on a promising Hollywood career to marry. As a result, as she puts it, she 'can't even get arrested' in the film or television community. Until she finds herself artistically, she will need the funds from my father's trust to live in the style to which she is accustomed.

"Placing my mother at the helm of the family enterprises makes perfect sense to me. Though she never had an office in the Ingraham Building, or had a title in the corporation, no corporate decision, large or small, was ever made by my father without first consulting my mother. As anyone who has ever worked for us knows, my mother and my father were true partners in the family business in every sense of the word. This is why theirs was such a loving and lasting marriage.

"As for myself, I am much too young and inexperienced to assume the stewardship of a company the size and complexity of Ingraham. At the moment I could not possibly run this company without my mother's help and guidance. And so both my mother and I are very happy with the present arrangement, as are my brother and sister. Though we will always miss our father, we are all happy that he left things as he did."

Cynics point out that it is lucky that the Liebling family is happy with the will. A stern final clause declares, "Anyone who makes the slightest move to challenge this Last Will and Testament shall be immediately stripped of any of its benefits." Asked to comment on this clause, Noah Liebling dismissed it as "routine." Asked about the tied-to-mother's-apron-strings factor, Noah Liebling replied, with a wink, "I can assure you that my mother has never worn an apron."

Mrs. Hannah Liebling, 62, was in Europe, traveling on company business, and could not be reached for comment.

All that, of course, was written twenty years ago, and many things have changed since then. For one thing, all the people mentioned in that story are now twenty years older. But, as you will see as our story unfolds, there are many things that have not changed. You may well ask: Was it the intention of Noah's father's will to keep his son from assuming the presidency of the company for this long a time? Or was it the old man's wish that his widow act as a sort of regent until Noah was a little older—four or five years, perhaps, or until Noah was in his mid-thirties? But Noah Liebling has now passed his mid-forties, and his mother is still very much, and very firmly, in charge of things, and has offered no visible sign that she is ready to let go. Was that what the old man really wanted, or expected, to have happen? By now quite a few people have asked that question.

But in the meantime, we have backed away from our story. We have left three of the principals—Hannah Liebling, her son Cyril, and her son Noah's daughter Anne—stuck in a traffic jam on Park Avenue, while we digressed backward to Hannah's late husband. It should be possible to tell this story in as straightforward and linear a fashion as possible, and avoid these flashbacks. But this may be hard to do. J. B. Liebling, twenty years dead, continues to influence his family as powerfully today as he did when he was alive. At certain intersections, as in a logjam of traffic, it will be difficult to bypass the old man.

Where are these three going? Where are they coming from? They are coming from Hannah Liebling's apartment at 1000 Park, where Anne has had tea with her grandmother. Anne is a freshman at Bennington, home on winter break. Ever since Anne reached her teens, these afternoon teas with her grandmother have become a ritual. Indeed, for Anne they are a command performance. They are always very formal, always preceded by a handwritten invitation on Hannah Liebling's embossed Cartier note paper:

> *One Thousand Park Avenue*
> *Dearest Anne,*
> *Your mother tells me you will be coming down from school on _____.*
> *Please join me here for tea on the afternoon of _____ at four o'clock.*
> *I look forward to seeing you.*
> *Devotedly,*
> *Nana Hannah*

Hannah Liebling pours from the big silver teapot. ("Lemon or sugar? One lump or two?") Then she hands the little teacup to Bridget, her parlor maid, who delivers it to Anne, who always sits in what is known as "the visitor's chair" opposite her grandmother in the glassed-in terrace that is called the morning room, since it faces east. Hannah then pours for herself, and Bridget passes the tray of thin finger sandwiches, cucumber, and watercress, followed by tea cakes and cookies. Hannah is determined that Anne shall at least be exposed to the kind of manners and social niceties which she herself was brought up to observe. She suspects that Anne's mother, Carol Liebling, is a little lax about such matters.

But Carol Liebling takes her mother-in-law's teas

every bit as seriously. "Glove inspection," Carol says cheerfully as her daughter prepares to depart. "Are they white-white-white? Clean-clean-clean? Good. Now keep them in your purse until you've rung her doorbell. Then slip them on. Have you got a clean white hankie, in case you need to blow your nose?"

"Moth-*err*!"

"And don't tease your grandmother," Carol says. "Remember, she holds the purse strings."

But Anne, blond and bubbly, knows she's pretty, and she knows her grandmother thinks she's pretty—a fair-haired Elizabeth Taylor, that same oval face when she was about Anne's age and played in *National Velvet*. (*National Velvet* is Nana Hannah's favorite movie.) And so she doesn't really mind dressing up and looking her prettiest for her grandmother, sitting with her ankles crossed in the visitor's chair, balancing her teacup in its saucer. And of course she can't resist teasing her grandmother a little bit. Not too much, just a bit. She has discovered that her grandmother actually enjoys the teasing—if it doesn't go too far, that is.

"Tonight there's a real sexpot coming for dinner," she said to her grandmother this afternoon. "I hear he's a real hunk."

"Really, Anne, such language!" her grandmother said. "If I talked like that when I was a girl, I'd have my mouth washed out with Fels Naphtha soap."

Have we mentioned that tonight is New Year's Eve? This accounts in large part for the amount of traffic on Park Avenue. Everyone is on his way to a party some-where else in town, or to a nightclub or restaurant, or to the theater. But New Year's Eve is another ritual in the Liebling family. It is the night that Carol and Noah Liebling have their annual family dinner and it, too, is a command performance, and that is where the Lincoln is headed now. Carol and Noah live at River House, on East Fifty-second Street.

At six o'clock, Cyril Liebling joined his mother and his niece in the morning room at 1000 Park. He did not have far to go, since he lives on the floor above. After Jules Liebling died, Hannah decided to divide the duplex apartment horizontally. "I don't need all this acreage," she said to Cyril, "now that I'm all alone. I'm going to have the staircase taken out and the upstairs sealed off. You can live up there. You'll have your own elevator entrance, complete privacy, and I'll pay the maintenance on both apartments."

It was not an arrangement designed to please Cyril, exactly. While the idea of a large, luxuriously furnished, and rent-free apartment at a splendid address was not without its appeal, Cyril did not much fancy the idea of living in such close proximity to his mother. With the income generated by his father's trust, he could easily have afforded an elegant place of his own.

"I suppose this is your way of keeping me under your thumb," he said.

"I'd like to keep my eye on you, Cyril. To make sure you stay out of trouble. You know what I'm talking about."

"But, Mother, that was a long time ago, and it was just a childish prank."

"A childish prank at age twenty-two? A little early to be entering your second childhood, don't you think?"

"Joey Fernandez was the child. It was all his idea, not mine."

"I do not wish to hear that name again! Anyway," she added in a gentler tone, "as I get older, living alone, I like the idea of a family member living close to me. You know—in case something should happen to me."

And so he had agreed to go along with her, though not for the reasons she outlined. It was because, secretly, for years he had been in love with that particular apartment. He had always hoped that when she died, she would leave that apartment to him. When it was his, he would reinstall that gracefully curving staircase between the two floors. He would redecorate the rooms to his somewhat more extravagant taste. He would turn the downstairs library into a screening room for his private collection of films. He would give large and lavish entertainments for glittering gatherings of his beautiful friends. "Darling Cyril," they would say to him, "no one lives as magnificently as you." And the magnificence of his final apartment would attract even more beautiful friends, and on and on. After dinner they would all file into his screening room for a film or two. The apartments at 1000 Park were all wonderfully soundproof.

None of his neighbors would ever suspect the intensity of the excitement that would be generated in his apartment. It was not such an outrageous dream. It made sense that his mother should leave the apartment to him, particularly if, when she died, he was already living in half of it. He'd already dropped little hints to her in this regard. "I'd love to see this place made *whole* again," etc. Meanwhile, half a loaf was better than none. With half the apartment he had his toe firmly in the door. And for the occasional dalliance there were always hotels.

But, of course, who would have expected that the old lady would live to be eighty-two? A number of years ago, she'd had a serious bout with cancer, and the family had gathered at Mount Sinai hospital around what was supposed to be her deathbed. Cyril had planned his funeral wardrobe. He had the perfect dark blue Sills suit. He would have the temple filled with white dahlias, her favorite flower. As the coffin rolled slowly toward the ark, he would utter an audible, uncontrollable sob, and grasp the back of the pew in front of him, as though about to collapse. For a month afterward, he would wear a black grosgrain ribbon on his lapel, and a mournful slouch.

But then she bounced back, healthier than ever. And year by year, Cyril has seen his beautiful dream recede before his eyes, as he has remained his mother's house guest. Is it any wonder he occasionally loses patience with her?

And whom will we meet when the Town Car finally arrives at River House? Well, Anne's parents, of course, Noah and Carol Liebling, the host and hostess. Cyril and Noah's sister, Ruth, will also be there, who still likes to be introduced as the Countess di Pascanelli, though she insists she uses her "good" name only because it is useful in making hotel and restaurant reservations. There have been a couple of other husbands for Ruth since that *Business Week* story was published in 1974, but none of them amounted to anything. They were totally and thoroughly undistinguished, and have no bearing whatsoever on this story. Tonight Ruth has asked if she may bring a new beau of hers along. It is interesting that, at fifty-five, Ruth still uses the term *beau*. Whether or not this beau will turn out to be husband material, who knows? We shall have to wait and see. Ruth has still not succeeded in finding herself artistically, though she continues to try. Recently she announced that she is writing a novel.

Noah Liebling now wears the title of executive vice president of H. & W. Ingraham Sons, Inc., the second in command. He commands a salary of over $500,000 a year. But his mother still holds the title of president and CEO, and Hannah has not yet found it "fitting" to turn over to Noah the controlling shares of stock as stipulated in his father's will. This, apparently, does not reflect any dissatisfaction on Hannah's part with Noah's work for the company. She has given him steady raises and promotions over the years, but has held back giving him full control. Some people believe that this is because Hannah does not yet quite trust Carol, Noah's spirited and independent-thinking wife. Hannah tends to think of Carol as *too* free-spirited, too independent, too much of an influence on Noah. Could it be that Hannah sees Carol as a rival, and thus a threat? Hannah is not a woman who likes to share control. And so Hannah thinks of Carol as a loose cannon, capable of capsizing the family battleship—or perhaps the family flotilla of battleships would be the better term.

Noah Liebling remains his mother's favorite son, just as he was his father's. To most people Noah seems like the ideal son—tall, athletic, affable, with the dark good looks of a *Gentleman's Quarterly* model. Once upon a time Cyril was the favorite son. But as a result of a series of differences and misunderstandings years ago, he no longer is.

In the winter of 1945, the telephone rang at 1000 Park Avenue. Jules and Hannah Liebling were at dinner, and Philip, their butler, conveyed the message to Jules Liebling at the dinner table. "Mr. George Litchfield of St. Anselm's School is on the phone, sir," Philip said. St. Anselm's was the boys' school in northwestern Connecticut where Cyril Liebling was a first-year student, and George Litchfield was its headmaster.

"Tell him I'll call him back."

"I told him you were at dinner, sir. But he insists it's urgent."

A look passed between Jules and Hannah. "Very well," Jules said. Looking pained, he placed his napkin on the dinner table, pushed his chair back, and went to take the call in the next room.

"I'm sorry to say that it has become necessary for us to expel Cyril, Mr. Liebling," Mr. Litchfield said.

A pause. Then Jules said, "For what reason, may I ask?"

"For—for unnatural sexual activity, Mr. Liebling," Mr. Litchfield said.

"What sort of activity?"

"They were—I believe it is called fellatio. He and another boy. They were discovered in the lavatory, by Mr. Smith, the dormitory master of Ward's Hall."

"Who was doing what to whom?"

"I—it's my understanding from Mr. Smith—they were doing it to each other."

"I see." Now Jules attempted what was intended to be an understanding chuckle between two men of the world. "Well, surely, Mr. Litchfield," he said. "Surely, in an all-male environment, at a school such as yours— two adolescent boys. I mean, certainly this isn't the first time this sort of thing has happened at a school like yours. Two young boys, experimenting—"

"Well, perhaps not, Mr. Liebling," the headmaster conceded, "but that sort of activity cannot be tolerated at St. Anselm's."

"And the other boy involved in the—incident? I presume he is being expelled also."

"No, in fact he is not," the headmaster said.

"May I ask why not?"

"It seems the other boy was an unwilling—at least a reluctant participant, Mr. Liebling."

"Hah! How do you know that? The boy could be lying!"

"It seems—well, it seems that your son was paying the other boy for this—activity."

"Paying? How can you prove that?"

"When Mr. Smith walked into the lavatory and found them there, the other boy had your son's personal check in his pocket. Apparently this has been going on for some time. The other boy has been cashing your son's checks in the bursar's office, and our bursar had begun to wonder about this. You see, the other boy is a lower-former, a scholarship boy from an underprivileged family in Harlem. He was only doing this for the money."

"The other boy is a Negro?"

"Yes. An honor student on a full scholarship."

"And so a Negro honor student on a full scholarship gets the benefit of the doubt, and a Jewish boy from a privileged family gets expelled—is that the way you work? Is that what you call justice?"

"Mr. Liebling, that has nothing to do with it."

"Give me the other boy's name."

"I am not at liberty to give that to you, Mr. Liebling," the headmaster said.

There was another pause. Then Jules said, "Look, Mr. Litchfield, there must be something your school needs. A new hockey rink perhaps? A new dormitory? An endowment of some sort? I'm sure you and I can work something out."

"I'm sorry, Mr. Liebling," the headmaster said. "We do not operate St. Anselm's that way. I'm afraid our decision is final."

"I see," said Jules.

"Cyril is in his room now. Mr. Smith, his dormitory master, is helping him pack up his things. He is to be off the school's grounds by midnight. Will you arrange for his transportation home?"

"I'll send for him," Jules said. "And you, Mr. Litchfield, can eat my shit." He hung up the phone.

He returned to the dining room, his face a mask, and picked up his napkin. His small, polished fingernails caught the candlelight.

Hannah's fork was poised in midair, though there was nothing on it. "Well," she said at last, "what did Mr. Litchfield want?"

"I'm withdrawing Cyril from St. Anselm's," he said.

"Oh, no! But why?"

"Other boys have been forging Cyril's name on his checks."

"But that's the other boys' fault! That's no reason to punish Cyril."

"He should be taught to keep his checkbook in a safer

place," he said. "I knew we should never have given him that checking account. That was your idea."

With a little sob she dropped her fork, got up from the table, and quickly left the room.

When Mr. Nelson, Jules's young chauffeur, arrived at the school that night to collect Cyril and his belongings, George Litchfield was a little surprised to see that Mr. Nelson was not accompanied by either of Cyril's parents. He found himself somewhat at a loss for what final words he might say to the Lieblings' driver. "Get some nice classical music on the radio," he said to Mr. Nelson. "In these circumstances I find that often helps."

That was the night, Cyril often thinks, that his parents threw him away.

That night, after Hannah Liebling had cried her tears and was about to turn off her bedside lamp, her bedroom door opened and her husband, in his dressing gown, stepped into her room. He closed her door behind him. He moved toward her bed and sat on the edge of it. At first Hannah was startled. It had been a long time since her husband had entered her bedroom. He reached out and began gently rubbing the back of her neck, her shoulder blades, and the soft flesh of her upper back. "I want us to make another son," he whispered.

There will be a seventh Liebling family member coming to Noah and Carol's house tonight. She is Rebecca Hower, Ruth's daughter by her third marriage or, if you count the two di Pascanelli marriages, her fourth. Rebecca, who likes to be called Becka, is twenty-five, and though she has been around all these years, she is something of a newcomer to the family, having only recently rejoined her mother after a long estrangement. This will be Becka's first appearance at a Liebling New Year's Eve. We will see how it goes, for Hannah Liebling barely knows this granddaughter.

In addition to Ruth's beau, there will be two other non-family members at tonight's dinner party. One is Melody Richards, who was Anne's best friend at boarding school and is now her roommate at college. Anne and Melody strike many people as an unlikely duo. It used to be said, with some truth, that two extremely pretty girls could never be best friends at that age. But here you have Melody and Anne, acknowledged to be the two prettiest young women at Bennington, and over the years they have become inseparable. The two girls' looks are like the opposite faces of the moon. Anne is blond and blue-eyed. Melody is dark, almost Latin-looking, with large, dark, wide-set eyes like an Andalusian girl's. In terms of personality, they are also opposites. Anne Liebling is as light and bubbly, and often as silly-making, as a glass of champagne. Melody is sober, quiet, thoughtful, often given to long silences. Anne is majoring in art. Melody, rather in keeping with her name, is majoring in drama. At school the two have been given the nicknames Toots and Caspar. We'll leave it to you to guess which name belongs to which.

Melody is also nearly a full year younger than Anne, making Melody one of the few seventeen-year-olds in their class. She has always been an intellectually gifted child. At the age of four it was discovered that Melody had taught herself to read. In grammar school, because she was so much more gifted than the others in her class, she was allowed to skip the entire third grade so she could be placed in a group where she would find the work more challenging. She has been challenging her classmates, and her teachers, ever since.

Melody, in further contrast to her best friend, is from a relatively poor family, and attends Bennington on a special scholarship. Her father, a career diplomat, holds a minor post in the U.S. State Department, and is presently stationed in Japan. Because her parents can ill afford to send their daughter halfway around the world for the winter break, for the past four years she has been spending these weeks with Anne and her family in New York. Noah and Carol have become very fond of Melody, and have begun to think of themselves almost as her foster parents.

There will be one other guest at the little family dinner party tonight, thanks to Melody. His name is William Luckman. You may have heard of him. Only twenty-one, he is the prodigal young Yale senior who has just published his first book, *Blighted Elms,* that has been climbing best-seller lists all over the country. His book's title is ironic. Taking as his central image the Dutch elm disease that has devastated Yale's once leafy campus, he wrote a book that is a startling exposé of the degree of sexual promiscuity that has afflicted, and diseased, a prestigious Eastern university. Names, of course, have been changed, but just barely. Yale, for instance, is called "Eli University" in the book, and several members of Yale's faculty and student body are said to be able to recognize themselves in Mr. Luckman's pages. There has been some sword-rattling talk of lawsuits.

Homosexuality and lesbianism account for only some of the tamer revelations. The amount of faculty-student sex is prodigious, according to the author. Incidents of sexual blackmail within the college community are rampant, as are cases of physical and sexual abuse and harassment of minors. A child pornography ring operates openly, while drug and alcohol abuse abounds. Male and female students in need of money sell themselves as prostitutes, while a prominent dean earns handsome sums as a pimp and a procurer. Orgies involving students, professors, and administrators are described in vivid detail, while the top administrators—from the president on down—and even the college's trustees provide an elaborate and cynical cover-up. In *Blighted Elms* Eli University emerges as a cesspool of degeneracy and depravity, crime and vice.

The book has become a succès de scandale. And, needless to say, Mr. Luckman's scorching depiction of this college and its sexual mores—and the book's sudden huge popularity and the publicity surrounding it—have left Mr. Luckman's future at Yale somewhat problematic. He has not yet been expelled—and has in fact almost arrogantly dared the college to expel him. "The only reason they haven't done it is because they know that will only generate more publicity for my book," he has stated. "I hope there are lawsuits, because lawsuits sell books, and whoever sues me will have to prove that what I say isn't true. They're scared to expel me. They're caught between a rock and a hard place. If they don't kick me out, they're admitting my details are accurate. If they do, I'll be crying all the way to the bank. The book's already been sold as a miniseries."

Melody Richards met the young literary lion in October, when she happened to be in Bloomingdale's White Plains store while he was autographing copies of *Blighted*

Elms. Curious to see what the notorious young author was like, she stepped over to his signing table during a lull in sales and fell into conversation with him. She found him witty, charming, and handsome. They exchanged telephone numbers. For the past month he has been on tour, promoting his book, and he called her several times from various cities. When Melody learned that he would be in New York for the Christmas holidays, she asked Noah Liebling if she could invite Bill Luckman to the family's New Year's Eve party.

At first Noah was dubious. "I haven't read his book," he said, "and I'm not planning to. From what I gather, it's nothing but a piece of smut in an academic setting."

"I think he's actually a very moral person," Melody said. "He was outraged by the things he saw going on there, and thought the public should know about them."

"Isn't he a little old to be dating you?"

She laughed. "He isn't a date, Mr. Liebling," she said. "I met him only once, in a roomful of people."

Carol Liebling was more sanguine about the idea. "I haven't read the book, either," she said. "But it's certainly causing quite a stir, and everybody's talking about it, and he's been on all the talk shows. He's very attractive. I think it would be fun for the girls to have him, Noah. And he'd help balance out the sexes at the table." Bill is the sexpot Anne was referring to.

And so Carol Liebling's dinner table tonight is set for ten, though only nine of these people are principal characters in our story: Hannah, Cyril, and Anne, Carol and Noah and sister Ruth, Ruth's daughter Becka, Melody Richards and William Luckman. Those are our ennead. Others—such as Ruth's new beau and Noah's and Carol's friends, Frank and Beryl Stokes, who also live at River House—will drift in and out of the proceedings, of course. But those nine are the ones to keep your eye on.

In the stalled traffic on Park Avenue, the horns continue to blow and the police whistles continue to shriek to no avail. Hannah Liebling leans across the back of the front seat of the Lincoln again and says, "Mr. Nelson, perhaps you'd better phone my son and daughter-in-law and tell them about this pickle we're in with this traffic. I know she's serving a lamb roast tonight, and she knows I like it pink, but not bleeding."

"Certainly, Mrs. Liebling." He picks up the car phone by his side and begins pressing buttons.

"And incidentally, Mr. Nelson. Which way does Third Avenue run—uptown or down?"

"Downtown, Mrs. Liebling."

"Ha!" she says to Cyril. "I told you so!"

The traffic inches slowly forward, the rain continues to pour down, and the windshield wipers of the Lincoln thrash furiously back and forth. *Manush, manush,* the wipers say.

Cyril thinks: Mr. Nelson knows which side his bread is buttered on.

2

An Intermezzo

One spring morning when she was fifteen (Hannah is remembering) and when the gardenia in the upstairs formal parlor was just coming into bloom, she tossed a blossom from the open front window into the street below. It was intended to land at her father's feet as he left the house on the way to teach his school. But she missed, and her father strode on in his purposeful way without seeing it. But a young sailor carrying a navy duffel bag happened to be passing the house on his way to a great adventure. He saw the flower fall to the sidewalk and stooped to pick it up. He looked up at the young girl in the window, and a breeze blew the parlor curtains aside. He smiled up at her, and she smiled back. Then he put the gardenia between his teeth, gypsy-style, and danced a little jig. Then he hoisted his duffel to his shoulder and walked on. But after a few steps he stopped and turned back. He removed his cap and hung it on one of the iron finials of her front gate posts. Then he walked away, whistling.

Later she read about his great adventure. At least, when she saw his picture in the newspapers, Hannah was sure that this was a photograph of the same young man with the same, slightly off-center smile. His name was Radioman First Class George Noville, and he had just completed a historic mission—the first radio-equipped transatlantic flight, in a trimotored Fokker monoplane, under the famous U.S. Navy Commander Richard E. Byrd. The year was 1926. A few years earlier Commander Byrd had circled the North Pole.

Two years later, her doorbell rang, and Hannah, who happened to be alone in the house at the time, went to the door. "I've come for my cap," he said. She let him in.

He brought with him a diary he had kept of his many travels since they had last seen each other. Pressed between its pages was her flower. "It brought me luck," he said. "And it brought me back."

All we know of what happened next is contained in a slender packet of letters, tied with a faded pink hair ribbon, which Hannah keeps in a shoebox at the bottom of one of her dresser drawers. The stamps are mostly foreign—from Tunis, Gibraltar, Malta, Tripoli, and other mostly Mediterranean ports—and the postmarks are faded, and the letters are undated, so it is impossible to tell how long the relationship lasted, and Hannah seldom looks at the letters anymore.

My darling—

It is midnight, and all my other shipmates are asleep, and I am writing this to you by flashlight so as not to disturb the others. And because it is hard to write with a flashlight in one hand and a pen in the other in this cramped bunk (the bunks in this #%$&## old tub are particularly narrow), this will just be to tell you that you are in my thoughts all day long, and in my dreams at night. Even an ocean and a half away, you are with me always. Nothing can ever separate us, my darling, but meanwhile I am working hard to get a stateside assignment so we can truly be together again.

The fellow in the bunk below me is snoring softly, making sounds that sound like manush, manush, *so I guess I should try to get some sleep now, too, which will be easy because I plan to see you in my dreams. Good night, my love.*

George

My darling Hannie—

Something you say in your last letter worries me a little. You say you hope *your father will like me. Well, I can promise you, my love, that I will do my #%&## best to* make *him like me! And your mother too! And your married sister, and her husband, and all the rest of your family, once I have a chance to meet them!*

Why would they not like me, my darling? I happen to think I'm a pretty nice guy, and so—thank God—do you, as the rest of your letter seems to indicate! You even use the word "love"—thank God!

Genoa is a dirty city, with very little to offer, it seems to me, so I am not going ashore with the others tonight. I would rather stay on board and write to you and think of you. Meanwhile, I expect to hear about my request for stateside duty very soon.

All my love,

G.

Darling Hannie—

Good news—I think! There's a rumor about that Cmdr. Byrd is planning another expedition—don't know where as yet. But he'll need a good radioman, and I know he was pleased with my work on that last flight of his, so I'm putting in a request for that assignment. That would bring me back to Washington, at least for the planning stages, and Washington is not far from New York, and that means perhaps it won't be long before you're in my arms again.

Don't worry that the expedition will be dangerous. Old Byrd knows what he's doing, and every detail is planned perfectly ahead of time.

I love and miss you so, my darling.

Ever,

G.

My dearest darling—

Please tell your father that I do have a future in the navy! In fact, I'm expecting a promotion any day now, and once I work my way up into the officer corps, there's going to be no stopping me! Tell your father that.

Yes, I know what you mean when you say our backgrounds, and our religions, are different, but what possible difference could that make to us as long as we love each other? Tell your father that, and I'm sure he will understand. And when he says he doesn't think I'll "fit in" with your New York friends, who says we have

to live in New York? There is a whole world out there
for us to live . . . and love in.

And as for "backgrounds," well maybe we Novilles
aren't high society. But we've always been ambitious,
and hard workers. And maybe your father, the famous educator, doesn't think too much of a fellow
with only a high school diploma, but things like that
shouldn't come between us. When I meet your father,
I'm sure I can make him understand. Trust me, my
love.

No word yet about stateside duty and/or Cmdr. Byrd,
but I'll let you know as soon as I hear anything.

Your always loving
George

My darling—

Please don't listen to what people are telling you!
When two people are in love as much as you and I
are, the only people they need to listen to are each
other.

Meanwhile, every time I take out that flower from
the pages of my diary, I see your sweet face and dream
I am holding you in my arms and kissing your sweet
lips.

Love always,
G.

My darling—

What is wrong? Reading between the lines of your
last letter, I feel that something is terribly the matter! If
something is happening that is troubling you, I'll go
AWOL and jump on the next ship to New York. I'll
be a stowaway!

What do you mean when you say something could
"stop" us? This is America. We were born free. We are
free to marry anyone we wish, aren't we? This isn't
the Dark Ages. My darling, your last letter worries me
terribly. Please write to me immediately and answer all
my questions. I know this: I can't live without you,
my love.

(unsigned)

My darling—

It has been a week since I've heard from you, and I am sick with worry. I can't think of anything else but what you may be going through. Please, please write. If only I could be at your side to help you . . .

But don't give in to them, my love. I know you're strong. Fight back! Fight hard! Our love is stronger and bigger and better than any of them—that is what you said yourself.

Write to me, my love. Write to me!

The correspondence breaks off at this point.

"Hannah needs a tour of Europe, Marcus," her mother said to her father. "All the other girls her age are having them, and I will accompany her as her chaperone."

"Can we afford it, Sadie?"

"I can, yes. I'm going to dip into my inheritance if need be."

"I won't have you doing that, Sadie. I can afford it."

"Very good. I've booked passage for us on the *Berengaria*. We sail for Hamburg Thursday week. The trip should be a broadening experience for her, I should think."

A few letters survive from that memorable European trip which, as it turned out, would last for the better part of a year.

Dearest Papa,

Today we visited the Cologne Cathedral, which is very beautiful and contains much beautiful stained glass above the chancel, depicting 48 queens and the Milan Madonna. The Shrine of the Three Kings on the High Altar was also beautiful and interesting. Tomorrow we visit three more museums, and will hear a performance of Parsifal *at the Offenbachplatz. . . .*

I hope Bridget is remembering to feed Pussy, and to see that her water dish does not go empty.

Mama joins me in best love.
                    Your loving daughter,
                    Hannah

My dear Marcus,

All has been going well for Hannah and myself until today when, after feeling unwell for several days, I consulted a physician, Dr. Ebert with the American Hospital in Berlin, who advises me that I am in the third month of a pregnancy. It all comes as something of a surprise to me, at my age, but Dr. Ebert assures me that this is a not uncommon occurrence for a woman of my age.

As you know, I have always had difficult pregnancies, and in light of this, Dr. Ebert strongly recommends that I not attempt an Atlantic crossing at this point, but rather that I remain here in Germany for my full term. Here, of course, are some of the finest physicians and medical facilities in the world. . . .

Please do not consider coming abroad to join me, dear Marcus. Such a trip would serve no good purpose, and I would not wish to see you interrupt your academic year on my account. I assure you that I am in the best of hands with Dr. Ebert and his staff.

Hannah will remain with me here, and I have enrolled her in some classes at the university, where she will be able to improve her German language skills.

Your loving wife,
Sadie

My dear Marcus,

Your beautiful baby daughter, weighing 6 lbs 11 oz, was born yesterday at 5:30 p.m., or 11:30 a.m. New York time. She is healthy and nursing lustily, and though I know you were hoping for a boy this time, I know you will fall in love with this little darling when you see her. She has your blue eyes and, it seems to me, your ears. What shall we name her? I am thinking of naming her after your grandmother Sachs.

As for me, I am doing well, though feeling somewhat tired and weak. Because of this, and because we are approaching the winter stormy season, and because I have never been a "good sailor," Dr. Ebert recommends that I remain in Berlin for at least another four weeks before attempting an ocean crossing. So I have advised Frau Stockelman that we will keep our little flat for that additional period.

    Hannah joins me in warm greetings.

Your loving wife,

Sadie

3

Placement

In another part of the city—on upper Fifth Avenue, to be exact—Mr. and Mrs. Truxton Van Degan IV are sitting in their living room overlooking the Metropolitan Museum. The Van Degans make it a point never to go out on New Year's Eve—it's such a cliché—though if you read the social columns you know that these two go out many other evenings, either here, or in Palm Beach, or in Southampton, whichever place they happen to be. Their butler has just brought them a bottle of chilled champagne, and the atmosphere in the room is equally icy. As often happens when Truck and Georgette Van Degan are alone together, they find that they have very little to say to one another. Perhaps the champagne will lift their mood. It hasn't yet, though Georgette is doing her level best.

"Well, darling," she says brightly, "are we happy to see 1993 come to an end?" She lifts her glass and tries to smile her most radiant smile. It's the smile she does for *Women's Wear*.

"Damn right," he says. "It's been a shitty year. I told you Bill Clinton would be bad for business. He sure the hell has been."

"Well, here's to a better 1994," she says.

"Yeah." He sits hunched forward in his chair, his glass cradled between two hands, not raising it in response.

She pretends to ignore this. "Patsy Collingwood called this morning," she says. "She's having a little dinner Thursday for William Luckman."

"Who's he?"

"The young man who's written that new book about all the nasty things that go on at Yale. Or it's supposed to be Yale. *Desire Under the Elms*, I think it's called."

"No, that's not it. That's the title of some other book."

"It's something like that. Anyway, I told her we had the thing at the Pierre on Thursday."

"Oh, yeah. That thing at the Pierre."

"Unless you'd rather go to Patsy's, darling. It might be amusing, and I could get us out of the thing at the Pierre, though I hate to do that to Marcella, who has her *placement* all worked out."

"Yeah."

"I do think the thing at the Pierre is really more important, darling. It will get more media coverage. And if we back out, Marcella will have to seat the entire party all over again."

"Yeah."

"And she has us *très bien placé,* at her most important table. With the Shugrues, the Dominican ambassador, and that divine new hairdresser everybody is insisting I've got to try."

"Yeah."

"So I won't call Patsy back."

Following this exchange, there is a long silence.

"And I'm going to try him, too," she says at last.

"Try who?"

"The new hairdresser. Philippe. They say it takes weeks and weeks to get an appointment with him, but if I'm seated next to him on Thursday, I'll work on him."

There is no immediate response to this, and another silence follows. Georgette extends one foot and studies her ankle critically.

Then she says, "He charges two hundred dollars just for a comb-out, but I'm sure he'd do me for less, considering."

"Who're you talking about?"

"Philippe! The hairdresser! Really, Truck, what's the matter with you tonight? I don't think you've listened to a word I've said."

"As a matter of fact, I haven't," he says.

"And you haven't touched your champagne."

He sticks his index finger in his glass. "There," he says. "I just touched it." He licks his finger.

"Really, darling, what's the matter? Something's on your mind, I can tell. What is it?"

"New Year's," he says. "Resolutions."

"Oh?" she says brightly. "What fun! I love New Year's resolutions. Mine's to get an appointment with Philippe as soon as I possibly can once these wretched holidays are over, before we go to P.B. What's yours?"

"I've made a resolution for you, Georgette."

"Oh?" She eyes him narrowly. "*You* made a resolution for *me*?"

"That's right, sweet tits."

"Oh, my, how romantic! You haven't called me sweet tits in years. Now tell me: Just what is this resolution that *you* seem to've made for *me*."

"I want you to do something for the Lieblings."

"For the *who*?"

"Noah Liebling and his wife."

"Oh. You mean the liquor people?"

"That's right."

"You mean you want us to enter*tain* them?"

"That's right."

"Oh, Truckie—puh-*lease*! No, never. No way. Are you quite *mad*? The Lieblings have just come down out of the *trees*!"

"Why not? I want you to do something for them, Georgette."

"All our friends would think we'd lost our minds. They're so N.O.C.D., those Lieblings."

"What's N.O.C.D. mean?"

"Not Our Class, Darling. They're definitely N.O.C.D. There's absolutely nothing they could do for people like us."

"Nevertheless, it's what I want you to do."

"But, darling. Don't you remember? Your parents moved out of one thousand Park when the Lieblings moved in. And they made a point of having their moving people come at exactly the same time as the Lieblings' moving people, so everybody in town knew what was happening. Roxy even put it in her column."

"My dad had some sort of business disagreement with old J. B. Liebling. But that was years ago. This is another generation."

"But that story is too well known. People still laugh about it. What would our friends say if we appeared to be taking up with people like that? One son is a faggot."

"So is that hairdresser you're so eager to sit next to Thursday night."

"Darling, that's quite different. Philippe is a great artist."

"Anyway, I'm not interested in that son. I'm interested in Noah Liebling."

"The son still lives at one thousand. With his mother. They say the Lieblings have ruined that wonderful old building. Nobody lives there anymore."

"Funny, but I walked past the building the other day. It looked fully occupied."

"I mean nobody *we* know. Park between Seventy-sixth and Ninety-sixth has gone way, way downhill. And the sister who calls herself a countess. Everybody says the title is bogus."

"I'm not interested in the sister, either."

"And the father was a bootlegger. He had people killed."

"The old man got his start in Canada, during Prohibition. But there was no Prohibition up there. So you can't call him a bootlegger. Everything he did was perfectly legal. Meanwhile, his son Noah—"

"Oh, Noah Liebling is all right, I suppose. He's *almost* attractive. But it's *her,* his wife, that nobody can stand."

"What's wrong with her?"

"Oh, it's so hard to explain," she says. "She's so pushy, so climby, so *enthusiastic*. She *smiles* too much. She's too *friendly*. She doesn't talk about the things people like us talk about. She bubbles. She bounces. She doesn't wear black at night. She doesn't even frost her hair."

"What's wrong with a bubbly, bouncy woman?"

"New York women don't bubble and bounce. They just don't, which is why she's never fitted in. She's from somewhere like Kansas, and she has a Kansas sort of face. People do imitations of Carol Liebling, and that sort of thing. When she first came to New York, she thought Porthault was only sheets. She'd never heard of the towels. Someone had to explain to her what Rigaud candles were."

"Of course, you, growing up in Cicero, Illinois, knew all about things like that," he says with more than a trace of sarcasm in his voice.

"Maybe not! But when I knew I was going to marry you, I learned—and I learned fast! And I learned to do party talk. She's never learned that. She'll get on a subject and just stick to it."

"When I first met you, Georgette, all you knew how to say was, 'Please raise your seat backs, place your tray tables in a fully locked and upright position, make sure that all carry-on luggage is securely stowed beneath the seat in front of you, and pass all plastic cups and glasses—' "

"So what! So I was a flight attendant! I wanted to better myself, and I did! Look where I am today—*le plus bien placé*! Patsy Collingwood probably isn't even going to have her dinner party if you and I can't be there. She as much as said so."

"You bettered yourself, all right. Thanks to me."

"Okay—thanks to you!"

"And my money."

"Okay—and your goddamned money. You got what you married *me* for, too! The best blow job you ever had!"

"One of the things I married you for," he says evenly, "was to do as you're told. And I'm telling you I want you to do something about Noah Liebling and his wife."

"Why? Tell me why you want me to entertain them?"

"Because I want his business, that's why. Old lady Liebling is getting up there in years. The old battle-ax can't live forever. She's either going to die or retire, and when she does one of those two things, the son is going to take over the company, and when that happens I want his business. Do you realize that for all the years the old battle-ax has been running Ingrahams, the biggest distiller in the world, she's never placed a single order from my bottling plant?"

"Probably because your father made a point of moving out of one thousand Park at the same moment the Lieblings moved in. Talk about royal snubs!"

"That's water over the dam. I want you to do something for Noah Liebling and his wife."

"Truck, I will simply not have those people in my house."

"Then invite them to dinner at a restaurant."

"And be *seen* with them? In *public*? What if Roxy, or

Liz, or Cindy, or Billy should see us? They'd think we were *friends*."

"Then they'd invite us to their place. They live at River House."

"How that board passed them I'll never know. She knows nothing about *placement.* She has a needlepoint pillow in her living room that has 'Thank you for not smoking' on it."

"Maybe she's allergic."

"No. She says the smoke would damage her paintings. Paintings! She hasn't got any, at least none that you or I would hang. Oh, she has a couple of Warhols. But nobody hangs Warhol anymore. After that disastrous sale at Christie's, I took our Warhol down. I was too embarrassed. Warhol is one of yesterday's painters."

"I wondered where the Warhol went. Where is it?"

"Stacked behind the dryer in the laundry room. Where he belongs. But Carol Liebling—she still hangs him. So you see what I mean." With her hand she gives her frosted hair a flip from behind.

He takes a sip of his champagne. "For someone you dislike so much, you seem to know an awful lot about her," he says.

"She has a daughter the same age as Linda. They were at Brearley together. I used to see Carol at parent-teacher meetings. And speaking of that, do you know what that woman had the nerve to say to me?"

"What?"

"She said, 'Have you thought about doing anything with your Chinese porcelains?' "

"What the hell did she mean by that?"

"Oh, she does some volunteer work for the museum." She gestures vaguely in the direction of the building across the street, which is invisible behind the drawn drapes. "She's on a couple of committees. I'm sure she's hoping to get on the board, which'll never happen, of course. She asked me if I'd consider giving our collection to the museum."

"Oh," he says.

"She even said—and this is the worst part—she even said, 'Just think, if you gave your porcelains to the Met, you could run across the street and visit the collection whenever you'd like.' Can you imagine a more gauche remark?"

"Actually," he says thoughtfully, "it's not such a bad idea."

"What's not a bad idea?"

"Giving that stuff to the museum. We'd get a nice tax deduction. My grandfather collected it. I've never given a shit about all that stuff."

"Truck Van Degan, are you out of your *mind*? That pair of Lang Yao *sang-de-boeuf* vases *alone* is worth a fortune! I had an appraiser in. He said you almost never find a pair. No way do you give any of it away. That collection is my insurance!"

"What do you mean—your insurance?"

"You won't buy life insurance. When you die, that collection is one thing I'll have to fall back on."

"I don't buy life insurance because I don't believe in it."

"Don't give me that, Truck. I know you too well. You won't buy life insurance because you're scared to take the physical."

"So," he says carefully, "you're getting ready for me to die. Is that it, sweet tits?"

"Well, after all, you are twenty-two years older than I am, darling. A girl has to think about her future, after all."

"Okay," he says, leaning forward in his chair, "let's talk about the future. Let's talk about the immediate future. I've asked you to do something about Noah Liebling and his wife. I haven't asked you. I've told you. I don't give a shit what you think about his wife. I don't give a shit what she knows about *placement*, or whether she hangs Andy Warhol or not. I happen to own a glass-manufacturing business. I make bottles. It used to be that we could do okay selling to the pharmaceutical companies. But the pharmaceuticals are all switching to plastics. It's killing us."

"Maybe you should get into the plastics business, darling."

"Shut up. Listen to me. There's a rumor on the street that Ingraham is about to launch an important new label. A new label means new bottles. I want the contract for those bottles, and you're going to help me get it. Is that clear? Can you get that through that thick skull of yours? The girls are the way to do it."

"What girls?"

"Linda and their daughter. They went to school together. That's your reason for inviting Noah and his wife to dinner."

"But I can't. Our friends would—"

"Don't tell me what you can and can't do, Georgette. I'm telling you what you *will* do. Understand?"

"Well, I won't." She jumps to her feet. *"I won't!"*

"You want to get into it with me, Georgette? Remember, I own this house. I own the porcelain collection. And I own you. You defy me, and you'll just have to accept the consequences."

"You're saying you'll divorce me? Listen, you son of a bitch, I've got enough goods on you—all documented, don't forget—that if you try to dump me, I'll get a lawyer to slap a divorce suit on you so fast you won't know what hit you! How would you like some of your recent shenanigans, up in Westchester and elsewhere, dragged through a divorce court? You think I had your daughter for the hell of it? I had your child so if you ever tried to dump me, you'd be paying alimony and child support till you bleed to death, you bastard! You think I'm kidding? When I finish with you, you bastard, you won't know your ass from chopped liver! You think business is bad now? When I finish with you, Van Degan Glassworks will be in Chapter Thirteen!"

From where he sits, he reaches out and seizes her left wrist, which is encased in a heavy gold bracelet. "Georgette . . . I'm warning you," he says.

"Let go of me!" she screams. She is a tall woman, five ten, and very thin, but also very strong. He, however, is easily a hundred pounds heavier than she. With his hand on her wrist, he tries to force her back into her chair again while, twisting her wrist in his grip, she tries to claw the back of his hand with her fingernails.

"You want rough stuff, bitch?" he says. "I can do rough stuff. Want a little rough stuff?"

"Stop! You're hurting me!"

He reaches for her other wrist, but she is too quick for him. With her free hand she reaches for her champagne glass and throws it in his face. A spot of blood appears above his left eyebrow.

"Bitch!" He raises his hand and is about to strike her when the butler appears at the door.

Pretending not to have heard the scream, or to notice anything unusual in his employers' situation, the butler says, "Dinner is served, Mrs. Van Degan."

The butler might have made one pertinent observation: Evenings when Truxton and Georgette Van Degan dine at home alone are extremely rare, but at least during this one they have been actually having a conversation.

River House! He must have been out of his mind, Noah Liebling often thinks, when he bought an apartment in this building, and he must have been further out of his mind when he agreed to be elected president of the building's board. Noah and Carol have discussed selling their apartment at River House, even though the market for apartments like theirs is soft right now. With Anne away at college, they hardly need these five bedrooms and five baths. But now that Noah is the board's president—well, selling would seem like a gesture of bad faith, wouldn't it? A coward's way out.

Besides, this is—River House! Thirty stories high, a full city block in width, and containing only seventy-three apartments—many of them duplexes, one of them a triplex with a two-story living room—when it was put up it was heralded as the most luxurious, and most expensive, apartment building in the world. It still is. It is also an unpluggable sinkhole for money. The building soaks up money like a blotter, like a giant sponge. It always has.

River House was built, Noah often thinks, as an act of sheer defiance, or an act of sheer folly—though not on the builder's part. He got his money out of it right away, and left the owner-tenants with the burden of maintaining his extravagance. Ground was broken in 1930, hard on the heels of the great stock market crash of 1929. "A symbol of the city's faith in its economic future," the *Times* called it at the time. But in 1930 the city's economic future looked decidedly grim, and during the next decade, as the Great Depression deepened, things got even grimmer. The building faces the East River, and when it was built, it had its own private marina for its tenants' yachts. Yachts were in short supply during the 1930s, and the tenants heaved a collective sigh of relief in 1941 when the city acquired the riparian rights from the building in order to construct the FDR Drive.

But this was only one economic burden lifted from the building. Another burden has always been the River Club, which occupies five floors and includes dining rooms, party rooms, tennis courts, a swimming pool, and twenty-one guest bedrooms. Originally, the River Club was to be for the exclusive use of the building's tenants. Of course, this didn't work when many tenants declined to purchase club memberships and pay club dues. The River Club was advertised as "a family club," just as River House was supposed to be a family building, meaning that bachelors and single women were discouraged. But soon the club found itself forced to sell memberships to families outside the building, and to rent out its party rooms for outside functions. The twenty-one guest bedrooms remain a problem. They were designed to be available for "overflow house guests" of the tenants. But since few families suffer from overflow house guests nowadays, these rooms are usually vacant and, in any cooperative building, vacant space stands for lack of revenue. When Noah suggested that these rooms might be rented out to transients, there was consternation among the tenants. "You mean running the building like a *hotel*?" cried one. "With total strangers coming in and out?"

"No new assessments!" Each new board president has made this valiant promise to his neighbors. At least Noah knew better than to promise such a never-never world. There will always be new assessments. The need for new assessments arises as often as once a month, at the monthly tenant meetings, and of course the owners of the largest apartments always scream the loudest. It is no wonder that the tenants' meetings often turn into name-calling, free-for-all shouting matches. Sometimes it seems to Noah as though no one in the building is really happy living there.

Tenants' meetings are designed to follow the format

of the New England town meeting, with each tenant permitted to have his or her say. As happens in New England, this means that very little actually gets accomplished. Here are some of the issues covered at the most recent tenants' meeting over which Noah Liebling attempted to preside:

The building's exterior badly needs a cleaning, and to sand-blast and steam-clean the facade will cost about a million dollars. (Everything that needs to be done to the building seems to cost about a million dollars.) Of course, that will mean a special assessment. There are cries of outrage over this. But the contractor has warned that sand-blasting may loosen the mortar between the bricks, and if that happens, the entire building will have to be repointed, and this will cost a good deal more.

Then Mr. Dellamore on fourteen got up to say that he has heard of a new method for cleaning buildings involving an acid wash. But Mrs. Corning on seventeen pointed out that acid washing would cause acid to drip down the sides of the building into the surrounding plants and shrubbery, killing it all, and Mrs. Ellinger on seven declared that she didn't want her section of the building washed with acid. Didn't acid have poisonous fumes? She had no intention of wearing a gas mask around her house for a month.

Mr. Gerridge on twenty-one suggested that only the building's facade that faced the street be washed, but Mrs. Conklin, on eighteen, pointed out that the side facing the river was the dirtiest and deserved the cleaning most, since that was the side the tourists saw when they went up and down the river on the Circle Line cruises. And speaking of views, Mrs. Townsend on nine interrupted, she would like to ask Mrs. Laidlaw, also on nine, to stop drying her panty hose from her windowsill, of which Mrs. Townsend's dining room had a full view. Mrs. Laidlaw hotly denied doing any such thing. In the end it was decided to appoint a committee to study ways and means of getting the building cleaned.

Next on the agenda was the matter of the building's entrance drive, which needed to be resurfaced. Caroline Taylor, on seventeen, claimed she had nearly broken an ankle when she caught her heel in a crack in the pavement. What if that sort of thing happened to a visitor, who might then sue? Very simple, said Mrs. Vadrick on nine. Simply tell your taxi driver to take you straight to the front door, and you won't have to walk on the pavement. Anything to avoid another assessment, she added, and besides, didn't the building have insurance to cover accidents of that kind?

That brought up another problem, Noah reminded them. The building's insurance carrier had announced a rate increase of fifty thousand a year. An assessment would have to be levied to cover the added premium. Mr. Sturtevant, on twenty-four, reminded the group that he was president of an insurance company. He was sure his company would give River House a new insurance policy at a much lower premium. It was decided to form two committees, one on the need for repaving the drive and another to look into new insurance policies.

Then there was the problem of Dr. Skidmore's storm windows. Dr. Skidmore, who lived on four, wanted to install aluminum-frame storm windows throughout his apartment. He was willing to have this done at his own expense, so no additional assessment would be involved, but a number of the other tenants thought aluminum-frame storm windows looked tacky. Leading the tacky contingent was Monica McCluskey, the mouthwash heiress. After Ms. McCluskey made her point, Dr. Skidmore got up and made a long, impassioned speech about the environment, and the importance of conserving energy, and stressed the fact that his aluminum-frame storm windows would help reduce the building's heating and air-conditioning bills, which were already staggering and getting bigger all the time. Ms. McCluskey replied that it wouldn't be so bad if the Skidmores occupied "one of the more desirable upper-floor apartments," such as her own, where storm windows would not be visible from the street. But as it was, from their "less desirable" space on the fourth floor, and in full view of passersby, "Dr. Skidmore wants to add tacky-looking storm windows that will make the whole building look tacky." Dr. Skidmore then called Ms. McCluskey "a post-menopausal old bag." Ms. McCluskey called Dr. Skidmore a "creep."

It was decided to table the storm-window issue for the time being, until tempers cooled. Sometimes it seems to

Noah that everybody in River House hates everybody else.

"But while we're on the subject of floors," Mrs. Curtis LeMosney rose to say, "as we all know, Mr. and Mrs. Hamilton, who live on the floor below mine, have recently, on their own and without the building's permission, hired a contractor and knocked down the wall between their living room and library in order to enlarge their living room. My apartment has the same configuration as the Hamiltons', or it did before they removed that wall. And now my living room floor squeaks when I walk across it, which it never did before." This drew no comment, since the knocked-out wall was a *fait accompli*. "I would like the board to reprimand the Hamiltons," Mrs. LeMosney added.

The last matter of business involved the canvas entrance canopy over the front door, which had been ripped in a recent storm and needed to be replaced. "The individual assessments for this should be relatively small," Noah added in what he hoped was an encouraging tone. Everyone agreed that the torn canopy looked awful, but there was considerable disagreement about what color the new canopy should be. A few traditionalists favored the same color as before, a sober dark brown. But others wanted something different for a change, dark green, perhaps, or a deep Venetian red, or dark blue, or black "to match the black marble in the entrance foyer." Each color, it seemed, had its small band of advocates. Monica McCluskey suggested a color that would be "bright, gay, and inviting," like yellow, orange, baby blue, or pink. There were boos and hisses when she got to pink. The argument over colors grew quite heated until it was decided to appoint a committee to study canopy colors and collect fabric samples.

There being no further business, Noah could always count on his old friend Frank Stokes to move that the meeting be adjourned, and on Beryl, Frank's wife, to second the motion.

Everyone who lives in River House is supposed to be rich. But, Noah sometimes suspects, some of the building's tenants may not be as comfortably off as they pretend to be. There is the curious case of the Darius Satterthwaites, for example. Joanne (called "Pookie")

Satterthwaite and her husband are in the *Social Register.*
Pookie and Darius Satterthwaites' names are often in
the columns and, in fact, Pookie Satterthwaite, Georgette Van Degan, and Patsy Collingwood are often referred to as "The Big Three" among New York's social
ladies. The Satterthwaites own one of the grander duplexes in River House, on the twenty-ninth and thirtieth
floors, and yet they have no furniture. Not a stick of
it. Where do they sleep, Noah often wonders—on the
building's famous mahogany parquet floors?

And then there is the perennial problem of Graham
Grenfell, the famous interior designer. Mr. Grenfell's
apartment is lavishly furnished in antique pieces of museum quality. In fact, some people suspect that Graham
Grenfell uses his apartment as his showroom, though
this is strictly against the rules. Graham Grenfell has
decorated a number of River House apartments, including Monica McCluskey's, who is said to have spent fifteen million on interior decor, including Fortuny wall
coverings and window hangings, marble bathrooms, and
a Baccarat chandelier in her dining room that cost a cool
million in itself. Too big for the freight elevator, the
chandelier had to be hoisted up from the street by a
construction crane mounted on the roof. And yet despite
assignments the size of this one, Graham Grenfell is always at least three months delinquent in his monthly
maintenance payments. Just when the board is about to
write him a letter, threatening to cut off his services,
meaning he will have to carry out his own garbage to
the street, Mr. Grenfell makes a partial payment and the
board withdraws the letter. Noah Liebling has promised
to do his best to put River House on a sound fiscal basis,
but with tenants the likes of Graham Grenfell, this is
going to be hard to do.

Noah and Carol Liebling own what is considered a
midsize apartment at River House, and on a middle
floor, the fifteenth. Their friends Frank and Beryl
Stokes—Frank is an Ingraham vice-president, and Noah
helped the Stokeses get into the building—have the
same apartment on the floor below. Tonight Carol has
set her dinner table for ten, with place cards. She has,
in fact, given considerable thought to *placement.* She and

Noah will sit at either end, of course, and since the sexes are not evened out—six women, four men—she will give herself two women: Noah's mother, on her right, in the place of honor, and Ruth's daughter, Becka, reunited with her mother at least for the time being, will be on Carol's left. Noah will then be given two women: sister Ruth, on his right, and Melody Richards on his left. Carol had thought it would be fun for the two girls to have the young celebrity author sit between them, and so she has placed Bill Luckman between Melody and Anne. Across the table, next to Becka, will go Ruth's new beau, whose name is Ector, and then Cyril, on Ruth's right. The table looks very pretty, with yellow tulips, out of season, as a centerpiece, but the candles have not yet been lighted. After receiving Mr. Nelson's telephone call from the car about the traffic situation on Park, Carol told Edna, her cook, to take the roast out of the oven so it won't be overdone. It can be slipped back in again when the last three dinner guests arrive.

Now the other seven are in the living room having cocktails. Mary, Carol's maid, is passing hot hors d'oeuvres. The lights from Long Island City, across the river, glitter from the tall windows, and William Luckman has assumed center stage, spreading his arms in wide demonstration before his temporarily captive audience. "The trouble is," he is saying, "is that the so-called modernist poets have lost the power to express emotions. *Feelings*. Lost it—they've thrown it away! When somebody like Keats talked about high-piled books in charactery, you could just see, you could almost reach out and *touch* all those wonderful, dusty old volumes. Thumb-worn, with heavy leather bindings—all piled in a sloppy sort of stack. Just in those five words you can feel the lamplight, feel the almost *runic* content of those books. Now someone like Merwin, on the other hand—"

"Oh, I agree with you," Carol Liebling says. "I've always loved the English romantic poets. They wrote with meter, and they wrote with rhyme. Meter and rhyme require work, and thought, and discipline. So much modern poetry seems just lazy to me. My friend Beryl Stokes is a former English teacher. She taught creative writing at the high school level. She said her kids would put any jumble of words on paper and call it a poem."

"They do the same thing at Bennington today," Melody Richards says. "The teachers try not to let them get away with it. We're asked to write an Alexandrian sonnet, a Shakespearean sonnet. They're not easy."

"You're both absolutely right," Bill Luckman says, nodding his approval. "Modern poetry is too easy to write. That's why no one reads it. And that's why no one wants to publish it. How long has it been since each of you has read a contemporary poem? Becka?"

"Months." Becka is trying hard not to look bored.

"Ector? I'm particularly interested in hearing your views."

"Uh—" He blows his nose into a paper cocktail napkin.

"Melody?"

"Well, at school we do read Eliot. And Pound. And—"

"They're almost classicists now, aren't they? Carol? How long?"

"Years. Years and years." He is a bit full of himself, she thinks, taking over the conversation like this. But he is certainly a nice-looking young man, with looks that suggest a young Tyrone Power. His eyebrows grow straight across the bridge of his nose, in a single dark, unbroken line along his brow. This is supposed to say something about a man's character, but Carol can't remember what it is. Like a cleft chin, or dimples. Does it indicate strength or weakness? "What about you, Noah?" he asks. "How long since you've read a contemporary poem?"

Noah is busy refilling drinks. "I've never been much of a literary type," he says. "But I think I do agree with you about the moderns."

He turns to Noah's sister now. "Melody tells me you're writing a novel, Countess," he says.

Ruth merely smiles.

"Can you tell us what it's about?"

She hesitates. "Love, I suppose," she says at last.

"Wonderful. Every great novel must contain a great love story."

Ruth has learned one thing from her days in films.

She has learned how to find the key light. She has found it now, in a tiny low-voltage ceiling spot that was placed to illuminate Andy Warhol's *Double Marilyn* with purple hair and green lips. When this light touches the tip of Ruth's nose, the tiny lines of aging, aided by periodic collagen injections, seem to fade away. Still, Carol thinks that Ruth, at fifty-five, has kept her beauty remarkably well, along with her figure. If only Ruth didn't always seem to be so unhappy . . .

". . . You're brave to hang your Warhols," Bill Luckman is saying. "A lot of people nowadays are nervous about owning Warhol. They're saying he's not a has-been but a never-was."

"Noah and I buy pictures we like. We don't think of them as investments, if that's what you mean."

"I admire your courage, Carol," he says. "I truly do."

"Have you ever thought of writing a novel, Bill?" Melody asks him. "Perhaps you should."

He gives her a sudden, hard look. "Are you suggesting that *Blighted Elms* is fiction?" he says.

"No, I only meant—"

"I assume everyone here has read my book," he says.

There is a brief, embarrassed silence, and Carol moves about the room with a plate of tiny sausages wrapped in pastry. "Do try one of these. My cook makes them herself. . . ."

Ector yawns noisily. ("It's Ector, not Hector," he said when introducing himself. "It's a Welsh name." And Carol has been so busy remembering this unusual first name that she has forgotten his last, which is something simple like White or Smith or Jones.) "Anything good on TV?" he asks now. "New Year's Eve, there ought to be some really neat shows." He looks around the room. "Hey, where is your TV?" he asks.

"There's a set in the library," Carol murmurs, "but—"

"You got a library here? Like the public library?"

"The room where we keep our books." She smiles brightly at him.

"You don't have a TV in the living room, where you can watch it? Are you shitting me?"

From the moment he entered the room, Carol suspected that Ruth's new beau was going to present a problem. For one thing, he must be less than half Ruth's age. For another, he is not appropriately dressed, in a blue windbreaker and an open shirt that is unbuttoned down to his chest hairs. He looks like a young thug, or a stevedore. He has heavy, pouting lips, like the young men who pose in leather zip-front bikini briefs for some of the kinkier menswear catalogues that show up in your mailbox. Carol Liebling suddenly has the wild thought that Ruth may have hired him for the evening from an escort service. He looks like a boy toy, and she wonders, with a sense of grim amusement, what Ruth's mother, when she arrives, will think of Ruth's newest romantic interest.

Ector, apparently sensing that he has said something out of place, stands up. "Gotta take a leak," he says. "Where's the john?"

"Straight down the hall, on your right," Carol says brightly. She glances at Ruth, who is following Ector adoringly with her eyes, and she hears Bill Luckman murmur the words "free spirit," but she is not sure whether he is referring to her, and her choice of artists, or to Ector.

Bill Luckman, without missing a beat and not wishing to lose his audience, turns to Ruth. "It's such a pleasure to meet you, Countess," he says. "I happened to watch *The Archbishop's Wife* on television the other night, and now that I've met you I can see that you would have been perfect to play the part of Rosalie. Brenda Scofield, who ended up playing your part, just didn't do the role justice."

"Thank you," Ruth whispers.

"Was it wonderful working with the great John Mardsen?"

She nods, and smiles, and spreads her hands in what-can-I-say gesture.

He turns to Carol. "You see, I've done my homework on the Liebling family," he says, and the implication is left floating in the air that the Liebling family has not done sufficient homework on him.

"I know you're all going to be impressed with Bill's book when you've had a chance to read it," Melody says. "It's really a blistering indictment of academia in the nineties."

"That's what the *New York Times* says," he says.

Ector has returned from the bathroom, and now makes a point of sitting in a loveseat next to Becka, rather than Ruth, which Ruth notices but pretends not to notice. "What do you do, Ector?" Becka asks him.

"Do?"

"For a living, I mean."

"Oh. Entertainment business."

"You're an actor?"

"More in the entertainment end, I guess," he says.

"Interesting."

Now there is another small crisis. Though he is sitting on a sofa next to a needlepoint pillow with the legend THANK YOU FOR NOT SMOKING, Bill Luckman has just casually reached into his jacket pocket, removed a pack of Dunhill cigarettes, and is lighting one with a slim gold lighter. There are several anxious glances in Carol's direction, but she merely says, "Let me see if I can find you something to use for an ashtray, Bill."

And as Carol goes to the drawer of a small table in search of an ashtray, Ector, seeing what Bill is doing, reaches in his own windbreaker pocket for cigarettes. Ruth raises her fingertip in a small warning gesture.

"Hell, if that guy can smoke, why can't I?" Ector says angrily. "What's so special about that fucker?"

"Let me see if I can find ashtrays for you both," Carol says, rummaging through the drawer, feeling suddenly short of breath.

There is something almost arrogant in Bill Luckman's smile, and in the way he holds the cigarette poised in his hand, waiting to be served an ashtray. Turning to Noah, he says, "Melody tells me you and Carol are almost like foster parents to her, Noah," he says, exhaling sharply.

"Surrogate," Noah says. "More like surrogate parents. At least at holiday times. We're all very fond of Melody."

"Tell me, Bill," Carol says. "Are you working on another book?"

"Yes, as a matter of fact I am," he says, looking pleased with the question.

"Can you tell us what it is? Or is it a deep, dark secret?"

"Well, *Blighted Elms* is about sex, as I guess you all

know. Sex is one of the two most powerful forces in human life. Sex itself is an act of raw power. In every sexual act there is one partner who is the victor, while the other is the conquered. Sex is an act of overpowerment. There is only one other source of power to equal it, in fact, to surpass it, and that is what I am writing about in my new book."

"Is sex really an act of overpowerment? Not for me." This is from Carol, in a bemused tone. "It seems to me more like a kind of sharing."

"Money," he says. "Sex is about physical power. Money is about emotional and psychological power. My book will be about America's secret rich."

"Oh? And who are America's secret rich?" Becka asks him. Becka, Carol thinks, does not much care for this young man.

"Take families like the Pritzkers of Chicago. They're enormously rich. They're a family of lawyers, but lawyers whose only clients are themselves. They're into all sorts of things. Hotels. Vast real estate holdings. But nobody really knows anything about them. Then there are the Weyerhaeusers of the Pacific Northwest—lumber barons. Except for the extraordinary number of vowels in the family name—six—nobody knows anything about them, either. But all these families have skeletons in their closets, family secrets that they make sure no one ever knows about. Shameful secrets."

"The secret rich and their shameful secrets," Becka says.

"Exactly," he says.

"What makes you so sure there are secrets? And if there are secrets, that they're so shameful?"

"There always are. There've got to be. If there weren't any secrets, they wouldn't be rich."

"Hmm," Becka says. "Interesting."

Melody, Carol notices, has been oddly silent through all of this, her eyes fixed on some indeterminate middle distance.

"And then there are the Lieblings of New York," he says.

Carol laughs lightly. "I'm not sure the Lieblings have any shameful secrets," she says. "But we're a family who've always enjoyed a certain amount of privacy. Most of us intend to keep it that way."

"Gotta take another leak," Ector says, standing up again, and Carol wonders briefly if he is possibly on some sort of drug.

"Some rich families have enjoyed too much privacy."

"And how," Becka asks him, leaning forward, "do you intend to go about extracting these secrets from the families you plan to write about? How do you go about shaking family skeletons out of closets?"

"That," he says with a little smile, "may take a certain amount of engineering."

Carol watches as Ector returns to the room and slumps in the loveseat again beside Becka, who barely seems to notice him.

"Engineering?"

"It's part of the creative process. Causing things to happen that wouldn't happen otherwise. It's part of the artist's job, molding the ordinary realities of life into what becomes a work of art."

"Do you mean to say you'll simply make things up?" Becka asks him.

"I assure you," he says sharply, "that my book will not be a work of fiction. It will, on the other hand, be a work of art."

"Fascinating," Carol says, to fill the little silence that has fallen across the room. "Another little quiche before they get cold?"

"Shit," Ector says, stubbing out his cigarette in the ashtray that Carol has provided. He turns to Ruth. "Is this all your family ever does? Talk about shit like this? Books and art and stuff? Let's see what's on TV."

But the moment is saved by the sound of the doorbell.

"They're here," Carol says, and hurries to the door to greet Hannah Liebling, Cyril, and Anne. There follow the usual apologies for being late, descriptions of the state of traffic on Park Avenue, the collecting of coats and scarves, greetings and kisses. Cyril kisses Carol on both cheeks, then turns to his sister, performs a deep bow, and lifts her thin hands to his lips. "My dear Contessa," he says. "Looking lovelier than ever, and younger than springtime." He turns to Ector and stares at him imperiously. "And this must be your new beau. Oh, my. Will wonders never cease."

"I need to tell Edna to put the roast back in the oven," Carol is saying.

"Yes. I like my lamb pink, but not bleeding. At least my slice. Noah, I'd like to have a few words with you alone after dinner."

"Sure, Mom."

During all this Becka returns to Bill Luckman. "You used the word engineering," she says. "Do you mean you can eng*ineer* family scandals in these rich families you'll be writing about?"

"I'm simply describing the artistic process," he says. "Turning life into art."

Not too many city blocks away, on upper Fifth Avenue, Georgette Van Degan is lying across her bed weeping. "Please, darling," she is saying to him, "please let me do what you like the most. Both your balls in my mouth at once. Isn't that what you like the most, darling? Isn't it? Let me do that for you now."

"Make that phone call first," he says. "Then you can do that."

"Please," she sobs. "Take off your clothes, darling. Let me get both of those fat juicy balls—"

"Make that call now! Call Carol Liebling now! Do you hear me?"

"But it's New Year's *Eve*, Truck! People don't call other people—people they hardly know—on New Year's Eve!"

"Make it now, I said. I want to watch you make it." He hurls the heavy Manhattan phone book onto the bed beside her. "Look up their number and *make that call.*"

She stifles one final sob, blows her nose into a Kleenex, wipes her eyes, and rolls over on her side and reaches for the telephone book.

4

A Telephone Call

"Your roast is perfect, dear," Hannah Liebling is saying to Carol at the table. "Just the way I like it. Pink, but not bleeding. And yes," she says to Mary, who is passing the lamb roast a second time, "I do think I will have a second slice." She helps herself from Mary's out-stretched platter.

"When I heard you were going to be late, I had Edna take it out of the oven," Carol says. "So it wouldn't overdo." And yes, she thinks, her table looks perfect, too—the Spode, the Baccarat wineglasses, the lighted candles in their heavy silver candlesticks, the flatware freshly polished by Mary just this afternoon, even though Ector has clearly had some trouble selecting which fork to use and left his dinner fork in the bowl in which the carrots were being passed. Mary quickly removed it, replaced it with a serving fork, and gave him another dinner fork. The yellow tulips in the centerpiece are drooping gracefully, just so, and Carol dares to hope that the rest of the evening will go well.

"I'm glad to see you using the Sachs family silver," Hannah says. "You're taking such good care of it, too, just the way my mother used to do. My mother always said that good silver should be polished every day."

Bill Luckman lifts a dessert fork and balances it between his thumb and forefinger. "This is German silver, isn't it, Mrs. Liebling?" he says.

"Indeed it is. In my mother's day, German silver was considered to be the best."

"How'd you know that?" Ector asks him from across the table. "How'd you know it was German silver?" His tone is almost aggressive, and the two young men, who are roughly the same age, exchange cool looks. This is the first acknowledgment that Bill has made of Ector's presence at this gathering.

"A Yale education, I suppose," Bill Luckman says, a bit drily.

"Huh!"

"Bill has written a book about Yale," Melody says, trying to be helpful.

"The traffic was really terrible coming down Park Avenue," Hannah says. "Bumper to bumper. I told my driver he would have done better to come down Third. There are more lanes, and the lights are synchronized."

"Excuse me," Bill says, "but isn't Third Avenue an uptown street?"

There is a little silence, and then Cyril says, "There is one thing you should know about our mother, Mr. Luckman. If she wants Third Avenue to run downtown, even for a few minutes and for just a few blocks, she will pay to have it done."

There is polite laughter at this, and then Hannah says, "And there was the most awful-looking group of young Negroes, with the strangest hairdos, who came right out into the street, and were jumping over cars, including ours. Right on Park Avenue! This isn't the same city I knew when I was growing up."

"But Mother has her pistol, and her can of Mace," Cyril says. "Our mother is always armed to the teeth, ready to do battle in any contingency."

There is more polite laughter. "New York just isn't the city it used to be," his mother says. "It just isn't. It's all those Negroes who came up from the South after the war."

Carol reaches out and touches her mother-in-law's wrist, and glances toward the kitchen door where Mary, who is black, is emerging to pass the vegetables a second time.

"It's true. That's what it is," Hannah says.

"Of course Mother is referring to the *first* war," Cyril says. "The Battle of Ardennes. Now, that was my idea of a battle. No, thank you, Mary," he says to the vegetable plates, one in each hand.

Now there is a little lull in the conversation.

"Beautiful tulips," Melody says.

"Tulips in midwinter."

"They force them in hothouses."

"Delicious roast. Be sure to tell Edna."

Bill Luckman clears his throat. "You're all so kind to include me in this little family gathering," he says.

"Of course," says Cyril, "it would be more of a family gathering if Aunt Bathy were here." He winks slyly at his brother, and Noah and Carol exchange glances down the length of the table.

"Aunt Bathy?" Bill says. "What a charming name. Who is Aunt Bathy?"

"My baby sister," Hannah says. "Her name is Bathsheba, after my father's grandmother, but we've always called her Bathy."

"Bathsheba? Wasn't Bathsheba an adulteress in the Bible?"

"Yes, but she and David repented, and the Lord forgave them. She gave birth to Solomon, whom the Lord loved."

"Of course, you're absolutely right," he says.

"Bathy is what my mother called her change-of-life baby. She's seventeen years younger than I am."

"With that much difference in your ages, she must have seemed more like your daughter than your baby sister, Mrs. Liebling."

"Well, perhaps. More like a little doll I could play with. My father used to call us his three graces—my big sister Settie, my baby sister Bathy, and me."

"And why isn't she here tonight?" he asks.

There is a little silence around the table, and then Cyril says, "Let's just say that some people in the family see Aunt Bathy, and some people don't."

"I see her all the time," Hannah says. "She lives in Brooklyn Heights. Bathy's tragedy was that she never married. And she was the prettiest of all of us. But she just never seemed able to find Mr. Right."

"Or perhaps Mr. Right turned out to be Mr. Wrong," Cyril says.

"She just never found her one true love," she says.

"Granny's one true love wasn't Grandpa," Anne says with a giggle. "Right, Nana Hannah?"

"Anne, whatever are you talking about?"

"You said so in the car."

"I said no such thing!"

"No, but I could tell it was true when you changed the subject, Nana Hannah."

"Anne, don't tease your grandmother," Carol says.

"What's this?" Ector asks as Mary places a finger bowl on the silver service plate in front of him.

"It's called a finger bowl," Bill Luckman says. "Remove the spoon and fork from the plate. Place the fork on your left and the spoon on your right. Now lift the bowl, *and* the doily, and place them both at eleven o'clock above your service plate."

"Why's there a flower floating in it?"

"Ignore the flower."

"What's this? More Yale shit?" He takes a gulp of his wine.

"Tell me more about your sister Bathy, Mrs. Liebling," Bill Luckman says, turning back to her.

"My father adored Bathy. She was the apple of his eye. My father was a famous educator, Mr. Luckman, but I suppose you knew that, since I gather you're interested in education."

"No, I didn't know that," he says.

"My father was Dr. Marcus Sachs."

"Should that name ring a bell, Mrs. Liebling?"

"Well, it would to a lot of people. He ran the Sachs Collegiate Institute. Of course, it died when he died. But he educated the sons of some of the finest families in New York City."

"She means some of the finest *Jewish* families, Mr. Luckman," Cyril says.

Ector looks across at Ruth. "You Jewish?" he says. "You didn't tell me that. I thought you said you was a countess."

Ruth merely smiles faintly and lowers her eyes. The key light now comes from the flickering flames of the candelabra.

"My father believed in discipline," Hannah says. "He did not believe in sparing the rod."

"Like some other fathers I could mention," Cyril says.

"And yet he turned out young men who went on to become some of the greatest business leaders in this city, including Bernie Baruch. My father taught that sort. Not someone like my husband."

"And you didn't even love him!" Anne says.

"That's not true, Anne. It's not true that I didn't love your grandfather."

"Then why—"

"This is Edna's famous chocolate mousse," Carol says brightly, picking up her spoon. "It's made with Demerara rum."

"The great Bernard Baruch," Bill Luckman says. "That really is impressive, Mrs. Liebling."

"He went on to become a family friend. Whatever money Papa left to my sisters and me, we have to thank Bernie for his advice to Papa on investments."

Bill turns to Carol. "This is all so interesting," he says. "Tell me about your family, Carol."

She laughs. "Not as distinguished as my husband's, I'm afraid."

"On the Sachs side, at least," Hannah says. "The Lieblings weren't anybody."

"My parents were quite ordinary, small-town people," Carol says. "My father died"—though this is not quite the truth—"and my mother is in a nursing home in Connecticut."

"So you're able to visit her fairly often?"

"Not as often as I should, I'm afraid," she says. "On her birthday, and at Christmastime, and whenever I feel particularly guilty about it. Those visits aren't easy—"

Anne giggles again. "Mom tries to think about Granny Dugan as little as possible," she says. "She even forgets where Granny Dugan is, and has to look the place up in her address book every time she goes up there!"

"Anne, will you pass that little plate of cookies?" Carol says, to change the subject.

"You visited her this Christmas, then?"

"Unfortunately, no, I—do try one of Edna's delicious almond macaroons."

Bill Luckman turns to Anne, on his left, ignoring the cookies. "What a rich mixture of genes you've inherited!" he says. "See how much I've managed to learn already about the secret rich?"

"The secret rich?" Anne says.

"It's a book he's writing," Becka says. "About little-known rich families in America. The Lieblings are going to be one of them."

Anne giggles. "This family has plenty of secrets, that's for sure," she says, and Bill Luckman gives Becka a look that says: I told you so.

"We most certainly do not," Hannah says sharply. "I assure you, Mr. Luckman, that my family will take no part in any such enterprise."

Now Mary enters from the living room and goes to Carol. "A telephone call for you, Mrs. Liebling," she whispers.

"Find out who it is, and tell them I'll call them back after I finish dinner."

"It's Mrs. Truxton Van Degan, ma'am."

Carol frowns. "Georgette Van Degan," she says. "I wonder what she wants. I guess I'd better take it. I'll take it in the other room. Excuse me." She rises and steps into the next room.

"The famous Georgette Van Degan," Bill Luckman says.

"A typical New York story," Cyril says. "One day she's pushing a cart down the aisle of a plane over Salt Lake City. The next day she's living in a penthouse over Central Park, the toast of New York society. Instant old money."

Hannah sniffs. "There used to be some Van Degans in our building," she says. "We didn't know them."

Ector takes another swallow of his wine. "Hell, I don't mind if you're all Jewish," he says. "I got nothing against the Jews. But it's just that the way you was all quotin' the Bible a while back, I thought you was the other way around."

"The Bible contains an Old Testament and a New Testament," Bill Luckman says.

Ector scowls. "I gotta take a leak," he says, and pushes back his chair.

But before he has completely left the room, or is fully out of earshot, Hannah says in a loud voice, "Ruth, where in the world did you ever dig up such a thoroughly unsuitable young man?"

And Ruth, who has said very little all evening, suddenly bursts into tears. She flings her napkin on the table, jumps out of her chair, tipping it over as she does, and runs after Ector, screaming, "Ector! Ector! *Take me home!*"

Noah reaches out and sets his sister's chair upright again, and her daughter Becka, red-faced with embarrassment, says, "Should I go with her? What do you think?"

"I'll see that you get home okay, Becka," Noah says quietly.

And in the long silence that follows Ruth's outburst, Melody Richards says, "I heard a cute joke the other day. It's about the nervous usher at the wedding. He's an usher at this big wedding, you see, and he's very nervous about getting all these people seated in the right seats. So when he sees a woman seated in the wrong place, he says, 'Mardon me, padam, but you are occupewing the wrong pie. Please allow me to sew you to another sheet.' "

Noah chuckles at the joke and thinks: Dear Melody! She must sometimes wonder how she got involved with this crazy family.

"That," says Bill Luckman, "in case you didn't know it, is called a Spoonerism, after William Archibald Spooner, 1844 to 1930, who for many years was warden of New College, Oxford. He was famous for his word transpositions, a form of metathesis. He once proposed a toast to Queen Victoria as 'our queer old dean.' "

There is more polite laughter among the seven remaining at the table, but Noah Liebling throws Bill Luckman a hard look. He has decided that Ector is just a stupid clod, but Bill Luckman is a wise-ass little prick.

"Ruth is so *touchy*," Hannah says.

Now Carol returns to the dining room, looking flushed and excited. "That was Georgette Van Degan," she says. "She wants to take me to lunch next week. I can't imagine why, I hardly know her. Unless—and this is a really wild guess—unless she's thinking of giving her Chinese porcelains to the Met. They really have a fabulous collection, including a pair of Lang Yao *sang-de-boeuf* vases that the museum would practically kill to have. Do you suppose that's it? I suggested that to her a couple of years ago, and maybe I planted a little seed in her mind. That must be it. Wouldn't that be wonderful? Wouldn't that be a feather in my cap—if I were the one who helped get the Van Degan porcelains for the Met?"

Then she notices the two empty chairs. "What became of Ruth and Ector?" she asks.

"I believe they went out to answer a call of nature," Cyril says with a tight smile.

"I see," she says. And then, "Well, shall we have our coffee in the living room?"

"I'd like to see you for a minute in the library, Noah," his mother says. "A little family business."

And now the little group, reduced to six—Carol, Bill, Cyril, and the three younger girls—has gathered in the living room, as Carol pours coffee. "The Van Degan collection is really fabulous," she is saying. "There are some eleventh-century bowls from the Sung period, for instance. Wouldn't it be great if the Met could get it all?"

"This is a beautiful room," Bill Luckman says, "and such a wonderful building. I understand that Noah is president of the building's board. That's quite an honor."

Carol makes a face. "I think he's finding it more of a headache than he bargained for," she says. "I think he's grateful that it's only for a year."

"The architects were Bottomly, Wagner, and White," he says. "And do you know that after they did River House, they never designed another important building in New York? River House was their *Arbeit,* and their swan song."

"What interesting tidbits of information you have at your fingertips, Bill," Carol says.

But despite the attempt at light chitchat, the atmosphere in the room is strained and tense. Becka, Ruth's daughter, still looks uncomfortable. She would like to ask Carol who, after all, has known her mother longer and better than anyone else in the room, to tell her more about her mother. But somehow, in the presence of non-family members, this doesn't seem appropriate.

Perhaps, Carol thinks, Melody senses this. Melody suddenly turns to Bill and says, "Would you like me to show you the rest of the apartment? It's really awfully pretty."

"I'd love that," he says matter-of-factly, setting down his cup.

* * *

As soon as they have left the room, Becka leans forward and says, "Aunt Carol, can you explain my mother to me?"

Carol hesitates. Then she says, "I've been wondering why you decided to come here, Becka."

"I didn't decide to come. She sent for me."

"This is the door to the library," Melody says, leading him across the long central gallery. "We can't go in there right now, because Anne's father and her grandmother are having a meeting in there. So. What did you think of them?"

"Who?"

"The Lieblings."

He shrugs. "Pretty ordinary. Nothing sensational."

"Not sensational enough for this new book you're writing?"

"Well, you know what Proust said—happy families are all alike."

"It wasn't Proust. It was Tolstoy."

"No, it was Proust."

"Have it your way," she says. "And this is what they call the blue guest room," she says, holding open a door. "You didn't tell me you wanted to meet the Lieblings because you were thinking of putting them into a book."

He smiles. "I guess I forgot to mention that."

"Do you think that was quite fair?"

"All's fair in love and war," he says with a little wink.

She gives him a sideways look. "Really? You disappoint me, Bill. I'd have expected a more original comment than that from the great writer."

His smile fades briefly, then returns. He says nothing.

"You see, it puts me in kind of an awkward position," she says. "After all, I asked if I could bring you tonight. The Lieblings are like a second family to me, and I've probably already told you certain things about them that I wouldn't want to see in a book."

"I think they're a little more to you than a second family," he says. "I think you're hoping they'll be your passport to a different sort of life."

She ignores this, opening another door. "And this is Anne's bedroom . . ."

"Tell me more about the countess."

"Poor Aunt Ruth. She's had a lot of problems. I'm sorry she ran out like that tonight. She can be quite sweet. But Nana Hannah tends to criticize her."

"Does she always wear that thick pearl choker?"

"Quite often, yes."

"She tilted her head at one point tonight, and I could see why. I saw the scars. The countess tried to slit her throat once, didn't she? See how observant I am?"

"Her romance with the count was pretty unhappy, I guess," she says. "It's funny to hear you call her the countess. She's always been plain Aunt Ruth to me."

"But I think she likes being called a countess, doesn't she?"

"I suppose so. But if you're looking for family scandals, there's sort of one there. When she married the count, he already had another wife."

"I know all about that. That's not good enough. Too ordinary. Too long ago. I'm looking for real family fireworks. Current fireworks. Current fireworks that have never been written about before. That's what'll sell a book."

"And I suppose if you can't find real family fireworks, you'll simply make some up."

He grabs her wrist. "What do you mean by that crack?" he says.

She twists her wrist free. "Nothing. But I've noticed you get very touchy whenever anyone suggests that everything in *Blighted Elms* isn't based on fact."

"It *is* fact. Anyway, with the Lieblings I've just scratched the surface. I'll be doing a lot more digging."

"Noah didn't like you. I guess you noticed that."

"Who cares? He's a cipher. It's obvious the old lady runs the show."

"I don't think Nana Hannah liked you, either. Watch out, Billy boy."

He stares at her. "*You* watch out," he says. "Don't start playing any games with me."

She opens another door. "And this is Noah and Carol's room," she says. "They each have their own separate dressing rooms and bathrooms. Pretty, don't you think?"

"You know, I usually like girls your age, Melody."

"Really? Why?"

"Because most girls your age have no history."

"You think I have no history?"

"Maybe you do. But I also think you're busy writing a new kind of history for yourself right now."

"Really? And this is the yellow guest room. It's the one I use. It has a small terrace with a river view. But it's too cold to go out there tonight." She starts to turn away.

"I observed something else tonight," he says.

"Oh? What's that?"

"You're in love with Noah Liebling."

"*What?* Don't be ridiculous."

"Oh, yes. I can tell. You didn't say much, but you couldn't keep your eyes off *mein* host. Think you'd like to be the next Mrs. Noah Liebling? Is that it?"

"Nonsense. Noah is Anne's father, and Anne is my best friend. And I happen to be devoted to Carol." She feigns a yawn. "You bore me."

"What's that got to do with it? It's lucky for you that Anne has popcorn for brains. I observed that, too. You know what? I'll bet you do Anne's homework for her at college. I'll bet Anne would have flunked out of Bennington long before this if it weren't for you. Am I right? But Anne is too useful to you for you to let her do that—*right?*"

"Wrong! You're so off base, Billy boy, that it's—"

"Listen. I know why you invited me here tonight."

"I invited you because you said you wanted to meet the Lieblings! Now please—"

"But you had a little different agenda—right? You know that Noah has a little bit of an itch for you. You invited me here to make him jealous. Is there a better way to whip up a man's interest than to make him a little jealous? You like to use people—don't you?"

"*Really!* You think I want to make Noah jealous of *you*?"

"Sure. I'm a hell of a lot younger and better-looking than he is, aren't I? Aren't I being called one of New York's most eligible bachelors? Aren't I getting more column mentions than that asshole John Kennedy, Junior?"

"Your craziness is only exceeded by your vanity, Billy boy."

"Sure, you invited me here tonight to build a little bonfire under Noah Liebling. And it worked. Of course he didn't like me. So this little dinner invitation was a little bit of a quid pro quo, wasn't it? Something for me, something for you."

She turns toward the door. "I'm not enjoying this conversation," she says. "Let's go back and join the others."

"Not yet," he says, and closes the guest room door behind them and turns the bolt. "Lucky for us, these old buildings are pretty soundproof."

"Soundproof?" She steps away from him.

He seizes her hand and plunges it against his crotch. "I promised you a nice, big fat reward if you introduced me to the Lieblings. This is it, sweetheart."

She pulls away from him. "That's not the kind of reward I had in mind," she says.

"What do you mean? You as much as said so. 'I expect a nice, big fat reward,' you said."

"I never said that!"

"Liar!"

"Well, if I said that, I've changed my mind," she says.

"This is what you've been wanting from the minute we met. You never fooled me once. You've been asking for this since you came over to me in the book department at Bloomingdale's. I read you like a book that afternoon. This is what you've been asking for, and now you're going to get it."

"No!"

"What about all those phone calls when you were trailing me around the country? What was that all about? What about Cleveland and all that dirty talk? Almost every night on my tour."

"I told you, I've changed my mind."

"Don't hand me that. You got me here. You got what you wanted, and now I'm gonna get what I want. I want my quid pro quo."

"You've gotten everything you're going to get from me!"

"Or are you just pissed off because I figured out what you're up to? Caught on to your little game with Noah Liebling?"

"Stop this! Stay away from me!"

"Not before I fuck you, sweetheart."

"Let me out of this room!"

"Oh, you want to play a little hard to get? Okay, I can play that game, too. Let's have some fun."

"I'll—"

He advances steadily toward her as she backs away. "You'll scream? Nobody'll hear you. Go ahead—scream. I'd like to hear you scream." With one hand he seizes her wrist again, then her other wrist in his other hand.

"No! Stop!"

"I like a little—resistance." Now he has both wrists grasped behind her in one solid grip, and with his free hand he is dipping deep into the front of her dress, pinching her breast hard, and at the same time forcing her with the weight of his body backward against the bed. "Give me a little more fight," he says.

"Stop! You're hurting me!"

"Good. It's better if it hurts a little. . . ."

"No! Stop! Oh, help!" she cries at the top of her voice. "*Noah—help me!*"

But now he has her pressed against the bed with the full weight of his six-foot-two, one-hundred-eighty-pound frame. One elbow is jammed forcefully across her throat, and with his other hand he snatches up the front of her dress and seizes her panties and roughly grabs her pubic hair. "Finger-fuck you first," he mutters in her face. "Warm you up."

"No! Oh, help! Someone help!" she screams again. "*Noah!*"

But now he takes his left hand and covers her mouth, while the right hand gropes and twists her panties, pulling them down across her knees, and there is the sound of fabric ripping. His own knee comes up hard between her legs, spreading them apart, and his finger penetrates her, first one finger, then two, then three, and she twists her head to one side and bites down, hard, on the fleshy part of the palm of his hand. There is a gush of blood, and he pulls sharply away from her and looks down at his bleeding hand. "You bit me, you little bitch!" he whispers. He says this in a tone almost of wonder and bewilderment.

"I told you to stop. I meant it," she says. Blood trickles from her mouth, and she spits it out.

He reaches into his jacket pocket for a handkerchief, and quickly wraps his bleeding hand in this. Then, in almost the same movement, he reaches into another pocket for a cigarette, and lights it with the gold lighter. Lighting his cigarette, his hand trembles, and he glares down at her with a look of purest hatred. "What did you want me to do?" he demands. "Did you want me to rape you? Is that what you wanted?"

"That's what you tried to do."

"Liar! That's one thing I've never had to do, thank God. But you wanted it. You know you wanted it. Why'd you ask me into your bedroom if you didn't want it? Why'd you make your bedroom the last room on the little house tour?"

"I told you. I changed my mind. Woman's prerogative. But this is a real first for you—right?"

"What do you mean by that?"

"It's the first time a girl has said no to the great Bill Luckman—and his big, fat cock. Well, frankly, it didn't feel so big and fat to me."

He steps toward her, and his right hand, still holding the cigarette, swings suddenly in a wide arc, and he strikes Melody hard and sharply across the face. Hot ashes from the cigarette fly into her eyes, and she cries out again. "Take that, you little cock tease!" he says. "I'll get even with you for this, you know."

"And I'll see to it that you never write anything about the Lieblings," she says.

He turns toward the door, unbolts it. "You're going to pay for this," he says. "I'm going to see to it that you keep paying for this. Writers work with words. I'm going to have the last one."

"And it was *Tolstoy,* asshole!"

He lets himself out of the room, closing the door behind him, leaving Melody sprawled, dry-eyed, across the bed.

She giggles briefly. Then, soon afterward, she hears a new set of footsteps in the hall, and she begins to sob.

From the hall, he goes into Carol Liebling's bathroom and runs cold water on his bloodied hand. He stanches the blood with toilet paper and flushes the paper down the toilet. In the medicine cabinet he finds a box of Band-Aids in assorted shapes and sizes, selects one, and covers his wound with a wide adhesive strip. Also in the medicine cabinet he sees a pharmacist's plastic bottle with a label reading, "Mrs. Carol Liebling—for sleep." For reasons that he himself may not entirely understand, he reaches for this and pockets it. Then he pees noisily in the toilet and flushes it again. Then he returns to the living room, his left hand thrust deep in his trouser pocket.

"I've had a lovely evening, Carol," he says. "Thank you so much for including me."

"Can't you stay till midnight? We thought we'd watch the ball drop in Times Square, and I've got some noise-makers, and we're going to open some champagne. It's sort of a tradition for Noah and me."

"Thanks, but I promised some friends that I'd stop by at another party," he says. "Thank Noah for me. It was wonderful to meet you both."

"Where's Melody?"

"Powdering her nose. Or she may have gone to bed. She mentioned that she was quite tired."

"I'll walk you to the elevator," Anne says.

Outside the apartment, as they walk toward the elevator, he says, "Actually, your friend Melody is pouting. She's quite a piece of work, isn't she?"

"Why do you say that?"

"Her little tour of your apartment ended in her bed-room. She tried to put the make on me. I told her I didn't do that sort of thing with minors." He presses the elevator call button. "She got mad. I told her to cool her jets. So, if she tries to bad-mouth me, that'll be the reason."

Anne giggles. "Melody did *that*?"

He shrugs. "Price of fame, I guess. Girls throw them-selves at me. It gets to be embarrassing. But you—I can tell you're different."

"Melody!"

"Oh, I suppose you have certain lesbian feelings for her. That would be natural at your age."

"I can't wait to have my first lesbian experience! But

it wouldn't be with Melody. I'd want it to be with a perfect stranger. Melody is my—muse!"

He studies her face in the soft hall light. "I think you're a little like your aunt Ruth, the countess—beautiful and glamorous, but a little . . . flighty, and easily hurt. You're very sweet." He bends and kisses her lightly on the lips. "Happy New Year," he says. "I hope to see you again." Then the elevator doors slide open. He steps inside, the doors close, and he is gone.

Anne stands for a moment in the elevator foyer, her fingers on her lips.

Now, as Noah is leaving the meeting with his mother in the library, which did not go well, he passes the door to the yellow guest room and hears what seems to be the sound of a woman sobbing. He hesitates, then taps at the door. When there is no immediate response, he opens the door a crack and sees Melody, fully dressed, lying across her bed, her shoulders shaking.

"Are you all right, Mellie?" She half rises, and he sees that the front of her dress is covered with blood. "My God, what happened, Melody?" he asks her, quickly closing the door behind him. She looks up at him, and he sees her red eyes and swollen face, and there is a fresh burst of tears. "Who did this to you, Melody?"

"Oh, Noah," she sobs. "It was so awful . . . so awful . . ."

"Tell me what happened, Melody."

"He . . . Bill Luckman . . . he tried to . . . tried to rape me. . . ."

"There's blood on your mouth."

"He bit me. He pushed me down on the bed and bit me."

"My God . . ." He steps quickly into her bathroom and runs cold water onto a facecloth. He returns to her, and though he can't see where the skin is broken, he wipes the blood from her face and lips. "My God," he says again, and he sits down beside her on the bed. His face is grim. "Now, tell me just exactly what happened," he says.

Through more tears, she tells him. Not just exactly, perhaps, but enough.

"Did he—?" He wants to ask her, "How far did he

get?" or something to that effect, but somehow he cannot bring himself to ask such a surgical question of a girl like Melody.

But she knows what he is thinking. "No!" she says. "But he was hurting me. When I started to scream, he stopped. Then he hit me in the face."

"Little bastard. Arrogant little bastard. I knew there was something about that arrogant little bastard I didn't like."

"Oh, Noah, I'm so sorry. It's all my fault. I asked him to come tonight. I thought he was—nice. He said I'd been teasing him, leading him on, but I swear to God I hadn't been. At least I didn't mean to be."

"Of course you weren't. And it's not your fault at all. He's just an arrogant little bastard and a bully, and now, thank God, you've found out what kind of a guy he really is. In a way you're lucky, Mellie. It's better he's shown his true colors now than later—if you'd gotten any further involved with a thug like that."

"Oh, Noah, I feel so—ashamed. And stupid."

"He's the one who's stupid—anybody who'd try a thing like that. He could go to jail. You know what's wrong with a guy like that? He's had too much success too soon. It's gone to his stupid head. He thinks because he's suddenly some kind of celebrity, he can get away with murder. He's got a stupid, sick mind to begin with. And when a sick mind gets hooked up with a swollen ego, you get—somebody like Mike Tyson, for Christ's sake."

"What should I do, Noah?"

"Do?" he says. His face grows thoughtful. "Look," he says at last, "unpleasant as it was, I don't think we should get the police involved in this. You could file charges. Criminal charges. But do you really want to do that? You'll just be asked a lot of terrible questions. Who invited him into your bedroom?—things like that. He'll deny everything. He'll say you led him on. All I can say is that I saw what he did to you. I didn't see him do it. It will be your word against his. He's been in the public eye a lot lately, and so there'll be publicity. Maybe even national publicity. And then a trial. Do you want to go through all that, Melody?"

She shudders and shakes her head.

"A thing like that could destroy your reputation, Melody. Even if we put him in prison, that sort of thing could follow you for the rest of your life. Everywhere you go, people will say, 'She's the girl who claimed—' And so on."

She nods. "But the only thing that scares me, Noah—the thing that scares me is that someday he might really hurt somebody, maybe even kill somebody. . . ."

"I don't think so. He's too much of a coward. Rape is a cowardly act, it seems to me. Maybe he's learned his lesson. Let's hope so. And as for you, you're young, Mellie. You've got an awful lot of years ahead of you. If I were you, I'd chalk this up to experience—learning that there are a lot of bastards out there like him. I'm not saying forget about it. I'm saying remember it, and maybe you'll be quicker to catch the signals next time."

"Should I tell Anne? Should I tell Carol?"

"What's the point? What good would it do? Why would you want to relive the experience all over again with them? Just keep it in a little secret drawer in the back of your mind."

"There's blood on the bedspread. How do I explain that?"

"You could always tell Mary that you—"

"Yes," she says quickly. "I know what I can say. But do I look just horrible, Noah?"

He smiles at her. "No, you don't look horrible. You look as though you'd been through a rough experience, but you don't look horrible. And I'm glad you told me about it," he says. He reaches out and covers her hand with his, and she squeezes it hard. "Let's keep this our little secret, Mellie, okay? No sense upsetting other people. This will be our secret," and he brushes his lips across the top of her dark head. And for a moment—oh, just for the briefest of moments—he asks himself why he has just done this. "Your secret will always be safe with me, all your secrets, always," he says, and there is one final small sob as she rests her head lightly on his shoulder. "I'm proud of you, Mellie," he says. "You handled a difficult situation in the best possible way."

"Thank you, dear Noah."

"Now, why don't you take a nice, long hot bath with

salts?" he says. "Then get into bed and have a nice, long sleep. Do you want a sleeping pill? Carol has some."

She shakes her head.

"And here's something else you should probably do." He rises, picks up the facecloth, and steps into her bathroom again. He rinses the cloth with fresh cold water and squeezes it out. Returning, he says, "Keep this over that left eye as much as possible. Keep adding cold water. Also hold it against your mouth. You may have a shiner in the morning, and also a fat lip where he bit you, though that doesn't look so bad now. We'll have to think up an excuse for that. Maybe you slipped in the shower or something." He presses the cold cloth against her face. "Do that, at least until you fall asleep."

"Thank you, dear Noah," she says softly. "I love you, Noah."

He laughs nervously. It was that fresh, clean scent of her hair that wouldn't seem to disappear.

"That wasn't meant to be funny," she says, not looking at him.

Carol Dugan Liebling is sitting in her nightgown at her dressing table, removing her makeup, using many tissues, when he steps into their bedroom. Hearing the door open and then close, she looks up at his reflection in her mirror. "Well, darling, how did it go?" she asks him. "The meeting with your mother." Then she says, "Not well. I can tell by the expression on your face."

"A ten percent salary increase. That's all."

"Not the big job."

"Not yet."

She sighs. "Well, darling, you've been patient this long. I suppose you can be patient a little longer."

"It's beginning to look as though I'll have to wait until she dies. And from the way she's going, it looks like I'll have a long, long wait. I'm beginning to feel like Prince Charles, waiting for the queen to die."

"She didn't even mention it?"

"Oh, yes. She mentioned it. But—"

"But with the usual condition."

He nods.

"Aunt Bathy."

He nods again.

"The same as last year."

"And the year before that."

She studies his face in the mirror for a moment. Then she turns in her chair and faces him. "Darling," she says, "perhaps it's time you told her why you can never accept that condition. Perhaps it's time you told her what you know. About Bathy. Wouldn't she understand why you feel the way you do?"

"I don't think so," he says. "She'd deny everything. She'd accuse me of having dreamt the whole thing. She wouldn't believe me. I know her." He removes his jacket, tosses it across a chair, loosens his necktie, and lies down across one of the pair of twin beds, staring upward at the ceiling.

She rises and goes to him, smelling of cold cream, a peppery, cucumbery smell. She sits on the bed beside him. "But look on the bright side, darling," she says. "A ten percent salary increase. That's not bad, is it? I think that's pretty nice. And the big job? You'll have it sooner or later. It's only a matter of time."

He says nothing. With one hand she smooths his forehead and pushes back his dark hair in which flecks of gray are beginning to appear, and with her other she begins unbuttoning his shirt. "Let's get some sleep, darling," she says. "It's been a long evening."

He brushes her hands away a little roughly. "Don't get into your mothering modality," he says. "Hell, I don't even think I want the damn job!"

"Now, darling, of course you do. You've worked for it for years."

"What makes you think I want to stay in this lousy business for the rest of my life?"

"Darling, I know it's frustrating at times, but—"

Still staring at the ceiling, he says, "There's always Aesop."

"Aesop? What are you talking about?"

"Aesop. A.E.S.O.P. It stands for An Exceptionally Solid Other Plan."

"Now, darling, don't talk like that. You know it worries me when you talk about quitting."

"Well, that's what I'm damn well talking about!"

She shifts her weight on the bed. "Well, slip out of your clothes and come to bed," she says. "It's late."

"I feel like lying here like this for a while," he says.

"Okay," she says. She rises and turns off the lamps beside both beds, and then slips between the turned-down covers of her own bed. In the darkness she says, "Becka told me your mother said something unpleasant to Ruth while I was on the phone. That's why she and Ector left."

He says nothing.

"I wish your mother could learn to be a little nicer to her children," she says.

He still says nothing.

"Poor Noah," she says.

"Now, don't start feeling sorry for me, Carol!" he snaps.

For a moment or two she, too, says nothing. Then she says softly, "Happy New Year, darling," and turns away from him in her covers, facing the wall.

But a little later, finding that she cannot sleep, Carol Liebling decides she must take a pill. But when she goes to her bathroom and opens the medicine cabinet, where they are always kept, her bottle of Seconals is nowhere to be found. She also notices that the toilet seat is up. She puts it down again.

Outside in the street, the Lincoln Town Car moves homeward toward 1000 Park Avenue, bearing but two passengers now, in the still heavy rain. Miraculously now, considering the congestion of traffic earlier, the streets are nearly empty. Theirs is the only car in sight. The windshield wipers thrash furiously back and forth, fighting the rain.

Cyril yawns noisily. "Notice, *Maman,*" he says, "that we are now on Third Avenue. And we are moving uptown."

"Snoring sailors," his mother says.

"Hm?"

"The sound the wipers make. *Manush, manush.* It always reminds me of the sound of snoring sailors."

"Now, when have you been around any snoring sailors, *Maman*?" he asks her.

She settles back in her seat with a smile. "Don't slouch, Cyril," she says.

5

Bike

A man, in his house, where he lies, and sleeps sometimes
with his wife (especially on summer nights when it is hot
and still outside and cool and air-conditioned inside,
when one can lie naked on the bed without covers or a
sheet) on one of the twin beds—pushed, at first, romantically close together, but now, because it is harder to
vacuum that way, separated by a prim nightstand, should
be a man at his bravest and best. And this man, when
he is lucky enough to have a wife he has once loved
thoroughly, and an apartment in a fine building that his
money has bought, and his own money manages to
maintain, is a man of countable blessings. But to be that
man, and to be, as he is, so sure that this man nearly
approaches the idea of the man he had once dreamed
of himself becoming (white-flanneled, randy, sipping
cool beer on warm afternoons after tennis, white-shirted
shoulders by Lacoste in the summer sunlight on some
lawn, a child playing happily somewhere in the distance)
was sometimes of little tangible comfort as you approached age fifty, and your contemporaries were suddenly talking of early retirement and needle fishing in
Florida, and here you still were, in this one of a pair of
twin beds (long ago, you agreed, tacitly, which one it
was to be), staring mutely at the changeful pattern of
night city lights on the ceiling, and getting a hard-on for
no practical reason. And then, too, though the apartment is yours and bought with your own money, and
though you worked closely with your wife on furnishing
and decorating the rooms, there were times when that
apartment had little reality except for the heat, which
sometimes sounded like Ross Perot's laugh when it came
on (There had been complaints about this in the monthly
tenants' meetings. Should the building invest in a new

heating plant? No!), and a small spot on the guest bathroom wallpaper that always reappeared, no matter how many times you repapered it (something to do with the Ryersons on the floor above, and he really should mention it to Harry Ryerson someday, but he never had), and the carpet in the long hallway which, unless you walked consciously up and down the edges of the carpet, which one tried to do, grew thin and bare at the center after a couple of years. And then, though your wife did not age like a rug or grow thin and shabby, or fade in the sun like drapes and wallpaper, your wife grew, too, after a time, to lose the precise outline she had once had in your mind, until, coming home, your home was merely a structure, and the picture of your wife in the dining room was no longer a picture of your wife when young, but merely a picture of a young woman full of spirit, and part of the dining room, which was a territory within the structure. With a certain deliberate aim at dissolving yourself this way in the familiarity of furniture and routine, you discussed things with your wife, made plans, agreed, disagreed, quarreled, made up, blamed, took the blame, apologized, and all these processes of course took time, and the time was charged to the future as part of the plans which were for the future and, if anyone asked, you would say this was half the fun. But the trouble was that after a few of these interactions, you both knew how and where they would end even before you had begun. But the discussions and the let's-talk-this-over idea were too sacred, too precious a part of whatever you believed your marriage to be, to be discarded, and so you observed the ritual and began and ended the discussions as time-honored custom decreed, politely. "I'm sorry." "No, you're probably right." "I didn't mean it." "I shouldn't have said that." Et cetera, et cetera. Looking at it this way, Noah tries to remember when, if ever, their talks had not had this quality of ceremony—the subject, deemed appropriate by a mutual nod, was opened, it was advanced a little, then thrust gently back, then was perhaps dropped altogether, for the moment, to be brought up again at a mutually agreed upon, more propitious time. He couldn't remember any times when it hadn't been this way, and he decided finally that for many years he had been walking cautiously up and down the edges of his wife, carefully avoiding the center where the fabric was tender.

He was once much more venturesome. Sometimes it startles him to remember how venturesome he once was. At the small elite men's college (now co-ed) he'd attended in New England, his father had offered to buy him a car. But Noah hadn't wanted a car. He'd wanted a motorcycle, and so his father (the apple of whose eye he then was) had let him pick out a big, muscular, 600 cc Harley-Davidson, bright red with scrollwork of reptilian design. In those days he thought of himself as Steve McQueen, Jimmy Dean, the young Marlon Brando, a rebel without a cause—not a Hell's Angel, exactly, but a What-the-Heck's Angel.

There were a number of other cyclists in the little college town, and with their bikes they formed an informal little club, tearing up and down the highways and country lanes, across fields and sand-lots, up and down the sides of quarries and gravel pits. The more experienced bikers taught Noah the tricks of the sport—front and rear wheelies, creek jumping, rock jumping, and stump jumping, and racing up and down the concrete steps of the hilly campus. On what had once been the college's football field (before the new stadium was built), they devised a game of motorcycle polo, using croquet balls and mallets.

Style is everything to a biker. They'd carefully prime their carburetors so their bikes would start on the first kick. A biker whose "hog," as they called them, wouldn't leap off like a rocket suffered a real stigma. It was tantamount to a gun jamming in combat, or an actor blowing a key line in a major speech: "To be or not to be, aye, there's the rub." If you flooded your carburetor on the first launch, you tried to atone for it by screeching off on one wheel, gunning your engine mercilessly to get up a head of steam before popping the clutch. There were injuries, of course, though none of them major. That was part of the game.

At college Noah had been invited to join Delta Chi Epsilon, which was considered one of the top fraternities. But after a while he began to sense that—despite the ritual hugging and handholding and singing of the sacred Delta Chi songs at the secret monthly meetings in the fraternity house's Goat Room, where members, rather like Klansmen, wore robes and hoods—he was not really a popular member of Delta Chi. He began to suspect that this had something to do with his bike and his "townie" biking friends. His fraternity brothers looked on disdainfully as his biker friends roared up to the Delta Chi house to collect Noah for an afternoon's adventure on their wheels. This, of course, made Noah even more defiant and rebellious as he slammed on his helmet, kick-started his Harley, and thundered off after the others, leaving his fraternity brothers in a cloud of dust and exhaust fumes. To hell with them, he said to himself, and their Mustangs and Corvettes. To hell with Delta Chi Epsilon and:

> Delta Chi, thy loving eye
> Is on us all today!
> All strong and true,
> We follow you,
> In brotherhood's grand w-a-a-a-y!

Then, in Noah's third year at college, there was an incident. It was on a Saturday night in February, after one of the monthly house meetings, when the brothers of Delta Chi gathered in the upstairs party room for drinks and beer before the jacket-and-tie dinner.

The president of the fraternity, whose name Noah has now forgotten, approached him rather haughtily and said, "I guess you know, Liebling, that you're lucky to be in this house."

"Oh?" said Noah warily. "What do you mean by that?"

"When your name came up during rush week, most of the members didn't want you," the president said.

"Oh?" Noah said. "Because of my bike?"

"It had nothing to do with your bike, Liebling. It's just that we've never taken in people like you. In fact, there's a clause in our national charter that we had to ignore to take you in."

"Okay," Noah said. "If nobody wanted me, why did you pledge me?"

"It was simply because, at our final pledge meeting, when you were about to be unanimously turned down,

Charlie Washburn said, 'But listen, guys. If we take this guy in, his old man will probably supply the house with free booze for four years.' That swung the vote the other way. That's the only reason we took you in. The chance for free booze. But we never got any free booze, did we? So it really wasn't worth it, was it, for us to take in our first Jew? And risk getting kicked out of the national."

That night he got very drunk. Around midnight he went outside, pulled the tarp off his Harley, hopped on her, and started her up. He swung her at full speed toward the fraternity house steps, mounted them, and threw his hog at full throttle into neutral outside the front door, shouting, "*Open up, you bastards!*", racing his engine until one of the brothers, in Jockey shorts, came down from his room to see what was causing the commotion. Once the door was open, Noah charged into the house at full speed. First he swung the bike to the right, into the room that was called the library, careening between sofas and chairs, knocking over tables and lamps. Next, on a wheelie, he charged across the entrance hallway into the living room, where the bike continued on its path of destruction through the furniture. He log-jumped a sofa, overturning it as he went, and headed for the big dining room, charging at chairs and tables that had been set up for the next morning's breakfast, sending crockery and glassware flying and crashing in all directions. Meanwhile, the brothers, in various stages of undress and sleepiness, were gathering on the upstairs landing to try to figure out what the hell was going on. "Take that, you bastards!" Noah shouted as he came down from his wheelie across the head table with a splintering crash.

Next he headed straight for the swinging doors that led to the kitchen, crashed through them and into the kitchen, where, at full speed, he circled the central cooking island several times, knocking over serving carts and steam tables as he went. Then it was back through the crazily swinging doors again, back into the dining room on an obstacle course between overturned tables and chairs. He slalomed out into the entrance hall again, and then, still at full throttle, galloped up the front staircase to the second floor where the bedrooms were, while the brothers cowered and hugged the walls to get out of his way. Then it was down the long central corridor, churning up the carpeting in great folds as he went, heading for the president's room, which, naturally, was the largest and best-situated room in the house, with its own bathroom. The door to this room stood open, and Noah and his bike sped through it and into the room, and around and around it, while Noah kicked out with his feet at every object in the room that could be knocked over and destroyed—stereo, radio, television set, nightstand, desk lamp, typewriter, everything in sight. With one neat shot that would have made his polo-playing buddies proud, he caught a tennis racket, in its press, with the toe of his shoe and booted it straight at a window, shattering the glass.

Then it was out into the corridor again, bounding down the stairs, across the entrance hall, out through the front door, which still stood open, and down the front steps into the night street. The whole episode had lasted less than five minutes, but in that short time he had trashed the Delta Chi Epsilon house.

At the street corner he stopped, idling his motor. He was breathing hard, and the cold night air burned in his chest. Six inches of fresh snow had just fallen, and the streets were eerily hushed and silent, that cushioned and cottony silence that always follows a snow-fall, though in the distance he could hear the rising wail of police sirens. What now? What next? Because somehow he knew he was not yet finished with them. His rampage must continue.

At the end of the street, bathed in the glow of a street-light, was the white Georgian mansion where the president of the college lived. Its windows were dark. He headed for that. On his bike he mounted the four curved steps that led up to the front door with its graceful fan-light, and stopped. Idling the bike at full throttle, he dismounted and unzipped his pants. Then, choosing a stretch of virgin snow as his canvas, he began to pee, writing in yellow on the doorstep of the president's house. He was able to write FUCK YOU—NOAH L before he ran out of pee. Then he remounted his bike, bounded down the four steps, and roared off into the night again as the sound of sirens drew closer and lights in the president's mansion began to come on.

The next morning—fined, released, and expelled—he headed home to his parents' house in Tarrytown.

It was a Sunday morning, and his parents should have been there. But when he entered the house, it seemed as eerily silent as the snow-bound streets of the New England college town the night before. He was still on an adrenaline high, and he walked through the empty rooms, calling, "Hey, Mom! Hey, Pop! Hey, Pop, I got kicked out of college! Hey, where is everybody?" He started up the wide double staircase.

The door to his parents' room was closed, and when he flung it open, he saw that the curtains were drawn, and it was a moment before his eyes became accustomed to the darkness. Then he saw a stirring in the room. "Hey, Pop, I got kicked—" he began. And then he saw a sight he would never be able to erase from his memory as long as he lived. He closed the door quickly and ran back down the stairs.

Later, his father said to him, "Son, I heard about what happened up there at that college of yours, and I want you to know I'm proud of you. You were insulted, and you fought back like a man. You didn't take the insult lying down. You stood up to the sons of bitches and showed them what you thought of them. Unlike that poor excuse for a brother of yours."

"What should Cyril have done? Lied?" He'd heard the Cyril story.

"He could have denied everything. That's what he should have done. Denied everything. Sons of bitches never could have proven anything. But your damn fool brother had to confess to the whole thing."

Noah said nothing.

"Anyway, I want you to know I'm proud of you, son. You're five times the man your brother will ever be. Ten times. Twenty times."

Noah still said nothing.

"And incidentally, son, what you may have thought you saw the other morning wasn't what you think."

Noah stared at his father, and then, feeling tears welling behind his eyelids, he turned his head quickly away. He had never known his father to lie to him before. But he knew what he'd seen. And now the only feeling he could summon for his father was a kind of blind, abstract pity. "Okay, Pop," he muttered.

His father touched his arm.

That summer he would sell his bike. In the fall he would set off for another college in the West.

"Too much success too soon," he had said to Melody tonight, blaming that. But what of the man who has had too little success too late? Where did one place the blame for this? Among his friends and contemporaries Noah was certainly considered a success. In the Ingraham Building, and within the organization, he was treated with deference and respect. After all, he was the only male member of the family in the company. At the same time—but perhaps this was only his imagination working—he was certain that some of the people who worked with him and under him regarded him with a certain amount of pity. Edith, his secretary, for instance. After all, he was also a man who worked for his mother and who, in the end, followed his mother's orders and did what she said. "Yes, Mom." He was now, technically, in charge of the production and marketing for all the Ingraham's labels—Ingraham's Royal Charter, Ingraham's Regency Rye, Ingraham's Colonial Gin, Ingraham's Imperial Vodka, Ingraham's Majestic Bourbon, Ingraham's Sovereign Blended Whiskey, and Ingraham's V.S.O.P. Scotch, a twelve-year-old single malt, where the initials stood for Very Special Old Pale. These were the so-called prestige brands, the only ones actually to bear the Ingraham name. These were the labels advertised in magazines like *The New Yorker* and *Town & Country*. These were the brands designed to give the company its high-class image. But, as everyone in the company knew, the real moneymakers were the lower-priced blends that were advertised on outdoor billboards and matchbook covers. When the apartment of the murderer Jeffrey Dahmer was photographed in the press, with an empty pint of Thunderclap Whiskey lying on his bed, no one, fortunately, noted that Thunderclap was also an Ingraham product.

When Rodney King was arrested for drunken driving

in Los Angeles, with a .19 alcohol count in his bloodstream, Thunderclap was what he had been drinking.

Thunderclap was ten times as profitable as Ingraham's
V.S.O.P., yet V.S.O.P. was promoted as the company's
flagship label. These were the ironies of this industry.
V.S.O.P. had been the only Ingraham's label to have
been granted a Royal Warrant, "By Appointment to
Her Majesty. . . ." and Noah's father had given his other
Ingraham brands their royal-sounding names—back in
Canada, where he first started—in the vain hope that
one day the British monarch might give him that rare
thing, a Canadian knighthood.

His father, who had always looked, even if he had not
always been, the picture of success, had been both proud
and fond of Noah—proud of him for, of all things, that
wild biking spree—even if Noah had not always been
fond or proud of his father. And before he died, Jules
Liebling (*geboren* Julius) had felt assured that he, as
Noah's father, would be to a great extent responsible for
whatever success in life his son might achieve. Noah
knew this was only partly true. Noah had come as far in
the company as he had not only thanks to his father,
but thanks to his own luck, charm, grace, smile, good
looks, poise, and better than average mind. But in
Noah's better than average mind he was under no illusions about his father's capabilities. His father had had
plenty of luck, but very little charm, grace, good looks,
or poise, and his father's mind had hardly been analyti-
cal or even very original. In fact, Noah occasionally wondered where it had all come from, all his father's
success . . . all the money.

Perhaps his father's secret was that he never took the
distilling industry very seriously. It was, he used to say,
a license to steal, a license to print money. The discovery
of the science of distilling, if you could even go so far
as to call it a science, was lost in history. The ancients
had known how to produce their equivalent of booze.
Any grain, fruit, or vegetable could be fermented to produce alcohol. The world's most primitive tribes have
been doing what Ingraham's does for centuries. Besides
alcohol, and various flavorings, the only other basic ingredient was the earth's most plentiful resource—water.
All the rest was packaging and promotion, and you had

something called the Distilled Spirits Industry. "I betcha even the caveman had his hooch," his father used to say.

The world's most primitive tribes, furthermore, drank without suffering from hangovers. They drank for days on end to glorify their pagan deities, and then passed out. But they awoke not with headaches or dry throats but with a sense of having been purified, renewed, redeemed, forgiven, blessed. It was only civilization that brought guilt to be associated with overindulgence in drink. Hangovers were nothing but an expression of guilt. All this was part of Noah's father's philosophy of liquor.

The distilling process was very similar to another ancient art, the making of bread, or "the other staff of life," as his father used to call it. The same chemical processes were involved. In fact, his father liked to tell the story of how, early on in his career, some ingredient—no one ever knew what it was—had fallen into a vat of whiskey at Jules Liebling's first distillery, and whatever it was had turned the whiskey, which still tasted like whiskey, an unappetizing purple color. Rather than throw out the vat, his father had suggested filtering the tainted whiskey through slices of bread. It worked, and the result was a clear, rich golden hue. "It took about four loaves of Wonder Bread at eight cents a loaf to do it," his father would say with a laugh. "We'd saved eighty bucks' worth of rotgut."

His father's mind was a vast repository of arcane liquor lore. He even knew the formula prisoners used to make Jailhouse Punch, which was also simple. You took a few slices of bread and soaked them with the canned orange drink they gave you at the prison breakfast table. In a few days fermentation would begin. Then you strained the resulting mess through a T-shirt. "It doesn't taste like much," his father said, "but it does the trick for the inmates." His father went so far as to claim that something very like the distilling process was what had caused the first organisms to emerge from earth's primordial ooze. Thus, in his mind, distilling was linked to Creation.

And so, with notions no more complicated than these, the former bartender had become a distiller. Of course, it didn't happen overnight. At Jules's bar in the little provincial town of Baie St. Paul, in Canada, one of his best customers had been a man named Henry Ingraham, the last of a dissolute line of Ingrahams, who had inherited a small, unproductive distillery on the banks of the St. Lawrence. "Henry could have made his own whiskey," Jules Liebling used to joke, "but it was easier for him to drink at my bar." Henry liked to drink rather a lot, and he preferred Jules's bar because Jules offered him a particularly generous line of credit. After several years, when Jules politely suggested that the time had come when Henry might consider paying his bar tab, a deal was struck. In return for the deed to Henry's distillery, Jules would forgive Henry his bar bill, and give him free drinks for the rest of his life. As luck would have it, that life lasted barely six months longer. Henry Ingraham, drunk, was gunned down one night in the streets of Baie St. Paul. The murder was never solved but, as it turned out, there were many other people in the town to whom Henry Ingraham owed money. No one ever suggested that Jules Liebling had anything to do with it. Why would he have? Henry's debt to Jules had been satisfactorily settled.

A little research—rather scanty, if the truth be told— revealed that the Ingraham distillery had been in the family for several generations before the intemperate Henry lost it. To Jules the Ingraham name had a respectable, Presbyterian ring to it, and so his first bottles bore the label "Ingraham's Fine Whiskey . . . Since 1789." Later, when "age" became a selling point for whiskey, Jules's labels began to read, "Ingraham's Fine Aged Whiskey . . . Since 1789." If customers thought the whiskey had been aging in oak barrels for over a hundred years, that was all right with Jules. Today the Ingraham Corporation letterhead bears the words "Distillers of Fine Spirits Since 1789," and five years ago the company made a promotional splash when it celebrated its "bicentennial"—"Two Hundred Years of Trust and Quality." Promotion of promotions, saith the preacher. All is promotion. It illustrated another maxim of Noah's father's: "If you say something loud enough and often enough, it becomes the truth."

Actually, the Ingraham label did not appear until 1917, when Jules launched it. He was twenty-three, had no more than a fifth-grade education, and had been bartending since age fourteen. These are the bare facts. None of them made its way into Jules Liebling's paragraph in *Who's Who in America,* though when the small western college that accepted Noah after he left his signature in the wintry New England snow presented his father with an honorary doctorate of science degree, he liked to be introduced on speakers' platforms as "Dr. Jules Liebling." If he could not be Sir Jules, then Dr. Jules would have to do.

Poor Pop, Noah thinks. *Poor Pop?* Back in 1917 he was on his way to becoming very rich. Around the corner was Prohibition. Jules always said that he had seen it coming, and perhaps he had. Once, when asked by a reporter for the secret of his success, Jules had answered, "The three P's—Packaging, Promotion, and Prohibition." He also once called Prohibition, with a wink, "The most important development in modern American history—more important than the atomic bomb." In fact, he claimed, Prohibition was responsible for the Bomb. "Prohibition created the Roaring Twenties," he said. "The Roaring Twenties created the Great Depression. The Great Depression created the Second War, and the Second War created the Bomb. Think about it!"

As for packaging and promotion, Jules had always believed in what he called "classy stuff." Classy was one of his favorite adjectives. Prohibition may not exactly have been a classy period in our nation's history, but to those who were around and willing to take advantage of it, it had turned out to be a nice little thing, and Jules Liebling was one of them. Jules was savvy enough to realize that Prohibition would never be enacted in the province of Quebec. The wine-loving French would never stand for it. And he soon discovered that Americans—even those who could not really afford it—would pay any price he and his friend Meyer Lansky asked, and they set their prices somewhat arbitrarily, for good liquor. With Prohibition the money came rolling in, and it has never really stopped.

And so, when Prohibition ended, Jules Liebling moved down to New York and built a castle called Grandmont in Tarrytown on a hill overlooking the Hudson River and the Tappan Zee, where Noah and his

brother and sister grew up, and where they were taught,
by nannies and governesses, that their father was the
kindest and wisest man in the world, their mother the
most beautiful woman, their home the most secure and
graceful, and they themselves the most fortunate of children. Now, of course, at age forty-eight, Noah is cynical
enough to know that none of this was really true. When
had he begun to realize that, though Grandmont was the
scene of many grand entertainments, his parents had no
real friends? Though Grandmont was surrounded by
other sumptuous homes and estates, the Lieblings had
never met their neighbors. Down the road lived the
Duchess de Talleyrand-Perigord. On the next hill lived
various Rockefellers. Noah's family did not know these
people. Nor was Noah's family invited to join any of
the various neighboring clubs where these people swam,
played golf and tennis, and sailed their boats in summer-
time. Instead, Grandmont had its own pool, tennis
courts, nine-hole golf course, and boathouse. Somehow,
Noah thinks, his father must have felt like Jay Gatsby
gazing across the bay at the inaccessible green light at
the end of Daisy Buchanan's dock, but without one of
Gatsby's great advantages: Nobody knew, exactly, what
Jay Gatsby did for a living. Everyone knew what Jules
Liebling did. Sheer money was not enough.

And why, Noah wonders, whenever he is thinking
thoughts like these, do his thoughts inevitably turn back
to money? Why should a man earning the salary Noah
earns be beset by money worries? And yet he is. Beset.
Besieged. Money is like somebody's law. Is it Parkin-
son's? It is the law that states that the more closet space
you add, the more clothes you will have to hang there.
The more bookshelves you put up, the more quickly
you'll run out of shelf space. The higher you promote a
business executive, the higher you must continue to promote him until he reaches such a level that he can no
longer do the job. Money was like that. The more you
had, the more you seemed to need. "Money's just a way
of keeping score," his father said. Not to Noah.

To Noah, the expenses of his family seem to keep
spiraling upward in a kind of endless Laffer curve. In
his mind he ticks them off. To begin with, more income
means more taxes. The maintenance on the River House

apartment has now reached six thousand a month, and the end is nowhere in sight. Certainly it will never go down. Plus there are the periodic assessments, which Noah himself, as the building's president, is now in the difficult position of imposing. Each assessment seems bigger than the last. He and Carol employ only two servants, Mary the maid/housekeeper and Edna the cook, and in terms of staff the Lieblings operate a household that is modest by River House standards. But add another five thousand a month for these two worthy ladies. Their daughter, Anne, attends what surely must be the most expensive college in the world, twenty-five thousand a year tuition, plus five thousand more for room and board, plus another three for books and equipment, plus library fees, laboratory fees, special lecture fees, infirmary fees, studio fees, gym fees, plus the cost of the little car she needs, plus insurance for a driver under age twenty-one, plus, plus, plus. Running a college, he thinks, must be like trying to run a co-operative apartment building, except that the tenants of a college cannot protest all the extra assessments as they come along. Then there are the costs of Carol's mother's care, in that place Carol prefers to call a nursing home, but which is really more than that, since Carol's mother requires constant supervision. Add another eight thousand a month for that. Plus the cost of ever changing, ever more expensive medications that seem to have turned the poor woman into an ongoing scientific experiment.

And these expenses he has just listed in his mind are only the fixed, immutable expenses which must be met each month before the members of his little family have even begun to live and feed and clothe themselves, to pay the doctor, the dentist, the butcher, the baker, and the candlestick maker, Rigaud candles. Sixty bucks a pop.

But would more money make all these worries disappear? Or is it power that he wants—the kind of power over his company that his father once had, and that his mother now has, the power of a clearly defined majority stockholder? He used to think that that was it, but now he is not so sure. And of course Carol was right, the power would come someday, it was only a matter of time, a question of patience. And patience, after all, is a virtue in itself.

And yet, you see, all that is not enough. There is something more that is just beyond his grasp. And yet, he thinks (and he is thinking all these things as he thinks of most things, while waiting for sleep to overcome him, to fell him with its golden bullet), there is still something restless and thirsty inside him that nothing—not the comfortable and safe apartment, not money, not power, not his job, his wife, his friends—is quite able to satisfy. It is as though there is a volcano that seems to be bubbling now inside him, on the verge of eruption, and what Noah wants is neither definable as love, or money, or knowledge, or a certainty of the future, but is a thing that cannot be expressed in any concrete terms, a thing with feathers. I have no offering, no grail, he thinks. But no, that is not it, either, for offerings or grails are not hard to come by if you want one. It is simply this: For the past two, or maybe three, years he has been unable to look forward to next week. So many next weeks have been the same as last weeks, and there is very little hope now that anything of importance or great joy will ever happen in any of them. Next week is sales conference. That is supposed to be important, and in one sense it is. Noah has an important presentation to make at this particular sales conference. A lot of the company's future hangs on it. A big investment is at stake.

Okay, but next week is also home again when sales conference is over, no different. Next week is also next year, and again no different, except for another birthday. And on and on the years arise and speed, over the past. You got out of the taxi, paid the driver, crossed the sidewalk to the gracious canopy that announced your building, crossed that stark marble foyer to the elevator, smiled at the elevator man who knew your floor, and returned to the apartment where you lived and slept, sometimes, with your wife, especially in the summer when it was warm outside and cool in the house. . . . And there she is, her breathing soft and regular now, in the other bed. And yet he is thinking of the scent of a young girl's dark hair, and the taste of her hair when he brushed his lips against it. "That wasn't meant to be funny," she said.

He reaches his hand under the covers of his twin bed, and begins the gentle, loving process of his hand on himself that will ease the path to sleep.

On his bike, defying death without goggles or a helmet, he had charged, at full speed, up a mountainside, jumping rocks and outcroppings, to the top, where he had stopped, suspended, left foot on a rock, in neutral but gunning the engine at full throttle to survey all the Berkshire foothills that lay in the distance and were waiting to be conquered. On his bike he had felt free.

And yet, still glimmering in his mind, is Aesop. Every Aesop fable had a moral at its ending.

Like most married couples who have been together as long as Noah and Carol, they do not always tell each other the truth. This is not to say that they lie to one another. Outright lies are too dangerous. It's just that they don't always tell each other the full truth about certain matters. After all, there are times when the full truth just complicates things. The full truth can be time-consuming, leading to unnecessary arguments and mindless tautology. Noah, for example, did not tell his wife the whole truth about his meeting with his mother that evening in the library. There seemed to be no point in telling everything that was said, especially since tonight's meeting was not much different from a similar meeting a year ago, or a year before that. What happened tonight was this:

They sat in the pair of wing chairs facing each other, and his mother said, "I'm ready to turn the business over to you, Noah. I'm even readier than I was last year when we talked about it. The time has come."

"I see," he said guardedly, because he was pretty sure he knew what was coming next.

"I'm going to be eighty-three," she said with a sigh. "I'm too old for this stuff. An old woman shouldn't be running a business like this. A woman shouldn't be running a business like this to begin with. This is a man's business, your father always said so. I want to put you in the driver's seat, Noah, where your father wanted you to be when you were ready for it. You're ready for it, and everybody knows it. My presidency was only meant to be an interim thing, and that interim's gone on long enough. I'm ready to turn over my shares to you, according to the terms of Pop's will. The lawyers have drawn all the papers up. Everything is ready for my signature."

"I see," he said.

"However—"

"There is a condition," he said.

"Yes."

"Same as last year's? And the year before that?"

She nodded.

"Sorry, Mom, but your terms are unacceptable," he said, and started to stand up, "Your terms have always been unacceptable. As far as I'm concerned, this meeting is over."

"Now, wait a minute," she said, holding out her hand. "Sit down, Noah. I intend to get to the bottom of this once and for all. Just what have you got against your aunt Bathy?"

"I won't have your sister working for this company. That's it. There's nothing more to say."

"Why *not*? She did wonderful things for this company over the years she worked for us. She can still do wonderful things. You're letting a valuable talent go to waste, Noah, by not finding something for Bathy to do. She could be a brand manager. She could be a regional sales rep—"

"Sorry, Mom. The answer is no."

"But what's your *reason,* Noah? Is it stubbornness, or is it—"

"For one thing, she's too old. She's past retirement age by now."

"*Old?* If *she's* too old, what does that make *me*?"

He said nothing, merely gave her a sideways look.

"People don't have to retire just because they reach retirement age. Look at your own father. He didn't retire when he reached retirement age. He retired by dying."

"Then let's just say I don't believe in nepotism," he said.

"*Nepotism!* You're the personification of nepotism! Where would *you* be if you weren't Jules Liebling's son?"

"Unemployable? Is that what you're saying, Mom? I don't happen to agree."

"Then *why*? Why won't you find a position in the company for her?"

"Let's just say I don't like Aunt Bathy, Mom."

"That's ridiculous! You used to be crazy about her when you were growing up! And she's always adored you!"

"It's a long time since I was growing up. My opinion of the lady has changed."

"But why? *Why?*"

"Look," he said. "Let me put it this way. If I'm going to run this company, I'm going to *run* this company, and I'm going to run it my way, without a lot of my relatives hanging around."

"Bathy wouldn't be just hanging around. She'd be working hard, contributing a lot. And it's not a lot of relatives. It's just one woman—my baby sister."

"One relative is too many. Sorry."

"Or is it just because this is something *I* happen to want you to do?"

"Yes," he said, "that's part of it, I suppose. Because it will look as though you're still running things from behind the scenes. Think of what the press will say— 'Mother Resigns Presidency in Favor of Son. Mother's Sister Named to Important Post.' That will get a lot of laughs in the trade, won't it?"

"Who the hell cares what the press says? Who the hell cares what the trade says? If we'd cared about things like that, we'd have gone belly-up years ago! We've always done exactly what we damn well wanted, and to hell with what people say!"

"Well, I care about what people say," he said.

"We wouldn't have to announce my resignation, your appointment, and Bathy's appointment all in the same *breath,* Noah. We could wait a few months—six months, perhaps, and then—"

"No. Because Bathy isn't going to be appointed—now or ever. Not while I'm around, at least."

"It's because she's a woman, isn't it."

"Yes," he said, "Perhaps it is. Perhaps that has a lot to do with it. Perhaps I've become a little gun-shy about working with women after all these years."

"That's supposed to be a slap at me, isn't it. But I've never ordered you around, have I, Noah? I've always let you do pretty much everything you wanted, haven't I? This new label you're launching, for instance. That's been your baby right from the beginning. I was against it, as you know. I was against taking that kind of a financial risk. But when I saw how much you wanted to do it, I gave you my go-ahead. Didn't I do that?"

"Yes, but it was an uphill battle to get that go-ahead," he said.

"I could have vetoed it outright! I had that power. But I didn't do that, did I?"

"No, Mom, you're a dream to work with. A real dream."

"Don't be sarcastic!" Now her eyes began to wander around the room, and he watched her as they settled on a single shelf of books. "Those books," she said, pointing. "All those books about education. Motivation. Human development. Boundaries of learning. All those books by authors with Jewish-sounding names—Seligman, Maser, Garber, Rosenhan—all with Ph.D.'s after them. Do you actually read those books?"

"They happen to be books on topics that interest me."

"It's not for that silly Aesop business, is it? Is it?"

"I said those're books that interest me."

"I don't want to hear any more about that Aesop nonsense, do you hear? You're in the liquor business, Noah. If you work for me, you're in *booze,* not crazy pipe dreams."

"You're changing the subject, Mom. We were talking about Bathy—remember? Not my reading habits."

Now she shifted slightly in her chair, and Noah knew his mother's body language well enough to know that this meant she was about to try a different tactic. "Suppose I told you," she began. "Suppose I told you that this was what your father wanted. Suppose I told you that your father wanted Bathy reinstated in the company. Suppose I told you that this was his deathbed wish. Suppose I told you that this was what he made me promise him with his dying breath."

"If you told me that, I'd know you were lying," he said. "If Pop had wanted that, he'd have said so in his will. His will was very specific about what he wanted for this company. No mention of dear old Bathy."

"Look at it this way, dear," she said—still another tactic, he knew, was coming when she began to call him "dear." "Think of it this way. It's all so unfair. We all have so much—you, I, Ruthie, and Cyril. We all have so much. But poor Bathy, who worked so hard for this company for so many years—she's wound up with nothing at all!"

"Then why don't *you* help her out, Mom? After all, she's your sister. It seems to me that you've got plenty to spread around."

"I've tried. I've tried again and again. I've begged her to let me help her out. But she's too proud. She'd never accept anything from me. But you, on the other hand— that would be a different story, dear. If you offered her a job, she'd be so thrilled!"

"Look," he said, "when Pop first asked me to come into the business with him, right after college, I said to him, 'Okay, but on one condition. Bathsheba Sachs has got to go.' He said okay, and that was that. He let her go. He knew how I felt about your sister."

"But why, dear—*why*? Why do you feel this way about her?"

He stared at the square of carpet between his feet. "Personal reasons," he said. "Private reasons."

"But don't I have a right to know what those reasons are?"

"Why don't you ask her? She knows how I feel about her—and why."

"I swear to you she doesn't, Noah! She's at a loss! She has no idea why you seem to hate her so, and it hurts her terribly! She only knows that something she may have done—she has no idea what it might have been—turned you against her years ago. She loves you, Noah. Can't you imagine what it's like for her, knowing that you hate her but not knowing why? She loves you almost as if—"

"If she knows how I feel about her, why would she want to come back into the company?"

"Oh, Noah, don't you understand? Don't you understand *anything*? It's not that she wants to come back into the company. She's never asked for that. She's never asked for anything, in fact. But whatever it was, whatever it was that happened between the two of you, it was all so long ago. Now you have the power, with one forgiving gesture, offering her a job, to erase all that, all the hate, all the old bitterness over—whatever it was. Don't you see? Don't you see that I want to see all the old wounds that have divided this family healed before I die?"

He looked at her, and she briefly averted her eyes; and for a moment he wondered whether his mother did, in fact, know exactly why he felt the way he did about her baby sister. Was it possible she had always known? In some ways, he'd never known her.

She dabbed her eyes now. "I don't want to die with my boots on," she said. "I want to die knowing that you're running the company, and that Bathy has been taken care of. I want to get out of my girdle and relax, and travel, and go to my quiet grave from some glamorous place—climbing the Spanish Steps in Rome, or in the lighthouse overlooking the harbor at St. Jean de Luz . . . St. Mark's in Venice . . . on the Charles Bridge in Prague. I'd like to die in the Juderia in Seville, or in the mosque at Cordoba, or at the Ritz in Paris, where I spent my honeymoon with your father. I want to die knowing that everything is in place, Noah. Is this too much for a mother to ask?"

"Now, don't start pulling your sympathy act, Mom. I know that act only too well. You're not dying. You're as healthy as a horse."

She lowered her eyes. "There are some things I haven't told you about, Noah," she said. "The doctor says I have an irregular heartbeat. He talks about fibrillations—"

"Come off it, Mom! Don't pull that crap on me!"

"It's not crap! But do you know what I think? I think you really don't want the top job. I think you're scared of it. I think you're like the Duke of Windsor. Wallis told me that once at Grandmont. She said, 'David wasn't in love with me. He just didn't want to be king. He used me as an excuse to get out of doing a job he didn't want.' I think that's the way you're using my poor sister."

"That's more crap! Would I have been standing

around on tiptoes all these years if I wasn't waiting to be kissed? It's just that I don't like the quid pro quo. You've always operated that way, haven't you—I'll scratch your back if you'll scratch mine."

Her voice rose. "It's just a *favor* I'm asking of you," she said. "That's what business is all about, isn't it? Favors? Doing favors in return for other favors? That's how business deals are made, young man! By calling in your markers. I owe you one, but first you owe me one! Your father made a fortune simply by collecting from all the people who owed him one!"

"And meanwhile, in the business community, I've become a joke," he said angrily. "A fucking joke, Mom, thanks to you. The mama's boy who can't get himself untied from Mama's apron strings. Because every time the little boy asks for a cookie, Mama says, 'No cookies until the little boy does what Mama tells him to.' Thanks to you, people laugh at me behind my back. Worse than that, people feel sorry for me—they pity me! 'Poor Noah, who's his mama's little puppet.' Even my wife pities me. How do you think that makes me feel? The only source of pride I've got left is that I haven't let you shove your sister down my throat."

"She's *family,* Noah. She belongs here. That's why I'm asking you this—tiny, tiny favor."

"Your sister is a lying, conniving, troublemaking, double-crossing little bitch! So, you know what you can do with your tiny, tiny favors, Mom? You can take them and shove them up that big fat ass of yours—one by one!"

Her eyes grew hard then. Just imagine her eyes, and the quick downward curl of her lip, something very close to a sneer. Now he was seeing the executive Hannah, the boardroom Hannah, the Hannah Liebling who sent $250,000-a-year executives trembling back to their drawing boards and, from there, still trembling, into the Biltmore Bar for many stiff drinks. She reached into her reticule for her spectacles, and placed them over the bridge of her nose, the way she often did at meetings when she had a final point to make.

Through her glasses she glared at her son. "You'll be getting a ten percent annual salary increase," she said. "I've already put that through. And there are some people who would consider that a not inconsiderable—even a very generous—raise. There are even some people who manage to make do on that amount of money a year. And I don't need to tell you that if you were CEO, your present salary could more than triple. You could pay yourself whatever you wanted, for that matter. And there would be other perks. The company plane. A fat wad of Ingraham stock. Bonuses and other benefits too numerous to mention, but of which I'm sure you are well aware. Your problem, Noah, is that you are stubborn. You were always a stubborn child, and stubbornness is a childish trait. A good executive is not a stubborn executive. A good executive must be flexible, be willing to go to the bargaining table, be willing to hammer out a deal. In addition to being stubborn, you have a terrible temper and a foul mouth. These are not attractive executive qualities. Your father could get away with that sort of thing because he was a roughneck to begin with. The role of roughneck doesn't suit you, Noah. You still look too preppy for the part. As a roughneck you just look silly. So perhaps you're not quite ready to be CEO, after all. But I want you to think about all this, Noah. Perhaps you should talk it over with Carol. See what she thinks. Let me know your decision within a week."

"I'm not going to talk it over with Carol, or with anyone else. I've made my decision. You talk about going to your grave from some glamorous place. I've got a better plan. I'm going to my grave with a headstone that says, 'He died without caving in to his mother. He died without kissing his mother's ass.' "

"Suit yourself," she said with a wave of her hand, her usual gesture of dismissal. "Someone's got to be boss. It'll still be me."

He got up and walked out of the room, leaving her there. But he still did not feel ready to join the others in the living room.

And that was when he heard the sounds of a young girl's sobs from behind the guest room door.

In her town house on Sutton Square, Ruth Liebling di Pascanelli is sitting on a long white sofa with Ector, watching the flickering image of the black-and-white film on the huge television screen that occupies one wall. "Here's where I make my first entrance," she whispers.

"Hey, that's not you!" he says.

"Of course it is!"

"I can't believe that's you!"

"Ssh! Listen to the dialogue."

From the screen, the actress named Ruth Radcliffe says:

> *Did you really mean you'd kill for her, Paul?*
> *I swear it, Roseline!*
> *Then the person you must kill is—*
> *Don't say it, Roseline. I know.*

"C'mon! That ain't you! That don't look a bit like you."

"Ssh!"

> *We'll be conspirators, Paul. You and I.*
> *You and I. Together.*

"They used the wrong take on that line," she says. "That was supposed to be my reaction shot. That was supposed to be my closeup. Instead, they gave it to him, and all you see is the back of my head."

On the screen, the scene has changed to calendar pages fluttering in the wind. One by one the calendar pages blow off the frame . . . December . . . January . . . February . . .

"If that was really you, you really used to be pretty," he says. "How old was you then? When was this movie made, anyway?"

"Don't you know it's rude to ask a woman her age?"

Now, on the screen, is a busy Arab street scene, mosques in the distance. The street bustles with women in face veils and men in burnooses, and the legend appears: "Marrakesh—1936."

"So that's when it was made. Nineteen thirty-six. Shit, man, I wasn't even born then." He yawns.

"That's when the story takes *place*," she says. "Look, do you want to watch this film or not?"

"Well, it's getting kinda late."

She presses the Off button on the remote, and the screen goes blank.

"So you're a movie star *and* a countess. And Jewish, even. Say, you're hell on wheels, aintcha?" He reaches out and squeezes her arm.

"Please don't," she says, moving away from him on the white sofa.

He looks at his watch. "Look, we got a little business to discuss," he says. "You know the rates. Hundred an hour, or a thousand for all night. I been with you—let's see, five hours. You want another hour or all night? I gotta phone the agency and let 'em know. What'll it be?"

"All night," she whispers.

"Okay. Where's the phone?"

She points.

He rises and goes to the telephone. Ruth's living room is all white, including the telephone. He talks quietly on the phone for a minute or two. "Say, this is quite a penthouse you got here," he says, returning to the sofa.

"It's not a penthouse. It's called a town house. What's it like being a male escort?"

"Not bad. I'm lucky. Got a good agency."

"A different woman every night."

"Oh, not *every* night. And I do johns, too. You know, businessmen. Conventions, that sort of thing. Makes for variety."

She shudders.

"Reason I'm successful is I always try to show a little affection. That's the secret."

She says nothing.

"Well, how about it?" he says. "Ready for a little roll in the hay? Satisfaction guaranteed."

She shakes her head.

"Not worried about AIDS, are you? Don't worry. I brought along plenty of protection. Choice of colors and flavors, ma'am."

She shakes her head again.

"You're funny," he says. "Most women I take out, older women like you, all they want is a little roll in the hay."

"No," she says. "No, thank you."

"You're not a dike, are you?"

"No."

"Don't get me wrong. I got nothing against dikes. I know a lot of nice dikes, some of 'em you'd never guess was dikes, no kidding. But if you'd wanted a girl for tonight, the agency would've sent one. Same charge."

"No."

"Speaking of which, if you want me for all night, the agency says payment in advance."

"In your ad . . . in the Yellow Pages . . . it said you accept the Visa card."

"Sure do! Got my little machine right in my ditty bag," and he pats the black zippered toilet kit on the sofa beside him, "But if you want me for all night, and you don't want a roll in the hay, what do you want?"

She turns her face away from him, facing the white-white wall. "Just someone to talk to," she says. And though he cannot see her face, a single tear slides slowly downward across her cheek. "Just someone common and ignorant to talk to. Common and ignorant like me."

6

Tables for Two

Jacques, the captain, has given Georgette Van Degan the best table at Le Cirque, as he always tries to do. This is the corner banquette on the right-hand side of the room, facing the door, where Georgette can see everyone who enters the restaurant and where, so much more important, everyone who enters the restaurant can see Georgette. To those faces she recognizes, she blows air kisses. Upon those she doesn't, she affixes a brief, icy stare.

Today she has been a few minutes late for her luncheon date, deliberately, but her guest, it seems, is going to be even later, and this has already put Georgette in a thoroughly sour mood. There is absolutely nothing in the world more infuriating to a woman than to be sitting alone at a table in a fashionable restaurant waiting for her luncheon partner, and to have people she knows walk in and see her sitting there, looking as though she has been stood up, and seeing on her friends' faces that look of gloating sympathy. Georgette has ordered a Lillet, and when not sizing up the room, she pretends to be studying the menu through a small gold lorgnette she wears around her neck, like a lavallière. Actually, it is not a lorgnette at all. It is a mirror, which Georgette uses to check her makeup as well as to see what is going on behind her back without turning around. Now she sees Carol Liebling, escorted by Jacques, moving toward her table, looking like something the cat dragged in. But no, that's not fair. Carol has made what Georgette would call a nice try, though she must have had a bad hair day. She is also lugging a briefcase.

Carol is wearing a new navy faille silk suit by Versace that she bought just for this occasion. The navy silk has tiny flecks of gold thread woven into it, and the suit was expensive. "Sorry to be late," Carol murmurs as she slides into the banquette beside Georgette. "My hairdresser kept me waiting." The two women do not kiss, as women often do at luncheon tables. They are not such good friends as that, though Georgette and Jacques always kiss when she comes into his restaurant, and they are not friends at all. Georgette does not even know Jacques's last name. Nobody does.

"Well, it was certainly worth the wait," Georgette says. "Your hair looks lovely, darling. You're doing something different with it, aren't you?"

"Do you like it? I let Michel try something new today. A little shorter."

"*Most* becoming, darling. So youthful-looking."

Actually, the waiting-for-the hairdresser story is a lie—a white lie but still a lie. In fact, Carol has spent the morning trying to get through to Mr. Corydon McCurdy, chairman of the Acquisitions Committee for the Metropolitan Museum. When he finally returned her calls, it was less than twenty minutes ago.

"Cory, the most extraordinary thing has happened," she said to him. "Georgette Van Degan has invited me to lunch today, and I think it might be because she wants to talk about giving their Chinese porcelains to the museum."

"Whatever makes you think that?" he asked her.

"Why else would she call me? I hardly know the woman. I really only met her once—at a Brearley parent-teachers meeting. But when I mentioned her collection—"

"Carol," he said, and there was a note of impatience in his voice, "the museum has been sending out feelers to the Van Degans about that collection for years. Mr. Van Degan expressed some interest for a while, particularly after the tax benefits had been explained to him. But Mrs. Van Degan has always been the stumbling block."

"That's what I mean," she said. "This luncheon invitation came from her, not him. And when I mentioned her collection to her a couple of years ago, I said something about how nice it would be to have her collection at the Met, right across the street from where they live—

and there was a definite reaction on her part. I think she may be about to come around, Cory."

"I doubt it," he said. "Everybody's approached the Van Degans. All the trustees, including Brooke Astor. And Brooke Astor's husband was some sort of cousin of Truxton Van Degan's."

"But I think I may have planted some sort of little seed in her mind. I mean, I really can't think of what else she'd want to talk to me about."

"Well, if you think taking her out to lunch will do it, go ahead. But I think you're barking up the wrong tree."

"Cory, she invited *me* to lunch. I didn't invite her."

"But if the Van Degans have already turned down Brooke Astor, why in the world would they approach the museum through someone like you?"

Carol had always known she disliked Mr. Corydon McCurdy, and now she decided the feeling was mutual. "Cory," she said carefully, "I merely called to ask you for your permission to begin negotiations on the terms of the gift—if she should bring it up."

"Sure," he said. "Sure, go ahead. But I can guarantee you won't get anywhere with her. If Brooke Astor can't do it, nobody can. . . ."

Now Jacques appears at their table. "Can I get you something from the bar, Mrs. Liebling?" Though Carol Liebling is not one of his regulars at Le Cirque, Jacques always makes it a point to know the names of Mrs. Van Degan's luncheon guests. Mrs. Van Degan likes to see her name mentioned regularly in the columns, and so does he. He will telephone this item to Roxy, Liz, Cindy Adams, and Billy Norwich this afternoon, and one of them is bound to use it. That's what makes a restaurant, the column mentions.

"Ingraham's V.S.O.P. and water, please."

Georgette fingers the stem of her wineglass and tries not to register any expression. But whiskey seems to her a rather *heavy* drink for lunchtime, and ordering the family brand seems—well, just a trifle crass. What if she were to order her wine served in a glass made by the Van Degan Corporation?

As though reading her thoughts, Carol smiles and says, "Sorry, but it's an old family rule laid down by

Noah's father. Whenever anyone remotely connected with the company orders a drink in public, it must be one of Ingraham's premium labels. Noah's father used to say, 'And say it loud—so the whole room can hear you.' I don't go quite as far as that, though."

"How amusing."

Looking at Carol, Georgette decides that Carol is actually a pretty little thing, though she will always have that problem with the Kansas face. The face is a little too scrubbed-looking for New York, a little too open and trusting. New York women did better who went for the bored look, or the suspicious look, or an artful combination of the two. The tiny freckles on Carol's nose and cheekbones don't help. Dermabrasion could get rid of those, of course, but nothing could be done with the wheat-colored eyes, except perhaps contacts. And Carol would look better as a blonde, she thinks, not with that reddish-chestnut hair, which must be a rinse. Certainly Georgette knows that *she* looks better as a blonde. Both women are at that age when all women look better as blondes. But would blond hair change that outdoorsy, milkmaid's heart-shaped face? Probably not. All Kansas women had that, and quite a few Texans, and there was nothing they could do about it. It was a face that had no corners to it, that simply looked too healthy for Le Cirque, though it might do all right for football games. Georgette guesses that, in high school, Carol Liebling was probably a cheerleader, and was voted Most Popular. And that navy silk faille suit. It is a Versace, but it was bought off the rack, and Georgette knows exactly where Carol bought it and how much she paid for it. It was a Kansas suit. "Love your suit, darling," Georgette says.

Eying her companion, Carol is thinking that Georgette merely looks costly. She looks costly in that special way that only very rich city women manage to look. Her hair looks expensive, her skin looks expensive, she smells expensive. Georgette Van Degan would look expensive in blue jeans and a faded Brooks pink shirt. She dresses simply but expensively, and today she is wearing a champagne-colored cashmere sweater dress with the sleeves casually pushed up above her expensive elbows, and along her slenderly expensive arms many chunky gold bracelets cascade down. A champagne-colored Chanel bag, in alligator, with a long gold chain lies beside her on the banquette seat, open, with many little Vuitton objects poking out at artless angles—a glasses case, a billfold, a notebook, a checkbook, a compact, a key case. Georgette Van Degan is by no means a beauty—handsome, yes, even striking, with a thin, strong-jawboned face that is composed of many flat, highly polished planes. It is a face, Carol thinks, that mostly has the look of money.

But it isn't just money, Carol thinks, that has bought that attitude that Georgette wears so comfortably—that air of brittle poise and utter self-assurance. If that could be bought, Carol might try buying a little of it for herself. Georgette looks as though she was born to sweep through the doorways of Bergdorf's, Harry Winston, and David Webb. Carol has learned to manage Bergdorf's now, but just barely. For years the haughty-looking saleswomen in that store intimidated her. If she paused to look at something on a counter there, and was approached by one of these sleek creatures, she would blush, mutter an apology, and hurry on. She has managed to overcome some of these country-girl feelings of inadequacy, at least where Bergdorf's is concerned. But places like Winston's and David Webb are still beyond her. She knows it is foolish, but stores like these are just too daunting. And then there is the little matter of Georgette Van Degan's Chanel bag, casually unclasped. Georgette Van Degan, Carol thinks, could walk down Fifth Avenue with an open handbag slung over her shoulder, the little Vuitton cases peeking out, and even the most intrepid thief would think twice before attempting to mug her. Carol, from years of habit, still clutches her handbag to her side when on the street. Seated at one of the best tables at Le Cirque with Georgette Van Degan, Carol does her best not to let Georgette suspect that women like this make her feel vulnerable and out of place. Even though they do. She smiles brightly.

After all, she reminds herself, Noah once told her that one of the things he loved about her was that she didn't look or act like a city girl. He meant that as a compliment. "I miss our Brearley parent-teacher meetings," she says to break the little silence.

"Yes, and how is dear Anne?" Georgette asks her now. "Let's see, she goes to—"

"She's at Bennington."

"And doing well?

"Oh, yes. Very."

"Such a *pretty* girl, I remember. Linda is at Vassar, and also doing well, I'm happy to say. Those two were such good friends back in the Brearley days."

"Yes." In fact, Carol can't remember that Anne and Linda Van Degan were friends at all. Classmates, yes. But perhaps they were friends. Anne was then at that age when daughters don't tell their mothers much of anything, at least not as much as they begin to tell them later on. Carol also has trouble remembering what Linda Van Degan looks like. She has a picture of a rather chubby little dark-haired girl, who unfortunately inherited her father's no-nonsense nose. But perhaps over the past three years Linda has grown taller and lost some of that baby fat. That can often happen to girls between the ages of fifteen and eighteen. Ugly ducklings can turn into swans.

Carol's drink arrives. "Tell me," Georgette says, "do you still have all those projects you were working on? I remember you always had lots of exciting projects going on. You were very active with the Met, if I recall."

"Still am. That's my main thrust, the Met. In fact, I was just talking this morning with Ivana Trump—"

"Ivana *Trump?* Forget her, darling. She can't do anything for you. She's on everybody's B list now. She's dead in the water. She's really become one of yesterday's people, I'm afraid."

There is a brief silence, and Carol sips her drink.

"But how I envy you all your projects," Georgette says. "I wish I could find time for things like that. But Truck and I always seem to be so busy, with travel, with keeping up three houses, and all the social life, which I absolutely *loathe,* but which I feel I simply must do for Truck's business."

"Yes, of course . . ."

"Do you and Noah find yourselves doing *much* too

much entertaining—much more than you really want to do?"

"Well, not *too* much, perhaps," Carol says, and then, lest Georgette think that she and Noah are a pair of boring stay-at-homes, she says, "I did have a small dinner party on New Year's Eve. Mostly family, but William Luckman came."

Georgette's eyes widen. "William Luckman?" she says. "The author?"

"Yes."

"*You* had *him* for dinner?"

"As a matter of fact, he was sitting at my dinner table when you called."

"Well, *well*!" Georgette says, looking at her guest with new appreciation. "How did you ever succeed in snapping *him* up?"

"He's a friend of a friend of Anne's."

"*Really*! Every hostess in town is after him right now. He's on everybody's most-wanted list, but he's terribly hard to get, always dashing off here and there, promoting his book. They say he's terribly attractive."

"Oh, he is."

"And I hear his book is fascinating."

"So is he. Very—articulate."

"And you had him for dinner. Did you phone it in to Roxy?"

"Roxy?"

"Roxy Rhinelander. I'm surprised she didn't have an item in her column."

"It was mostly a family dinner," Carol says modestly. "I didn't want any publicity."

"Carol, I think you are an absolutely fascinating woman!" Georgette says, meaning it, and calling Carol by her first name for the first time. "You have a dinner for the hottest new man in town, and nobody even knows about it! I call that *class*!"

"Just a little family dinner," Carol says for what must be the third time, but very much aware that she has made a strong impression on the famous Georgette Van Degan, and pleased with that.

"And you say he's a friend of Anne's."

"A friend of a friend of hers. Melody Richards."

"Is she Loyce Richards' daughter?"

"A different family. Her father's a diplomat, stationed in the Far East. But I know Loyce Richards. She's on our museum board."

"Loyce and Peter spread themselves too thin, if you ask me. They're on *every* board, and when you're on every board it stops meaning anything. People forget which board you're on, and pretty soon they stop caring and you're dead in the water. You become one of yesterday's people."

"I suppose you're right, yes."

"But what *you* do is so much cleverer, darling. You concentrate on just one thing, the Met Museum. That's your main thrust, as you put it. As a result, when I think of the museum, I think of you, and when I think of you I think of the museum."

"And I envy *you*, living right across the street from the museum," Carol says, feeling sure now that the conversation is leading to what this lunch date is all about.

"It's absolutely the best place to live, I think."

"Being able to step across the street and be among all those treasures . . ."

"Well, there's that, of course," Georgette says. "But the best thing is the security. The museum has fabulous security, around the clock, and we get all the benefits of that. The blocks between Eighty-second and Eighty-fourth have got to be the safest blocks in town."

"Of course. I hadn't thought of that," Carol says.

"Anyway, that brings me to what I wanted to chat with you about."

"Yes," Carol says, leaning forward and giving Georgette her best smile, but trying not to appear too eager, though she is now quite certain what is coming next.

"I was thinking," she says, "about the way some things are fashionable. Then they go out of fashion. Then they come back into fashion again. Then they go out again. But then they can come back again."

"But some things, like great art—"

"Yes, but the point is always to be one jump ahead of the fashion. To spot the trends before they become *too* trendy. That's always been my motto, to be a jump ahead of the pack. Timing is everything, particularly in this town, if you don't want to become one of yesterday's people. And that's why I think the timing is just right for this idea I have for you and me."

"I absolutely agree," Carol says.

"You do? But I haven't told you what my idea is yet."

"Let's say a little bird told me."

"Who told you? Have you been talking to Patsy Collingwood? She's the only one I've told. Besides Truck. And Truck doesn't talk to anybody."

"Let's say I guessed it. From conversations you and I had, back when our girls were at Brearley."

"Oh. Well, if you know what it is, what do you think of the idea?"

"I think it's absolutely wonderful," Carol says. "And I'm honored that you'd let me have a part in it."

"You'd have a big part in it. We'd share it. It would be wonderful publicity for both of us."

Carol covers Georgette's hand with hers. "No, the publicity should be all for you. You and your husband. After all—"

"No, you and I should share it, fifty-fifty."

"I don't care that much about publicity, Georgette."

"Nonsense. It could help you with the museum. They might put you on the board."

"I don't really care about getting on the board, Georgette. All I care about is what's good for the museum. Why, those two Lang Yao vases alone—"

"As centerpieces, you mean?"

"Perfect centerpieces for the whole thing!"

Georgette looks dubious. "We're not supposed to put water in them. Perhaps dried arrangements, but I think dried arrangements are tacky. I'll ask Truck. Anyway, I was thinking of about a thousand people."

"To announce it, you mean? Well, perhaps we could get two of the Annenberg galleries."

"Oh, I wouldn't want to have it at the museum— would *you*? Too stuffy. I was thinking of the Piping Rock Club, under a tent. And I don't think we want boomp-chink-boomp-chink Whatsisname, do you? Lester Lanin. Wouldn't you rather have Peter Duchin? And I assume your husband's company could provide the liquor, which would save us both a lot of money."

All at once Carol is lost. "I'm sorry, Georgette," she

says. "I don't think I quite understand. You're talking about a party?"

"Of course. A coming-out party for Linda and Anne. In June. A drop-dead party to end all coming-out parties, and we've only got six months to get it all together."

"For Linda," Carol repeats numbly. "And Anne." She feels her cheeks grow red.

"Coming-out parties were all the rage in the fifties. Then they went out of fashion in the sixties. Then they started to come back in the seventies and eighties, and then they went out again. Now we're going to bring them back again for the nineties—you and I. That's what I meant about fashions, how they swing back and forth, back and forth. But we're going to set the trend for the nineties. We're going to be right out there on the cutting edge."

"A coming-out party," Carol says.

"Won't it be fun?"

Their waiter appears. "Your usual lunch, Mrs. Van Degan?"

"Yes, Felix. Two four-minute eggs and half a slice of dry whole wheat toast."

Carol stares blankly at the menu, which she has not even studied, and where she sees no mention of four-minute eggs. So that's how she stays so thin, she thinks. Her eyes alight on the Maryland crabs, though somehow she has lost her appetite. "I guess I'll have the crabs," she says, putting the menu down.

"The first thing we've got to do is pick a date," Georgette continues without missing a beat. "Somewhere between when school gets out and the Fourth, when everyone goes away. It's got to be a night when nobody else is doing anything, when there'll be no competition, and when we can get Peter Duchin, because we want Peter him*self*, of course, not just one of his orchestras. Then we've got to think of a theme and get the invitations ordered. For engraving Cartier wants at least a month. Each girl would invite her own list of friends, and as for the boys, there's a formula. You want at least two and a half boys for each girl, so there'll be lots of competition for the girls and no wallflowers. There's an agency that will supply lists of suitable boys from the various schools and colleges. What do you think of making it white tie instead of plain old black tie? That would make it so much more of an *occasion,* don't you think— a really grand ball? The point is to do the really surprising thing. You have to keep surprising people if you want to stay on top—in this town, at least. If you don't, you're dead in the water. We want to get lots and lots of press, of course, because we want this to be the most important debutante party *ever,* for Linda and Sally."

"Anne," Carol says.

"And I'm so thrilled you're as excited about this as I am, and I can't believe you guessed that this was what I had in mind. You're obviously a woman of many facets, darling—getting William Luckman to your house for dinner ahead of everyone else. What a coup! And what is it they say about great minds?" She throws Carol a quick look. "You *are* excited about this, aren't you, darling?"

"Well," Carol says, "to be honest with you, I'm a little disappointed, Georgette."

"Disap*pointed?* Why?"

"Frankly, I thought you'd asked me to lunch to discuss giving your collection to the museum. I mean, I couldn't think of any other reason."

"Collection? What collection?"

"Your Chinese porcelains."

"Oh, that," Georgette says with a wave of her hand. "You'd have to talk to Truck about that. It's really his collection. His grandfather started it. But frankly, darling, I can assure you that Truck has no interest in donating any of that."

"But could we talk about that for a minute?" Carol says. "You see, under the new tax laws there are certain advantages in making such an important gift now. In fact, I've put together a few facts and figures for you, and listed various ways in which the gift could be made. You might want to take this home and discuss it with your—" She starts to reach for the envelope in her briefcase.

"Forget it," Georgette says. "No way, darling."

"—husband."

"If you want to talk taxes, I don't see why our party couldn't be deductible," Georgette continues. "After all, it would get lots of publicity for Van Degan Glass, and for the Ingraham Corporation. Truck and I have the most marvelous accountant. He's just a little bit crooked, and his motto is, 'When in doubt, deduct it.' They can't put you in jail for deductions. But we don't have a minute to lose, darling—June is only six months away. And as for the costs, you and I will split them right down the middle—for the catering, the flowers, the orchestra. I'm thinking of perhaps two orchestras—one for regular dancing and then a rock group, perhaps in a separate tent. And it's wonderful that your husband's company will supply the liquor. That will save us—oh, at least ten thousand dollars. Maybe more."

"I'll have to discuss all this with Noah," Carol says. "And with Anne, of course. But frankly I'm not sure—"

"They'll be thrilled. And I'll call the Duchin office the minute I get home, to make sure we get Peter him*self.* My dear, we're going to have the party of the *decade*! Of the century!" Suddenly she lifts her mirrored lorgnette. "Don't turn around," she whispers. "But look who the cat dragged in. Dina *Merrill.* Oh, good. Jacques has given her a really lousy table. One of yesterday's people. You have to be so careful in this town, don't you? If you're not, everybody will simply forget who you are, and you're dead in the water. Since your daughter Sally knows him so well—"

"Anne. My daughter's name is Anne."

"That's what I *said.* Since she knows him so well, we should invite William Luckman to our party. That would draw the press, too. Unless he's turned into one of yesterday's people by June, which could easily happen. Celebrities have such a short shelf life these days, don't they? Tell me, do you get back to Kansas often, darling?"

"Kansas?"

"Isn't that where you're originally from, darling?"

"I was born and raised in New Hampshire," Carol says.

Their lunches arrive, Georgette's soft-boiled eggs in a silver bowl with two points of toast perched on the rim like the wings of a bird.

"Oh, yum-yum-yum," Georgette says to the eggs.

In another part of town, two other women are also having lunch. They are Hannah Liebling and Bathsheba

Sachs. They lunch at least once a month, and Hannah has chosen the Café des Artistes out of consideration for Bathy. The restaurant serves excellent food at reasonable prices; the two women split the check, and Bathy's budget is limited. Both have ordered, as always, martinis on the stem with Ingraham's gin.

"I just realized what day this is," Hannah says. "It's Jules's birthday."

"My goodness, you're right."

"If he were alive, he wouldn't let us forget it, would he? Let's see," she says, counting on her fingers. "If he were alive, he'd be a hundred and one!" She raises her glass. "Well, here's to the old s.o.b.," she says with a wink.

"Yes," Bathy says, smiling and lowering her eyes. They touch glasses.

Bathy, Hannah thinks, has somehow managed to keep both her looks and her figure, though Hannah, by her own admission, has thickened somewhat in the hips and middle. Bathy still has that slender blond loveliness, though she has let the blond hair go to gray—pulled back, behind her neck, in a trim chignon that shows off her wide, pale, smooth forehead, her best feature, because set in that forehead are the same merry blue eyes, the Sachs eyes. All Sachses have them.

Hannah says, "Do you remember that time in Harry's bar in Venice when he kicked up such a godawful fuss because the bartender didn't have any Ingraham brands in stock? Oh, there was going to be hell to pay for that poor Italian bartender. I thought that bartender was going to burst into tears—didn't you?"

"He just couldn't understand why any bar in the world wouldn't stock his labels. And then if they did, he always made the bartenders rearrange their shelves so that the Ingraham brands would be displayed front and center, with their front labels facing the customer. Do you remember who that Italian bartender turned out to be?"

"Harry Cipriani himself!"

"Right, and he raised such hell about the stock being displayed that most bartenders were afraid to change it back again. He might come back and raise even more hell."

"Of course, I usually slipped the bartender fifty dollars when Jules wasn't looking," Hannah says.

"Of course! So would I."

"Under-the-counter payoffs. It still goes on, except nobody talks about it."

"Except you and I."

"Except you and I." The two women exchange smiles.

"If your husband could have had his way, Ingraham bottles would have been one solid label. He hated that government regulation that no more than thirty percent of a bottle's surface can be covered with labels."

"Hated it. He said it was worse than Communist Russia."

"Oh, my. What you and I went through with that man."

"But what fun we had. Sometimes."

"Remember the time he threw the telephone out the window?"

"Someone had phoned him with bad news. Thank goodness it landed on the street and not on someone's head."

"I can't remember what the bad news was, can you?"

"Neither can I. Something from the state liquor commissioner, I imagine. That was usually what it was."

"Incidentally," Bathy says, "I was touched to see that you ran my Christmas ad again this year."

"We'll always run it, as long as I have anything to say about it. It was one of the best ideas you ever had, Bathy dear."

Were you aware that Bathsheba Sachs was for many years the advertising director for Ingraham? She started with Hannah's husband's company after graduating from the Fieldston/Ethical Culture School and after what was then the mandatory year's grand tour of Europe. At first she was little more than a messenger, delivering mail and memos to the various offices in the building, but soon the company was letting her try her hand at writing advertising copy. She turned out to be a clever writer, and in 1960 Jules Liebling named her as his director of advertising. She was only thirty-two and, at the time, she was the youngest person, and the only woman, in the distilling industry to occupy such a position. With her unusual name and her even more unusual beauty, she soon became something of a legend in the business. In 1965 *Advertising Age* named her its Woman of the Year, and devoted its cover story to her. Alas, this is a business that forgets its legends very quickly.

The so-called Christmas ad has appeared in mid-December every year since 1960. Those years—the 1960s—were not good ones for the liquor business. Public tastes seemed to be changing. Up to then vodkas seemed to dominate distillers' sales charts, the theory being that consumers believed that vodka left no telltale breath. This was not really true, but the industry had been delighted to encourage the notion that by drinking vodka, a man or woman could be a secret drinker. Ingraham's had capitalized on this misconception, too, with ads for Ingraham's Vodka that employed the slogan, "It Has the Secret!" And a competitive brand claimed, "It Leaves You Breathless!" But in the 1960s vodka sales began to go soft. Younger people, it seemed, preferred to get their highs from other chemical substances, while the more traditional market seemed to be turning from distilled spirits to wines, wine spritzers, light beers, soft drinks, and bottled spring or mineral waters. Distillers panicked.

Ingraham had tried to get into the bottled-water business by buying a brand called Yukon Spring Water, but despite heavy advertising Yukon Spring failed to take off. The "designer waters," Evian and Perrier, continued to dominate. Bathy's idea, then, for the 1962 Christmas ad had been an unusually subtle means of appealing to the changing public attitudes toward drinking. It was an all-type ad, and appeared as a full page in national newsmagazines, as well as in major newspapers across the country, headlined: A HOLIDAY MESSAGE FROM THE H & W INGRAHAM COMPANY. "The holidays are a time for joy and high spirits everywhere," the copy began. But the copy then went on to warn drinkers not to take the term "high spirits" literally. "As distillers, we know only too well the tragic results of overindulgence in spirits at this time of year," the copy said, and it cautioned drinkers to approach liquor with respect, especially when they intended to be behind the wheels of motor vehicles or any other piece of machinery. There were other commonsense tips and suggestions about alcohol, its effects on the brain and central nervous system, and readers were urged to refuse to have "one for the road." "As distillers," the copy concluded, "we have always believed that spirits should be approached with moderation and respect, and that the safest place to drink is in the home."

At first Jules Liebling had been almost violently opposed to the Christmas ad. "*What?*" he screamed. "In our biggest selling season you want us to run an ad telling people not to *drink*? This is crazy!"

"Not *not* to drink, Jules," Bathy said. "Just telling people not to drink too much, to be careful how and where they drink. Not to drink if they're going to be handling a car, in particular."

"You're telling them to drink at home! My bar business is seventy percent of sales! How do they get to the bars if they don't drive there in a car?"

"I'm just urging them not to drink too much."

"You are crazy, Bathy! What will my competition think? They'll laugh at me. They'll think I've gone meshugge!"

"Just try it, Jules," Bathy persisted. "In terms of public relations, I think this could pay off in the millions."

"Public relations, public shmelations," he said. "This is a meshuggener idea your sister has."

But Hannah had agreed with Bathy. "Just try it," they both urged him.

"People nowadays are turning away from hard liquor because they're afraid of what it will do to them," Bathy said. "This ad will tell them there's a way to enjoy drinking without getting into trouble. This is very reassuring copy."

"There's a difference between drinking and getting intoxicated," Hannah said.

He agreed initially to run the copy, or an abbreviated version of it, in small print at the bottom of Ingraham's regular schedule of holiday ads, much the way the government-mandated warnings now appear on labels. But Bathy insisted that for the ad to have any impact at all, it must run in full pages in newspapers and magazines, and make a big splash. And finally he gave in to "this crazy experiment of your sister's."

The effect of that first Christmas ad was immediate

and overwhelming. Newspapers across the country editorialized on it, praising "this sober and responsible distiller" who "cares more for humanity than profits" (*New York Times*), and citing Jules for his altruism, honesty, civic spirit, and concern for the public welfare. The ad was even quoted, verbatim, on radio and national television newscasts, publicity that could never have been bought since liquor advertising is not accepted by the non-print media. Women's magazines, many of which also refused liquor advertising, published laudatory articles about Jules Liebling, his company, and his praiseworthy stance, and *Fortune* put him on its cover. Reporters who had never referred to Jules with epithets much kinder than "the billionaire booze baron" now called him "this caring, public-spirited citizen."

Jules was invited to appear on radio and television talk shows, where he cheerfully took full credit for the ad, and even managed to get across the dubious point that Ingraham products were "more purely distilled," and "contained fewer harmful esters," making them less likely to cause hangovers, thereby reducing absenteeism in the workplace. One TV talk show host went so far as to call Ingraham "the Tiffany of distillers," but the adjective most commonly used to describe Jules was "responsible," and wasn't responsibility the closest thing to respectability, the commodity Jules longed most to attain? Jules Liebling was not used to hearing himself called civic-minded, and he found he thoroughly enjoyed the experience.

Passing him in the corridor a few weeks after the Christmas ad's appearance, Bathy Sachs greeted him with a wink and an "I told you so."

The competition was more than envious. It was furious at the way Ingraham's and Jules were being extolled. But since Jules had effectively preempted the anti-drunk platform, there was nothing they could do about it. ("Fucker's walking around like he's Jesus Christ," muttered one rival.) The competition could do no more than wince as, guided by the knowing hand of Bathsheba Sachs, the words *responsible* and *trustworthy* began appearing with increasing frequency in Ingraham's advertising copy, and the slogan for Ingraham's V.S.O.P. became "The Only Scotch You Can Always Trust," and other labels became touted as "A Trusted Brand from the Trusted House of Ingraham."

Jules began receiving letters from teachers, saying that they were incorporating the text of the Christmas ad into their lectures to young people on substance abuse. One letter from a fourth-grader said, "My teacher says that when I'm old enough, and want a drink of whiskey, I should always ask for Ingraham's because they want to save people's lives and not make people drunk." "Let's offer this kid fifty thousand dollars if he'll let us use this as a testimonial," Jules suggested, only to be reminded that federal laws prohibited the use of minor children in liquor advertising. Instead, he had settled for having the letter framed and hung prominently on his office wall.

A woman from Montana wrote to Jules to say that she had stitched the words from the Christmas ad into a sampler, and sent him a Polaroid photograph of the result, asking Jules if he would be interested in buying it. Another wrote asking for permission to set the words from the Christmas ad to music. Indeed, the public response to the ad was so resoundingly positive that Jules began wistfully to suppose that he might be considered for the Nobel prize.

Nor was the Christmas ad the only important or innovative touch that Bathsheba Sachs managed to apply to Ingraham's advertising. From repeal through the 1950s, an unwritten rule of the liquor industry was that no woman could be shown drinking in a liquor ad. Women could appear in illustrations, but only as background figures, and never with glasses in their hands, and most certainly never to their lips. No federal regulation dictated this. It was simply a gentlemen's agreement within the industry itself, and as a result, all liquor advertising was aggressively masculine in tone. Again, over Jules's objections—what he and others in the business feared most were changes that might bring about further government controls—Bathy succeeded in producing a series of Ingraham's ads that actually depicted women enjoying the cocktail hour. The general public scarcely noticed this revolutionary step. But the reverberations from the "women's campaign," as it became known, were profound within the industry itself.

Typically, of course, Jules Liebling never thanked his

wife's sister for any of her contributions to his company
and its prestige—not even when, in the quarter following
the publication of the famous Christmas ad, Ingraham's
sales figures rose fourteen percent above the correspond-
ing quarter the year before, and Ingraham became the
industry's acknowledged leader. To Jules they were always "my advertising campaigns."

"How are the children?" Bathy asks Hannah now, sipping her martini.

"Oh, much the same," Hannah says with a sigh. "Ruthie came by Carol's on New Year's Eve with a most
inappropriate young man. I just hope she's not planning
to embark on another of her marital adventures. And
Cyril is—just the same. Slouches to annoy me."

"And Noah?"

She frowns. "Noah is a good boy," she says. "He's
always been a good boy. Noah works hard, and does a
good job for the company. It's just that he's so—stubborn. He's always been stubborn. I'm trying to work on
that stubborn streak of his."

"You don't suppose he could have inherited that from
his mother, do you?" Bathy says with a wink.

"He's so headstrong and determined."

Bathy laughs softly. "We certainly don't need any
more headstrong and determined people in this family,
do we?" she says.

"I gave him a nice raise this year. That should satisfy him."

"But not the job he's been promised."

Hannah lowers her eyes. "No. Not yet," she says.

"Not experienced enough? Is that it?"

"No, it's not that. Not exactly. It's just that—"

"What is it, Hannah?"

"It's just that I don't know what the boy would *do*
with that much power."

"The boy will be forty-nine years old this year. Isn't
he getting to be a little old to be called a boy, Hannah?"

"I can't help it. I think of him that way. If he were
given all that power—all that stock, all that money—
what if he were to blow it all on some harebrained
scheme?"

"Aesop," Bathy says. "Does he still talk about Aesop?"

"No. He hasn't talked about that for a long time. That's what worries me."

"Why should it worry you? Maybe he's forgotten all about that."

"I worry more about the things he doesn't tell me than the things he tells me. Or maybe it's some other harebrained scheme. Save the world! I've lived long enough to know that nobody's going to save the world. Jesus Christ tried it, and look what happened."

"In other words, you still don't trust him."

"I just don't know what he'd do with all that independence. Go off on some crazy tangent, like the Aesop business. Save the world."

Bathy twirls the stem of her glass. "So," she says carefully, "because you can't be sure what he'd do with his independence, you keep him—dependent."

"It's because I just can't bear the thought of him getting all that money and all that power, and then— *poof!*—seeing everything I've worked so hard for go down the drain."

"And everything Jules worked for. And everything that I worked for. Don't forget Jules and me."

"That's what I meant."

"And Carol, too. She's done her share. I'm sure Carol wouldn't want to see that happen, either."

"You bet your socks she wouldn't!"

"What do you think Carol wants?"

"For him to run the company, of course."

"And that's what Jules wanted, too."

"Yes. Eventually."

"Well, you haven't asked for my advice," Bathy says, "but I think eventually is now. Of course there's a risk. This is a high-risk business. But I think the longer you wait, the greater the risk that he'll—"

"Fly the coop?"

Bathy nods. "Give him the company now. I think you'd feel a lot happier with yourself if you did this now."

"Happy? Are you saying I'm not happy?" She puts down her glass abruptly. "You're right," she says. "I'm not happy."

"I know. I can always tell. Give him the company now. And with no strings attached."

"Strings? He's the one who keeps attaching strings!"

"Are you quite sure, Hannah?"

Hannah looks away. "Well, maybe one little string," she mutters.

"Detach that string. It isn't getting anybody anywhere."

"Oh, I just wish you could be back in the family again, Bathy," she says a little distractedly. "All of us, the way it used to be. We could discuss things, argue about things, even fight about things. Didn't we used to have the best doggone fights? The fights were the best times of all, looking back! We were all a family. Maybe we weren't exactly happy. But we were us. But now—"

"Don't, dear," Bathy says, lightly touching the back of Hannah's hand. "I know how Noah feels about me. I'm used to it. It used to upset me, but it doesn't anymore."

"But it hurts *me,* knowing how you—how much you gave up."

"Hush," she says. "It was just that Noah idolized his father so as a little boy. Worshiped the ground he walked on."

"That was my fault. I raised him to think his father was a kind of god, that his father could do no wrong, that his father was an absolutely perfect father in every way!"

"That's a good way to raise a son, if you ask me."

"It was wrong! No mortal being is a god. There's no such thing as a flawless human being, and Jules Liebling was hardly a flawless human being. I was wrong to lie to him like that."

Bathy hesitates. "Hannah," she says at last, "do you think it's time we told Noah the truth?"

"We promised never to do that, Bathy."

"I'll tell him my part of the truth, Hannah, if you'll tell him yours. But your part, I think, has to come first."

The two women's eyes meet.

Hannah's eyes withdraw first. "Are you ready for another cocktail?" she says. "I think I am. Waiter—" she calls out loudly. "Two more martinis, with Ingraham's gin!"

"Don't change the subject, Hannah," Bathy says. "Let's tell him the truth—but you first. Then give him the job, but with no strings. I have my own life now. Don't try to use my life to control Noah's."

Now Hannah blurts it out. "But if you were back in the company, you could keep an eye on him. You *could* help keep him under control. After I'm gone, that is."

"That is not going to work, Hannah," she says. "I can never control Noah. For that matter, neither can you. You have got to let Noah become his own man. But if you want someone who might help control Noah, there's only one person who can do that—and you know who that is."

"No. Who?"

"Carol."

"*Carol*? But she's only his wife. I'm his mother!"

"Yes, dear," Bathy says with a smile. "That's always been your problem."

Once more their eyes meet, then withdraw.

Their drinks arrive.

"Now might be an especially good time for you to start being especially nice to your daughter-in-law," Bathy says.

From Roxy Rhinelander's column the following day:

Glimpsed at Le Cirque yesterday, with their heads together like a couple of li'l ole magpies, were **Georgette Van Degan** and **Carol Liebling,** the wife of **Noah,** who's the son of **Jules Liebling,** the late billionaire booze baron. What was on the ladies' minds? Well, Topic A was the lavish coming-out bash the two will be tossing for their deb daughters, **Linda Van Degan** and **Anne Liebling,** who've been best of chums since grade-school days. An early June date is planned. And who'll supply the bubbly and the Barleycorn for the 1000-plus-guest dinner dance? Aw, you guessed it. And Topic B? Could it be the ultra-exclusive dinner party **Carol Liebling** gave on New Year's Eve, honoring best-selling author **William Luckman,** who's so-o-o tall, so o o dark, so-o-o handsome, so-o-o successful and so-o-o sexy that every deb's mother's got her eye on him? Has peppy **Carol Liebling** got the lead position? Watch this space, kiddies.

The morning newspapers, including the one containing this item, are delivered to Hannah Liebling on her breakfast tray.

Carol Liebling reads it while sipping her coffee in her dining room at River House. She jumps up from her chair, spilling her coffee all over the newspaper in the process. Her reaction is one of frustration and rage. She hasn't even discussed Georgette's plan with Noah—or even with Anne—and already Georgette has made it official!

"I have an interesting proposition for you, Hannah," her mother said to her that morning in their house in Park Slope.

"Oh? What's that?"

"I met an interesting man at the Joint Distribution Committee reception last night. He was the only gentleman not wearing a dinner jacket, but I suppose that's understandable. It takes these Russians a while to get accustomed to our American ways. His name is Jules Liebling."

"Oh?"

"He knows who you are, and of course he knows who *we* are. He'd like to marry you. Isn't that nice?"

"*Mama*! I'm not going to marry anyone!"

"Now, wait a minute, young lady," her mother said sharply. "This is a very serious matter we're discussing— a matter of life and death, as it were. You don't want to go to your grave a spinster, do you? That would be a shame and disgrace, and it seems to me you've brought enough shame and disgrace on us already."

"It isn't a shame and a disgrace if no one knows, is it?"

"I'm talking about the shame and disgrace you've brought upon yourself, and upon me, even though your father, God rest his soul, never knew." Her father had died the year before.

"But I'm not going to marry a man I don't even know!"

"I'll tell you everything you need to know about him. To begin with, he's very rich, and that's important. He's in the liquor business, unfortunately, but he's made a lot of money."

"You mean he's a bootlegger?"

"No. He made his money in Canada, where liquor is perfectly legal. In fact, he doesn't like to be called a bootlegger. He calls himself a distiller. He told me repeal is right around the corner, and he's come to New York to establish his business here, so he can be ready as soon as repeal goes through. They can be smart, those Russians."

"Liebling doesn't sound like a Russian name to me."

"They all do that. They change their names from something like Liebowitz to something that sounds more German. It's easier for them to get credit that way, you see. Oh, they're very clever, there's no gainsaying that. Last night he pledged one hundred thousand dollars for the Joint."

"But that doesn't mean I'd want to *marry* him, Mama."

Hannah had already begun to suspect that her mother was not being entirely truthful in her account of this startling proposal. It seemed quite unlikely that two virtual strangers would casually encounter each other at a large, formal Joint Distribution Committee reception, and that the gentleman in question would proceed to ask for the woman's daughter's hand in marriage. There was more to it than that, Hannah was certain. But she knew it would be fruitless to ask. Her mother was much too skillful a liar.

"But you've got to marry *some*body," her mother said airily. "I admit he's not one of our sort, and not one of our class. But he's a decent Jewish man, and at least he's not a Bolshevik, as so many of them are. And remember, Hannah, beggars can't be choosers."

"What do you mean by that, Mama?"

"There are certain facts you've got to face, Hannah. If you were to marry one of the nice Jewish boys from the families we know, he would discover right away, on your wedding night, that you had been—well, that you had been tampered with. That would never do, would it? It would be all over town in no time, and he'd throw you out into the street, and that scandal would follow you for the rest of your life. But being a Russian, this Mr. Liebling probably wouldn't even notice anything that was—well, a little off. I mean, they're used to that sort of thing, the Russians."

"But why does he want to marry *me*?"

"They all want to do that. As soon as they make some money, they want to marry *up*, into one of the fine old Jewish families like ours. It helps them in their businesses. And I'll tell you something else, Hannah. When a man marries up, his wife almost always manages to elevate him to her level. But when a man marries down, his wife drags him down to hers. Don't ask me why this is, but it always works out that way. It's a rule of thumb. It's another reason why you should accept Mr. Liebling's proposal."

"But I don't want to get married!"

"My dear, you must. Think of your future. Think of little Bathy's future." Bathy was a toddler then.

"What's Bathy got to do with it, Mama?"

"A great deal, I'm afraid. You see, Dr. Lowenstein has told me I have cancer. I'm afraid I don't have much longer to live, Hannah. You can't take care of Bathy on your own."

"I can take care of Bathy!"

"My dear, you cannot. Your father did not leave us a great deal of money. Your father was a great man, and a great scholar and educator, but scholars and educators do not make a great deal of money. When I die, there will be very little left for you. You will need a husband, a husband with money, like Mr. Liebling. I explained this situation to Mr. Liebling."

"Explained what situation, Mama?"

"That there is very little money on your side. That I am ill, and that after I am gone Bathy will be in your charge, and he has promised me that after I die, he will take care of Bathy."

And so that was it. It was to be one of those Old World arranged marriages, between two people who scarcely knew each other. And in such an arrangement there was always a quid pro quo. Hannah would provide Jules Liebling with the luster and cachet of her Sachs name. In return Jules Liebling would provide her and Bathy with a comfortable life. Weeks, even months, of delicate negotiations had doubtless taken place before a deal had been struck. And it wasn't hard for Hannah to guess who the principal negotiator in this transaction had been. Sadie Sachs had performed the same role as a matchmaker in a European shtetl.

"It was very gentlemanly of him, I must say," her mother said, "for a Russian."

Hannah was silent for a moment. Then she said, "Why do you keep saying, 'for a Russian'?"

"Well, there's a matter of class, for one thing, no matter what you say. Class and background. We Germans came to America of our own volition, and at our own expense. They came because the czar threw them out. He couldn't tolerate their socialist ways. For another thing, in Germany we were a highly cultivated and respected people. Mendelssohn was my distant cousin! In Russia those people were riffraff. Most of them couldn't read or write. They spoke a language—Yiddish—that nobody could understand."

"Yiddish is Judeo-German, Mama!"

"*We* never spoke Yiddish. They did. Still, all things considered, I think Mr. Liebling is the best choice you're going to have, and I told him so."

"You mean you've already promised me to him?"

"Yes, more or less. I told him I thought he was an excellent choice for you. I didn't tell him that he might be your only choice."

"But I don't love him, Mama!"

"That doesn't matter. To be honest with you, I didn't love your papa when I married him. In fact, I hardly knew him, Met him once or twice. It was one of those marriages that were worked out between our parents. That sort of thing may sound old-fashioned to you but, believe me, those were the best marriages. They lasted. As for love, that will come later. When you children started to come, then love started to come, too. It will happen to you also. You'll see. And remember, Mr. Liebling is very rich."

"I know I'll never be in love again, Mama."

"You'll see," her mother said again. "He's not bad-looking, Mr. Jules Liebling. "He's a few years older than you, which is fine. Your papa was a few years older than I was when we were married, and ours was considered an ideal marriage in every respect."

"Was it, Mama?"

"Of course it was!"

"Oh, Mama—why couldn't you and Papa have let me marry the man I *was* in love with?"

"That was out of the question, and you know it. What would the rest of the family have said? We'd have lost all our friends." Her mother picked up her stitchery canvas—a field of yellow poppies, as Hannah remembers it, against a pale green background. It would become a sofa cushion in the upstairs parlor, the sofa on which Sadie Sachs would die two years later. "I've invited Mr. Liebling to tea on Thursday, so you can meet," she said, pulling a stitch through the canvas. "I want you to put on your prettiest dress—the blue, I think, with the ruffled sleeves. And when he proposes marriage, I want you to say yes to him. Remember, I was at your side during your time of desperate need. Now you must come to my side at mine, when I need most of all to know that your future, and Bathy's future, are settled and secure before I'm gone. You owe that to me, Hannah. And remember—Mr. Liebling may not be the husband I'd have chosen for you if things had gone otherwise. But he's the bird in the hand, and he's very rich."

And so he had come to tea that Thursday, and she had worn her best dress, the blue with the low waistline, belted at the hips, and sleeves of pleated chiffon. The dress showed off her shoulders, which she considered her best feature. She was a little disappointed with his looks. He was not, as her mother had said, bad-looking, but his head seemed disproportionately large, and he was shorter than she might have wished, and he had small, almost feminine hands. Her mother left them alone for a few minutes in the parlor.

"Your mother is a remarkable woman," he said to her, studying her over the rim of his teacup, his eyes grave.

"Yes. I quite agree."

"Widowhood must be difficult for her."

"Yes, it has been."

"A man doesn't really need a wife," he said. "But every woman needs a husband. Don't you agree?"

"I suppose," she said carefully. "I hadn't really thought about it."

"It's true," he said. He set down his teacup on the table beside his chair. "Now let me meet this little sister of yours," and he stood up.

Astonished, she realized that what he had just said had been his marriage proposal to her.

They were married in a large ceremony at Temple Emanu-El, with a reception afterward at the Plaza. Her mother wanted a fancy wedding, with all the families of the Uptown Jewish elite invited—the Schiffs, the Warburgs, the Lehmans, Loebs, Seligmans, Strauses, and Sulzbergers. "It will show people that we're not embarrassed, that we're still able to hold our heads up high," Hannah's mother said. And of course Jules Liebling paid for everything.

And they all came, all the best people. Still, at the time there was some whispering among the wedding guests that they had only come out of curiosity.

Years later, Bathy asked her, "How could you have married, and stayed married to, a man you never loved?"

"Love is hunger. Marriage is three square meals a day," was Hannah Liebling's reply. It was only partly true.

In 1935, when Hannah's mother was dying of the cancer that had been riddling her body for the past several years, though she refused to let Dr. Lowenstein prescribe medicine for the pain she was now almost constantly in, she summoned Hannah to her bedside, and said, "Just promise me one thing, Hannie. Promise me you'll stay with Jules no matter what happens. Do this for me, and also for your own sake, and also for little Bathy. I did something important for you once. Now you must do this for me. Bathy will go to you and Jules now, where she belongs. So you must make this marriage last and last and last. No matter what happens. Promise me you'll do this."

"I promise, Mama."

"And here's something else you must keep," she said. "It's very important." She reached into the drawer of her bedside table and withdrew a slim leather case. She handed it to Hannah. On the front of it was stamped, in gold letters, BATHSHEBA MARCELLA SACHS.

"What's in it, Mama?"

"Open it."

Hannah opened it and pulled out a slender green booklet.

"It's her passport," her mother said. "If she should ever need to travel outside the United States, she will need a passport. Notice that it lists her place of birth as New York City. Ordinarily to obtain a passport, you need to produce a birth certificate, but a birth certificate lists both parents' names. A passport does not. Bathy's birth certificate has been removed from the records at the American Embassy in Berlin. There is no longer an official record of her birth. But now that you and Bathy have this passport, you will always have proof that she is a United States citizen in good standing, and no one will ever ask any questions. So it's important that you must keep her passport valid. It must be renewed every five years. You must not let her passport expire, Hannie. Do you understand? You must keep this in the safest possible place for her—I suggest in a safe deposit box. It's the only document she will ever need. You see, Bathy must never know the truth. It would hurt her so."

"I understand, Mama. But how were you able to do this?"

"Mr. Baruch. Mr. Baruch is very close to President Roosevelt. Mr. Baruch was able to do this for me, with the help of the White House. Mr. Baruch was always grateful for the fine education he received at your papa's school."

"I see," Hannah said, studying Bathy's picture in the passport. It all seemed so long ago, those months in Europe, when her mother had taken charge of everything, inventing what would become their story as they went along. Hannah herself had been too frightened of the situation in which she found herself to do anything but exactly what her mother told her to. And there had seemed to be no one else, no one in the world to whom she could turn, besides her mother. "You're young," her mother had said. "When this is all over, you'll simply forget that any of this happened. It will be easy, wait and see." But it hadn't been easy, and she couldn't forget. How could she? It had stayed with her, every living day of her life since then, it seemed: that memory. And the terror and confusion of those days.

Now her mother said, "Always remember that you are a *Sachs*. We Sachses take care of our own." Then her mother said sharply, *"Don't do that, Hannah!"*

She had just pressed the passport picture to her lips.

Anyway, that was how Bathy came to live with Jules and Hannah when she was not quite seven years old.

And now Patsy Collingwood and Pookie Satterthwaite have just been seated at one of the skinny tables at Mortimer's. The skinny tables are the ones at the front of the restaurant, by the windows, where fashionable diners are displayed for viewing by the passersby on Lexington Avenue, and they are called the skinny tables because no woman larger than a size eight is permitted to sit there. Larger women are relegated to the back of the room. This is said to be the arrangement preferred by Glenn Bernbaum, the ethnically laundered proprietor who, looking like an English country squire in his Tattersall tweed hacking jacket and doeskin slacks, moves about greeting, with studied indifference, his socially prominent clientele.

"I'm sure you asked me here to discuss Topic A," Pookie says, perching forward in her chair and resting her elbows on the table.

"Exactly," says Patsy. "I'd like to know what you think Georgette Van Degan is trying to pull."

"A coming-out party, of all the un-chic things. And for that fat daughter of hers, of all people. Perrier with lime," she says to the waiter.

"The same," Patsy says. "Exactly. It's all so fifties-sounding. The *Times* hasn't covered coming-out parties for years."

"And Roxy wouldn't touch them with a ten-foot pole. I'm surprised she even mentioned that this one was being planned."

"Exactly."

"The *Times* doesn't even report weddings anymore."

"Well, not exactly. I've heard that you can pay the *Times* to do a wedding."

"But this isn't even a wedding. It's a *debutante* party,

of all things. Can you pay the *Times* to write up a debutante party?"

"Perhaps. But Georgette wouldn't do that. That's not her style at all."

"No. She's definitely up to something."

"Exactly."

"I smell a rat."

"And with Carol Liebling, of all the B-list people."

"C-list."

"D-list."

"They live in our building," Pookie says. "In fact, he's president of the board. He only got the job because nobody else would take it. Nobody can stand him. He's always trying to slap new assessments on us. Actually, he's kind of cute."

"Speaking of cute," Patsy says, "did you notice our waiter? I haven't seen him here before."

"Hmm," Pookie says, giving the distant waiter a long, appraising look. "Adorable."

"Probably gay."

"Shall we try to find out?" Pookie giggles.

"Now, darling, we've got to learn to keep our hands off children," Patsy says. "Let's get back to Topic A. What's Georgette up to?"

"Georgette never does anything unless she's got a plan. She's definitely got a plan with this latest bit. The point is, what is it?"

"Exactly. That's what we've got to find out."

"And how did Carol Liebling get William Luckman to her dinner party? How'd she pull that one off?"

"Exactly. I was supposed to have him at my house last Thursday night. Then Georgette pulled out. Then he pulled out. I had to call the whole thing off."

"Oh? And you didn't ask Darius and me?"

"Darling, I just told you. I had to call the whole thing off."

"Hmm."

"You know, Pookie," Patsy says. "Sometimes I wonder about those Lieblings. Are they on everybody's B-list because they're *too* rich? I mean, I'm rich, and you're rich, but they're richer than everybody else combined. Are people jealous of them? Is that why they're on the B-list—and don't even seem to *care*?"

"No, darling, that has nothing to do with it. It's because his father was a bootlegger, and even had people *killed*, or so I've heard. And because his mother is a foul-mouthed old battle-ax. And because they're"—she silently mouths the word—"Jewish."

"You think that's it? I'm not so sure."

"Well, the only thing I'm sure of, darling, is that we've got to draw our wagons into a circle until we find out what Georgette is up to."

"Exactly. Of course, I have one theory."

"What's that?"

"I wonder if Georgette is trying to humiliate Carol Liebling in some way by dragging her into doing this unchic thing. I mean, I adore Georgette, but you know how she likes to humiliate people, how she likes to drag people down so she gets the upper hand. There's nothing Georgette loves more than dragging people down, humiliating them."

"But why would she want to humiliate Carol Liebling?"

"Jealousy? Because they have too much money?"

"But she's doing this debutante thing *with* Carol. If she humiliates Carol, she's going to humiliate herself, too, isn't she?"

"Darling, *nobody* has ever succeeded in humiliating Georgette, though all of us have tried."

"Nobody has succeeded except—"

"Except."

"Truck Van Degan."

"Exactly."

At first the newlyweds, Jules and Hannah Liebling, lived at Hampshire House. In those days most of the best apartment buildings on Manhattan's Upper East Side were quite flagrant in their refusal to accept Jewish tenants, stopping just short of placing signs in their lobbies to that effect. And so the answer, for affluent Jewish families, became the Upper West Side or, for some, apartment hotels like Hampshire House, which was neither really East Side nor West Side, but sort of in the middle, on Central Park South. Hampshire House was already known as "the Hollywood hotel." It was where all the movie moguls stayed when they were in town.

The figure 2600 sticks in Hannah Liebling's mind, though she is not sure now whether that was their apartment number or the rent.

Oh, and Hannah has to admit that though she might not have been in love with him, it was exciting being married to Jules Liebling. Those were exciting years, those last years of American Prohibition, with the money simply rolling in. They were exciting years, but they were also terrifying, dangerous years. People *were* killed—particularly people on the periphery of the liquor trade. But then there were people who had to be killed, traitors who deserved to be killed, or who did things they knew they might be killed for. There were people who tried to work both sides of the Prohibition laws, for example. There were U.S. Government Treasury agents who collected their government salaries and then tried to sell the liquor they had confiscated, proving the unwisdom of trying to serve two masters. In fact, Jules pointed out, by 1929 most of the men who were called bootleggers were on the payroll of the U.S. Government. In a chaotic situation like this, how could mayhem be avoided?

Of course, Jules's principal distilling operations were still located in the province of Quebec, where everything was perfectly legal and things remained relatively calm. One American exception was a distillery he owned in Kentucky, which was licensed to produce alcohol for medicinal purposes, and was supposed to be dispensed only with a doctor's prescription. But if doctors chose to bend the law and prescribe liquor for people who didn't need it, Jules Liebling had no control over this.

The real trouble, Jules explained to her, was on what was called "the South Shore"—that is, the southern, or American, side of Lake Erie. The South Shore had become a war zone, a killing field. Some liquor shipments were confiscated by revenuers, but most were simply stolen at gunpoint. Boats and trucks were hijacked, their drivers murdered and their corpses tossed by the side of the road. Jules usually tried not to get involved with what was going on on the South Shore, but by February 1929 things had reached such a state—with so many of his shipments being stolen before they reached their rightful purchasers in the United States—that Jules decided to step in and do something about it. He summoned his Midwest distributor, Mr. Alphonse Capone, to New York for a meeting. In fact, Mr. Capone was one of Hannah's very first dinner guests in her new home at Hampshire House.

The newspapers, of course, had branded Mr. Capone a bootlegger. But the use of this term was forbidden in the Liebling household, and to Hannah he was simply one of her husband's many American distributors, the one who had the exclusive contract to distribute Ingraham products in the Chicago area. Mr. Capone's arrival in New York was well chronicled in the press, and there was no doubt that he enjoyed the publicity, and that his was becoming a household name throughout the world. He arrived at Grand Central in his own private railway car, known as a Palace Car, with his own retinue of servants and bodyguards. A special red carpet was rolled out along the station platform to greet him. At Hampshire House, four of his bodyguards stationed themselves about the hotel lobby. Two more were posted outside the front entrance to the apartment, and another two guarded the rear service door.

Though she knew that Mr. Capone had other business interests in Chicago besides her husband's products, it was hard for Hannah to think of Mr. Capone as a gangster. In fact, in those days nobody really thought of him that way. He was simply a fabulously rich man. In the year 1927 alone, when he was only twenty-seven, he had an income of $105,000,000, the highest gross income received by a private U.S. citizen in all of history—$35,000,000 more than Henry Ford would ever earn in his best year. Now, still under thirty and looking even younger, Mr. Capone seemed to Hannah simply a sweet, plump, baby-faced little man, with impeccable manners, who was one of her husband's best customers. He bought his liquor on consignment, and paid Ingraham a royalty of thirty percent on every case he sold. And he always paid his bills on time, and always in cash. Hannah knew this because she often helped Jules with the books.

Mr. Capone, she discovered, was also a deeply religious man. He bowed his head and crossed himself before picking up his fork, and did the same thing, she learned, whenever he passed a church or a cemetery. He told her that as a youth he had served as an altar boy at St. Francis of Assisi Church, and had been so trusted for his honesty that he had been given the job of counting the money in the collection baskets.

Because she knew Mr. Capone was of Italian extraction, she had asked her cook to prepare an Italian dinner for him, and he had declared her lasagne the best he had ever eaten. For dessert, she remembers, he ate a full dozen of her cook's famous brownies, and after dinner insisted on going into the kitchen to give the Negro cook a kiss. The poor woman nearly fainted dead away. She was that thrilled. The richest man in the world had kissed her!

Hannah also remembers the after-dinner conversation.

"Our overhead was particularly high last month, Alphonse," Jules said.

"Yes. Three of your shipments failed to reach their destination."

"Do you think they might still be in the Chicago area?"

"Jules, I simply have no idea."

Jules puffed on his cigar. "There's a garage in North Clark Street," he said at last. "Number three-oh-five, I believe. Are you familiar with the building?"

"I am. It belongs to Georgie Moran."

"After hours, I gather, he uses it as a distribution center."

"So I'm told," Mr. Capone said.

"I'm also told that cases of my labels have been turning up there," Jules said.

Mr. Capone looked pained. "Georgie's a good Irish Catholic boy," he said. "He's a good friend of mine. We're competitors, yes, but friendly competitors. Georgie wouldn't do a thing like that to me."

"But what about some of the people working for him? Can they be trusted?"

Mr. Capone ran his finger under the collar of his shirt. "I've never had any trouble with Georgie," he said. "I wouldn't want any trouble with Georgie."

Jules's face grew thoughtful. "Perhaps," he said, "it would be useful if I had a little talk with George Moran, Alphonse."

Mr. Capone looked enormously relieved. "Yes, that would be a big help, Jules," he said.

Then the conversation turned to other matters. "More coffee, Mr. Capone?" Hannah asked him.

Mr. Capone returned to Chicago, where he was welcomed with much fanfare, the next morning.

But then, a week later, the newspapers blazed with lurid headlines. Seven men had been machine-gunned down in a North Clark Street garage in Chicago. All of them, it seemed, worked for Mr. George Moran. Immediately the press and the police as well were claiming that the murders were the work of Al Capone, though there wasn't a shred of evidence to support this thesis. The press gave Alphonse Capone the nickname "Scarface," though Hannah hadn't noticed any scars, and George Moran was nicknamed "Bugs"—all of which made the principals sound more sinister and romantic. And because the shootings occurred on February 14, the press christened the event the "St. Valentine's Day Massacre."

"Do you really think Mr. Capone could have had anything to do with it?" Hannah asked Jules.

"Nonsense. You heard Alphonse say he and George Moran were good friends."

"What about Mr. Moran? Could he have done it if his men were cheating him?"

Jules sighed. "I suppose it's possible," he said. "I guess anything is possible in these troubled times."

And then, at the end of the month, working on the books, Hannah noticed some invoices made out to George Moran. Was this some mistake?

"I pointed out some inefficiencies in his operation," Jules said. "He's repaying the favor by giving me some of his business."

"But I thought Mr. Capone had exclusive distribution rights for Chicago," she said.

"I persuaded Alphonse to share distribution rights with Mr. Moran," he said. "At least for the time being, until things settle down a bit."

The perpetrators of the St. Valentine's Day massacre were never apprehended. In fact, the government was never able to get any of its charges against Mr. Capone to stick. Finally, in 1931, they got him for a white-collar crime, income-tax evasion, which could have happened to anybody, and which Mr. Capone regarded as an insult. He was given a light prison sentence and a fine of $50,000. Which he promptly paid, in cash. Hannah used to have a box of her cook's brownies sent to him once a month in his prison cell, and he always wrote her a charming thank-you note. To Hannah, no matter what terrible things they said and wrote about him, Mr. Alphonse Capone was always a true gentleman of the old school.

By 1933, of course, Prohibition was a thing of the past. That wonderful Age of Innocence was over.

7

"Uncovered Treasures"

When Carol Liebling first began to fall in love with the work she was doing at the Metropolitan Museum of Art, she was already a little bit sick of it. The year was 1988, one of the most uneventful years in the history of the American republic. After taking a scary 500-point tumble the year before, the Dow Jones Industrial Average had begun gliding comfortably upward again—past 3,000, then 3,500, and finally flirting with the seemingly impossible 4,000 mark, while Carol could remember a day when the magic goal to overtake had been a mere 1,000. The twinkly smile and ruddy complexion of Ronald Reagan seemed to reassure the country that all was well, or at least that nothing was really amiss, as the rich got richer and the poor went elsewhere, where they were probably better off. The president's way of dismissing unwelcome news was comforting. He would simply cock his head, grin, shrug, and say, "W-e-e-ll . . ." And Carol was restless.

Working at the Met could be a lot of fun. It certainly had its rewarding moments. And, a not unimportant consideration, it was the kind of work that pleased her mother-in-law to see her do, and that pleased Noah. "It's just the kind of community service work you *should* be doing as Noah's wife," Hannah often said to her approvingly, even though it had sometimes seemed to Carol like the kind of community work that used to be endorsed by her mother's *Ladies' Home Journal.*

She had started her museum work not long after Anne was born, as a lowly volunteer, selling art books, gifts, and postcards in the museum's shop two afternoons a week. But having minored in art history at college, she soon found herself being given tasks with greater responsibilities. By 1986 Anne had successfully weathered the

transition to Brearley's Middle School, and didn't seem
to require that much mothering anymore. Noah was still
expecting his mother to turn over the reins to the company at any moment, and was working very hard with
that in mind, and Carol had been given the official title
of the Met's head of volunteers. She had also been given
the unofficial title of museum archivist.

Being head of volunteers for the museum was not
without its moments of frustration. A good deal of paperwork was entailed, arranging and rearranging schedules for
her volunteer staff, most of whom were well-to-do
women who really didn't want to work very hard. She
began to see herself as a kind of glorified dispatcher for
a radio cab company. And Carol—feeling young, impatient, overqualified, and underused—had already begun
mentally casting about for something else to do. She had
no idea what. But she decided before quitting her job
at the Met, and moving on to whatever it was that might
lie ahead for her, she was going to make some sort of
contribution to the museum that would be significant
enough for Carol Dugan Liebling to be remembered for
it. When she quit, it was going to be on a note of triumph, not defeat. And it was in her secondary capacity
as archivist that she felt she had found what she was
looking for.

For two years prior to that forgettable year of 1988,
she had been spending most of her time on a project
she had named "Uncovered Treasures."

It had all started when, poking around in the museum's basement storage rooms, and in various warehouses
around the city where the Met stored items from its
collections, Carol turned over a canvas which she immediately recognized as an early Velazquez painting of St.
John in the Wilderness. Looking through catalogues of
early exhibitions, she could find no evidence that this
painting had ever been shown. This Velazquez did not
appear anywhere in the museum's inventories. Her only
conclusion was that this was an important piece that the
museum did not even know it owned.

Wondering whether "her" Velazquez was simply an
isolated oversight, she rummaged in the museum's vaults
some more. She soon discovered that it was not. Within
months she had compiled a list of twenty-six works that

had never been catalogued, inventoried, or exhibited, including a Delacroix, an El Greco, two Matisses, a Picasso mother and child, and a second Velazquez. With help from her volunteer staff, she was certain that she would discover even more. That was when she took her idea for "Uncovered Treasures" to the museum's director.

"Think of it," she said. "A special exhibit of pieces from the museum's treasury that the museum didn't even know were there!"

He responded with his usual quick enthusiasm. "Go for it!" he told her.

Soon her list grew to sixty works of art, then to seventy-three, then eighty. In all, Carol spent eighteen months working on her presentation for "Uncovered Treasures—Secrets from Our Lost Archives," as she subtitled it. When it was finished, it ran to more than two hundred pages. It included a complete index of the works themselves, a chronology of their discovery, and a bibliography of textbook sources. Carol drew up a detailed blueprint of how the exhibition could be arranged and hung and lighted. She compiled a budget of the show's probable costs, and appended a list of possible corporate sponsors who might be expected to underwrite the show, at least in part. Needless to say, she did not include the Ingraham Corporation on this list. She even composed an outline and a table of contents for the show's catalogue, and wrote a proposed introduction for it. When she was finished, she sent all her material to a printer and had it bound in blue leather with gold lettering. Then she presented this to the director, who promised to submit copies of her proposal to the board of trustees for consideration at their next meeting.

But when, a week or so later, the director summoned her into his office, his face was long. "Everyone agreed that you'd put a lot of hard work into this," he said, tapping a copy of "Treasures" with his fingertip. "But I'm afraid there wasn't much enthusiasm for the idea among the members of the board, Carol."

"I wonder why not," she said, trying to conceal her profound disappointment.

"There was a general feeling that the timing isn't quite right for this sort of thing," he said.

"Timing?" she said. "What's timing got to do with it? These are works of art that have never before been seen by the New York public. The timing could be anytime."

"It doesn't quite seem to fit in with our regular schedule of upcoming exhibits," he said.

"It's a show that could be mounted this year—or next year—or five years from now."

"But it's a show that doesn't seem to have any clear focus. It doesn't focus on any particular time period, or artist, or event."

"The focus is on the museum *itself,*" she said. "It's a show that says that, like everybody else, the Metropolitan Museum has an attic in which valuable things get lost, or misplaced, and then turn up later. My idea was that this show would humanize the museum—make it seem more personal, less like an institution."

"I'm sorry, Carol."

"What else did the trustees say?" she asked him.

"Well, of course I can't quote you verbatim each trustee's individual comments," he said rather crisply. "But there was a general feeling that this show wouldn't have legs."

"Legs?"

"That it wouldn't be a big box office draw."

"You sound as if we're in show biz," she said.

"Well, in a sense we *are,*" he said with a small, pained smile.

"Funny," she said. "But I thought the museum was in the business of education, not entertainment."

He threw up his hands. "But what's the point of mounting a big, expensive exhibition if nobody comes to see it?" he said. "I'm sorry, Carol. If it's any comfort to you, I personally thought you had a hell of a good idea there."

And all at once she knew that he was lying, or at least that he was not telling her the whole truth. There was more to it than that, but there was nothing she could do. "Well, thank you, Roger," she said, and rose to go, and he turned to paperwork on his desk.

And so that was the end of it. The board of trustees was all powerful, and the director was their highly paid minion. She was a mere unsalaried volunteer. But she could not help but think that if she herself had been able to make her presentation to the board, she could have sold them "Treasures." But that was not the way Things Were Done at the New York Metropolitan Museum of Art.

For the next few days her thoughts centered mostly around the big antique silver coffee urn that stood on the Boulé sideboard in the Trustees Meeting Room, and the little array of Limoges demitasse cups arranged around it. If she could only figure out a way to lace that coffee with arsenic . . .

It was only the coldest sort of comfort to her when she noticed, some weeks later, that Velazquez's *St. John in the Wilderness* had been hung in a position of some prominence in a room devoted to seventeenth-century Spanish painters.

She also knew that she could not quit her job now. The challenge to somehow leave her stamp on the museum had become even greater.

One night she came home to River House to find Noah and her mother-in-law in the library with huge sheafs of architectural drawings spread out on the carpet between them.

"Plans for the new Ingraham Building," Hannah explained. "We've decided to build our own building."

"We've outgrown our space in the Chrysler Building," Noah said. "We've had some cost studies done. This turns out to be the most economical way to solve the problem."

Carol studied the plans, which called for a huge square box, thirty-eight stories tall, made of shiny pressed aluminum, dotted with hundreds and hundreds of little windows, row upon row of them. Over the top of the building the architect had indicated a tall illuminated sign, reading INGRAHAM—THE TRUSTED NAME IN SPIRITS. The floor plans showed a maze of tiny offices.

At first Carol didn't know what to say. Finally she said, "Does Ingraham really need this much space now?"

"Of course not," Hannah said. "That's the point. What we don't need, we'll lease out. As we need more space, we can take over the leases. This is going to be a real moneymaker for us, Carol."

"Who are the architects, Nana?"

"Frankel and Steiner—tops in the business. They deliver the lowest cost per square foot in town."

"And you want—pressed aluminum?"

"It turns out to be the cheapest way to sheathe a building this size," Hannah said.

"And it's extremely durable," Noah added helpfully. "Keeps the heat in winter and reflects the sun in summer, making it more economical to air-condition."

Hannah Liebling tapped the plans approvingly with her forefinger. "I like the sign best," she said. She turned to Carol. "Well, what do you think?" she said.

"What do *I* think?" Carol said.

"Yes. What do you think? Pretty impressive, isn't it? Particularly with that sign up there on the roof. The architect says you'll be able to see that sign from the George Washington Bridge."

"You really want to know what I think?" Carol asked her.

"Of course!"

"If you really want to know what I think, Nana, I think it's the ugliest design for a building I've ever seen in my life," Carol said. "And I think that sign is—absolutely vulgar." She looked quickly at Noah, who was merely smiling. His smile said, *I've been trying to tell her that all along.*

"Well!" Hannah said, tossing aside the plans. "Who asked you your opinion about it, anyway?"

"You did," Carol said. "You asked me what I thought of it, Nana. And I just told you."

"Well, maybe I did," she conceded. "But—ugly? What's so ugly about it? It seems like a perfectly nice building to me."

"I'm not sure you really want my opinion, Nana," Carol said.

"Of course I do. I just asked you, didn't I?"

"Well, then let's start at the top. That sign—"

Noah cleared his throat. "That sign was Mother's idea," he said. "It was an afterthought. Actually, the architect wasn't entirely sure—"

"They'll be able to see it from New Jersey!"

"Let me just say one thing, Nana," Carol said. "If you're going to build your own building and attach your corporate name to it, I think you have to be terribly careful about what sort of a statement this building makes, because whatever it is, it's going to be a statement about your company. And it's going to be a statement that will be there for a good long time. I wouldn't worry about New Jersey. It's going to be a building that will be seen by hundreds of thousands of people who pass by it every year, people from all over the world. We're going to have to assume that people will see that building on the New York City skyline long after all of us are in our graves. That means that it should be an important building, a building that will register in people's minds, not just a building that's energy-efficient and was cheap to put up."

"Huh!" Hannah said. "You're saying that a building should be a work of art?"

"Yes, but in a rather special sense, Nana. It isn't like a book that you don't have to read if the subject doesn't interest you. It's not like a painting that can be passed by, or a piece of music that you don't have to listen to if you don't like it. A building—particularly a corporate building, and a building of the size you have in mind— imposes itself on people. If you have business to do there, you have to find the building on the street, enter it, and find your way around inside. Buildings envelop us, wrap themselves around us, so they should be both pleasing to the eye and pleasing to the spirit."

"Huh!" she said again. "And you don't think this one is?"

"I really don't, Nana. It seems to me that when a business organization decides to build a building, it takes a moral position. And it's up to the architect to try to express that moral position."

"And you don't think Frankel and Steiner have done this?"

"Frankly, in this case, Nana, no."

"Well," Hannah said, "I don't suppose you have anybody better in mind, do you?"

"As a matter of fact, I do," Carol said.

"Who?"

"His name is Jean-Pierre Selancy. He's a Frenchman—quite young, only twenty-eight. He's won prizes for a theater complex he designed in Paris and an office

tower in Marseille. His work has never before been represented in the United States. He's quite wonderful."

"Hmm," Hannah said. "If he's never worked in this
country before, then he might be willing to work for
less—for the opportunity to design an important New
York building."

"That's a good point, Nana," Carol said. "He just
might."

"Make a note of that name, Noah," his mother said.

The subject of the new Ingraham Building did not
come up again for several months. Carol made a point
of not mentioning it to Noah. She knew the situation
was a tricky one, and she knew that Noah was on her
side. She had heard that invitations to submit designs
had gone out to four more architects. But she didn't
know whether Jean-Pierre Selancy was one of these, and
she was a little too afraid to ask. She did know that, in
the end, the decision would be Nana Hannah's. Though
Hannah always made a great point of insisting that she
bowed to Noah's judgment on many matters, Carol knew
that it was still Hannah who had the final word.

Then, one evening, Noah came home beaming. "I've
got great news," he said. "She's chosen your French architect. Congratulations, darling."

Carol clapped her hands. "Wonderful," she said.
"We've won!"

He hesitated. "But then, the bad news is—"

"Wait," she said. "Let me guess what the bad news
is. The bad news is that she's taking all the credit for
having found Monsieur Selancy. Am I right?"

He gave her a rueful look. "Well, yes," he said.

"That doesn't surprise me in the slightest," she said
with a shrug.

The next morning she picked up the *New York Times*
and saw, on the front page, the headline:

Design for New Ingraham
Building Is Unveiled

The illustration showed the architect's rendering of a
slender, graceful tower to be built of bronze and glass,
facing a plaza landscaped with trees, pools, and foun-

tains. Paul Goldberger, the *Times*'s architecture critic, went on to praise the design's "splendid simplicity," its "fluidity of upward motion," and its "timeless grandeur and glowing elegance."

And toward the end of the article, Carol read:

> The building's prize-winning architect, Jean-Pierre Selancy of Paris, has never before been represented in America. His design was chosen, over many other candidates, by Mrs. Hannah S. Liebling, the farsighted CEO of Ingraham's. . . .

"You're not upset, I hope," Noah said to her that night.

"Heavens, no. I'm used to the way she operates. I'm just happy that you're going to have a beautiful new building, and not that upended egg crate she wanted in the beginning."

A few days later, Hannah mentioned it to Carol. "What did you think of the *Times* story?" she asked her.

"I thought it was absolutely wonderful," Carol said.

"They called me farsighted," Hannah said.

"It was exactly what you wanted, wasn't it? Of course, I noticed the misprint. It should have said the architect was chosen by Mrs. Noah Liebling, not Mrs. Hannah Liebling. But that's understandable. The names—Noah and Hannah—are so similar."

Her mother-in-law gave her one of her narrow looks. Then she said, "I think you ought to be spending more time on your museum work, Carol. And try not to get too involved with the distilled spirits industry."

And that, in fact, was precisely what Carol planned to do. Just that morning, in *Art & Antiques* magazine, she had read:

> Perhaps the most extensive, and valuable, collection of antique Chinese and Japanese porcelains is in private hands, and has never been seen by the public. This is the collection begun by the late Truxton Van Degan, the glass manufacturer, in the late 1800s, and greatly added to by his son, Truxton Van Degan, Jr., in the 1920s. The bulk of the Van Degan collection remains

in the vaults of several New York banks because of
the enormous insurance costs that would be entailed
if it were to be removed.

Carol decided that this would be her next project. She
had met Mrs. Truxton Van Degan several times at
Brearley parent-teacher meetings. At that point she and
Georgette Van Degan were little more than nodding acquaintances. But that would be a good place to start.

In the darkness of their bedroom, Noah said to her,
"I'm sorry your 'Uncovered Treasures' wasn't a go."

"I think I made a mistake," she said. "I thought all I
needed was the director's approval. I think I should have
spent more time lobbying among the trustees—taking
them to lunch. That sort of thing. That might have made
a difference."

"Kissing asses," he said.

"Yes."

"But you want to know what I think?"

"What?"

"I don't think your director ever showed your presentation to the board of trustees."

"Really, Noah? What makes you say that?"

"I think he decided it didn't make him look good. I
think he decided it would look like sloppy housekeeping
on his part. All that valuable art lying around in warehouses, and he didn't even know it existed. He killed
your idea to cover his ass."

She hesitated. Then she said, "You know something,
Noah? I think you may be right."

"I'm sure I'm right. Think about it for a minute. He's
the chief honcho of the Met Museum. And suddenly all
this important stuff he's supposed to be in charge of gets
turned up by a mere—woman."

"And a mere volunteer," she said. "Of course."

"Kissing asses. Covering asses. That's what business is
all about."

She lay in silence, thinking about this. Then she heard
him rise from the bed next to hers. She felt him pull
back the sheet and coverlet from her bed, and kiss the
hollow between her bare breasts. "Uncovered treasures," he said.

8

A Delicate Matter

You may have got the impression, from the story thus far, that Cyril is something of a cipher in the Liebling family. He is in some ways, but in some ways he most definitely is not. Certainly Cyril himself does not think of himself as a cipher. In fact, Cyril often reminds himself, if it were not for Cyril, his younger brother would never have attained the position he did. One could go even further and point out that if it were not for Cyril (and Cyril's misdeeds in his father's eyes), there might never have been a Noah Liebling at all. Without Noah there would have been no Carol. Without Noah and Carol there would have been no Anne; without Anne there would have been no Melody Richards; without Melody, William Luckman would never have come into any of their lives, and none of these people would have come together so explosively as to create a homicide case, as became clear at the trial.

Looked at this way, Cyril becomes the pivotal figure in the ennead. And so, though it involves a matter of some delicacy, Cyril's story deserves to be told fully and honestly.

Cyril's engraved business letterhead reads:

CYRIL DE R. LIEBLING
Public Relations
1000 Park Avenue
New York, NY 10028

The "de R" is something of an affectation. Cyril's actual middle name is David. But Cyril does not object too strenuously if some of his clients suppose that "de R" stands for de Rothschild, and that Cyril is somehow connected to the European banking family. Cyril is not above inventing relatives. He might say, "My cousin, Baron Guy de Rothschild . . ." Just as often he will say, "My sister, the Princess di Pascanelli . . ." This is all right. This is all part of what is called public relations.

Which brings us to the matter of clients. If you ask his mother, she would no doubt snort and say that Cyril doesn't have any clients. Where his mother is concerned, Cyril encourages this view. Living, as he does, on the upper floor of what used to be her duplex apartment, Cyril does his best to keep his mother's nose out of his business. He will often speak mysteriously of having to leave for "an important client lunch" or "an important client dinner."

"Who's the client?" Hannah will demand to know.

"I'm not at liberty to say."

"Huh!"

Actually, he has several clients. One is a young dress designer whom Cyril is trying to establish as a fashion force. Another is a hair stylist from France who calls himself simply "Philippe," and whom such powerful and important New York women as Patsy Collingwood and Pookie Satterthwaite and, more recently, Georgette Van Degan have begun to use. Cyril's plan for Philippe is to help him launch his own line of hair products. That's where the money is in the hair business, not in doing comb-outs. Cyril has promised to make Philippe the next Vidal Sassoon. Or at least to try.

In 1956, however, Cyril was involved in a much graver matter. It was a summer Sunday evening in Tarrytown, at Grandmont, and Hannah, Jules, and Bathy were gathered in what was called the music room—watching *The Ed Sullivan Show*. Just a month earlier, Ruth Liebling had run off and married the Brazilian copper heir Antonio Fernandez-Just, much to her father's displeasure. There had been much publicity about this, mostly centered on the fact that Ruth was only eighteen, while Sr. Fernandez-Just, who had had four previous wives, was fifty-seven. Jules had been spending quite a lot of time on the telephone to Sao Paulo, trying to persuade Ruth of the unwisdom of this union, but without success, and so this was not the most relaxed of times in the Liebling household. Still, *The Ed Sullivan Show* was one of Jules's favorites, and the three of them had planned to spend a quiet evening at home.

Cyril, who was twenty-two, had taken his car to join a friend and drive to Manhattan to see a performance of *My Fair Lady*. Little Noah was in his room being read to by his governess. The other servants had been given the afternoon and evening off, as they always were every other Sunday. One of Ed Sullivan's guests was a trained chimpanzee, and Jules was laughing at its antics. Hannah was passing a bowl of fresh popcorn that her cook had made earlier in the day. And in the middle of this almost tranquil scene, the telephone rang. Jules, thinking that it might be Ruth ready to capitulate, picked it up on the first ring, and Bathy reached out and lowered the volume on the TV set.

"*Pop!*" he heard Cyril's voice shout. "Pop! I've been kidnapped!"

"Kidnapped? What do you mean? Where are you, Cyril?"

At the word "kidnapped," the others in the room froze. Hannah dropped the bowl of popcorn, and it scattered across the carpet. Bathy jumped to her feet and turned off the television. It had been one of their worst fears, not so much for Cyril, their grown son, as for little Noah.

"Tell me what happened, Cyril."

"Two men. I was coming down the drive, headed for New York to pick up my friend and go to the show. When I got to the gate, there was a car parked across the drive. . . ."

"What kind of a car?"

"I don't remember. I think it was black. I got out of my car to see what the matter was. . . . It was dark, I couldn't see . . ."

Bathy stepped quickly to the phone and whispered to Jules: "Keep him on the phone as long as possible. I'll call from the other line and see if they can trace this call." Jules nodded, and Bathy ran to the next room.

"And then what happened?"

"Two men came out of the bushes. They were wearing ski masks. They had guns. They grabbed me. I tried to fight them off, but they knocked me down in the gravel. I struggled, but one of them put his gun at my head and

told me not to move. Then they tied me up, put a blind-
fold on me, and put a gag on my mouth. Then they
carried me, and threw me in the backseat of their
car. . . ."

"Where did they take you, Cyril?"

"I don't know. They drove a long time—maybe a half
hour. We crossed two bridges. At least it *sounded* like
we crossed two bridges. So I don't think I'm in Westchester County anymore."

"You don't know where you are?"

"I'm in this *room*, Pop! I don't know where it is.
There're no windows. I can't see out. They carried me
up two flights of stairs to get me here, I know that. . . ."

"Can you describe the room, son?"

"Pop, they're right *here!* They're here in this room
with me. They're both sitting right here with me. Pointing guns at me. Wearing ski masks. They've got me tied
to a chair. One of them is holding the phone so I can
talk to you. . . ."

"Does either of these men wish to speak to me?"

He heard his son's voice say, "My father wants to
know if you want to talk to him."

Then a man's voice came on the line. "Mr. Liebling?"
the voice said. "We have your son. He is quite safe, for
now," and Jules thought he detected a foreign accent.

"What do you want?"

"For your son's release, we want two-point-five million dollars. The terms of his release, and how the
money is to be delivered, will come to you by mail. Until
the money is paid, your son will be unharmed. We will
give him food and water."

"And if I can't pay? Don't pay?"

"Your son will be—dispatched."

"What do you mean, 'dispatched'?"

"Exactly what I say. No more questions now, Mr. Liebling. Wait for your instructions in the mail. Everything
will be made quite clear in our instructions, Mr. Liebling.
Do you wish a final word with your son?"

"Yes, please," Jules said.

Then Cyril came on the line again. "Please, Pop," he
said. "Please pay them what they want, Pop. I'm scared,
Pop! I'm scared they're going to kill me, Pop! Help me,
Pop!" Then Cyril began to cry, and the line went dead.

Bathy stood at the music room door. "Any luck with tracing the call?" he asked.

She shook her head. "The phone company needs at least an hour to set up tracing equipment."

"Have them set up tracing equipment on every line coming into this house. Also the New York apartment. Also my office lines."

"Already done," Bathy said.

"Also I want tape recorders set up on all these lines, so we can tape all incoming calls."

"Already ordered," Bathy said. "They'll be installed in a half hour."

Jules reached for the phone again.

"Who are you calling?"

"The FBI."

"Don't," she said, reaching out and pressing the receiver buttons down. "If you call the FBI, that'll mean the police, and the police will mean the press. The press will make a circus out of this, particularly after the business with Ruth. I think we should try to deal with the kidnappers on our own."

"She's right, Jules," Hannah said. "If the press gets wind of this, it could frighten them. They might try to—"

"They might decide to kill Cyril," Bathy said evenly. "It's happened before. I have a friend, Kevin Shaughnessy, who's a private investigator."

"Call him."

"I already have," she said, demonstrating the quick efficiency that was already making her such a valued member of Jules Liebling's business team. "He's on his way to Tarrytown right now."

Jules stood by the telephone muttering, "Trouble . . . trouble. Nothing but trouble. First the St. Anselm's thing. Now this."

"Oh, Jules!" Hannah cried. "You can't blame Cyril for this!" Then she burst into tears.

"Surely you have the money, Jules," Bathy said, almost contemptuously. "Surely two and a half million dollars isn't too much to pay for your son's life!"

"Cyril's car must still be at the foot of the drive," he said. "Somebody should get that and put it back in the garage."

"I'll do that," Bathy said. She hurried out of the house

and down the long drive. At the turning, she saw the
headlights of Cyril's yellow Mustang facing her. Its con-
vertible top was down. Both doors hung wide open. Its
engine was running. Just beyond, the heavy iron gates to
Grandmont, with their scrollwork of reversed L's, were
closed. She jumped into the car, closed both doors, taking care not to touch any areas that might contain fingerprints, threw the Mustang into gear, drove it back up
the hill to the house, and parked it in its regular space
in the garage. Then she removed the keys and locked
the garage doors.

In the music room, still weeping, Hannah knelt on the
carpet, picking up the spilled popcorn, piece by piece.
Suddenly, to her surprise, her husband was kneeling on
the floor beside her and took her into his arms.

Kevin Shaughnessy, age thirty-eight, a former Pinker-
ton man, turned out to be a heavyset redheaded Irish-
man who exuded an air of solid authority. He had driven
immediately to Grandmont from his home in Yonkers,
and had spent a half hour scouring the grounds of the
estate with a powerful flashlight. It was nearly ten
o'clock when he sat down opposite Bathy and the Lieblings in the music room. A bulge under his jacket indicated where he carried his service revolver in a shoulder
holster, and as he hitched up his trouser legs, a second
bulge in his left sock revealed where he carried a second weapon.

"There's really nothing more we can do until we hear
from the kidnappers again," he said. "But there are a
couple of aspects of this case that puzzle me a little.
Mind if I smoke?"

"Certainly not," Hannah said.

He lighted a cigarette, igniting a wooden kitchen
match with his fingernail. "So let's talk about those aspects. To begin with, there's the position of the Mustang.
Your son told you that he was driving down the drive,
toward the gate, when he saw another vehicle, just beyond the gate, blocking him. And yet when Miss Sachs
found the vehicle, with its motor running, it was headed
back up the drive, away from the gate, toward the house.
Any explanation for that?"

"Perhaps they turned the car around."

"Perhaps. But why?"

"To throw us off?"

He inhaled deeply and blew out a sharp stream of smoke. "Perhaps," he said again. "But again—why?"

No one said anything.

"And then there's the position of the car doors. Both doors were open, on the passenger's and on the driver's side. Your son told you he got out of his car to see what was the matter. Assuming he got out on the driver's side and left that door open, why were both doors opened when Miss Sachs found the car?"

There was another silence.

"Now, your son indicated that he was attacked outside the gates. That would mean the gates were open. And yet when Miss Sachs found the vehicle, the gates were closed."

"They could have closed the gates behind them when they left."

"Yes, but most kidnappers are in a big hurry, Mrs. Liebling. They don't take the time to close gates behind them, or to reverse the direction of the victim's car. And here's another thing. Your son says he struggled with his assailants on the drive. I assume this would have happened just outside the gates. Your drive is composed of fine, loose gravel. Long Island grit, I believe it's called. I found no signs of a struggle in the gravel outside the gate—or inside it, for that matter. Or in the grassy areas alongside the drive, on either side. Odd, don't you think? What's more, a car passing along on a gravel drive like yours leaves tread marks. And yet when I examined your drive just now, the only tread marks on it were the ones made by Miss Sachs when she drove the car back up to the garage. There were no tread marks from any second vehicle, either inside or outside the gate."

"This isn't rescuing my son!" Hannah said angrily. "Talking about tread marks!"

"I'm sorry, Mrs. Liebling," he said. "But we don't know where your son is yet, or who's got him, or how we're going to get him back. Right now I'd like to get to the bottom of some of the puzzling aspects of the case."

"He's right, Hannah. Let him talk," Bathy said.

"Now, let's talk about the time of day," he said. "You

said you were watching *The Ed Sullivan Show*. That comes on at eight, and the trained chimp was in the first segment. That means that your son's call came through at about seven or eight minutes past eight—correct?"

"Correct," Jules said. "In fact, I looked at my watch."

"Your son said he had been driven by his assailants in their car for about a half hour. That means the kidnapping must have occurred at around seven-thirty, or a little after. Today is July twenty-ninth. Your son said that he couldn't identify his assailants' car because it was too dark. But the sun doesn't set as early as seven-thirty this time of year. There would have been at least another hour of sunshine this afternoon. The kidnapping must have occurred in broad daylight."

"He was probably terrified. He could have easily been confused."

"Of course. And yet when Miss Sachs found the car, its headlights were on. Odd, don't you think?" He pronounced the word "odd" with a Down East vowel sound: *Awed*.

"Yes," Jules said. "Very odd." His face was grim.

"Now, let's turn for a minute to the conversation you had with the kidnappers," Shaughnessy said. "Admittedly, this was very brief, but a couple of things interest me. To begin with, you said the man had what sounded like a foreign accent."

"Yes."

"Any clue as to what kind of foreign accent?"

"French perhaps. Or Italian. I can't be sure."

"And when he mentioned the ransom figure to you, he used the expression 'two-point-five million.' Correct?"

"Correct."

"Doesn't that strike you as a little odd, Mr. Liebling?"

"No. What's odd about it?"

"Two-point-five million. Not two and a half million, or two million five hundred thousand. Two-point-five million sounds like the way an accountant would talk. Or a real estate man."

"What the hell difference does it make?"

"You see, what I'm trying to do, Mr. Liebling, is to draw up a psychological profile of the perpetrators, from what little evidence we have. And when you told him that you might be unable to pay, or be unwilling to pay, such a sum, he responded that in that case it might be necessary to have your son 'dispatched.' He used that word. You're sure of that."

"Absolutely. I remember it distinctly. I asked him what he meant."

"Odd word. Dispatched. Such a—such an almost *dainty* word. He didn't use the word killed, almost as though he was afraid to use it. You see, Mr. Liebling, if it's any comfort to you, I'm beginning to get the impression that our abductors here are not men who are essentially dangerous. I feel that these people are amateurs, not professionals, which could be to our advantage. They want to extract money from you, of course. But I get the strong feeling that they definitely don't want to harm your son, and won't, unless—"

"Unless we do something that causes them to panic," Bathy said.

"Correct."

"That's why we wanted someone like yourself to handle the initial negotiations," Bathy said. "Without notifying the police, or alerting the media."

"Of course. Now, you said that your son's plans for this evening were to pick up a friend, drive to Manhattan, and then attend a performance of *My Fair Lady.*"

"I think he said he was going to drive to Manhattan first, and pick up the friend there, and then go to the theater. I'm not sure."

"It doesn't matter. He and the friend were to meet somewhere between here and the theater. Was dinner mentioned?"

"I don't think so, no."

"What time did he leave the house?"

"I didn't make a note of it. Around six, I think."

"Six would get him to Manhattan at around six-thirty. That would give them time for dinner before an eight o'clock curtain. That's the usual thing. Now, do you have any idea who this friend of his was?"

"No. He didn't say."

"And you didn't ask him?"

"No. It didn't seem important."

"It's become important now. Does your son have any special girlfriend?"

"No."

"Any male friend that he'd be likely to go to the theater with?"

"Not that I know of."

"So the friend could have been male or female."

"Yes."

"But you see, Mr. Liebling, the odd thing is, if he left the house around six, and the alleged kidnapping took place in the vicinity of the front gates at around seven-thirty, what was he doing in the intervening hour and a half?"

"Don't use the word 'alleged'!" Hannah said. "Perhaps he forgot the tickets, drove back to the house to get them. That would explain the way the car was headed, and—"

"And the two opened front doors. If the friend was with him when it happened. But that's not the way he said it happened, Mrs. Liebling. He said he was on his way to New York. He said he was alone."

"When he called, he was obviously frightened and confused."

"Mr. and Mrs. Liebling, there is another small problem here."

"What's that?"

"*My Fair Lady* is playing at the Mark Hellinger Theater. Today is Sunday. On Sunday nights there are no performances at the Mark Hellinger. On Sundays the theater is dark. So are nearly all New York theaters."

There was a long silence, and then Hannah said, "Perhaps he didn't realize this. Perhaps he was just hoping to pick up two tickets at the box office."

"For the hottest new show on Broadway? For a show that has people lined up around the block for tickets that have to be bought weeks—even months—in advance? Is your son that naive? I shouldn't think so."

When there was no immediate reply, he added, "Mr. and Mrs. Liebling, I can only conclude that your son was not being entirely truthful when he told you about his plans for this evening."

It was nearly midnight. Hannah leaned forward in her chair. "Mr. Shaughnessy, will you spend the night with us tonight?" she said. "There are plenty of spare bedrooms."

"Yes, please do!" Bathy said.

"I'd very much like to do so," he said. "In fact, it would be helpful if I could use your son's bedroom. I'd like to go through his things, if you don't mind. And I may ask to spend several nights with you while we try to get to the bottom of this. These things take time, I'm sorry to say."

The ransom note arrived in the next morning's mail, bearing the postmark of a Manhattan substation. It was carefully printed, in pencil, on lined yellow paper. It read:

> *Mr. Liebling:*
>   *We have your son. He is safe with us, and will remain safe until such time as our demands are met, at which point in time he will be safely returned to you. It is not our desire to have to dispatch your son, but we are fully prepared to do so if our demands are not met. Our demands are unconditional. We demand $2.5 million, which must be paid in bills of small denominations, no bill to be larger than $20. Their serial numbers must not be sequential. We realize that it may take you some time to aggrandize this much cash, so we suggest you begin doing this immediately. We will telephone you tonight at 6 p.m. for a report on your progress in this direction, and to deliver you the issuance of further instructions.*

"The postmark tells us nothing," Kevin Shaughnessy said. "The letter could have been dropped in any one of over a hundred different mailboxes in lower Manhattan. But, again, notice the odd formality of the language. The word 'dispatch' again. 'Aggrandize,' and 'issuance of further instructions.' I get the impression that we're dealing with someone who's learned English rather recently, and who's trying to use it very carefully and precisely. At least tonight's call, if it comes, will be traceable."

"Please don't say 'if it comes,' " Hannah said. "It's bound to come."

"Did you find anything in my son's room?" Jules asked.

"Nothing I wouldn't expect to find. I found a small

black address book, with names and telephone numbers. Every young man keeps a little black book. The names meant nothing to me, but I'm running a check on all of them to see if anything turns up. Until the phone call comes, there's nothing much more we can do except wait."

Throughout the day, on Mr. Shaughnessy's instructions, Jules and Hannah and Bathy did their best to act as though nothing at all had happened. To the household servants, who asked where Mr. Cyril was, the answer was that he was out of town for a few days. Kevin Shaughnessy's presence in the house was explained by saying that he was "an old family friend," nothing more.

Then, at precisely six o'clock, the telephone rang. Jules immediately picked it up, and Mr. Shaughnessy moved into the next room to pick up an extension.

"Mr. Liebling, did you receive our letter?"

"I did," Jules said.

"Are our demands quite clear?" This was, Jules thought, a different man's voice from the one he had spoken to the night before—younger-sounding somehow, but with the same trace of an accent.

"Your demands are very clear," he said. "Raising that amount of money will be no problem. But I don't think you fellows have thought this through very carefully. Two and a half million dollars, in small bills, is quite a lot of paper. I've figured that it will take at least eighteen large suitcases to hold that much cash. We'll need a truck to deliver that much cash to you, and you'll need another truck to pick it up."

"Excuse me? How many suitcases?"

"Eighteen," he said, and then, on a sudden inspiration, he said, "*Diez-y-ocho. Diez-y-ocho maletas muy grandes.*"

"*Claro.*" Then, in the background, Jules thought he heard the sounds of a whispered conversation.

"How do you expect me to handle that?" he asked.

"A few moments, please. I will call you back."

"May I speak to my son, please?"

"He is not with me at this moment."

"Where is he? I thought you were guarding him."

"There are two of us, as I believe you know. We take

turns doing the guarding duty. I will call you back shortly."

"Spanish," Jules said when Shaughnessy returned to the music room. "Probably Puerto Rican."

"Yes. That was clever of you, Mr. Liebling. The call was placed from a pay telephone in the Flatbush section of Brooklyn. I have the exact location of the booth, but you weren't on the phone long enough for me to get one of my operatives over there. But I think it's safe to say he's being held somewhere in Brooklyn."

"Brooklyn! The largest borough in the city!"

"Yes, but the scope of our search is narrowed considerably. He said he felt their car crossing two bridges— that would be one into Manhattan and the second into Brooklyn. Let's wait for their next call."

But then there was no next call. Monday evening passed, then Tuesday, and then Wednesday, and there was no further word from the kidnappers.

"If we don't hear something soon, I'm afraid we may have to turn this over to the FBI," Kevin Shaughnessy said.

"Oh, please—let's wait as long as we can," Hannah said. "If the media get hold of this, it could frighten them, and—"

"I know what you mean," he said. "Meanwhile, I've run a check on all the names in your son's address book. They all seem to be legitimate. Most of them are young males, incidentally. And none of them were planning to see *My Fair Lady* with your son."

Then, on Thursday morning, there was a call. This time it was the older of the two men's voices on the other end of the line. "Mr. Liebling, we have modified our demands somewhat," he said. "The figure remains the same—two-point-five million dollars. But the money can be in hundred-dollar notes, wrapped in packets of one thousand dollars each. The serial numbers, however, must not be in sequence. We appreciate that it will take some time to prepare the money in this fashion. We are giving you twenty-four hours to do so. We estimate that this amount of money will fill two, or at the most three, large plastic garbage bags. This is how we want the money delivered, in large green plastic garbage bags. In exactly twenty-four hours you will receive a final telephone call with full instructions as to how and where these bags are to be delivered. Is all this clear to you, Mr. Liebling?"

"Quite clear," Jules said, and the line went dead.

"Another pay phone in Brooklyn," Kevin Shaughnessy said. "But we're narrowing down the neighborhood—Flatbush and Brooklyn Heights."

The next few hours were something of a mystery to the household staff at Grandmont. Why had a large bale of what appeared to be old newspapers been delivered to the house, along with an industrial-size paper-cutting machine? Why were Mr. and Mrs. Liebling, Miss Bathy, and their house guest Mr. Shaughnessy locked in the music room with all this material? Well, it had always been a strange household, and it was not the servants' duty to ask questions. The answer was that the four of them were busily cutting, stacking, and banding twenty-five hundred little piles of paper and stuffing them into large green plastic garbage bags.

"I wonder if our perpetrators know that any deposit larger than ten thousand dollars must be reported to the IRS," Kevin Shaughnessy said at one point. "The IRS and the FBI are all T-men. These guys are taking a big risk. Or else they're damn fools."

Later he said, "When their call comes tomorrow morning, I want you to tell them one thing. I want you to tell them that you absolutely cannot deliver the money until you have talked to your son, and have been given his assurance that he's alive and well."

Jules nodded.

"In return, promise them that the police will not be called."

"No police. No publicity."

"Unless—"

"Unless what?"

"Unless it's publicity they actually want," Kevin Shaughnessy said. "I'm beginning to wonder."

"Why would they want publicity?"

"Why did Booth murder Lincoln?"

"Oh, please don't talk about murder!" Hannah cried.

Nevertheless, they were all up at dawn the following morning and waiting in the music room, which had become their operations center.

At eight o'clock the telephone rang.

"Mr. Liebling?"

"Yes."

"You have the money ready?"

"Yes."

"Good. Then follow these instructions carefully. Cyril tells us you own a dark green Chrysler station wagon, New York license plate LZT-897."

"That's correct."

"Very well. You will be driving that tonight. You will be alone."

"Now, wait a minute," Jules said. "I've never driven a car. I don't know how to drive. My son will confirm that. I'll need a driver."

A pause. Then, "Very well. You may be accompanied by your driver. But no one else."

"Fine," Jules said.

"There is a restaurant called Billy's Grill at one-two-four Fulton Street in Brooklyn. The proprietor closes his restaurant promptly at midnight, and just before locking up, he places his garbage, in big green bags, on the sidewalk outside the front door. At exactly ten minutes past twelve, you will drive your station wagon past this restaurant. The street must be empty. There must be no pedestrians on the street. There must be no other vehicles moving on the street. If there are, you will go around the block until the street is empty. Someone will be watching to make sure that this is the case. If there is any possibility of a witness to your delivery, it will be necessary to dispatch your son. Is that clear?"

"Yes."

"If the street is clear, you will deposit your garbage bags on the sidewalk alongside the restaurant's garbage. Then you will drive away as quickly as possible and not attempt to return. Once the money has been satisfactorily delivered to us, your son will be released, and you will hear from him."

"There's just one thing," Jules said.

"Yes?"

"Before I deliver this money, I must talk to my son. I need to hear him say he's alive and well."

"I'm sorry, but your son is not with me now."

"I didn't figure he was. But I'm not leaving this house with your money until I've talked to Cyril."

There was another, longer pause. Then, "What time do you plan to leave your house, Mr. Liebling?"

"To be in Brooklyn by ten after twelve—no later than eleven-fifteen."

"Very well. You will hear from your son shortly in advance of your departure." And once again the line went dead.

"Another pay phone in Brooklyn," Kevin Shaughnessy said when he returned to the room. "Different number, but within the same fifteen-block radius as the others. I think we're close to getting your son back, Mr. Liebling."

But the rest of the hours of the day dragged on with painful slowness.

Then, shortly before eleven, the phone rang again. "Pop!" Cyril's voice cried. "Pop—are you going to pay them their money? Are you going to get me out of here?"

"Are you all right, son?"

"All *right*? I've been sitting tied to a kitchen chair for almost a week, Pop! With one or the other of them sitting here pointing a gun at me! I've hardly slept for nearly a week, Pop! They only untie me to go to the bathroom! They—"

"Have they treated you well?"

"Well? Well, they feed me, if that's what you mean. Not that their food's that great. Oh, Pop, *please*—please do what they say, Pop! Just pay them their money and get me out of here! It's been just hell, Pop! It's been like living in hell! I want to go home, Pop, *please*!" Then he heard his son's voice, suddenly calm again, as though turning to speak to someone else in the room, ask, "How'm I doing?" Then Cyril said, "Oh, please, Pop, help me. Just do what they say!"

"Tell them I'm on my way with the money," Jules said. "Tell them I have their instructions, and I'm on my way now."

"Be careful, Pop! They're dangerous! Be sure to do exactly what they told you, Pop, or they'll kill me!"

"Be patient, son. Just stay where you are, and be patient."

"Stay where I *am*? How can I go anywhere, tied to a chair?"

"You'll be home soon, son," his father said.

"*Wahoo!*" shouted Kevin Shaughnessy, bursting into the room. "We know where he is! Thirty-four Joralemon Street, Brooklyn Heights, apartment 3-C. Let's go!"

Quickly they loaded the three heavy garbage bags into the back of the station wagon. Kevin Shaughnessy took the wheel, and Jules slid into the passenger seat beside him. "Two brothers named Fernandez," Kevin said as they headed down the gravel drive toward the gate. "Both bachelors. Older brother, Miguel, is twenty-five. Younger one, Jose, is fifteen. Older one works as a security guard on Seventh Avenue. Younger one is still in high school. No P.C.R. for either one—prior criminal record. Moved into this apartment six weeks ago. It's a one-bedroom efficiency, third floor walk-up. Your son said he'd been carried up two flights of stairs, so this must be where they've got him. Don't know much about them yet. Quick check of neighbors reveals zip. Neighbors say they keep to themselves. No suspicious noises from the apartment, no suspicious comings or goings. Very quiet. Typical perps. Homebodies. Still, it's a little odd. . . ."

"What's a little odd?"

"The name. Fernandez. Didn't your daughter just elope with a man named Fernandez?"

"Antonio Fernandez-Just. A Brazilian."

"Yeah. Would any of his relatives have wanted to kidnap your son?"

"Antonio Fernandez-Just is supposed to be very rich. Why would he want to extort money from me?"

"I dunno. That's why I asked you."

Jules shook his head. "It doesn't make any sense," he said.

"Maybe it's just a coincidence. Fernandez is a pretty common Hispanic name. Like Smith or Jones. New York phone books have dozens of pages of Fernandezes. Still, it's kind of funny. All the people causing your family trouble seem to be named Fernandez."

Jules said nothing.

"I wonder what your son meant when he suddenly

turned away from the phone, and said, 'How'm I doing?' "

"Perhaps they told him to sound desperate. After all, they're desperate for my money."

"Yeah, maybe that's it," he said.

They were nearly a half hour early when they located Billy's Grill in Fulton Street and drove quickly past it. They spent the rest of the time figuring the shortest distance to the building at 34 Joralemon Street, some ten blocks away. At ten minutes past twelve they returned to the restaurant, which was now dark and shuttered, with garbage bags stacked outside it. The street was quiet and empty. Quickly, Jules and Kevin tossed their bags from the car against the others and sped on. They did not wait to see a slight figure emerge from the shadows between two buildings and load the big bags, one by one, onto a Safeway Stores shopping cart. After all, except for a few hundred-dollar bills placed on the outside of the wrapped packets as decoys, the rest of the "cash" consisted of cut-up newspaper.

"We don't have much time," Kevin said as they pulled up in front of the apartment building on Joralemon Street and got out, leaving the engine running. Kevin pressed the doorbell for 3-C. "I'm counting on him thinking it's his brother returning with the cash," he said.

"Wouldn't he use his own key?"

"He's loaded down with three big bags—remember?" And, in response, the buzzer sounded, and Kevin pushed the door open.

He bounded up the two flights of stairs and ran on tiptoes down the narrow corridor toward the apartment marked 3-C, with Jules close behind him. Kevin whipped his service revolver from its shoulder holster, and stepping back a short distance, he aimed his shoulder at the door and, charging at the door, crashed it open. "Everybody freeze!" he shouted.

They were in a kitchen, and a television set was going. Steve Allen was hosting *The Tonight Show*. An open window let in the warm summer night's breeze, stirring cretonne curtains, and across the street a neon sign advertising Budweiser beer flashed on and off.

A tall dark-haired young man, who would have been

Miguel, the older Fernandez brother, immediately jumped to his feet. "Hands against the wall!" Kevin ordered, and the young man quickly obeyed. In a kitchen chair sat Cyril, with his upper body bound in what appeared to be clothesline, though his hands were free. He appeared to have been drinking a beer. "Hey—Pop! *What the hell*?" Cyril cried.

A revolver lay on the kitchen table, and Kevin quickly pocketed this. "Untie your son," he said, and rapidly began to frisk the other man, who leaned, hands upward, face forward, against the kitchen wall.

But when Jules started to undo the knots, which seemed rather loosely tied, the clothesline, which looked seriously frayed in several places, immediately broke apart into pieces and fell to the floor, and Cyril was instantly freed.

Then Kevin Shaughnessy yanked the telephone from the wall, and hurled it out the open window. "Now let's get out of here," he said, and herded Jules and Cyril out of the apartment, down the stairs, and out into the waiting station wagon. Putting the car into gear, Kevin and his two passengers headed for the Brooklyn Bridge. The plan was for Kevin to drive them to the greater security of the apartment at 1000 Park Avenue. Hannah and Bathy were driving from the country to meet them there.

"Did you pay them the money, Pop?" Cyril asked as they headed for the bridge.

"You weren't very well tied up," his father said drily. "The rope they tied you with broke the minute I touched it."

"If I'd tried to break loose, they'd have shot me, Pop! You saw he had a gun!"

"You told me the room you were in didn't have any windows."

"I told you what they *said* to tell you, Pop!" He turned to Kevin. "Who're you?"

"An old friend of the family," Kevin said.

"Did you pay them the money, Pop?"

"What difference does it make?" his father said. "You're free now."

"Do you know that's the biggest ransom demand in *history*, Pop? The biggest in history! I wasn't sure you'd pay it. But why wasn't there anything in the papers, Pop? Why wasn't it on TV?"

"I took care of that."

"Every day they'd buy all the papers, looking for something. Every day they'd watch the TV news. But there was—nothing. The biggest ransom in history—but it didn't even make the news. We thought it would make big headlines."

" 'We' thought?"

"They thought. Why didn't it make big headlines? You did pay them the money, didn't you, Pop?"

"No, I did not."

Cyril looked crushed. "But, Pop," he said. "I don't understand. Then how did you—?"

"We'll discuss all this when we get home, Cyril," his father said.

They rode the rest of the way in silence, while Kevin Shaughnessy chain-smoked cigarettes.

At the apartment, Hannah Liebling greeted her son with open arms. "Oh, my poor baby!" she sobbed. "What a terrible thing you've been through! Oh, look at you, my poor baby! Look at the circles under your eyes. How tired you must be, my poor baby. Just get some rest now, darling. It's so late. You must get some rest. . . ."

In the library of the apartment, Kevin Shaughnessy had fixed himself a stiff drink. When Jules and Hannah joined him there, it was nearly two in the morning. "Well, Mr. and Mrs. Liebling," he said, "this has been an unusual case. But I think my job for you is finished."

"Thank you so much, Mr. Shaughnessy," Hannah said. "We couldn't have done any of this without you. And everything worked out just the way you said it would. You were brilliant . . . brilliant."

"There's just one more thing," he said, and he reached into his pocket. "When I was searching Fernandez, I found these. Three ticket stubs. They're for *My Fair Lady,* Wednesday night's performance. The night before last. The tickets were purchased with your son's American Express card." He handed the stubs to Jules.

"Obviously they stole his credit card," Hannah said.

"If so, they were very nice and returned it to him. I

checked his billfold, and everything was in order, including three hundred dollars in cash."

Jules stared at the ticket stubs.

"Mr. and Mrs. Liebling, I am left with the strong impression that while your son was claiming to be tied in a chair at gunpoint, he and the Fernandez brothers were off enjoying a Broadway musical."

Jules tore up the stubs and tossed them in a wastebasket. "I see your point, Mr. Shaughnessy," he said at last. "I presume you'll have your bill prepared for me in the morning."

And that should have been the end of the episode. But it was not, not quite.

The next morning a policeman stood at the door of the apartment. "Mr. Liebling, we have a warrant for the arrest of your son, Cyril Liebling."

"On what charge?"

"Contributing to the delinquency of a minor."

"Who is bringing this charge?"

"Mr. Miguel Fernandez, who is the legal guardian of his younger brother, Jose Fernandez, a minor. The senior Mr. Fernandez charges that while your son was a guest in his house, he caught your son in the act of sexually molesting his younger brother."

And so Cyril was led away from 1000 Park Avenue in handcuffs.

This event generated enough headlines to have satisfied anyone, particularly in the New York tabloids, the *Post,* the *News,* and the *Daily Mirror:*

HEIR SEIZED ON SEX CHARGE!
—*Post*

BOOZE BARON'S SON CALLED PEDERAST!
—*News*

BILLIONAIRE MOLESTED H.S. HONOR STUDENT,
VICTIM CLAIMS!
—*Daily Mirror*

Meanwhile, Ingraham lawyers tried to arrange for Cyril's release on bond. The New York County Prosecutor's Office had set bail at $5,000,000.

Then, two days later, the telephone rang in the apartment. "This is Joey Fernandez," the boy's voice said. "My brother Mike says to tell you that we'll drop all charges if you'll pay us one-point-two-five million dollars."

"Let me handle this one," Hannah said, seizing the phone from her husband. "Mr. Fernandez," she said, "I don't know who you are, or what you are, or what you represent. But I know this. I know that molesting a minor may be a felony, but kidnapping is a high federal crime, carrying a sentence of up to life imprisonment. I have your ransom note, written in your or your brother's hand. All your telephone calls to our homes in Westchester and New York have been recorded, including this one, and I have the tapes. We also have a witness who will testify that he found my son in your apartment, tied to a chair, and guarded by your brother with a gun in full view. If you do not drop all charges against my son within fifteen minutes, I will turn all this material over to the Federal Bureau of Investigation. Good-bye." She dropped the receiver in its cradle.

Ten minutes later, the phone rang again. It was the New York City chief of detectives. "Mrs. Liebling, the Fernandez brothers have dropped all charges against Cyril," he said. "They have admitted that this was all a hoax."

"I see," she said.

"Would you like us to press charges, Mrs. Liebling? Hoax or not, it was still an extortion attempt."

"I think not," she said. "There has been too much about this case in the press already."

"I'm making arrangements for your son's immediate release."

"Thank you. May I ask what was the purpose of this hoax?"

"Publicity. It seems the younger Fernandez wants to be a rock 'n' roll star. Believe it or not, it seems that, as a result of this, young Fernandez has already got himself an agent. It's a strange world we live in, Mrs. Liebling."

"It certainly is," she said.

"You know," his father said to Cyril that night, "the trouble with you is that you've never been able to do anything right. If you'd been able to conceive of a really clever extortion plot, and been able to carry it out, I'd have been impressed. I'd have actually admired you for it. I'd have thought: This young man has brains! This young man has moxie! He's really going places. But your little plot was stupid from the beginning. You lied about where you were going that evening. You said you were going to see a show that wasn't even playing. You had the car headed the wrong way. And on, and on, and on—one stupid blunder after another! Your plot was so stupid and transparent that it wasn't even laughable. It was just pathetic. Because you'll never be able to do anything right, nothing will ever work for you. You have no future. You are completely hopeless. Now let me show you a young man on whom the future of this family rests."

He had ordered Noah's governess to wake him up and bring him downstairs to the music room. Noah stood there sleepily in his pajamas, rubbing his eyes, unaware of what any of this was about. He was eight years old.

"This is the young man on whom the future of this family hangs!" his father declared. "This is my hope! This is my promise! This is the future of my company, my family, and all my dreams! This is the real man in the family, Cyril—not you. Do you know what my first impulse was when you called last Sunday night? It was to let them *dispatch* you—you stupid, worthless piece of scum!"

"Oh, Jules," Hannah sobbed. "Jules . . . Jules . . ." As Noah's governess, equally mystified, led him back upstairs to bed.

To this day, Noah Liebling has never been able to forget that scene.

It wasn't a very happy funeral. That may sound like an odd thing to say, but there are such things as happy funerals, when family members and old friends stand up and offer happy reminiscences, and tell funny stories about the deceased; they joke a little, and no word is unkind. And everyone leaves feeling a little better, somehow believing that death isn't such a bad thing to have happen to you, after all. But Jules Liebling's funeral in the winter of 1974 wasn't one of those.

It wasn't happy because it was obvious, from the stony expression on her face, that Hannah Liebling was mad as hell about something. What she was mad about was that there were so few people there. But what did she expect? Thousands of mourners? There'd been no public announcement of this funeral. The death notices of the Billionaire Booze Baron had all concluded with the sentence, "Funeral plans are as yet incomplete," which was what Hannah had requested. There'd been no further publicity. Perhaps Hannah was angry because, although she insisted she wanted her husband's funeral to be small and private, she'd really been hoping that the funeral home would somehow miraculously fill to overflowing with mourners. But since so few people knew about it, that hadn't happened, and so Hannah was sore.

The services were held in one of the smaller rooms at Frank E. Campbell's on Madison Avenue. The only flowers were an arrangement of Hannah's giant white dahlias, from the gardens at Grandmont, at the head of the coffin. An organist played a few riffs and variations on "Happy Days Are Here Again" because, believe it or not, Jules had been a lifelong Democrat and an ardent supporter of the New Deal. After all, FDR supported repeal. A rabbi said the Kaddish, first in English, then in Hebrew, though Jules had never been a pious Jew. The visitors' book contained no more than two dozen signatures.

A few of Jules's more important distributors had been notified, and they were there with their wives. They had come to provide a show of loyalty to the new boss. Noah and Hannah had come in together, and were seated in the front row. Ruth Liebling Hower, who had not yet reverted to being a countess, flew in from California and joined them there. Noah saw Bathsheba Sachs come in and quietly take a seat in the back row, but he did not look back in her direction again, and when it was time for them all to get up and go, she had already left. There were a few other close associates of Jules's from the office. The only person visibly weeping was Jules's long-time secretary, Edith Ackerman, who had brought her niece, who was severely retarded, but who nevertheless behaved herself very well. Noah, seated between her and his mother, noticed that Ruth was drunk, and she tripped and nearly fell when leaving the pew, but no one else appeared to notice anything. There were a few other people whom Noah didn't recognize.

After the service, there was no trip to the cemetery because there was to be no burial. The hearse departed with the coffin to the crematorium, and there was no cortege. When it was over, Hannah went directly home without speaking to anyone.

Noah went outside to the front steps of Campbell's to have a cigarette. In those days everybody smoked. Later, it became so dangerous to light a cigarette within shouting distance of another human being that Noah had finally said the hell with it and quit. As he stood there, patting his jacket pockets in search of a book of matches, he became aware of a tall, older, slightly stooped man standing on the steps with him. The man seemed oddly dressed for a funeral, in a full-length lynx coat that nearly touched the tops of blue suede Gucci loafers. And something about the older man looked familiar, but Noah couldn't place him.

"Need a light?" the man said. The man's voice sounded familiar, too, but still Noah couldn't attach a name to that middle-aged face.

"Oh, thanks," Noah said, and the older man lighted Noah's cigarette with a gold Dunhill lighter. That little gesture—the way he flipped the lighter open—also rang a bell, and Noah thought: This is someone I've met before, but who?

"And so now, I suppose, the mantle will fall upon your shoulders," the man said.

"I beg your pardon?" Noah said.

"You don't recognize me, do you."

"I feel I should, but no, I'm afraid—"

"It's Cyril."

"Cyril!" The afternoon was chilly, and now a cloud passed across the sun, and a wind swept up Madison Avenue. "Cyril," he said again. A gesture was called for, and Noah extended his hand, and the two shook hands.

"It's been a long time."

"Yes, it has."

They stood there awkwardly a moment, suddenly shy in each other's presence, their eyes averted. Though it embarrassed Noah not to recognize his brother, it was understandable. He had not seen Cyril in over ten years. Cyril had let his hair grow longer, nearly shoulder length, and now it was silvery, the color of his long lynx coat. He had also taken to wearing a single gold earring in his left earlobe, long before this sort of thing would become a fashion commonplace, and an affectation that Cyril would later abandon. There had been another episode—not as serious as the kidnapping one—and Cyril had finally been banished from the Liebling household by their father. Noah knew about this episode, of course, but no one in the family ever spoke of it. Cyril had been treated as a non-person: out of sight, out of mind.

Cyril had been banished to the West Side because, in those days—the early 1960s—it was felt that people who lived on the West Side could live exactly as they wished. If one wished to live differently from the way normal people lived, one could do it on the West Side. The West Side was like a foreign country, and West Siders never ventured East. Cyril had been provided with a generous living allowance. His father would not have thrown his son out on the street. Still, he had been banished from Grandmont and from 1000 Park Avenue, and that banishment would not end until some time after his father's death, when Hannah came up with the idea of dividing the apartment horizontally and giving Cyril the upper floor.

Because of the difference in their ages—Noah was now twenty-five and Cyril was forty—Noah and his brother had never been close. Still, this meeting with Cyril on the steps of Frank E. Campbell's Funeral Chapel was difficult for Noah, and he stood there mutely, trying to think of something to say. But it was difficult because too much time had passed, there was too much ground to cover, and besides, all that ground had slipped away. He stood there, rocking on the balls of his feet, while the wind whipped up the canyon of the street, carrying with it the smell of coming snow. He felt he should deliver to his brother some sign of affection— a hug, a slap on the back, a soft punch to the shoulder—

but the moment for that seemed to have passed. He felt he should say, "Gee, you're looking great!" But in fact, Cyril did not look great. He merely looked strange, and foreign. And he could not simply say, "Well, good-bye!" So he found himself shaking Cyril's hand again and saying, "Cyril. Well!"

"Yes. Well. Well. Indeed."

"Well."

"And so now I assume the mantle of the Ingraham Corporation is about to fall upon your shoulders," Cyril said.

"Yes, I suppose it is."

"It was supposed to fall on mine, you know. The mantle. But that was years ago."

"Yes, I know. Would you have wanted it?"

"Oh, yes, I think so, though that's a forlorn hope now. This is supposed to be a disreputable business. And, as you know, I've become quite a disreputable person. I think I'd have been admirably suited to it. I think I'd have done quite well with it." There was a sudden twinkle in his eye, and the ice seemed finally to be beginning to break. "And what about you, baby brother? Are you ready to assume it? This golden, disreputable mantle?"

"Yes, I think so," Noah said.

"Only think so? Don't you *know* so? Don't you want it?"

"I guess so," Noah said. "But I used to think of doing something else."

"What sort of something else?"

"I used to think about a career in the social sciences," Noah said. "But now—"

"My dear fellow, I don't have any idea what the social sciences *are*," Cyril said. "And please don't tell me. I don't want to *know*. But don't worry. You'll do fine wearing the golden mantle. You'll get married to some nice girl. You'll have children. You'll live at a fine address. And I? Well, let me just say that I bear you no ill. You were always a good boy."

"Thanks, Cyril."

"It's too late for me to try to turn back the clock. But, you know, I'll always miss him."

"Who?"

He nodded toward the chapel door. "The old bastard," he said. "Our father."

"Look," Noah said quickly, "let's get together soon, Cyril. For lunch, or dinner. Or just for a drink. Let's get to know each other better, Cyril. We really need to."

"I'd like that," Cyril said with a little smile, and their eyes made contact again, and in that little smile Noah suddenly saw again the Cyril he remembered as a boy.

"In fact—want to go somewhere for a drink right now?"

"Not now," Cyril said, glancing at his gold Cartier tank watch. "I must be on my way."

"But let's get together soon, Cyril. Call me."

"I will," Cyril said.

They shook hands again and parted, Noah walking east and Cyril turning toward the west.

But, as it turned out, they did not get together soon again. It was not, in fact, until Carol, in an attempt to draw this fractured family together, began having her little family dinners on New Year's Eve at River House.

9

Choices

Why is it that our lives can become polarized about some small, seemingly insignificant event? A call from a stranger, a knock on the door, entering a familiar room unannounced and hearing unfamiliar sounds, a scene of a father vilifying his older son in front of the rest of the family. Or a decision as to whether or not to pack a pair of swimming trunks for a business trip.

At River House now, Noah Liebling, at a crossroads in his life, is faced with this decision.

Noah has always been a careful packer. He is as meticulous about packing as he once was reckless on the wheels of his bike. He considers the swimming trunks he holds in his hand. Ingraham's sales conference, which begins with a kickoff cocktail party tonight, is being held this year in Atlantic City. Atlantic City would not have been Noah's choice as the venue for this annual event. But by tradition, the salesmen are given a choice of a half dozen possible locations, ballots are passed out, and Atlantic City received the majority vote this year. Why? A lot of the salesman, it seems, like to gamble. This should come as a surprise to no one. The distilling industry is a business designed for gamblers. Everything about it is high-risk. This is why, they say, it has become a predominantly Jewish industry.

Back to the swimming trunks—green, with a white stripe down the side and a Polo logo. On the one hand, he thinks with his logical mind, in January it will obviously be too cold for the beach. On the other hand, the hotel where they will all be staying may have a heated indoor pool. A lot of hotels have those things nowadays—the pool, the spa, the health club. A swim would be pleasant at the end of a busy day. Or it may not have a pool. Noah can't remember from the brochure, and the brochure is at the office. Tentatively, he places the trunks on the top of the open suitcase. Swim trunks always go on the top of the suitcase, just as shoes always go on the bottom, followed by socks, underwear, shirts, ties, etc., etc., because that is the order in which everything is unpacked when you get to the hotel. The trunks take up very little room, and they weigh next to nothing, so what the hell?

But then, he thinks, indoor pools are unappetizing places, caustic with the smell of chlorine, and noisy with the screams of splashing children and their endless water games. And there will be no time for swimming or other relaxation, either. He will have too much to do, too many hands to shake, too many faces to try to remember. Thank God for name tags! He removes the trunks and replaces them in his dresser drawer.

But then, Atlantic City is not the sort of place one visits with small children—not anymore. Atlantic City's din is from the grownups at the tables and the slots. The pool, if there is a pool, will be peacefully empty, and he can swim a few laps before bedtime. He puts the trunks back on the top of his suitcase. And yet, if he packs the trunks and ends up never using them, he will feel the same impatience with himself that his mother feels when she has to let the space in front of her go "wasted" when entering a revolving door. Decisions, decisions! He removes the trunks again.

In another open suitcase is the carousel of color transparencies that Noah will be using when he makes his major presentation to the entire conference on Friday afternoon, just before the wrap-up cocktail party of the week of meetings, along with his notes for the script he is still working on. So far these color slides and the content of the accompanying script are still Top Secret. Only a handful of others in the company knows about them. On the program for the day, the only clue as to the importance of this event is in the words: "Friday, 12:30 P.M., Luncheon in the Grand Ballroom to be followed by a Major Presentation by Mr. Noah Liebling."

And, seeing his notes for the script, Noah suddenly realizes that he has almost forgotten to pack another Very Important Thing. This is the President's Message that he is to deliver at the kickoff party tonight. The

President's Message, triple-space-typed by Jonesy, Hannah Liebling's secretary, is still on the top of his dresser. He quickly retrieves this and places it on the top of his suitcase, where the swimming trunks were, glancing at the opening words: "In our more than two-hundred-year history . . ." This is a lie, of course, and Hannah damn well knows it. Their history is not even a hundred years old, but does it really matter? He looks at his watch. It is two-fifteen.

"I've got a car ordered for us both at two-thirty," Frank Stokes said to him that morning. "If you finish packing in time, drop down to my place for a drink before we head off to the wilds of Atlantic City."

"Fine," Noah said.

Frank Stokes is Ingraham's vice president for sales. Frank and Beryl Stokes have the apartment on the floor below the Lieblings', on the same elevator stem. In fact, it was Noah who helped them get into River House, over the objections of some board members who said, "Don't we have enough liquor people in the building? Are you trying to turn River House into the Ingraham Building?" Anyway, there will not be time for that drink now, and Noah is about to snap both cases closed when he realizes he is not alone in the room. He turns and sees her standing in the doorway.

"Going out of town?" she asks him.

"Oh, hi, Mellie," he says. "Was I talking to myself?" He did not realize that he and Melody were alone in the apartment together.

We should pause here to insert a word or two about the Bennington Plan. Those of you who know about the Bennington Plan can skip this section, but the Bennington Plan accounts for Melody's somewhat awkward position.

When Bennington College for Women was founded in the 1920s, it was something of an anomaly. To begin with, it was never really a college for women. There have always been men at Bennington—not many, but a few—and Bennington was established primarily for young people interested in careers in the arts: drama, dance, music, literature, film- and television-making, and so on.

Part of the Bennington Plan is what is called the Winter Work Period. Every year the school closes for the months of January and February, and during these months students are expected to find work off the campus in their chosen fields. Cynics have pointed out that one of the world's most costly colleges, situated on a hilltop in the mountains of southern Vermont, manages to save a great deal of money in heating bills by closing during the coldest winter months, but that is neither here nor there. In its woodsy setting, laid out to suggest a sprawling New England farm—with dormitories posing as farmhouses and studios disguised as barns—the campus atmosphere is intended to be conducive to artistic endeavor, and in many ways it is. Bennington students take their studies, and the winter work program, very seriously. Otherwise, rules are very few, and loosely enforced, if at all.

Of course, not all Bennington students go to work during the winter work period. Some simply travel, visiting European museums and architectural wonders, taking notes on what they have observed, and this "work" will count for academic credit when they return to the school with the crocuses and daffodils. Some actually find jobs. Anne Liebling, as an art history major and using her mother's museum connections, has found a winter job as a file clerk in the Catalogue Room of the Met. She started work there the first of the year. The pay isn't much, of course, but at least she is working in her field.

Melody, as a drama major, has been less fortunate, as anyone who has tried to work in the theater well knows. To her credit, she has been looking for something—answering casting calls, following the course of Broadway rehearsals, offering to do everything from painting flats for scenery to running out for coffee and doughnuts for the stagehands.

"What I'd like," Melody has said to Carol, "is to find something in the theater that would pay me enough so I could afford to share an efficiency, or a loft in SoHo."

"Nonsense," Carol said. "You can always stay here. We love having you, and there's plenty of room. Don't worry about finding some other place to stay."

Still, though Melody has stayed with the Lieblings for

shorter periods in the past, a two-month house guest is something else again. Melody realizes this, and so does Carol. Still, both the guest and the hosts are trying to make the best of the situation, at least for the time being.

Meanwhile, the fact that Anne has been able to find employment while Melody has not has created a not imperceptible rift between the two best friends. We have not progressed very far into January, and Anne Liebling has already learned, at the end of a working day, not to ask her friend, "Well, how did job hunting go today?" She knows what the discouraged reply will be.

And is Melody the slightest bit resentful of Anne for having found a job, however boring, so easily? If so, Melody has given no indication. (Anne does not know that Melody, writing home to her mother in Tokyo, said, "It's funny, but it's much easier to find a job when you don't need one—if you're rich already, that is.")

"Sales conference," he says now. "We do this every year in January. This year it's Atlantic City."

"How long will you be gone?"

"Just a week. Back Friday night."

She moves to the open suitcase and lifts the sheets of typewritten paper. "What's this?" she asks him.

"President's Message," he says. "I have to deliver it tonight at the kickoff party."

She reads, " 'In our more than two-hundred-year history . . .' Not a very exciting opening line, is it?"

"My mother's words," he says. "They're carved in stone, I'm afraid." He's glad to see there's no black eye, no swollen lip.

She makes a face. "I could do better than that," she says. "How about, 'As we plunge fearlessly into our third century—' "

"Okay, okay," he says. "I'll let you argue that one with Hannah Liebling."

She looks at him. "Is it hard working for your mother, Noah?" she asks him.

He decides to give her an honest answer. "Yes, it is, as a matter of fact. But I consider it one of the challenges of my job."

Now she lifts the handwritten notes from the case containing the carousel of color slides. "And this?"

"A script I'm working on."

"A script?"

"To go with a slide show. I'm pitching a new Ingraham brand at the end of the week. Script still needs a lot of work."

"Want me to help you?"

He glances at his watch. "No time, I'm afraid. I've got to be out of here in ten minutes."

"Take me with you," she says.

He tries to affect an easy laugh. "Sorry," he says, "this trip is strictly business." But this is not strictly true. To a lot of the salesmen this week in Atlantic City will be an outing, a holiday, a company-paid vacation.

"I'm serious," she says. "Take me with you, Noah. I'll help you write your script. I've taken playwriting courses. I can type sixty words a minute. I won't be in your way. I'll make this part of my winter work program. What do you think of that?"

"No, no . . ."

"Please, Noah. It will give me something to do. I'll write a report on it when I get back to school. 'The Business Sales Conference as Theater.' My adviser would like that! Because it is a form of theater, isn't it? Meetings to get the sales staff excited about what's coming up in the year ahead? Whipping them up—"

"I think of it more as employee relations," he says. "Making the people who work for you feel they're appreciated."

"But that's show business, too! So much of business is really show business. A girl in our class is working for some trial lawyers. She's going to analyze trials as theater pieces. How many people will be at this conference?"

"All together, about a thousand."

"Would one extra girl, sitting in the back of the room, taking notes, be even noticed?"

"They'd think you were a spy from the competition, Melody."

"That's just like the theater! In the theater everybody's always spying on what everybody else is doing.

And in between the meetings I'll help you with your script. Oh, please, let me come, Noah."

"No, that sort of thing is strictly against the rules," he says, and yet he knows that this is not strictly true. A lot of the salesmen, and in this business they are mostly men, use sales conference to leave their wives and families behind, and connect with girlfriends. And in the bars of Atlantic City, the girls will be lined up, waiting. . . . "Besides," he says, "how would we explain this sort of arrangement to Carol—and Anne?"

She looks at him. "Very simple," she says. "We wouldn't tell them. It would be our secret, like our secret from the other night. I'll make up something. I'll say I've found a week's work in another city. You see, I've thought this through very carefully, Noah. You see how serious I am."

He feels his cheeks redden. "No, it wouldn't work, Melody," he says. "I'm sorry." And yet why is he thinking that it could work? If only . . . If I were only still that boy on the Harley.

She turns away from him. "It doesn't have to be sex," she says. "I didn't say it had to be sex. I know that's what you're thinking. You've probably been thinking that all along. It's true I like you—very much—but it doesn't have to be that. Mostly, I want something to *do*—something exciting. I can't just sit around this big apartment, day after day, doing nothing!"

"Something will come along for you, Melody," he says. "I'm sure of that." Her mention of sex startles him. Had he been thinking of that, too?

"Fat chance. I hang around the theaters, trying to sneak through stage doors, trying to interview performers, the production crew. . . . I'm treated like a trespasser, a nuisance . . . trying to watch rehearsals from backstage . . . being kicked out . . . it's so humiliating . . . and meanwhile that asshole keeps telephoning all the time!"

He is a also little surprised to hear her use the word *asshole*. "What asshole?" he says.

"That asshole I brought here on New Year's Eve. Bill Luckman!"

"What's he been doing?"

"Calling me up. Three, four, five times a day. Sometimes he disguises his voice so I'll think it's a job offer. But then he calls me a tease. Tells me to stop holding out on him, to stop stringing him along. Sometimes, when I'm alone here and hear the phone ring, I feel like I want to scream!" She stares at him defiantly now.

"What do you say to him when he says things like that?"

"Sometimes he says worse things! I just hang up on him."

"Good girl. That's the only thing to do. He'll get the message after a while."

"Will he? Sometimes, when I'm alone in this apartment, I think, what if he should come to the door?"

"There's no way he could get up here, Mellie. You're in the most secure building in New York. But if anything should happen, just dial eight on the house phone for the security office."

"That's another reason why I wanted to go with you."

"Look, if this—this asshole gives you any more trouble, I'll be staying at Resorts International in Atlantic City. Just give me a call, okay? If I'm in a meeting, say it's an emergency, and they'll bring me out. Okay?" He starts to reach out to touch her arm, but then he checks himself.

Just then the telephone rings, and both of them look quickly at the phone on the bedside table. "I'll get it," Noah says.

"Hey, Noah." It is Frank Stokes's voice. "You about ready? The car's waiting downstairs."

"I'll be right down," Noah says, and hangs up the phone. "I've got to go," he says, and snaps his two suitcases closed.

Grabbing the suitcases, he turns toward the bedroom door, then turns back to look at her. She is standing there, her arms crossed across her bosom, hugging her shoulders. Her chin is up, but there are tears in her eyes. "Don't worry about me," she says. "I can take care of myself. I always have. And I didn't say there had to be sex. Remember that."

"I'm sorry, Mellie," he says, and turns and heads out the door.

Alone in the apartment, she walks down the long corridor to the living room, and parts the curtains to look down on the entrance courtyard below. She watches as Noah and Frank Stokes emerge from the building and walk to a waiting limousine. She watches as the driver loads their luggage into the open trunk. She watches as the driver opens the rear door of the car, as the two men climb inside, and as the door closes, concealing the passengers behind tinted glass. She watches as the car pulls out into the street and drives away.

Then, directly across the street, she sees the figure of a young man. He is wearing tight black spandex running shorts, and he is standing on one leg, braced with one hand against the trunk of a tree. His other hand grasps his ankle, and he is flexing his knee up and down, as though to relieve a cramp in a peroneus muscle.

Recognizing him, Melody bangs on the windowpane for his attention, but he is too far below her on the street to hear her.

She flings open the window and leans out. "Hey, Luckman!" she calls down to him. "*Hey, Luckman!*"

He puts his other foot down and, shielding his eyes with a bandaged left hand, looks upward, into the sun.

"Hey, Luckman!" she calls again. "How's your hand, asshole?"

Then she raises her fist and gives him the finger. She slams the window shut, and then, laughing, runs down the hall to the yellow guest bedroom, knowing exactly what she is going to do.

As the limousine enters the Lincoln Tunnel, heading for the New Jersey Turnpike, Frank Stokes turns to Noah and says, "You're kind of quiet this afternoon. Something on your mind?"

"Thinking about Friday's presentation," he says.

"B-Day, huh?" Frank is one of the few people in the organization who know about the new label, and B-Day is what they have christened the day when it will be unveiled.

"That's right."

"Don't worry. Something tells me we're going to have a hit on our hands."

But of course Noah is not thinking about Friday's presentation, or B-Day, or about anything remotely con-

nected with that, though perhaps he should be. He is
thinking about Melody.

He has been aware for some time that Melody has
developed some sort of schoolgirl crush on him, and he
is ambivalent about what to do about it. There is something about the way she looks at him, and then, of
course, there was this afternoon. It is not an unflattering
situation. What man Noah's age would not be flattered
to have a beautiful eighteen-year-old—no, not even eighteen, because Melody's eighteenth birthday is still five
months away—form a schoolgirl crush on him? The very
phrase "schoolgirl crush" probably dates him, he thinks.
Do college-age girls have crushes anymore? They certainly
don't call them that. They have affairs—light, casual, un-
committed affairs, with no consequences expected or
even considered. Has Anne had affairs? He hopes not,
but he cannot be sure, and if she has, it would be hard
for him to condemn her for this, in today's atmosphere,
with condoms being freely dispensed in boarding school
infirmaries. Today a teenager's parents are expected to
roll with the punches, or else go back to the dinosaur
age.

Anne must have been eight or nine when Carol decided to explain the facts of life to her, and Carol had
told him about it later. "I was trying to tell her as honestly as possible about what happens when a man and a
woman make love," she said. "And I was trying to describe it in a way that was—well, you know, both scientific and poetic. And she suddenly turned to me, and
said, 'Mother, are you talking about fucking?'"

"And *zen* what did you say?" he asked her with a
grin.

"I couldn't believe my ears. I *think* I turned red as a
beet, and I *know* I fought a terrible impulse to slap her
across the face. But then I laughed and said, 'Yes, I'm
talking about fucking.'"

And so here he was now, in this situation, or Situation,
capital S, as in Seduction. He had seen it beginning to
happen—oh, perhaps eight months ago, when both girls
were home from Ethel Walker on spring break. There
had been a bowl of peanuts on the coffee table, peanuts
in their shells in a silver bowl. Odd, the way details stand
out. He had noticed Melody shelling peanuts, cracking

the papery husks between her fingertips, dropping the husks in an ashtray, then carefully removing the brown skin from each nut, taking care not to let the two halves of each nut fall apart. Then, when she had a handful of perfectly shelled, perfectly skinned nuts in her hand, she extended her cupped palm and offered them to him. That gesture, the outstretched hand, the offering of the nuts, and the faint smile on her lips when she offered the nuts to him, told him everything. There were no words needed, and his heart opened like a door. "Thank you" was all he had been able to say.

In the days of his bike, there had been plenty of easy sex. Girls loved his bike. They loved the speed, and they loved the noise and the wind in their faces as they clung to his waist from the buddy seat behind. These were the town girls, of course, the townies upon whom his brothers at Delta Chi Epsilon looked with undisguised disdain. The "nice" girls from Wellesley, Smith, or Holyoke were either too prim or too timid to accept bike dates. Or perhaps they knew what bike dates usually led up to. Bennington girls, of course, were always a little different. They enjoyed their reputation of being a little wild, a little Bohemian. They even called their campus The Left Bank—the Left Bank of Pownal Creek. But even Bennington girls would not accept bike dates. Why had they sent Anne to Bennington? Because that was where she wanted to go, naturally, and one reason she wanted to go there was because that was where Melody, her best friend, wanted to go.

There was one town girl he remembers in particular— Loretta, or Lorena, or Louella, or something like that. If he ever knew her last name, he has forgotten it now, but she worked as a telephone operator for New England Bell, and he had made her acquaintance while placing a long-distance call. Sight unseen, she had agreed to a date on his bike.

As they sped through the soft spring night, she gripped his waist from behind, clutching the waistband of his jeans, her thumbs hooked under his belt. Then one hand moved below his belt, and then with the other hand she was unbuckling it. And then came the point when there was nothing else to do but to slow down the bike, pull off into a dark country lane, cut the engine,

turn off the headlights, and dismount. And that was that.
No words were spoken. Loretta, Lorena, Louella, Louisa, whoever you were, where are you now?

And why is he suddenly also thinking now of his
brother? Cyril, who caused so much trouble for the family over the years, is rewarded by being free to do whatever he chooses, by being free to fuck whomever he
wants. Cyril has been handed a totally carefree life.
While Noah, who always tried to be the dutiful son—
who tried to do his father's wishes and to fulfill his father's dynastic dream, even long after he lost the respect
he once had for his father, because that was what he saw
as his duty—now finds himself lashed—no, chained—to
that duty for the rest of his life.

The limousine enters the toll plaza.

"Do you have brothers or sisters, Frank?" he asks
him now.

"No, I was an only child. Why do you ask?"

"Just wondered."

"You're sure in a damned funny mood," Frank says.

The limousine speeds south on the turnpike. NO HITCH-
HIKERS, NO MOTORCYCLES, a sign warns. That is the story
of Noah's life.

And, he thinks, if I hadn't spent all that time dith-
ering, waffling, trying to decide whether or not to pack
the goddamned swimming trunks, I'd have been out of
the room and out of the house long before she even
came to the door, and what took place this afternoon
would never have taken place at all.

And now he can't even remember whether he ended
up packing the goddamned swimming trunks or not.

Shit, he thinks.

It is nearly four o'clock when Carol Liebling gets
home from a meeting across town, a Friends of the Museum meeting at which very little seemed to get accomplished, and the apartment seems strangely quiet. Noah,
of course, has left for Atlantic City, and Anne is still at
work. "Melody?" she calls, dropping her gloves and bag
on the bench in the front hall. "Melody?"

Mary appears. "She left here in a real hurry, Miz Liebling," Mary says. "About an hour ago. Packed a bag

and everything. She left this for you." She hands Carol an envelope.

Carol opens the envelope and reads:

> *Dearest Carol . . . and Anne . . .*
>
> *Guess what! I got a call from the stage manager of a play that's trying out at the Shubert in New Haven, and he offered me a job! It's not much of a job—assistant to the prop manager—and, frankly, it doesn't sound like much of a play, but they're hoping to bring it to Broadway, and at least it'll mean working in the theater. So that's where I'm off to. Will call in a couple of days to let you know how things are going.*
>
> *Yours, in haste,*
>
> > *With love,*
> > *Melody*

Carol slips out of her mink jacket and hands it to Mary.

"Miz Stokes called three, four times while you was out," Mary says. "She says it's real important."

"Okay," Carol says. "Thanks, Mary." She steps into the library and dials Beryl's number.

"Well, hello . . . stranger," Beryl says, and Carol detects a note of resentment in Beryl's voice.

"Hi, Beryl," Carol says brightly. "How're you?"

"Funny you should ask," Beryl says in the same voice. "Funny you should ask, because I'm feeling—well, I'm pretty well ticked off at you, if you want to know the honest truth."

"Really, Beryl? Why?"

"Frank said I shouldn't call you about this," Beryl says. "Frank said, 'They can have anyone they want for dinner. They don't always have to invite us.' But now Frank's gone to Atlantic City, and I just can't be in denial about this any longer. I've just got to let you know what my true feelings are about this, Carol. And my true feelings are that I'm terribly, terribly hurt. And I thought you were my best friend."

"Now, wait a minute," Carol says. "I don't have any idea what you're talking about."

"No, I don't suppose you do," Beryl says in a distant voice. "No, that would be just like you. Not even knowing how deeply you can hurt another person. Not even caring. Well, maybe someday you will care about your friends. Maybe someday you'll try getting in touch with your friends' feelings and not just your own."

"Please, Beryl," she says, beginning to be annoyed. "Please tell me what it is you think I've done."

"You had a dinner party for William Luckman. I know, because I read it in Roxy. . . . And you didn't invite Frank and me."

She sighs. "Now, Beryl," she says. "It wasn't a party *for* Bill Luckman."

"Roxy's column said it was. Roxy Rhinelander said *honoring* William Luckman."

"She got it wrong. She gets a lot of things wrong. It was our annual family New Year's Eve dinner—Noah's mother, his brother and sister. Anne's friend Melody, who's—or was—staying with us, brought Bill Luckman along. It was a last-minute thing. That's all it was."

"And Frank and I were home alone, right on the floor below you, and you never even asked us up. Me, of all people."

"Why you of all people, Beryl?"

"William Luckman was my star pupil."

"What do you mean—your star pupil?"

"I taught him English in the eighth and ninth grades. He was my star pupil. I've told you that."

"Honestly, Beryl, I don't think you told me that."

"Well, I did. I know I did. But obviously you've forgotten. That would be typical of you, I guess, to just forget how much William Luckman meant to me. Oh, well. Frank told me not to make this call, but I just couldn't stay in denial about this all my life."

"Beryl, I swear to you I didn't know you had any connection with that young man. If I'd known, I would've—"

"Oh, well. It probably doesn't matter. Now that he's so successful, and so famous, and all over the TV talk shows, he probably doesn't even remember little old me, who was his eighth and ninth grade English teacher. But I like to think that some of that success, just a little bit of it, may have been due to little old me."

"Oh, I'm sure he'd remember you, Beryl."

"Well, I just thought I should let you know how you

hurt me, Carol," she says. "How you hurt your best friend."

Sometimes Carol wonders who appointed Beryl Stokes as her best friend. Personally, Carol finds Beryl a terrible whiner. But Noah has great respect for Frank Stokes, the two men work closely at the company, and so Carol always tries to be nice to Frank's wife. "Look," she says quickly, "what are you doing Wednesday night?"

"Wednesday? Day after tomorrow? Frank's out of town, of course. But—nothing. Why?"

"Come up and have a drink. I'll invite Bill Luckman. I know he's finished touring for his book."

"*Really?*" Beryl squeals. "Really? Oh, that would be super-super-super, Carol!"

"Good. And I'll ask Georgette Van Degan, too. *She* wants to meet Bill Luckman, and he wants to meet *her,* and you want to see him again, so it works out perfectly. Come around six."

"Three women and only one man? Will he like that?"

"And Anne will be here, too, of course. But I have the impression that Mr. Luckman doesn't mind being surrounded by admiring women. On the contrary."

Beryl giggles. "While the boys are away, the girls will play, huh? And he's grown up to be so handsome!"

"He's a good-looking fellow, yes."

"And he was always so bright! Are you going to tell him I'm coming? Because he just might not remember—"

"Suppose I just tell him I'm having a mystery guest— a woman from his past?"

Beryl squeals again. "Oh, that would just be super-super-super. Can I bring anything? Want me to stuff some mushroom caps?"

"No, no. Just bring yourself."

"And I'm going to get to meet Georgette Van Degan, *too*! Oh, this is so exciting. What shall I wear? My pink Adolfo, I think, with the lace. Oh, this is the sweetest thing you're doing, Carol. I forgive you now. I forgive you for *everything.*"

"Thanks," Carol says a little drily. "Do the pink Adolfo."

"When I first knew Bill Luckman, I was just a frumpy

little old schoolteacher. That was before I landed Frank. He'll hardly recognize me now, will he? Oh, I'm so excited I can't *stand* it! I can hardly wait. Thank goodness Frank is out of town. Oh, and by the way, that's exciting about the coming-out party you're giving with Georgette Van Degan for the two girls. Of course, don't feel you have to invite Frank and little old me to *that*."

"Roxy jumped the gun on that, too," Carol says. "Nothing's been decided. I haven't even discussed it with Noah, or with Anne. And Noah's mother will have something to say on that, too, if I know her. It was Georgette's idea, and it's still very pie-in-the-sky for now."

"Well, don't feel you have to invite Frank and me to that," she says. "We'll understand."

"Oh, you'll be invited, Beryl. *If* we have it."

"Goodness, now that you're moving up on the social ladder like this—with people like Georgette Van Degan, Patsy Collingworth, and Pookie Satterthwaite and all *that* crowd—you probably won't have time for little old best friends like me. Don't worry. I'll understand."

"Now, Beryl," Carol says carefully, "I'll always have time for you. . . ."

Now Anne is home from her job, her cheeks pink from the January cold outside, wearing jeans, fleece-lined boots, a down-filled parka, a stocking cap, and carrying a backpack. Girls don't dress for the office the way they used to, Carol thinks, as Anne unslings the backpack from her shoulders. Right at the moment Anne certainly doesn't look like a debutante.

"What would you think of having a coming-out party in the summer?" her mother asks her.

"A coming-out party?"

"Yes. Being a debutante."

"Do girls still do that, Mom?"

"They're coming back. Or so I'm told."

"Gee, Mom, I don't know. But it might be—well, really neat. I guess."

"It would be with Linda Van Degan."

"Linda Van Degan? Who's she?"

"Don't you remember her from Brearley?"

Anne frowns, wrinkling her nose. "Was she—kind of fat, with big boobs?"

"She's slimmed down a lot lately," Carol says, hoping this is true.

"Gee, Mom—like I say, it could be—well, really neat, I suppose."

"We'll have to see what your father thinks about it. This was Mrs. Van Degan's idea. It strikes me as a little silly."

"I'd rather it could be with Melody. Where's Melody?"

Her mother hands her Melody's note.

"I must say Carol Liebling didn't turn handstands at my idea for us giving a party together," Georgette Van Degan is saying to her husband that evening as she sits at her dressing table, preparing her face for the night ahead—another benefit.

"Party? What sort of party?"

"Oh, just a little party," she says vaguely. "Co-hosting a party with me, you'd think she'd be thrilled."

"Yeah. Nothing too expensive, I hope."

"Just a few friends. But she didn't exactly turn handstands when I offered to go halvesies on it with her, which you'd think she'd be thrilled. The bitch. And I picked up the lunch check, too."

"Maybe you oughta suggest something else."

"*What*? You mean and cancel this? I can't cancel this now! Roxy's already had it in her column. If I tried to back out now, I'd be publicly humiliated. It was you got me into this, remember."

"Maybe you oughta suggest something that's more down her alley than a party. Some people, parties aren't everything. Think of something else, Georgette."

"Like what? What could be more glamorous than co-hosting a party with me?"

"Yeah, you're the bee's knees, Georgette. But didn't you say she's big with the Met? Like on the board or something?"

"The board of *trustees*? Her? Never! Though she'd probably like to be, the little climber. She's just some sort of volunteer."

He gestures around him. "Like tell her we're ready to

give this Chinese stuff to the Met. They want it, you know, and I could use the tax break right now."

"Never! That collection stays with me!"

He looks at her narrowly. "Georgette," he says, "do I need to remind you that the collection belongs to me?"

"But it was to be for my—"

"You want to get into it with me again, Georgette? Is that what you want? If you want to get into it with me again, Georgette, I'm ready."

She bites her lip. "Well, maybe we could offer them *part* of the collection," she says.

"Okay. Call her and tell her that."

"What if I told her we're just *thinking* of making a gift?"

"That's okay, too. String 'em along. Get 'em excited. The more excited they get, the higher the appraisal they'll put on whatever I decide to give 'em. Remember, it's whatever *I* decide. So call Carol Liebling and tell her I'll be discussing the terms of the gift with my lawyers in the morning."

"Of the *possible* gift."

"Okay. Call her."

"Now?"

"Now."

"Carol, darling, it's Georgette."

"Yes, Georgette . . ."

"I just wanted to let you know, darling, that Truck and I are thinking of perhaps giving some of our porcelain collection to the Met. Truck wants to talk to his lawyers about it."

"Georgette, how wonderful!"

"Just *thinking* of *perhaps* giving *some* of it, you understand."

"Of course."

"But meanwhile, Truck is absolutely *wild* about the idea of us giving a coming-out party for Linda, and whatsername, your daughter."

"Anne."

"Right. I've never seen him so mad for an idea as he is about this one, darling. When I mentioned it, he went absolutely *ape*! So we've got to move ahead with our plans as fast as we can, darling. If there's the slightest glitch in our plans, Truck will be *furious*. . . ."

"Cory?" Carol says. "It's Carol. Guess what? The Van Degans are now considering giving at least part of their Oriental collection to the museum. Mr. Van Degan and his lawyers are going to meet to work out terms for a gift proposal. I should have those terms to present at our next meeting. What do you think of that?"

"Well, I'll be damned. I'll be God-damned."

"Yes—me, of all people. Did I get further than Mrs. Astor?"

Carol never knew Noah's father, who died not long after Carol and Noah met, but she will never forget the afternoon Noah took her to meet his mother. The year was 1975, and they had been secretly married, that morning, at City Hall. That was how much in love they'd been. That was how young they were. Holding hands, they ran out into Chambers Street in the rain, shouting, "We did it! We did it! Hallelujah, and praise the Lord!"

But now, less than an hour later, they were both very nervous.

Carol had been overwhelmed by the vast apartment at 1000 Park Avenue, two full floors at the top of the building—the black and white marble entrance foyer, the double staircase curving upward with its banisters upholstered in red damask (this was before the apartment was divided horizontally in half to accommodate Cyril), the pleated rosewood paneling, the portrait, by John Singer Sargent, of Noah's grandfather, Dr. Marcus Sachs, gazing austerely from the library wall above the fireplace. On the entrance floor there was a ballroom, seldom used nowadays, Noah explained, that was two stories high with a stained glass ceiling that depicted Orion in pursuit of the Pleiades, with its chandelier in a dust bag and little gilt chairs lining the walls. The entrance to the ballroom was flanked by a ladies' cloakroom and a gentlemen's cloakroom and a smoking room. In the room called the Music Room, two Steinway concert grand pianos stood back to back in a bay window with a view of Central Park, while a golden harp stood in one corner. The lighted picture frames in this room, Noah told her, contained original Mozart manuscript scores in the composer's own hand. In illuminated glass cases were a quartet of stringed instruments—two violins, a viola, and a cello—signed by Stradivarius, and the cello was the last one the master had made, in 1725, known as La Belle Blonde. There was even a room called the Telephone Room, with nothing in it but a chair, a table, a pink pad of crested paper for making notes, and a silver bowl filled with freshly sharpened pencils. And, of course, a telephone.

And then there was the major domo in his swallowtail coat trimmed with gold braid—the initial L embroidered at the cuffs—who addressed Carol's new husband as "Master Noah," and backed out of the room, saying, "I will notify Madame that you are here." He was not to be called a butler, Noah whispered, because he supervised two footmen, along with the housekeeping and kitchen staff. And there were the little uniformed maids, in white lace caps and lace-trimmed aprons, who appeared across long vistas of open doorways, scurrying about unnecessarily wielding feather dusters against nonexistent cobwebs, and needlessly plumping up fat cushions in chairs that looked as though no one ever sat in them. To Carol, the whole apartment looked like a Donald Oenslager film set. And then, suddenly, Noah's mother appeared in one of the doorways—an immense woman, or so she seemed to Carol, dressed in black, with three strands of large Oriental pearls across her bosom.

"Mom, I want you to meet my wife," Noah said.

"Well!" she said, standing there, looking Carol up and down.

Carol waited for Hannah Liebling to say more, but when she didn't, Carol stepped toward her and held out her hand. "I'm so happy to meet you, Mrs. Liebling," Carol said.

Noah's mother's hand brushed against hers. "So," she said, turning to Noah, "I am being presented with a fait accompli. What happened—did you get her pregnant?"

Noah's face flushed. "Mom," he said, "when you get to know Carol, when you see how bright and sweet she is, you're going to love her every bit as much as I do."

"That," she said, "would be patently impossible, since

you are a man and I am a woman. Unless you take me for a lesbian. I dislike surprises."

"Mom, we're just so very much in love. We—"

She dismissed him with a wave of her hand. She turned to Carol and, speaking to her for the first time, said, "My son is a very stubborn young man. He was stubborn as a child, and he continues to have a very stubborn nature. He is also impetuous, headstrong, impulsive. If you stay married to him, you will learn all these things about him. I hope it works out, for your sake, and if it does, perhaps you can do something to curb this stubborn, willful nature of his. Do you think you can make him grow up, young woman? I wish you luck. Dine with me tonight at eight o'clock. Just the two of us. You and I have matters to discuss." Then she was gone.

"She likes you," he whispered to her as they left the apartment.

"She *does*? I got the impression she hated me."

"She wants you for dinner," he said. "That's an important sign."

Later, Carol would joke that she'd spent her wedding night with her new husband's mother. Hannah Liebling's dining room walls were covered with pale blue watered silk, and the long table was lighted with as many as forty candles. At one end of the room hung a portrait of Hannah Liebling as a younger woman, much slenderer and looking almost pretty with wide blue eyes, and at the other end hung Jules's portrait, older, with a down-drooping mustache, with one hand inserted partway into the pocket of a double-breasted vest. The two footmen served them, removing service plates between each course and placing each new course in front of both women simultaneously while, standing just to the left of the kitchen door, the majordomo, whose name was Albert, announced the courses in French. "*Ris de veau à la mode de Calais,*" he said as the footmen, each carrying a single plate, made their entrance from the pantry. With each course, Carol noted, the china pattern changed. "*Pêche flambée au rhum.*"

Hannah Liebling did most of the talking, seemingly

heedless of the servants who padded about the room on slippered feet.

"Did you marry my son for his money?" she asked Carol.

"No," Carol said.

"Good, because he hasn't any," Hannah said. "Someday he will, of course. Someday he will control this whole company, but that day will not necessarily come soon. At the moment he is just one of our salaried employees. He owns no stock in us at all. The two of you will be living on a fixed income."

"I understand all that," Carol said. "Noah has explained his situation to me."

"If you didn't marry him for his money, what did you marry him for?"

"Because we happen to be very much in love!"

"Love," Hannah said. "I was in love once, or thought I was. I found love to be not a very useful experience, even though the young man was—very attractive, and even rather famous at the time. Fortunately for me, there were wiser heads around me who were able to explain to me the unwisdom of my ways. Why did you choose to get married in this fashion? By running off and getting married without telling anyone?"

"Frankly, it was because my mother disapproves of Noah—on religious grounds."

"I can understand that."

"My mother is a very devout Catholic. In some ways, almost too devout."

"And your father?"

"My father—disappeared when I was a little girl. I don't really remember him at all. I was an only child, brought up by my mother with the help of a parish priest. My mother has always worked."

"I work, too, you know."

"I know that, Mrs. Liebling."

"And I suppose you thought—I suppose you both thought—that *I* might disapprove of *you*."

"That thought crossed our minds," Carol said.

"Of course it did. It was right to cross your minds. So that's why you ran off and got married like this."

"We decided to get married *first*. And to face any

disapproval on our parents' part later, when it was too late for anybody to try to stop us."

"Of course. You decided to present me with a fait accompli. I can understand that. Years ago, I considered that possibility, too, though, as I say, wiser heads prevailed. Let me say that I don't disapprove of *you* personally. But I do disapprove of mixed marriages. I have seen too many of them that did not work out. My own was to have been a mixed marriage. I know now that it would have not worked out. Of course, I was much younger than you at the time."

"Noah and I discussed all this. We decided from the beginning that things like this would never matter to us."

"Because you were so much . . . *in love.* Tell me, do you think that with great wealth comes great social position?"

"Frankly, I never thought that much about it," Carol said.

"Then let me tell you that it does *not.* We are very rich. We have been called the richest Jewish family in America, and perhaps we even are. And yet, socially, the Lieblings are riffraff. That is a fact of life you will have to face now that you are married to my son. My husband made a fortune, but he made it in *booze.* Don't give me that skeptical look—I'm telling you the *truth!* The polite term is 'the distilled spirits industry.' My husband disliked polite terms. He called an undertaker an undertaker, not a funeral director. He called a garbage man a garbage man, not a sanitation engineer. His money was made in booze. This is not a glamorous business, or even a respectable one. It is not like banking, insurance, or the law. My husband was called, first, a bootlegger, and then he was called an ex-bootlegger, even though he never was either of those things. It's been said that my husband had people killed. Well, plenty of people were killed in this business, but my husband never killed anyone. It's been said, too, that my husband had connections with the Mob. Well, while my husband was manufacturing booze in Canada, Meyer Lansky and Al Capone were the people you had to deal with if you were going to supply the American demand for booze on the other side of Lake Erie, and I personally found both Mr. Lansky and Mr. Capone to be perfect gentlemen. Mr. Lansky, in particular, is a gentleman of the old school. He still sends me cards at Christmas and on my birthday. But all those things are held against the Lieblings here in New York. As far as New York society is concerned, the Lieblings don't rank much higher than the garbage man. I hope you realize all this, and don't think that because you're married to Noah Liebling you're going to be asked to Mrs. Astor's house to tea. Because you won't be."

"Noah has explained all this to me," Carol said.

"Money can buy a lot of things, but it can't buy you social acceptance—not in a city like New York, or anywhere else, for that matter. In New York, you'll discover that you've married into a disreputable family, and that's that. And then there's the fact that we're Jewish. We're secular Jews, as it happens, but in the outside world nobody knows what that means. We're still Jews. You'll hear it said that there's no anti-Semitism in this city. Baloney. It's there, all right. It's just not polite to talk about it. It's not just all the clubs that won't take in Jews. There are law firms that don't want Jewish partners. There are banks that don't want Jewish officers. There are insurance companies that won't promote Jews to anything higher than a clerk. There are schools that only want a certain number of Jewish children. There are apartment houses that don't want Jewish tenants. This building used to be one of them. When my husband and I bought this apartment, there was at least one Christian family here that was particularly unhappy about it. They made a point of moving out the same day we moved in. Their moving vans pulled up to the curb just when ours did. It was not very considerate of them, of course, because it caused a traffic jam for blocks in all directions, but considerateness was not on their minds. They had a point to make, and the point was that they would not tolerate a Jewish family living, even for a minute, under the same leaky roof. Later, I overheard someone saying that this building had 'gone Jewish.'

"You'll hear that there's no anti-Semitism here because this city needs its Jews too much. They say that without the Jews there'd be no culture in New York because the Jews support the theater, the opera, the symphony, the ballet, and the museums and so forth.

This may be true, but it's not necessarily a good sign for the Jews, and I'll tell you why. You see, the Christian community regards us as a kind of service class. They'll go to a Jewish doctor, use a Jewish stockbroker, shop from a Jewish merchant, hire a Jewish lawyer—particularly if it's for something that could be ugly and expensive, like a messy divorce. My husband used to say that the Christians used the Jews to clean up their messes for them, and he had a point.

"You'll hear it said that Hitler was a fluke, and there could never be another Holocaust. I don't believe it. Have people forgotten about the czarist pogroms, the Spanish Inquisition, the destruction of the First Temple? Throughout history the Jews have tended to become too important, to become *too* needed by the Christian community, too necessary. They've seemed to get too big for their britches. When that happens, there's resentment, there's anger, there's jealousy. A reaction sets in, and Jews are accused of poisoning the wells. Then all you need is someone who can organize that reaction, and you have another Adolf Hitler. Sometimes when I hear people say how much New York needs its big Jewish population, I think—thank God they don't need us even more! Don't laugh! I am not being funny!

"And what do they need the Lieblings for? They need us for *booze*. Christians have a lot of guilt about booze, though Lord knows they knock back enough of the stuff. They don't like to admit that they need us to get them plastered at the country club. And so they blame us for drunk drivers, for the Bowery bums, and for all the winos on skid row. My husband had a theory. He used to say that Christians secretly believed that booze ought to be free, that it was part of their birthright, and that if drink and drugs were free there'd be no more crime, and poor people would stay home where they belonged and not go out causing trouble for the rest of us. Lord knows, at least once a week I get a call from some Christian charity asking if we'll give them free booze for some party. When I say no, they accuse us of being greedy. Then they ask if we'll give them liquor *at cost*. When I say no to that, they think it's because we don't want them to find out how little the real cost is, and how enormous our markup is. In this business, there's no way to win.

"A few years ago, our company ran an ad at Christmastime, urging drinkers not to overindulge in booze during the holiday season. That ad created a big stir, and we've repeated it every year since. The ad wasn't even my husband's idea, but he got all the credit for it, and for a while it even began to seem as though the Lieblings might be beginning to be accepted as respectable members of the New York business community. For a while. It didn't last. The stigma of the booze business was too great. There's just no way to overcome it, and my husband and I gave up trying.

"Meanwhile, there's a group of fine old German-Jewish families in this city. At least they *think* they're a group of fine old families. But the Lieblings will never be accepted by that crowd. My family, the Sachses, were a part of that. I'm sure Noah has told you about my father. He was Dr. Marcus Sachs, a famous educator—part of the service class, of course. He had his own school, the Sachs Collegiate Institute, and he turned out boys who were ready for Harvard by age fourteen. Discipline was his secret. That's Father's portrait over the mantel in the library. He was widely admired and respected, and he and Mama had dinner at the White House. But I lost all that status when I married Jules Liebling. Even my Sachs relatives look down their noses at me now, because I was forced to marry so far below my station in life."

"*Forced* to marry, Mrs. Liebling?"

"Chose to marry, then. Or, let's say that at the time I had no other choices. I'm sure you've heard it said that the Jews have always had to live in two communities. But with the Lieblings it is a little different. Outside, we have the Christian community. Then we have the Jewish community. Then we have just ourselves, this small family, isolated from both communities, not a part of either one. Just us. That's why I care so much about who marries into this family. As Lieblings, people come to us for money but nothing else. When Noah takes over the company, as he will someday, people will come to you for money, but for absolutely nothing else. You will probably find it a rather lonely feeling, being Mrs. Noah

Liebling. But if you are going to stay married to Noah
Liebling, you will have to get used to it. I am telling you
all this because these are what I call the Liebling facts
of life. I understand you are from a small town in New
Hampshire, where you certainly cannot have experienced anything like what you will experience as Mrs.
Noah Liebling. In a way I feel sorry for you. I hope
you're up to it. There are other small problems that go
with it. Noah's brother is a pansy. His sister tried to
work in films, and then began marrying unsuitable men.
No, being Mrs. Noah Liebling will be no bed of roses
for you. It won't be easy. That's why I feel it's necessary
to warn you of all the problems you will have to face. I
hope you understand."

"Yes," Carol said, her eyes flashing. "But as Mrs.
Noah Liebling, I intend to change all that!"

Hannah Liebling smiled at her for the first time.
"Dream on," she said. "But I must say I admire your
spirit, my dear. Shall we have our coffee in the library?
We can talk to Papa's portrait there."

As they were leaving the dining room, Carol paused
in front of one of the two Boule sideboards. "This is a
lovely Ming Yellow jar," she said, touching it. "Chinese
Export porcelain is something of a hobby of mine."

"My husband's ashes," Hannah said.

But, remembering all this, Carol sometimes asks herself: Have I really kept my promise? Have I really succeeded in changing anything? Nearly twenty years later,
Georgette Van Degan wants me to give a party with
her. Is that the kind of change I was talking about? Will
that change anything at all?

When she got home that night, Noah took her in his
arms. "I suppose she gave you her standard Liebling
Facts of Life lecture," he said.

"Yes, but she smiled at me, and she called me 'my
dear.' "

"It doesn't matter. We have each other," he said.

A few months later, they were celebrating Noah's
thirty-first birthday, and were opening his birthday cards,
which were mostly from other people in the company.
There were a great many cards. The company, Carol had

discovered, operated rather like a large college fraternity, with Hannah Liebling as its fond but firm house
mother, a role similar to the one she had played when
Noah's father was alive. There was a strong feeling of
family in the company. People kept track of one another's
birthdays and other special days, and a certain number
of people in the company were actually Noah's relatives.
Jules Liebling had had an older brother, Nathan, who
had been severely crippled by polio as a child. Still, a
position had been found for Nathan, and now Nathan's
three sons all worked for Ingraham in various capacities.
And there were other cousins, some of them so distant
their relationship was barely traceable—young men who
had arrived from the old country, looking for work in
"Uncle" Jules's business—and jobs had been created for
most of these people and, in time, for their sons and in-
laws. Jules Liebling had been a benevolent despot. He
rarely fired anybody, unless it was for some gross mal-
feasance, such as stealing. When it was felt that an employee had reached his fullest potential, he was not let
go. He was just kept on in whatever capacity he had
ended up in and was promoted no further. Thus the old
gentleman who supervised Ingraham's mail room was
some sort of Liebling "cousin." For social life most Ingraham employees entertained one another. Thus, Frank
and Beryl Stokes would become Noah and Carol's closest company friends. It was a comfortable, if somewhat
closed and insular society, as Carol's mother-in-law had
warned her. On formal occasions, such as at meetings
with one of the company's worldwide network of advertising agencies, the company was usually referred to as
"the house" or, even more formally, as "the House of
Ingraham." But among those who worked for Ingraham,
the company was nearly always called—almost lovingly—"the mill."

They sat in the living room of their first apartment, at
25 West Seventy-second Street, and Carol slit open the
envelopes, read off the salutations on the cards, and then
handed them to Noah, who identified the senders.

"George and Barbara," Carol said.

"That would be George Billings. Shipping Department. Toronto."

Then Carol opened a card and paused, reading the

inscription a second time. "This one's signed, 'All my love, Bathy.' Who is Bathy? And what a strange name!"

He quickly snatched the card from her and tore it up, tossing the pieces in a wastebasket. "Never mind," he said.

"Darling—who is Bathy?"

"None of your business," he snapped.

"Who is she? Some old girlfriend of yours, I suppose?"

"I said it's none of your business!"

"I thought we weren't going to have any secrets from each other," she said. *If you stay married to him,* her mother-in-law had said. "I want to know who Bathy is, Noah."

He still looked very angry. "Her name is Bathsheba Sachs," he said at last. "She's my mother's younger sister."

"You mean she's—your aunt?"

"She has no business writing to me."

"Why on earth not? Your own aunt?"

"It's a long story," he said. Then he told her about the trouble with Bathsheba Sachs.

10

Rumney Depot

Having grown up in the little town of Rumney Depot, New Hampshire, the only rich people Carol Liebling— who was Carol Dugan then—had known were her friends the C. R. McClarens, who lived in a big white colonial house on Cobble Hill Road. C. R. McClaren ran a prosperous dairy business, and owned a prize herd of Golden Guernsey cattle. The milk cartons on the Dugans' breakfast table always bore the label of McClaren Farms and featured a picture of one of Mr. McClaren's most famous cows which, reportedly, commanded a breeding fee of thirty thousand dollars. At the Laconia First National Bank, where Carol's mother worked, and where C. R. McClaren did his banking, Mr. McClaren always tipped his favorite teller fifty dollars at Christmastime. Unfortunately, Carol's mother was not that teller.

C. R. McClaren was even nationally famous, or almost, since he was president of the American Guernsey Cattle Association and, it was said, United States presidents occasionally asked his advice on agricultural matters.

Carol remembers one Halloween, when she was in the fifth or sixth grade, when the rumor circulated to the effect that the McClarens were handing out twenty-dollar bills to trick-or-treaters. She and three friends, in their costumes, trekked up to Cobble Hill, under the big porte cochere, and nervously rang the front doorbell. A maid appeared and asked them to go around to the back of the house, to the kitchen door. There the children were handed hot chocolate in paper cups. Through the kitchen they were able to glimpse Mr. and Mrs. McClaren at their dinner table.

Because of their prominence, the McClarens' doings

were heavily chronicled in the weekly Laconia *News-Leader* and to Carol, growing up, these reports made heady reading. When Mr. and Mrs. McClaren left for Europe for the summer, the newspaper printed the story, and the McClarens' stately progress from one European capital to another was also dutifully reported. When they returned, there was always a headline, WELCOME HOME, CYNTHIA AND C. R. McCLAREN! When the McClarens and other business leaders in the state were entertained at the governor's mansion in Concord, this news made the front page of the *News-Leader*.

The McClarens had three daughters, Beth, Monique, and Stacy—all several years older than Carol. Of the three, Monique McClaren was Carol's favorite. It was something about her name, alliterative, with all those smart, clicking consonants. Her second favorite was Stacy, who, though she didn't have Monique's glamour, sounded peppy and lots of fun. Beth McClaren sounded a little dull. When, one by one, the McClaren girls went off to boarding school and college, or became engaged, or were married, these events were also reported, with weddings again making the front page, and Carol read about them avidly.

Carol Dugan had never actually met any of the McClaren girls, though she had occasionally seen them speeding by in their snappy little sports cars, and her mother had once waited on C. R. McClaren at the bank, when his regular teller was on vacation. Still, having read so much about them while she was growing up, in a little town where not much happened that wasn't McClaren-oriented, she began to feel she knew them well, that they were her special friends, the beautiful Monique, especially. This feeling was so strong that, years later in New York, meeting a man from Laconia at a party, Carol found herself asking him, "And how is Monique McClaren? Is she still married to Tim Tyler? Are they still living in Boston?" It was not that she was envious of the McClarens, exactly. It was just that their lives seemed so much more interesting than hers.

Her own Roman Catholic upbringing was strict and, as she looks back at it, also downright strange. Her mother, Anna Dugan, was proud of her position at the bank because tellers were required to be well mannered, well spoken, well dressed, and ladylike. Gum chewing was grounds for dismissal. Also, no teller was permitted to leave the bank at night until every penny in her cash drawer, from that day's transactions, had been accounted for. "My drawer has always balanced out," her mother used to boast.

Carol's father, she was told, had simply disappeared. Her mother would tell her nothing more, and Carol has only a vague, blurry memory of a man in the house, who she supposes must have been this disappeared father, though she is not even sure whether this is a true memory or a dream. Once, on television, she had watched an old movie called *The Invisible Man* and this is still the way she imagines her father's disappearance—simply being made invisible through some mad scientist's alchemy, yet still able to make his presence felt through an ability to make objects move mysteriously about the house. A pair of pinking shears left on her dresser would reappear on the kitchen table. The Invisible Man had moved them.

At the all-girls' convent school that Carol attended, the nuns told their charges that if they touched themselves *there* all their fingers would fall off. Today, though she knows better, that thought still manages to frighten her. Carol once asked her mother where babies came from, and her mother replied, "From the river." Sometimes, after school, Carol would wander along the banks of the Pemigewasset River, hoping to find a baby ready to be scooped out. Finding a baby would certainly relieve the boredom of her days. She also asked her mother if boys were any different from girls, and her mother told her, "All children are alike and identical in the eyes of God."

Anna Dugan spoke of God often, and also of something she called the Eternal Verities. In the paintings she did in her spare time—watercolors of towns and landscapes recalled from memory, wistful renditions of Christ's suffering on the cross, or of the Blessed Virgin holding the Infant Jesus—she was always trying to express the Verities: Truth, glittering like a sword in the shadows; Virtue so unchallenged as to defy the lightest touch of humanity; Honor, like a flower bursting forth from the rubble of the world. Anna Dugan rarely spoke of her own past, though when she did she implied that her family origins were genteel. Looking back, it sometimes seems to Carol that her mother existed not only in another century but on another planet—a planet surrounded by angels. "I am sure the angels heard that," she said every night as she and her daughter knelt by the sofa in the living room of the little house that Anna Dugan owned outright—"free and clear," without a mortgage (mortgages, even though she worked for a bank, Anna considered an invention of the devil)—to say their prayers.

Aside from her daughter, her no-gum-chewing job, and her paid-for house, the only other comfort in Carol's mother's life was Father Timmons, who called nearly every evening after work. Father Timmons and Anna Dugan sat on the sofa, evening after evening, sipping perhaps a little cream sherry that Father Timmons often brought with him. Cream sherry was not *drink,* Father Timmons explained. It was no different from sacramental wine, which was Our Lord's blood, and therefore holy. And so the two of them sipped their holy wine, and sometimes got a little giggly while they discussed the affairs of the human mind and soul. Discussing the Immaculate Conception, Anna Dugan sometimes became a little shrill. "I'm having a vision!" she would suddenly cry out.

Anna Dugan always had an urge to do a particular religious watercolor—her interpretation of the Ecstasy of St. Teresa, she had had a vision of it—and the two of them often discussed that project. "I'm still not quite ready for it, Father," she would say, "though I feel I'm getting closer to it." And closer to it she always got, though never, finally, close enough. It was her conscience that bothered her most. After all, who was she to think she could express on paper what poets and mystics and princes of the Church had been trying to get straight in their minds for centuries? And Father Timmons, wisely, did not encourage her to begin, but always advised her to wait until she was sure, absolutely sure, that she had her vision as clear as crystal in her mind's eye before attempting anything. And so, instead, they would perhaps discuss one of Anna's completed watercolors, and Father Timmons would comment on the use of color and chiaroscuro, or the effect of sunlight she had managed to achieve across the waves or on a barn roof. "I just dabbed a little yellow right *there*—and there it was, just like *that!*" she would explain. "A complete accident."

But nothing was ever an accident, no, Father Timmons would insist, for everything was part of a plan, and the plan Anna's picture had was merely an expression, on a smaller scale, of a larger one. And sometimes their talk would turn to Carol, and how well she was doing at St. Catherine's School, and how much the sisters liked her, and how bright she was (which was true), "though a bit too independent-minded for her own good" (also true, Carol supposes). And perhaps Carol would be brought into the room then, and the three of them might sit, quietly talking, and then perhaps Father Timmons would put some of his old 78 r.p.m. records on the old windup Victrola that Anna had bought at a yard sale, and they would listen to old songs. If cream sherry had been served, Carol's mother and Father Timmons might dance the fox-trot. During these times Carol would be able to see, and believe clearly, that there was indeed, somewhere, a shady nook by a babbling brook.

And then, at the end of these musical interludes, unless Father Timmons had brought along his multiband shortwave radio (in which case they would listen to music playing from such far-off places as Chicago, Minneapolis, or Atlanta, depending on the reception, which depended on the weather), they would kneel and thank the angels and all the saints and the Blessed Virgin for all the bounties that life bestowed, and for all the heartaches, too, that teach us lessons. And Anna Dugan would rise to her feet first with tears glistening in her eyes and, with a wide gesture of her arms that took in both her loved ones, say to Carol, "You know that God the Father and Father Timmons are the only real fathers you'll ever have."

And this was true enough. And as an adult Carol has occasionally wondered whether Father Timmons might actually have been more of a father to her than that, more than a foolish and doting old family friend in a reversed collar who also happened to be the parish priest. It is a notion, she has decided, that does not bear much thinking about. In the little town of Rumney

Depot, she heard it said that her mother was "peculiar." She set her jaw and said nothing when she overheard comments like that.

One incident stands out particularly in Carol's mind from those growing-up years. It was a summer Saturday, when she was nine or ten, and her mother had planned a picnic at Stinson Lake. Father Timmons was to go with them, of course, but at the last minute he had been called to say Mass at a funeral, and so her mother announced that the picnic would be called off, even though the picnic lunch was already packed. In her bitter disappointment Carol had staged a regular temper tantrum. Though Stinson Lake was only a dozen miles north of town, it seemed to Carol as though they never went anywhere, while, from the *News-Leader* it was clear that the McClarens were always on the go. She screamed and sobbed and stamped her feet and pounded her fists on the kitchen table, and in the end her mother relented, and they drove off for the lake in her mother's blue Plymouth coupe, though her mother was not in the best of moods.

Anna Dugan brought her paints and brushes and easel, and set up her easel on the strip of beach, and began painting the mountains on the far side of the lake. Carol sprawled on a beach towel in the sand. Out on the water, a speedboat pulled a girl on water skis, her blond hair streaming behind her, and Carol imagined that this might be Monique McClaren. On the beach, some teenage boys in swimsuits were engaged in a game of volleyball.

At noon her mother opened the picnic basket, and began laying out their lunch on a blanket on the beach— tuna salad sandwiches, deviled eggs, pickles, olives, potato chips, and a chocolate cake. Carol had been watching the volleyball game. "Mom," she asked almost idly, "what's that funny bunched-up business boys have between their legs?" Her mother seized her by the armpits and jerked her to her feet. "Impure thoughts!" she cried. "You've been having impure thoughts!" Then she struck her across the face with a slap so hard it sent Carol flying backward into the picnic lunch, into the sandwiches, into the deviled eggs and chocolate cake. "You are an evil, evil little girl!" her mother screamed at her. "You will rot in hell for your impure thoughts, and your eyes and tongue will be eaten by the devil!" The volleyball players paused in their game to watch this scene, and from nearby on the beach, other heads turned, though of course no one said or did anything.

Anna Dugan gathered up their ruined lunch, which was now little more than garbage, into the folds of the blanket. "You'll get no lunch," she said. "And you'll get no dinner, either. And you'll never, ever come to this beach again!" Then she marched Carol, sobbing, back to the car.

Her mother kept those promises.

A year or so later, an older schoolmate explained and described to Carol what the funny bunched-up business was, and its function—in perhaps more vivid detail, and in somewhat more colorful language—than was actually required. And somehow, after those basic anatomical facts, and their implications, had been revealed to her, Carol became even more unforgiving of her mother than before.

She met Noah Liebling on a blind date when she was twenty and a senior at the University of New Hampshire. "A nice young businessman up here on business from New York," her friend had described him. At first she hadn't been particularly impressed with him, though she was pleased with his dark good looks and amused by his habit, when ordering drinks, of always asking for an Ingraham brand, and in rather too loud a voice. "I work for Ingraham," he said with a shrug. "Company policy," and he let it go at that. He did not mention that his family owned the company. This was in the winter of 1972. The name Liebling meant nothing to her.

They began exchanging letters, nothing particularly personal, certainly nothing passionate. Presently, though, he was flying up to Portsmouth on weekends to see her. He would rent a car, and they would drive to one of the nearby ski mountains. There he would rent skis and poles and boots for them both, and give her skiing lessons. "A New Hampshire girl ought to know how to ski," he said.

This was true. The McClaren girls, she remembered from the days when she had followed their activities so

closely in the *News-Leader*—though they were all off
and married now, with children of their own—had often
been pictured on one ski slope or another. She mentioned the socially prominent McClarens. He had never
heard of them. She decided they had nothing in
common.

He liked to ski fast. As a beginner she was more cau-
tious. Still, he slowed down to keep pace with her own
slowness, and that was nice of him.

Meanwhile, she was working for her M.A. in psychology at the university. She decided that he must have a
very good job indeed to be able to afford all this flying
back between Portsmouth and New York, all these rent-
als of cars and ski equipment and lift tickets. But he
wasn't show-offy about his money, and that was nice of
him, too.

She noticed he didn't talk much about his job, beyond
saying he was "in sales." And he talked even less about
his family. He hardly ever mentioned his father, and she
gathered he was somewhat intimidated by his mother.
"My family is peculiar," he said once.

"My family is even *more* peculiar," she said. "I'm
sure, when it comes to peculiar, my family has your family beat."

"We have a lot in common, then," he said with a
smile. This struck her as the opposite of the truth.

Long before meeting him, Carol had decided it was
time she lost her virginity, though she hadn't decided
how, or when, or where, or with whom she was going
to do it. All her friends, if they were to be believed, had
already lost theirs. All the lurid admonitions of the sisters at St. Catherine's School—fingers falling off if you
touched yourself, tongues falling out if you kissed a boy
too deeply—she now knew were nonsense. She had even
encountered two of the sisters—Sister Margaret Mary
and Sister Barnabas—in an embrace that was far from
sisterly. But she decided that if she was going to lose
hers, it was not going to be with Noah Liebling. Their
relationship was more of an outdoor, not an indoor,
thing. After kissing him good night outside her dormitory door, she would step quickly inside, and that would
be that.

It was not until she saw his father's obituary in the

New York Times in 1974 that she realized who Noah
Liebling was, that his sister was the one she'd read
about, several years before, when she eloped with a Bra-
zilian copper heir nearly three times her age and, later,
when she became involved in a messy marriage to an
Italian count. At first Carol couldn't believe that this
could be the same family. And yet there it was, in black
and white, in the nation's newspaper of record. Jules
Liebling *was* Ingraham's. He'd started it from scratch, a
Horatio Alger success story. Rags to riches. There was
Noah's name, listed as one of Jules Liebling's two sons.
She decided not to telephone him. Let him call her.

But then, a couple of days later, she did call him. She's
not sure why she did, but she did. He'd just come, it
seemed, from his father's funeral, and he told her about
encountering his older brother, whom he hadn't seen in
years, outside the funeral home, and not recognizing
him. She'd also read that this banished brother had been
left, in trust, a sizable inheritance, while Noah, who had
worked for the company, had been left nothing at all.
All this sounded to Carol too strange and sad, and she
decided immediately that she'd never see him again, that
she wanted nothing to do with this strange, sad family.

But then he said, "Look, I could use a little company
right now. Why don't you hop on a plane? Fly down
here. We'll have dinner."

"All right," she said.

"I'll meet your plane," he said.

And so he took her out to dinner. To this day, she
can't really remember where they went, but during dinner he said to her, "Carol, I don't quite know how to
say this, but I like you very much."

"And I you," she said.

"And I you," he repeated with a faint smile on his
lips. "And I you," and their eyes met, and locked, and
suddenly the air between them was charged, electric, and
Carol felt a sudden ringing in her ears, a tightness in her
throat, a yawning feeling in the pit of her stomach, and
she knew that what was going to happen was going to
happen, and that he knew it, too, and that there was
nothing either of them could do to stop it from happening, try as they might. For the rest of the meal, toying
with their food, they said little and ate almost nothing,

preparing for the inevitable. The time had come, the time was right, the time was then. The taxi ride from the restaurant to his handsome bachelor apartment on Seventy-second Street seemed to take an eternity.

Later, when it was over—and it was sweeter, gentler, and far less violent and painful than anything her friends had ever described to her—he lifted himself on one elbow in the bed and studied her face. "I love the way you look," he said. "Your looks don't match."

"Don't match?"

"Your hair—what color do you call it?"

"Sort of a chestnut color, I guess."

"And your eyes?"

"Hazel. I've always hated the color of my eyes."

"More like amber. But you see? Chestnut and amber—that's an unusual combination. They don't match." He touched the tip of her nose. "And look—a freckle. And here's another."

"I've had those since I was a kid and got sunburned at the lake." She giggled. "You've kissed all my makeup off."

"Dark-haired girls don't usually freckle. That's what I love about your looks. Nothing really matches, but it all comes together beautifully."

"Oh, I'm not beautiful—not beautiful like my friend Monique McClaren."

"That's another thing I like about your looks. You don't know you're beautiful, do you?"

"No!"

"You know who you look a little like? A little like Audrey Hepburn before she started playing princesses."

"Thank goodness it's dark in here!"

"Audrey Hepburn, when she still had a little baby fat." He touched her again. "Here. And here. Don't ever change your looks, Carol."

"I'm afraid it's too late to try."

"Most of the girls I've known have been city girls. You're not like one of them. My mother would probably like me to marry some blond debutante type. Or one of our own skinny, lacquered Jewish princesses, with no hips and no rear ends. But you—you look—well, just natural. Just like yourself. Just like Carol Dugan ought to look."

"Thank you, Noah . . ."

"I've known some bike girls, too. Thank God you're not like one of them, either. Not tough."

"Not tough enough, maybe."

"Maybe, maybe not. I think a man could hurt you, Carol. But I promise I'll never hurt you. But look—I've made you cry." He touched her eyelids with the tip of his tongue. "I love the taste of your tears," he said.

She sobbed and flung her arms around him again. "Oh, I really am your girl now, aren't I, Noah?" she said. "I really am your girl. Oh, Noah, I love you so!"

He looked deep into her eyes in the half-darkened room, and said, "And I you."

Later, she wondered if it was callous of them to have made love so soon—and so often—after his father's death. And yet, in some way, his father's death seemed to have released him, and in releasing him, it had managed to release her as well. She decided she'd been in love with him all along.

She decided she was going to make him marry her. As it turned out, that wasn't necessary.

"Do you find solace in the Catholic Church?" he asked her as they walked west on Fifty-ninth Street the next afternoon after seeing *The Godfather,* with Marlon Brando.

"Solace? Funny word. But no."

"Did you ever?"

"No, I don't think so. That's why I'm a lapsed Catholic. I haven't been to mass in nearly ten years."

"I'm not a very good Jew, either. But you still *are* a Catholic, aren't you? I mean technically. Officially. Baptised, and all that."

"Well, I guess so," she said with a shrug. "But it doesn't mean anything to me anymore. My mother, of course, is another story. One reason I'm studying psychology is to try to understand my mother."

"That's the only thing," he said.

"What only thing?"

"The only thing to stop us from getting married."

"It wouldn't stop me!" Carol said.

THE WRONG KIND OF MONEY

They had reached the park. "Sit down a minute," he said, gesturing to a bench.

They sat, and he reached into his jacket pocket and produced a small blue box from Tiffany. "Open it," he said.

She opened it, and inside was a square-cut diamond solitaire, two and a half carats in weight.

"I'm putting my money where my mouth is," he said. "I'm asking you to marry me."

"Oh, Noah!" she gasped. He slipped it on her finger. "How did you know my ring size?"

"Last night, when you were asleep, I looped a piece of string around your finger."

She burst into tears. "Oh, Noah," she said, "it's just the most beautiful ring! It's just the most beautiful ring I've ever seen!"

"Better not wear it in front of your mother until you've explained a few things to her," he said.

But she decided to ignore that piece of advice. The next day she flew back to Portsmouth and drove directly to Rumney Depot, with his ring on her finger.

Her mother noticed it immediately. "Where did you get *that?*" she demanded.

"It's my engagement ring," she said. "I'm engaged to be married."

Her mother looked at her narrowly. "To *whom?*"

"His name is Noah Liebling."

"Liebling? What kind of a name is that—Liebling?"

"It's a Jewish name, Mama."

Of course, Father Timmons was immediately summoned. "You cannot marry a Jew in my parish church," he told her. "I cannot say a nuptial mass for you. I flatly refuse to solemnize this union."

"I haven't asked you to, Father," she said. "I don't *want* you."

"But Father Timmons is our family priest," her mother wailed. "If my daughter marries, Father Timmons must perform the mass!"

"Don't worry. We'll find someone. Someone with some sense."

"I have great influence with the bishop. This union will not be recognized in the eyes of God. In the eyes of God you will be living in mortal sin. In the eyes of

God you will have renounced your faith. As an apostate you will be excommunicated. You will never be able to go to Confession. You will not be permitted to receive Holy Communion. You will be denied the Blessed Sacraments. When you die, your soul will be doomed to wander in eternal purgatory, Sheol, Gehenna, Tophet, the abode of the damned. Are you prepared to face all this, my child, in order to marry some—Jew?" As he spoke, he fingered his beads. "Have you had impure thoughts about this Jew?" he asked her. "Have you—*sinned* with the Jew? If you wish, I will hear your confession now."

"I have nothing to confess," she said. "Your threats mean nothing."

"Abaddon, Naraka, jahannan, avichi," he intoned, reciting the circles of damnation.

"All my life I've slaved for you," her mother sobbed. "Slaved, night and day, slaved like a dog to raise you in a Christian home, to teach you the eternal verities, to guide you in the paths of righteousness in His name's sake . . . slaved, and this—*this* is the thanks I get!"

"Amen," said Father Timmons.

"A dirty Jew!"

"Don't use that expression, Mother!"

"Never to be reunited with my only child at the gates of Heaven!"

"Let us pray," Father Timmons said. "Let us pray for the immortal soul of this lost child. Heavenly Father . . ."

"A Jew—who killed our Christ!"

"That's not true! Nowhere in the Bible does it say that the Jews killed Christ. Christ was killed by the Roman soldiers."

"My child, you are speaking of Canon Law. Canon *Law!*"

"In their secret rituals they slaughter little children and drink their blood!"

"That's another stupid lie. Nothing you've said is true!"

"In the *Protocols of the Learned Elders of Zion* it says—"

"That's a proven fake. Noah and I have discussed all this. Judaism is a religion just like ours, except the Jews don't accept the divinity of Christ, who was a Jew himself. The Jews simply believe that the true Messiah is still to come."

"You see? What did I just tell you? The Jew has poisoned her soul!"

"Noah also says that when someone has more than ten million dollars, he's no longer considered Jewish. He's merely rich."

Her mother looked up from her sodden handkerchief. "He has ten million dollars?" she said.

"Not him perhaps, but his family does. Maybe even more. Someday Noah is going to be very rich."

There was a short silence.

"Is that a real diamond?" her mother asked.

"Of course it is. From Tiffany."

"He could always convert, Anna," Father Timmons suggested helpfully. "I could give him his instructions. We'd be bringing another soul into our Mother Church."

"He isn't going to convert," Carol said. "He's proud of what he is."

"And if Carol were to agree to raise any children in the Roman faith, then perhaps the bishop might—"

"I won't agree to that, either," Carol said.

"Of course they're all rich," her mother said. "All the Jews are rich. They have an international conspiracy to control—"

Carol rose to her feet. "I'm not going to listen to any more of this garbage," she said. "I'm going to marry Noah Liebling."

"She has forsaken God for Mammon," Father Timmons said.

"Ten million dollars," her mother said. "How did they get all this money? What kind of business is his family in, anyway?"

"They own distilleries," Carol said.

"Liquor! The devil's brew! I might have known it. Typical, typical. The Jews are always in the liquor business. They do it to try to befuddle the minds of honest Christians, so they can take over the world—"

"Has he tried to urge liquor on you, child?" Father Timmons asked her. "Has he tried to instill in you a taste for spirits?"

"Slaved . . . all my life . . . like a dog . . . slaved . . . for a Christ killer . . ."

Carol reached for her car keys. "I'm going now," she said. "Good night."

"My child, you are flying in the face of Holy Writ!"

"To hell with Holy Writ," she said.

"Carol!" her mother cried. "You know the Blessed Virgin weeps when she hears you talk like that!"

"Screw the Blessed Virgin," Carol said, and turned on her heel and walked out of the room, and out of the house. Behind her she heard Father Timmons chanting in Latin some arcane ritual of exorcism, and her mother sobbing, "It's no use, no use. . . . The Jewish devil has got her soul. . . ."

She half expected a bolt of lightning and a clap of thunder to halt her as she ran down the drive to her car, but there was none. She drove back to New York that night. It was nearly midnight when she got to Noah's apartment. There were blood tests to be taken, and there was a license to obtain. They were married on a Friday morning in City Hall, and then went uptown to meet Noah's mother in the scene you already know about.

Somehow the Laconia *News-Leader* got word of the marriage. RUMNEY DEPOT DEB WEDS LIQUOR HEIR, the front-page headline read.

Remembering this, Carol often smiles, wondering what the McClaren girls, if they still got the paper, made of that one: "Rumney Depot Deb."

11

The Mill

Now, in his hotel suite in Atlantic City, Noah Liebling has unpacked his suitcase—discovering in the process that he must have left the swimming trunks behind, after passing, as he came through the lobby, the hotel's indoor pool looking sparkling, inviting, and mercifully free of small children—and now he has set up the carousel of color slides and is going over, once again, his notes for Friday afternoon's presentation. Why, as he does this, does he experience a sudden sinking feeling, a feeling of dread and apprehension? It is just that so much time and money have already gone into this, and so much is at stake? What if the product fails to take off, as they say in the business? What if it fails to fly?

It all began—and has been proceeding with some secrecy ever since—nearly two years ago, when Noah was in London. A distributor told him of a private distiller in the tiny Scottish village of Ballachulish who was producing a single-malt whiskey of remarkable lightness and color and "nose," and Noah had made the trip north to Ballachulish to investigate.

He had found the owner of the distillery, Mr. Angus Kelso, to be a jolly, rosy-cheeked, redheaded Scot who insisted that the best use of his whiskey was to pour it over pancakes for breakfast. It was equally delicious, he added, over mashed potatoes and haggis at dinnertime, and over ice cream for dessert. Indeed, his whiskey was the pale amber color of the finest maple syrup, and its flavor was equally light and buoyant, with just a touch of sweetness and none of the heavy, peaty taste of many single malts. "The ladies love it," Mr. Kelso said with a wink. "It doesn't have the mannish airs of a lot of the scotches around here." Though American tastes preferred an 86-proof scotch, Mr. Kelso bottled some of his stock at a heady 105 proof. "*That* makes the ladies sit up and take notice!" he said.

His whiskey, he explained, was aged a full fifteen years in charcoal-charred oak barrels, but the secret of his whiskey was neither in the aging nor in the malt. "The secret is me water," he said. His hillside farm was situated above deep limestone caverns filled with springwater, but the limestone was only part of it. He pointed at the tall stands of Scotch pine that lined his hillsides and descended into the valley below. Rainwater entering the limestone caves was filtered through a thick layer of pine needles that covered the valley floor. That unusual combination, the limestone caves and the filtering blanket of needles above them, gave his water its extraordinary quality. "Sweetest water you'll ever taste on God's green earth," he said, and offered Noah a glass. Noah had to agree.

Mr. Kelso's caverns contained, he estimated, roughly two million cubic feet of this water, constantly replenished by natural springs and Scottish rainfall. "And in this part of the country it rains every day but Sunday," he said, "which is so I can play the golf to the sounds of church bells ringin'."

And suddenly Noah had an idea. What if he could arrange to market both Mr. Kelso's whiskey *and* his water? A lot of American drinkers called for "Seven and Seven." Could the marketplace be persuaded, instead of Scotch and water, to call for "Kelso and Kelso"—or whatever name might finally be given to the kindred labels? It was an exceedingly long shot. But with the proper marketing and promotion, it might be possible to pull it off—giving Ingraham's a new prestige whiskey as well as a new designer-label bottled water.

Mr. Kelso made a number of extravagant claims about the restorative powers of his whiskey—claims which could never be made in advertising, to be sure, but which were interesting nonetheless. He had mixed small quantities of his whiskey into the feed for his herd of Guernsey cattle, and the butterfat content of his dairy's milk had increased thirty percent. He had added whiskey, mixed with clover honey, to the mash he fed his chickens, and his hens had doubled their laying capacity. Women who had been barren for years would, under a regimen of Kelso's whiskey, soon find themselves pregnant, no matter what their age. Men who suffered from impotence became as randy as young stallions. A neighbor who had been bedridden with terminal cancer was prescribed a tot of Kelso's whiskey once an hour, and now the man was up and about, doing his chores and feeling fine. Mr. Kelso introduced Noah to this fellow, who did indeed seem to be the picture of health, and Noah listened to the man's stirring testimony. But it was the taste and color of Kelso's whiskey—and the tingle of his water—that excited Noah the most.

It was a gamble on two fronts, of course. But Noah worked out a licensing arrangement with Angus Kelso whereby Ingraham would be given exclusive distribution rights to his whiskey in the United States, Canada, and Japan, the three largest scotch-drinking markets outside the British Isles. Why the Japanese were so fond of scotch was always something of a mystery. The Japanese even produced a "scotch" of their own, though it could not be labeled or sold as such outside their own country, except as "scotch-type" whiskey. Noah obtained rights to Kelso's water for the United States and Canada only since, for reasons equally mysterious, the Japanese had never been interested in bottled water.

Angus Kelso's terms were on the stiff side—ten percent of wholesale—but Noah agreed to them. And he accomplished all this in the face of considerable skepticism from his mother. Hannah worried that Kelso's whiskey, or whatever they ended up calling it, would undermine sales of their flagship label, Ingraham's V.S.O.P. But Noah argued that Ballachulish-15, the working name he had given to the whiskey, was aged for a full fifteen years, whereas V.S.O.P. was aged for only twelve. The new brand would be higher priced and positioned in a more upscale market. Also, V.S.O.P. sales had been flat for the past several years. Demographic studies showed that the public conception of V.S.O.P. was of an "old-fashioned" scotch; it was not appealing to the yuppie crowd of baby boomers.

Noah also pointed out the recent trend toward "lite" beers and wines and soft drinks, and "light" and "ultra-light" cigarettes. Whatever advertising program was worked out for Ballachulish-15, Noah felt strongly that this scotch's special lightness should be its theme. Finally, he reminded his mother that his father had always encouraged competition between various Ingraham brands. Competition made the brand managers, division heads, and even the salesmen work harder to keep their labels performing strongly in the marketplace. It was even possible that Ballachulish-15 could spur the market performance of V.S.O.P., and wouldn't that be a welcome development?

His mother was also dubious about the Ballachulish bottled-water tie-in. "The seven-and-seven thing was just a fluke," she said. "Just a lucky coincidence. The makers of Seven Crown and Seven-Up had no connection with each other, and nothing in common except the number seven."

"Let's think of this as a planned coincidence," he said. And so, reluctantly, Hannah Liebling gave Noah the go-ahead on his two-pronged project. And now B-Day, as they had begun to call it, was at hand, and Noah had begun to feel that his future in the company depended on the success of this presentation and how the men responded to it. After all, other successes of the company had been brought about largely by his father. This one was his own. His mother even said so. "This will be your baby, Noah," she said, and it was impossible not to detect a note of warning in her voice.

"Doesn't your mother ever appear at sales conferences?" Frank Stokes asked him once.

"She tried it once," Noah said. "But you may have noticed that my mother doesn't exactly have a slap-you-on-the-back, hail-fellow personality. I think all the salesmen's figures went down the following year. She's a bit pigheaded, but I guess she figured there might be some connection."

And of course, after the presentation, a great deal more would remain to be done. A final name, a perfect name, would have to be chosen for the brand, and Noah had decided that there would be a contest for the name among all Ingraham employees and their agencies—a contest with a fat cash prize. That meant that thousands of names would be submitted for consideration. Then labels had to be designed, along with distinctive bottle shapes, and advertising and marketing plans, and a special media strategy, all had to be devised. Ballachulish water could be advertised in media—television, radio, the women's magazines—that would not accept liquor advertising, and that meant that, with luck, the two prongs of the project would promote each other. It would be at least a year, and millions of dollars would have been spent, before Angus Kelso's whiskey appeared on the shelves of liquor stores, or before his water found its way to supermarkets.

Noah's presentation to the sales force, he decided, would begin almost like a travelogue, with colored slides showing Angus Kelso's farm, his fat cattle and plump hens, then his distillery, then the entrance to the limestone caves, then the pine-clad hills with their blanket of pine needles, then the endearing Mr. Kelso himself, and—for a touch of humor—some of his wilder claims, that it restored fecundity in women and virility in men, and was the cure for everything from the common cold to cancer. He had considered putting all this onto a video, but decided against it. A slide show was more old-fashioned, more intimate, more in keeping with the rustic subject matter. And Noah felt that he could sell his ideas more effectively standing on his feet in front of them than as a disembodied offscreen voice.

Then there would be a question period. During this Noah would explain how the promotions for Mr. Kelso's two products could ride piggyback on each other.

The program would conclude with a blind taste test of the new products in comparison to other labels in a similar class. This, he hoped, would turn into a celebration party designed to send the salesmen home in a happy, enthusiastic selling mood, and pleasantly drunk. Once you had the salesmen on your side, that was half the battle.

Now, in his hotel suite, the telephone rings, and Noah reaches for it. "Mr. Liebling? I have Mrs. Hannah Liebling for you," her secretary says.

"Thank you, Jonesy."

"Noah," his mother's voice says, "what's all this nonsense about a party?"

"The cocktail party doesn't start till six," he says. "And I've got your President's Message to read. And while I've got you on the phone, do you think we could punch up the opening line a little? 'In our more than two-hundred-year history' sounds a little flat. What about, 'As we plunge fearlessly into our third century'? Or 'As we face the challenges of our third century'? Or something like that?"

"What in blazes are you talking about?"

"Your President's Message, Mom."

"No, no, no, no. That's fine. I'm not talking about *that* party. I'm talking about *this* party—this party you and Carol are planning to give for Anne."

"A party for Anne? You mean my daughter, Anne?"

"Of course! Is there any other Anne? It was in this morning's paper. Some sort of coming-out party, in June."

"I don't know anything about that, Mom."

"We've never had coming-out parties in this family. And the paper says Carol is giving it with that Van Degan woman, of all people!"

"Georgette Van Degan? What's wrong with her?"

"*Wrong*? Don't you *remember*? When your father and I bought One thousand Park, the Van Degans made it a point to move out the same day we moved in. They had their moving vans pull up at the same time ours did. Everybody in New York was talking about it."

"Mom, I wasn't even born when you bought the apartment. And I think it was the present Truck Van Degan's father who did that. He's been dead for a number of years."

"It doesn't matter. It's the same family of Jew baiters. People will think I've lost my marbles to have my family involved in anything that has to do with those Van Degans. They're in the glass business. Your father refused to buy bottles from Van Degan Glass as a result of the way they treated us."

"But, Mom, I really don't know anything about this," he says. "Why don't you call Carol and ask her?"

"No. I want *you* to ask Carol what's going on. After all, you're her husband."

"All right. As soon as this thing in Atlantic City is over, I'll—"

"No! I want you to find out now. I've had several calls about it already. Several people think it's pretty funny, us and the Van Degans. They're laughing at us, Noah. I want to know what's going on before I read anything more about this party in the papers."

"Okay, Mom, okay."

"And this story also says that we've agreed to supply all the liquor for this—this coming-out party for Anne and the Van Degan girl. Who agreed? Did you agree?"

"No. I told you, Mom, this is the first I've heard about it. Carol hasn't mentioned any party to me."

"You know we've always had a policy *never* to supply free liquor to parties. Every *week* I get asked to supply free liquor for some benefit or other. The Heart Ball, the Public Library dinners, the—"

"Well, a party for Anne isn't quite the same as a charity benefit, is it? But never mind, I'll—"

"Bathy even called me about it. She thinks it's a perfectly terrible idea in terms of our public relations. Not only will it bring back all that old Van Degan business from years ago. But in today's economy she thinks it'll look terrible for us to be throwing a big, expensive dinner dance for a couple of teenage *girls*."

"Please don't quote Bathy's opinions to me, Mother," he says.

"Well, Bathy happens to be smart, and if that's what Bathy thinks, other people will think the same."

"Okay, okay," he says. "I'll see what I can find out from Carol."

"Good. Call me back as soon as you've found out. I want to see this thing nipped in the bud, whatever it is."

"Meanwhile, you might wish me luck with Friday's presentation."

"Friday? What's that?"

"Friday is B-Day—remember?"

"Oh, that. Well, it's a little too late for luck on that one, isn't it? You're already in so deep. It's too late to turn back on that one. You're either going to sink or swim on that one. Fish or cut bait."

"Thanks, Mom," he says. "Thanks for those fine, stirring words of encouragement."

"Now, don't be sarcastic. But this *is* your baby, after all," she says.

He replaces the phone in its cradle. Now it is time to change for the kickoff cocktail party, and go downstairs to the ballroom, and smile, and shake hands, and hug, and slap backs, and make nice to all the hundreds of people he is supposed to know on a first-name basis. Oh, thank God, thank God for name tags, he thinks. He would like to leave the guy who invented name tags something in his will. Noah has long ago mastered the art of looking straight into a man's eyes and at his name tag at the same time.

"Good speech," Frank Stokes is saying to him now as they leave the ballroom and the cocktail party, and walk across the lobby toward the elevators. Frank is a little tight, but that, after all, is the point of a kickoff cocktail party, before everyone settles down to the more serious business of the rest of the week. "I really liked that part about facing the challenges of our third century . . . and the country approaching its third millennium. That was really neat. I didn't know your mother was—you know, that articulate."

Noah gives him a wink. "Sometimes I give her a bit of editing," he says.

"And at the end, when you said something like, 'We need every one of you who work here at the mill.' That was really neat. Calling it the mill. That's what got the big hand. I mean, you know, like everybody calls it the mill. But some people—I mean a lot of people—would be a little nervous about calling it the mill in front of your face, and nobody would dare call it the mill in front of *her*. But to hear you call it that—or I mean to hear *her* call it that—that was a really neat touch, Noah. They loved that!"

"Editing again," he says.

"The mill. As in treadmill. Or gin mill. Is it tough working for your mother, Noah? No, I shouldn't have asked that. That's none of my business. Forget I asked that."

"It has its ups and downs," he said. "I'm used to it. I know how to handle her."

"Shouldn't have asked that. None of my business."

"It's a question a lot of people ask."

"So. Why don't we change into some more comfortable clothes, meet for a drink at the bar, and then try our luck at the tables?"

"Sounds good to me," Noah says.

They step into the elevator, and Frank punches the buttons for their respective floors.

"Hey!" Frank says suddenly as the elevator door begins to close. "Isn't that—?"

"Isn't that *what*?" Noah asks sharply. For he, too, has seen the girl.

"That girl sitting in the lobby. With a suitcase. Isn't she that friend of Anne's from school? That Melody?"

"*Nonsense*! Don't be ridiculous. What would she be doing here?"

"But, golly, I could have sworn—"

"Well, it wasn't her. Looked a little like her maybe. But it wasn't her."

There is a little silence as the elevator rises.

At the sixth floor the elevator stops, the door opens, and a whole flock of giggling young women push into the elevator, perhaps a dozen of them, most of them in fanny-hugging mini-skirts, lacy semi-see-through tops, and high-heeled platform shoes. They are clearly party girls, lured here by the word of Ingraham's sales conference. They push the button for the twenty-first floor, where the company's hospitality suite is located. They press their backsides a little too closely against the two men; Noah and Frank are pressed against the rear of the car, and the elevator is overwhelmed by the complicated commingling of musky perfumes and chewing gum.

"So," Frank says to Noah. "Meet you in the bar in half an hour?"

"Who—*me*?" squeals one of the girls.

"No, I don't think so, Frank," Noah says. "I've got to work on Friday's presentation."

"All work and no play—"

"*All work and no play!*" squeals the same girl, and the others all laugh noisily.

"And I've also got a headache, Frank. I've changed my mind."

"I've got a friend who can take care of head!" says another girl, and there is more shrill and noisy laughter.

"Okay . . . okay," Frank says. "Don't bite my head off, buddy."

"Oooh . . . oooh," say the girls. "Somebody's just bit *his* head *off!*" And there are great shrieks of laughter at this.

Noah says nothing, merely stares at the elevator door over the heads of the laughing girls, a smooth mirror of brushed chrome. In the door the reflection of his face is pale, opaque, moonlike.

"Whatever it is, something's sure got you in a grouchy mood," Frank mutters. "That's for sure."

"I've got a goddamned important presentation to make on Friday, in case you don't remember!"

"Okay . . . *okay,*" says Frank.

"*I've got a goddamned important presentation to make on Friday, in case you don't remember!*" mimics the girl standing just in front of Noah in a piping voice, wiggling her butt against him. There is more loud laughter.

"Jesus!" Noah says as the elevator comes to a stop on seventeen. "Ladies, this is my floor. Will you let me get off, please?"

"Oooh . . . oooh . . . He *needs to get it off*!"

"You have a roommate," she says. "I'm sorry. I tried to get a room, but your convention has taken over the entire hotel."

"For Christ's sake, what the hell are you doing here, Melody?"

"I can sleep there—on your sofa."

"You're goddamned the hell not sleeping here anywhere! What the hell do you think you're doing here, anyway? How the hell did you get here?"

"On—a bus."

"Well, you're damn well getting on the next bus back to New York. You're not staying here with me."

"Please don't be angry with me, Noah," she says.

"*Angry!* This is just the goddamned most inconsiderate thing—"

"I know it is." Her chin trembles, but she is not crying. She reaches for her suitcase. "Well, I'm sure I can find a place to stay. I had at least six propositions made to me in the lobby while I was waiting for you to come out. Somebody in this hotel will take me in for a few nights, don't worry about that."

"Now, wait a minute," he says. "Tell me what happened. Tell me what made you do this."

"If I had a home I could go to, I'd have gone there," she says. "But I can't go to Japan! He's started stalking me, Noah—Bill Luckman. After you left, I looked out the window. He was standing there, in the street. He's got the building staked out, Noah. He looked up at me, and said—I could read his lips—'I'm watching you.' And then he—then he gave me the finger, and he looked up at me with—with a look of purest hatred. I can't describe it. He frightens me, Noah."

"Why didn't you call the police?"

"You told me not to."

"Or the building's security?"

"They can't do anything about someone who's outside on the street, can they? Anyway, I was too shocked—too terrified. I felt trapped. I just had to get out of there. I decided to sneak out of the building through the service entrance in the basement, so he wouldn't see me leave. I thought—I thought if I could just stay here with you, just for a day or two, then maybe he'd realize I'd gone away. Then I could come back and be able to go out on the street again, to look for a job, without thinking that he's following me everywhere I go. I guess it was a crazy thing to do, to come here, but I just couldn't think of any other place to go. I was desperate, Noah."

"What did you tell Carol?"

"I left her a note. I said I'd gotten a job with a theater company in New Haven. I hated to lie, but I just couldn't think of anything else to say!"

"Sit down, Mellie," he says, and she sits down in one of the pair of armchairs that flank the sofa.

"If you let me stay here, Noah, just for a day or so, no one will ever know."

"That's not the point," he says. "The point is that this is a five-day business conference. I've got meetings to go to every day. And when I'm not in meetings, I'm expected to be going around here socializing. Right now, right this very God-given moment, Mellie, I should be down at the bar, or in the casino, or upstairs in the hospitality suite, shaking hands, talking it up with these people who work for me, telling them what a great job they're doing, smiling, being nice to all these—these stupid sons of bitches who are in the bar down there getting drunk and trying to pick up girls in the lobby! I just don't have time to look after you, Mellie, or entertain you. I just can't do that while I'm here."

"I don't need to be looked after! I don't need to be entertained! I'll stay out of your way, I promise you!"

"But I'll need to do some entertaining in this suite. I'll need to have people in. I'll—"

"If you have people in, I'll go somewhere else. I'll go to the pool. There's a movie theater. I'll go to the movies."

"But—"

"You think I'll leave traces of myself around? My shoes under the chair? My panty hose drying in the bathroom? I was brought up in Japan, Noah. I'm a very tidy girl. If I'm not here, there'll be no signs of me, I promise you—not even lipstick on your facecloths. I'd never embarrass you, Noah."

"Well," he says, hesitating. "Well, perhaps. Perhaps just for tonight. You can have the bedroom. I'll take the sofa—"

"No! I want it to be the other way around. I'm the uninvited guest."

"But just for tonight. Tomorrow we'll work out something else."

"Oh, thank you, Noah!" She jumps from her chair and kisses him on the lips, and there it is again, that scent of her. "Thank you, dear Noah." Just then the telephone rings, and Noah goes to the desk to answer it.

"Hello, darling," Carol says. "I just called to see how things were going. Is Atlantic City pretty awful?"

"Pretty bad. This hotel is full of call girls."

"Well, you just keep your hands off them," she says.

"Oh, I will. You can count on that."

"Are you alone, darling? Or is someone with you? Somehow you sound as though someone's with you."

"Frank Stokes just dropped by for a drink."

"Oh, then I won't keep you. Beryl's coming by for cocktails Wednesday night. Some people she wants to meet. Oh, and Melody's found a job, with a play that's trying out in New Haven."

"I know."

"You know? How did you know that?"

"No, I mean—yes, she told me about that before I left this afternoon. She was pretty excited about it."

"Yes. Well, darling, I just want to wish you all kinds of success on Friday. Notice I didn't say luck. I said success. Ballachulish is going to be a big hit, I know it is."

"Keep your fingers crossed."

"I will, darling. I love you, darling."

"Love you, too."

"Bye."

He replaces the receiver in its cradle, realizing that he has forgotten to ask her about the party for Anne and the Van Degan girl.

"You lied for me," Melody says. "You told two lies for me. They were white lies, but they were nice lies. Thank you for lying for me, Noah."

He looks at her face, upturned in the lamplight. He clears his throat. "Have you had any dinner?"

"No."

"Hungry? Want me to have something sent up?"

"Nothing much. Something simple."

"Chicken sandwiches?"

"Perfect."

"There's some champagne in the fridge. Would you like a glass of champagne?"

"Yes," she says.

But later, in the dark bedroom of the suite, Noah cannot sleep, and his thoughts race uncontrollably. The drapes at the windows do not close properly, and from some invisible neon advertisement outside, lights flash white, then yellow, then blue, then white again. The red-lighted numerals of the digital clock at his bedside mark the time, and all the primary colors assail him in this mysterious, pulsating room where nothing will come to rest. For the better part of an hour he lies there, trying to keep his body still, trying to force his thoughts to separate themselves from himself. And just as he feels he is finally succeeding, and drifting off to a place where he feels his thoughts will float away from him, no longer be a part of him, but be rejoined with some vaster universe beyond this room, he is roused to consciousness by the sound of a door opening, and he raises himself on one elbow. There is a noiseless whisper of fabric moving, and the door closes again. Again there is a whisper of fabric, as though dropping to the floor, his bed sighs softly as it gives to the weight of a second person, and there is that fresh, clean scent of her hair.

"Hush," he hears her say. "Don't turn on the light. Don't say a word. I just want to lie down beside you for a while. I just want to make sure of something. I want to try something."

"Melody," he says. "We mustn't." But he is well past caring.

"But," she says, "we already are, my dear Noah."

Much later, he hears her say, "Have you ever been unfaithful to your wife before?"

"No," he says into the pillow.

"Then you have no reason to feel guilty. It was I who seduced you."

"It's not that. It's just that I'm—that I'm not—"

"Not free?"

"Yes."

"But, my dear Noah, that's the thing I love about you most—that's what's best about us—that you're not free. I know you love Carol, and I know Carol loves you, and I also love Carol, and I love Anne, and I never want anything to come between you and all those people you love, and who love you so much. You see, it's because you're not free that we can make love. Not being free, you are safe, and therefore so am I."

He takes her in his arms again.

12

Brief Encounters

"Thank you for showing me your script, Noah!" she says.

She is sipping coffee from their breakfast tray.

"A travelogue," she says. "Yes, I see what you mean. I like that idea. Now, go back to that third or fourth shot, the one of the ferry dock in the little Scottish village. Try starting with that one. That's how you'd enter the village, right? If you were just stepping off the ferry . . ."

"Right," he says, finding the slide she wants and placing it at the head of the conveyor of transparencies. "This one?" he says as the image appears on the screen: the ferry dock, the little village, the houses of the picturesque town rising from the grassy banks of the loch.

"That's it." She sits, in her stocking feet, her legs tucked beneath her, on the sofa beside him, while he, in his shirtsleeves, operates the carousel. She begins to talk, in a low, calm voice that is also rich with excitement, and he immediately sees that she is writing his presentation for him: "*For me it all began in the tiny Scottish village of Ballachulish, population three hundred and sixteen, not far from the entrance to the Firth of Lorne. It was in the early summer of 1992, and the air was crisp and fresh and new. What was I doing in this little town, so small and remote that it doesn't appear on most maps, a town that reminded me of Brigadoon, that magical town that reappears only every hundred years, and only for a day? It was because I'd heard that here lived a man named Angus Kelso, who distilled a single-malt whiskey that was like no other in the world. . . .*"

"Hey, this is great!" he says eagerly. "One of us should be writing this down!" He rises and begins pacing the floor.

"Don't worry, I'll remember it. I'm a quick study when it comes to lines. But I'm thinking, Noah—what about a little music? Not all through the show, of course, but just right here, at the beginning? A tape playing, very softly, one of the songs from *Brigadoon*. And then maybe, at the very end, a reprise of the same song? What do you think of that?"

"I think that would be—just great!"

"A tape shouldn't be hard to find. I'll pick one up today. Now let's cut straight to that close shot of Mr. Kelso."

He rearranges the slides again, and the image of the redheaded, smiling Scotsman appears on the screen, and she continues her narration: "*Meet Mr. Angus Kelso. What would you guess his age to be? Forty? Forty-five? Mr. Kelso is actually sixty-nine, and the secret of his eternal youth may just be his whiskey, which he tells me he pours on his breakfast pancakes every morning.* Pause for a laugh. *He also assures me that his whiskey cures barrenness in women and impotence in men.* Pause for laughter. *Incidentally, his whiskey also cures the common cold. Oh, and I almost forgot—it also cures cancer. I hope all you advertising people are taking notes, because these are pretty impressive claims—claims no other distiller has ever dared to make.* Pause for more laughter. And we'd cut the music right here, I think."

"Melody, this is just wonderful. Wonderful!"

"Now I think we could move to the picture of the caves. Can you find that one?" He finds it, inserts it next, and the dripping white limestone caverns appear, their pools receding mysteriously into the dark interior of the earth, and Melody continues: "*But Mr. Kelso also told me that the secret of his whiskey's extraordinary flavor and lightness, as it is in the case of every single-malt, lies in his water, which is drawn by hand from these deep limestone caves. He calls his water 'the sweetest water you'll ever taste on God's green earth.' I tasted some, and I had to agree. . . . And now the shot of the hillsides. . . .*"

He finds the shot, inserts it: pine-clad hills. "*But there's more to this water of Ballachulish than just the deep limestone caves,*" she says. "*The rainwater that has been gathering in these caverns for centuries is first filtered through a thick blanket of pine needles. In some places on these hills the blanket of pine needles is more than three feet thick . . .* Now the close-up of those pine needles. . . ."

He finds that, pine needles adrift like golden snow.

". . . And very slippery. I know, because I tried to climb those hills. . . . And now the shot of you landing on your fanny in the pine needles. . . ."

He finds it, and she laughs and claps her hands. "Pause for laughter. I like it, don't you?"

"I love it!" he says.

"And now a close-up of Mr. Kelso's whiskey in the glass. *But it was when I tasted Mr. Kelso's whiskey . . .*"

"Melody, we've got to get all this down on paper."

"All I need is a typewriter."

"I'll have one sent up."

"And paper, of course. Or do you want it on cue cards?"

"Cue cards maybe?"

"That could be risky. You'll be standing at a lectern. If you drop one, or get one out of place, then you'll be all fouled up. I think a triple-spaced script would be better."

"You're right. Melody, you're certainly going to be earning your credit for your winter work period." He studies her. She is wearing a slim blue skirt, to the knee, a matching cashmere sweater, the sleeves pushed up to her elbows, a gold circle pin, and her dark hair is pulled back in a simple ponytail. "You know, it's funny," he says.

"What's funny?"

"You don't look like a Bennington girl."

She laughs. "What's a Bennington girl look like?"

"From the ones I've seen on campus, it's jeans, battle jackets, knapsacks, boots and Reeboks. It's either grunge or long, flowing Mother Hubbards. And little felt hats."

She laughs again. "Those're for the *heavier* girls," she says. "It's the heavier girls who go in for muumuus. Remember, I'm an actress. You dress for the part. You dress for the casting call. If the part calls for a slut, I dress like one of those girls hanging around your hospitality suite. But for this assignment I decided I'd dress like someone's executive secretary. Anyway, I'll have your script typed up for you by the time you get back from this morning's meeting."

He frowns. "Following this meeting there's a lunch."

"After the lunch, then. Whatever."

"And after the lunch I've got two more meetings, back to back. I told you I wouldn't have much time to spend with you this week, Mellie."

"That's all right. Whenever you get back here, I'll have a draft of the script ready for you to look over."

"And, at six o'clock, I've invited some people up here for drinks."

"Don't worry. By six o'clock you won't find hide nor hair of me. Not even the typewriter. Unless—"

"Unless what?"

"Unless when I finish, you'd rather I just hopped on a bus back to New York," she says. "The way you said last night."

He hesitates, looking at the square of carpet between his feet. "No, I don't want you to do that," he says. "By about nine o'clock I should be free."

"All right. I'll phone the room at nine o'clock."

"And then we—"

"Can have a bite to eat."

"Chicken sandwiches." He sits down again.

"Our chicken sandwiches. Have you ever seen the movie *Brief Encounter,* Noah?"

"No."

"Celia Johnson and Trevor Howard. David Lean directed. It's about two people, neither of them free, who meet and have a—well, that's the title of the film."

"Brief encounter. Mellie, I—"

She holds up her hand. "Don't say it. I think I know what you're going to say, but I don't want to hear you say it." She glances at her watch. "You'd better hurry and finish dressing, Noah, or you'll be late for your meeting."

He rises and looks down at her as she sits, very still, on the sofa, her legs tucked beneath her slim blue skirt.

Without returning his look, she carefully picks up her coffee cup again and takes a small sip. "And do something about *that,*" she says. "You can't go to your meeting in that condition."

* * *

Now she is saying to him in the darkened bedroom:

Me? You mean you want to hear about my childhood, and all that? It really wasn't all that interesting, at least it wasn't up to a point. At one point it did get interesting, but by then I wasn't exactly a child anymore.

As you know, my father works for the State Department. I used to think my father was some kind of god. After all, he worked for the United States *government,* and in Japan anybody who works for the government is considered *very important.* A businessman may make more money, but to work for the government is supposed to be this great honor. As a kid it seemed to me we had all sorts of special privileges. The government gave us a car, for instance. We didn't even have to pay for gas. We could park our car in places that said "No Parking" because our car had diplomatic plates. We could shop at the military post exchange and get lower prices. If my father had to travel for his job, he could fly for free on a navy plane, at least if the navy plane happened to be going where he had to go. If not, the government paid for the travel. There were other little things, discounts and so on, that you get if you work for the U.S. government. It was also considered good that my father was paid in U.S. dollars, not in yen, though for the past few years that hasn't meant so much. Anyway, I grew up thinking that my parents were the greatest thing since sliced bread. All my Japanese friends were envious of me, and I liked that. I must have been a horrid little snot.

Later, I found out that my father wasn't any kind of god at all, and wasn't even very important. My Japanese school friends were so impressed because we had an autographed photograph of the president of the United States in our living room. Later, I found out that everybody at my father's level got one of those.

But the trouble is, my father *looks* like a god—tall, and blond, and handsome, with the body of a Greek warrior. He has those long, smooth swimmer's muscles, and he always has a golden year-round tan. The Japanese think he looks like Errol Flynn, and that's what they call him—*Ellor Frynn.* My father knows he's good-looking. He's very vain.

What my father *is* is a translator and interpreter. Well, it's a little better than that. He's assistant to the head of that department at the embassy in Tokyo. He spends his days translating documents back and forth between English and Japanese, which sounds kind of boring, translating all those boring, official documents. My father taught himself to speak and write fluent Japanese at the Fort Ord language school in Monterrey, and when I was growing up, I was led to believe that this was a great accomplishment. Maybe it was. Japanese is a difficult language, with all sorts of different vowel sounds that can completely change the meaning of a word. The word for *wander,* for instance, is very close to the word for *shit.* If you wanted to say, "I think I'll go out and wander in the garden," it could come out as "I think I'll go out and shit in the garden" if you use the wrong vowel sound. I speak some Japanese. But I've never learned to read or write it.

It was my father's mastery of the Japanese language, I was always told, that led to his being posted to Tokyo. But later I became not so sure whether this was the whole reason. My mother is a very bitter woman. She was always very bitter about the State Department, and when she and my father quarreled, which they often did—though not so much anymore—she used to imply that my father had been sent to the other side of the world as a punishment for something. Punishment for what? I really don't know, but sometimes I think I can guess. My mother has always hated Japan. She hates Tokyo. She hates the Japanese and has never learned to speak a word of the language, not even hello on the telephone. She absolutely loathes Japanese women, and she has no Japanese friends. Her only friends are the other American wives, who are just as boring and bitter as Mother is about how they hate living in Japan. Tokyo is an important post, but not to hear my mother talk about it. She'd much rather be in one of the more glamorous cities—London, Paris, Rome, or even Vienna or Budapest. If there's one thing Tokyo isn't, it's glamorous. But the place she'd most like to be is Washington, D.C., right at the heart of things. She's from Virginia, and has family there. She's bitter because it doesn't look as though my father will ever be assigned to Washington, and she blames my father for the fact that she's stuck for the rest of her life on the other side of the world. It's not a very happy household, my parents'.

When I was thirteen or fourteen, I wanted to start to date. All the other girls my age were dating boys by then—at least all the American girls. But my father was very opposed to this. He said he preferred the Japanese system, where girls—girls of good family, that is—are very much sheltered and protected until they're ready to get married, and by that time most of the marriages have been arranged for them. In Japan teenage girls are expected to stay home and help their mothers, and learn the tea ceremony and all that, and to do their fathers' wishes. It's still very much a male-dominated society in Japan, and it's terribly strict and confining for women, particularly young women. As Japan gets more Western-ized, it's beginning to change, and women are starting to rebel, but my father was in favor of the old-fashioned ways. He wanted me—literally—to fetch him his pipe and slippers when he came home from the office at the end of the day, and to fix him a drink. Then he liked to have me sit on a footstool beside his chair, while he smoked, and sipped his drink, and stroked my hair while he read the evening papers. And I—well, I liked these quiet evenings with my father, up to a point, because I still thought my father was some sort of god. But I wanted more out of my life than that.

There was one boy I began seeing secretly. His name was David, he was a few years older than me, and we—well, we were convinced that we were very much in love. He was my first sexual experience, and I—well, I liked it very much! He was very sweet, very gentle, a lot like you in many ways. My mother had told me nothing about the facts of life—absolutely nothing at all. She hadn't even warned me about getting the curse. But for-tunately I have an older sister, Cassie, who'd told me pretty much everything I needed to know. Cassie's mar-ried now and lives in Australia. There must have been some romance between my parents, back in the days when Cassie and I were being born. They gave us these romantic names. Cassandra. Melody.

David was the first person who ever told me I was pretty. He told me I was beautiful. He told me I was beautiful enough to be a movie star, and it was he who said I ought to study to be an actress. But when my father found out I was seeing David—he saw me getting out of David's car one Saturday afternoon—he was furious. There was a terrible scene. He said David was too old for me. He said David wasn't good enough for me. He said David's family was trash. He said David's father was a war profiteer. This was because David's father, who'd been too young to be in the war, had come to Japan after the war and bought up a lot of military equipment, and sold it, and made a fortune in what I guess is called the scrap metal business. David was in business with his father at the time.

My father told me I was never to see David again, but of course I did. David and I began making plans to run away together. I guess I've always been a runaway at heart. I ran away to be with you here, didn't I? David's family owned a cabin in the mountains north of Kyoto, which they never used, and that was where we planned to run away to. I'm sure it wouldn't have worked. That cabin would have been the first place our families would have looked for us. Still, we made all these elaborate, secret plans.

Meanwhile, my father began taking me on outings on the weekends, just the two of us, far outside the city. These outings were so David and I would have no chance to meet. Because David worked and I was in school, the weekends were the only times we were able to get together. My father would get me into the car on a Saturday morning, and we'd drive—I'd never know where we were going till we got there. "Surprise," he'd say. "Surprise, surprise." One afternoon that summer our destination turned out to be a tiny island in Toyana Bay, on the west coast, where he'd rented a speedboat and scuba-diving equipment for us both. My father knew I loved scuba diving, and he did, too. He was in a good mood. He'd had a meeting at the Imperial Palace the day before.

Once or twice a year he'd have to attend a meeting at the Imperial Palace, and after each of these meetings he'd bring home a little souvenir. They were just trinkets, really—a whalebone letter opener, a silver pen, a crystal paperweight, things like that. He used to tell us these were gifts from the emperor himself. I don't believe that. I don't believe he ever met the emperor. The emperor and empress of Japan lead very secluded lives, and hardly ever meet with people outside their family and members of the imperial household. They don't give audiences, like the pope, or hold press conferences, or make speeches. I think his meetings at the Palace were just with minor functionaries of the household. And the trinkets? I believe he stole them—just picked these things up when no one was looking and dropped them in his pocket. Members of the imperial household don't give out little souvenir gifts to visitors. No way.

The Japanese are funny about crime. They like to say that theirs is a crime-free society. They talk of America as the land of the criminals. There's plenty of crime in Japan, of course, but it's not considered polite to talk about it. And so, if a member of the Japanese imperial household noticed some small object missing after one of my father's visits, it would be beneath his dignity to mention it to anyone, much less the American embassy. This was how my father was able to get away with pinching little things from the palace. At least this was David's theory, and he understood the Japanese mentality and customs much better than I did. And I think David was right.

Anyway, it was a lovely day, and we were diving in clear water, not very deep, no more than twenty feet, among the coral reefs, and I noticed my father gesturing at me, pointing at something. At first I thought he'd found an unusual shell, or coral piece, and I swam closer. I saw what he had in his hand was what looked like a child's bracelet, or perhaps a napkin ring, of pink onyx. At first I wondered what a bracelet could be doing at the bottom of Toyana Bay, and then I guessed he'd got it from the palace. And then—and this is difficult for me to talk about—he unzipped the front of his wet suit to show me his erection. He placed the bracelet on it, smiling, gesturing to me, suggesting I could have it if I would reach out and take it off.

I shot up to the surface of the water like a bullet, and climbed back on board the boat. I think if I'd known how to manage the boat, I'd have pulled up the anchor and driven off and left him there—escaped! He came to the surface a few minutes later. He'd pulled himself together, the pink onyx piece was nowhere to be seen, and he was acting as though nothing at all had happened. He was in a very jolly, almost carefree mood, and I began to wonder if I'd imagined the whole thing. But I knew I hadn't. Who could imagine a thing like that? "Don't you want to dive some more?" he asked me. "I want to go home now, Daddy," I said. "I have an earache." I couldn't look at him. And so he got out of his diving gear, and we headed for the shore and home. In the car, he talked a lot but about nothing in particular. I couldn't think of what in the world to say to him. At one point he reached out and touched my knee. I pulled away from him. "I was only joking," he said. I didn't answer him. He didn't frighten me. He disgusted me. I pitied him.

I couldn't bring myself to tell my mother what had happened. I couldn't bear to look at my father. And I couldn't even bear the thought of ever seeing David again. I was too ashamed. Ashamed of my father, and ashamed of myself for having a part in it. I felt as though I'd been a part of a terrible crime that he'd blame me for, that he'd hold me accountable for in some way, and so I just stopped seeing him. When he'd call, I'd hang up on him. He wrote me letters. I tore them up. It wasn't that I hated him. I hated myself, and felt I wasn't worthy of him anymore. I suppose he must have wondered what had happened, but I didn't care. All I knew was that whatever we'd had between us was over. Not long ago I heard that he married a Japanese girl. I hope they're happy.

But I did tell Cassie about Toyana Bay. Somehow, I had to tell somebody. She sat very still for a long time, looking worried and scared, and then she said, "That was how he started with me, too—exposing himself." Started? Started what? She wouldn't say. All she would say was that there had been other things. She'd been younger than me, too young to really understand what was going on. She hadn't known there was anything wrong with it, that it wasn't normal to have these secret things go on between fathers and their daughters. She thought all fathers and daughters did these things, and she said she was glad to see that I knew better. I asked her, "Does Mama know?" She just bit her lip and said she didn't think so. That was when she told me she was going to marry this boy who had a cattle ranch in Australia, a boy she really didn't love at all, just to get as far away from home as possible.

That was when I decided that I was going to leave home—run away, if necessary. I began to make my second runaway plans. I told my parents I wanted to go to boarding school in the States. My father said he couldn't afford such a thing. I would have to settle for the American School in Tokyo, where the children of American government employees could go for free. So, on my own, I wrote to Ethel Walker in Connecticut. I applied and got accepted on a full academic scholarship.

"Look at this, Daddy," I said to him, showing him the letter.

"Where are you getting the money to travel to the States?" he said. "Not from me."

And so, faced with that, I began scheming of ways to get enough money for my ticket. It became a crazy time for me. I thought of forging his name on a check. I thought of trying to steal one of his credit cards. I thought of trying to blackmail him, threatening to tell my mother what had happened that afternoon. I knew he'd just deny it. "But what about Cassie?" I'd say to him. "Is Cassie lying, too?" But I knew I couldn't drag Cassie back into it. She was already making her escape. I even thought of going back to David and his family, and asking to borrow the money from them. But, as I say, I just never wanted to see David's face again.

Then one day my mother came to me and handed me a check. It was only enough for a one-way ticket to New York, but it was all the money she'd been able to scrape together. "I know why you want to go," she said. "And I know why Cassie wants to go." There were tears in her eyes.

"Mama—you *know?*" I said to her.

She looked away from me and just nodded.

"Mama, *how could you?*" I cried. "How could you stay with a man who would do things like that to Cassie and me?"

"Don't you dare blame me!" she screamed. "You two can both escape from here. I can't."

"Why not?" I asked her. "Why can't you?"

"It's the only life I have," she said. "It may not be perfect. It may not even be any good at all. But this is the only life I have." Of course, that was a crock, and I told her so.

And so that's how I got away from them. That's why I go back to Japan only when I absolutely have to. That's why I mooch on people like you and Carol. Once I graduate from college and I'm on my own, I'm never going to go back at all. That's why I'm never going to let myself fall in love again. Love only leads to disillusion. But it's funny. You're the only other person I've ever told about all of this, besides Cassie. I've never even told Anne, my best friend.

"Love doesn't have to lead to disillusion," he says into the darkness.

"Oh, yes. It does. It always will. For me, at least. When I was growing up, I thought my father was some kind of god."

"And here's another funny thing," he says. "My own father let me down—betrayed me—in much the same way. And I was just about your age. No, a little older."

"And it doesn't go away, does it?"

"No. Mellie, I—"

She covers his lips with her fingertips. "Hush," she says. "Don't say another word. This is just a brief encounter—remember? Remember we only have three more nights together."

"And then what's going to happen?"

She switches on the lamp beside the bed. "Now I want you to take a look at the script I've written for you," she says.

But much later, in the darkened bedroom, Noah Liebling cannot sleep. Through the narrow slit in the window curtains, neon lights from the sign outside flash perpetually from white, to yellow, to blue, to white again in a changeless rhythm, while the red numerals on the digital clock mark the sleepless minutes as they pass. *For me, it all began in the tiny Scottish village of Ballachulish, population something-or-other.* No, for me it all began in an overdecorated hotel suite in Atlantic City, with a girl whose name was a tune, a girl who is even younger than my own daughter, but who somehow seems much more worldly. Statutory rape. That is the legal term for what has happened here, for she is a minor, still a child, and there are laws, terrible laws, designed to punish men like me for what I have done. Her father is a child molester, but who can blame him? So am I. Curled here on the pillow beside me, her dark hair—the scent of her hair—across her face, breathing quietly and evenly, she looks, in the dimly flashing colored lights, even younger than she is.

I should have sent her home right away. She would have been safe from that asshole at River House, the most secure building in New York. He would have not got beyond the broad shoulders of Peter, the doorman, in his heavy greatcoat with epaulets of gold braid, the uniform of a Ruritanian hussar. I should have sent her home, but I didn't, and I didn't because I didn't want to. I wanted her here, with me, like right now, and right now it is too late. The deed is done. The crime has been committed. Like her own father. He that is without sin, let him cast the first stone, or however the hell it goes.

This will last only a week, that was her promise. But this will be a week that will change my life forever, Noah thinks, and what will happen when it is time for us both to go home again? Nothing? How can it be nothing? How can she and I continue to live in the same house with Carol and Anne after this? It cannot happen. That simply will not work. No, but I could give her some money, help her find her own place to stay, turn her into a kept woman. Could I really do that to her, to Carol, and to Anne, or have I already done it? What is wrong with me? *For me, it all began* . . . and I'm offering a thousand dollars to any man or woman in this organization who can give me the name of what is wrong with me.

It is a feeling at the base of my skull and at the pit of my stomach, an aching. Is there something the matter with me, Doctor? Am I going crazy, or have I already slipped past that thin barrier between sanity and lunacy? When I was a little boy, I used to worship my older brother, Cyril. He seemed so elegant, so wise, the man of the world. I used to follow him around, and he hated that, and his favorite word for me was crazy. "Are you crazy, Noah? Stop acting crazy!" At night, before going to sleep, I used to break into cold sweats with fears that I was losing my mind. "That's where they ought to put you, Noah," Cyril said as they drove past the place. "Bloomingdale's." Not the store, but the hospital for the criminally insane outside White Plains. Criminal, and crazy. The doctor will say, "Yes, Noah, you are criminally insane." Should I see someone? Yeah.

Is this what being in love is like? It is certainly unlike any feeling I ever had for Carol, and yet the strange thing is that the feeling I have now seems to draw me to Carol more powerfully than ever, and makes me appreciate how much I have, or had, in Carol, and how lucky I am, or was, to have her. No, Carol is not as young as she once was, but she is kind, and gentle, and thoughtful, and giving, and loving, too. If love is sacrifice, as Melody says it is, Carol has sacrificed a great deal. And yet, if I love Carol so much, how can I have let myself do this terrible thing to her and to the child we had together? There is no sane answer.

"There is insanity in the family, you know." Where had he heard this? There were supposed to be two crazy aunts, his father's sisters, who were considered "strange." But what the nature of their strangeness was he never knew. He had never met these aunts. Both his brother and his sister had spent years seeing psychiatrists. "Do you want to see what an erection looks like?" his brother asked him when Noah was eight or nine, walking into Noah's room to show him. "My psychiatrist taught me how to do this." Crazy.

The carousel of color slides turns in his mind, along with the white, yellow, and blue lights from the pulsating sign outside the window. Come with me to Ballachulish, Melody, or somewhere, anywhere that's been lost in time and isn't on any map, and we'll make the population grow by two more people. We'll go to Ballachulish, where no one knows us or anything about us, and we'll start a whole new life together. We'll swim naked in the limestone caves, and we'll make love on a thick mattress of smooth, golden, silky, slippery pine needles. Because Ballachulish is a magic place, and only appears out of the mists for one day every hundred years, each day for us will last a hundred years, and in a thousand years we'll be the same age. Perhaps I'll work in Angus Kelso's distillery, under a different name, of course, and we'll leave everything else behind—my wife, my daughter, my family, my career. Does that make any sense to you? Crazy. He is a man of forty-eight who has been having sex with a child, but he is the one who is thinking like a child. He is Errol Flynn. He is Roman Polanski. The names of men like him fill the crime stories of the newspapers day after day. . . .

It's no use. A memory as simple as the small, flat brown mole just above her navel fills him with yearnings more huge and harsh and overpowering than all the vastness of Carol's trust and love. With tears in his eyes he reaches out and touches her soft, dark hair with his fingertips. Lifts it. Smells it. Presses it against his lips, and her dreaming arm falls across his chest, producing almost an electric shock of feeling.

"I still have this funny dream," he said to her before they came to bed. "It's something I started thinking about in college. It would be that whenever I get my inheritance—the money, the stock in the company that I'm supposed to get—that I'd like to do something really *moral* with it. Take the curse off it, as it were.

"You see, from the time I was a little kid I was aware that my family's money wasn't made in a very moral way. People looked down their noses at the way we'd made our money. It was considered dirty money. I used to think: Why couldn't we have made our money in some other way? Banking! Real estate! Railroads! Publishing! Coming up with some medical discovery that would cure some terrible disease. But no, our money was made in booze. We made it from skid row winos and Bowery bums. We called it the Distilled Spirits Industry. But we were nothing but a bunch of *tummlers*— that's all we were."

"What's a *tummler*?"

"Someone who's paid to make a lot of noise to keep the party going—a guy who runs around the room with a lamp shade on his head, trying to make people think they're having a good time. A professional buffoon. My old man used to say that the liquor business was a part of show business, part of the entertainment industry. What do you do when you entertain? You bring out the booze and pour it down people's throats until everybody's laughing and feeling better. My old man said that drinking was like going to a Broadway show, only the ticket was cheaper, and the sensation lasts a little longer. Okay, I'll buy that. But how do you feel when people from an organization like MADD march up and down in front of your building with pickets calling you a murderer?"

"So tell me about your dream."

"It's that when I get my inheritance, I'd like to use it—or a lot of it—to establish a foundation to support something I decided to call the American Experimental School of Parenting. You see, there's a lot of talk in the press these days about the deteriorating quality of education in this country—crowded classrooms, poor teachers, lack of funds, guns and knives in the schoolyard, drugs, gangs, sex, and violence. My theory is that by the time a kid reaches school age, it's too late to do much of anything to change him. Any behavior patterns—good or bad—are pretty much set by then, and any attempts to change them should have begun long before that—at birth, or even before. Minority groups may cry 'racist' at this, but I really think men and women should be *licensed* before becoming parents. After all, it's a lot harder to learn to be a parent than to learn to drive a car, and you need a license to do that. At least some sort of training in parenting should be required. But no adult education programs in this country have really addressed this. Instead, parenting has gone out the window. Parenting is becoming a lost art. Instead, kids are dumped in malls or stores while their parents do something else, or they're placed with grannies and sitters or in day-care centers, or dumped in front of TV sets where we fret that they're seeing too much sex and violence. 'Get after the networks,' we say, but that's not the answer. The answer is 'Get after the parents.' My foundation would look into ways that parents could be coerced—or shamed—into education, to show them that parenting just doesn't work without some sort of preparation. Of course, none of this is going to be easy. It's a lot harder to educate an adult than it is a child. But I think that's the only solution to the mess our society is in right now—to try to teach parents how to raise better children. If we could only do this—train mothers to be better mothers, and fathers to be better fathers—I think a lot of the questions we argue about, including abortion and race relations, would become moot. Sound like pie in the sky to you? Maybe it is, but I think we've got to start somewhere, and my foundation could offer some kind of start. I even like the acronym I've given it—AESOP, because every Aesop's fable had a moral at the end. Anyway, that's my little speech."

She looked thoughtful for a moment. Then she said, "Do you hate your job, Noah?"

"Sometimes," he said. "Not right now, but sometimes."

"Did you ever discuss this dream of yours with Carol?"

"Hell, no."

"Why not?"

"I mentioned it to my mother once. Needless to say, she was horrified. She thought it was sheer craziness."

"Do you still want to do this?"

He laughed. "Maybe. If the day comes when I finally get the company stock I'm supposed to get. But that day seems to be getting further and further and further away—along with the dream. My magnificent obsession."

She said nothing.

"So what do you think of the idea, Melody?" he asked her.

She thought a long time before answering him. "Well, it's a lovely idea," she said at last. "It really is a lovely dream. But it still seems to me like throwing away everything you've done with your life so far."

"I don't see it as throwing it away," he said. "I see it as redeeming it. Salvaging it somehow."

There was more he could have told her. He could have told her about the considerable number of books he had collected on the subject—that shelf full of books "by authors with Jewish-sounding names, all with Ph.D.'s after them." He did not tell her that two years ago he had hired an outside researcher, an associate professor from the University of Pennsylvania's Department of Human Resources—yes, a professor with a Jewish-sounding name and a Ph.D. tacked onto it—who regularly provided him with new statistics, new materials, new studies on the subject. Or that his literature on the subject now filled five fat filing-cabinet drawers in his office at the Ingraham Building—files under such headings as "Self-Improvement and Psychotherapy," "Anxiety," "Theories of Change," "Education and Religion: Paths Toward Excellence," and "Why We Fear Our Children." Or that the more his future with the company seemed to recede before him, the more time he spent annotating, updating, and cross-referencing these files.

"Of course, it's always something you could do as a hobby," she said.

"As a hobby," he said. "Like collecting stamps? Building model airplanes?"

"It just doesn't seem very practical. I mean, if parents are going to need licenses to have children, who's going to give out the licenses? The federal government?"

"I was just using that as a metaphor," he said. "I just meant they could be offered some sort of job training. Look—your own parents are something of a case in point, don't you think?"

She looked at him steadily. "If my parents had needed a license to have me, I wouldn't be here," she said. "And if your parents had needed a license to have you, you wouldn't be here, either. But here we are. Two illegals. Do you consider yourself a good parent, Noah?"

"Listen," he said, "I didn't ask you to follow me down here. I didn't ask you to crawl into bed with me."

"*Crawl?*" she said. "Is that what you think of me? As some kind of crawly creature? Like a worm?"

He threw up his hands. "This conversation isn't getting us anywhere," he said.

She had been sitting tailor-fashion on the bed in her short nightie. Now she uncrossed her legs, stood up, and stretched her arms high into the air toward the ceiling. "Nothing is getting us anywhere," she said. "Nothing is going to get us anywhere. I don't like the way this whole scene is going. Let's run through this whole scene again. Take it from the top."

"I don't think you feel anything for me at all, Melody."

"Tell me what a *tummler* is."

"A *tummler* is—"

"Tell me something else. Were you ever in love with Carol?"

"What?"

"Were you? Ever? Really in love with her?"

"I think—I don't know."

"I think—I know you never were, Noah. Why have you just told me things you were never able to tell her—important things?"

"I don't know."

"I know. Because you're in love with me. And don't ever say I don't feel anything for you, because I do feel—deeply. I'm in love with you, Noah. I think I have been since the day I met you. It can't be a brief encounter anymore, can it? It's gone too far. It's too late now, and we can't turn back the clock. We're in love with each other. It's as simple as that. There's nothing more to say. Admit it, Noah—that it's true."

"What are we going to do?"

"Marry me, Noah. I want you to marry me, Noah."

It has been another long and busy day, and Frank Stokes sits by himself at the bar, nursing an Ingraham's and soda. A blonde in a tight black mini-dress that appears to have been made of Naugahyde hops onto the stool beside him. "Hi," she says. "What's your name?"

"Puddin' Tane," Frank says.

"Mine's Estelle," she says. "Care for some conversation?"

"I guess I don't mind," he says.

"Where's your friend?"

"What friend?"

"We seen you both in the elevator Monday night. Me and my girlfriends. Remember?"

"Oh, yes," he says.

"He's in suite seventeen-fourteen, your friend."

He looks at her. "How did you happen to know that?" he asks her.

She giggles. "Days, I work here at the hotel. In housekeeping. I'm not supposed to be here. They don't like us hanging around here after hours, socializing with the guests. But I say what they don't know won't hurt 'em—right? I thought he was kinda cute, your friend. What's his name?"

"Puddin' Tane."

"Same as yours? Aw, come on, You're kiddin' me."

"Yeah."

"Suite seventeen-fourteen is one of our deluxe suites. Five-ninety a night. He must be pretty rich, your friend. What's he do?"

He hesitates. "Executive v.p. of the company," he says.

She whistles. "Gee whiz," she says. "That sounds pretty important. What about you? What're you?"

"Janitor," he says.

"You kidding? You look, like, too well dressed to be no more than a janitor. Aw, I'll bet you're kiddin' me again. I bet you're pretty high up, too."

"Well, maybe I am," he says.

"Who's his girlfriend?"

"Whose girlfriend?"

"Your friend's."

"He hasn't got a girlfriend."

"He's with his wife, then."

"We don't bring our wives to things like this," he says.

"Well, then it's gotta be a girlfriend. She's staying in seventeen-fourteen with him, that's for sure. And she's a lot younger than he is, I can tell you that."

"I don't know what you're talking about," he says.

"I seen her. When I came in to do the room yesterday morning, she was there. Brunette. Long, dark hair. She was working at a typewriter, typing something."

"Probably some kind of secretary," he says.

"Oh, yeah? She asked me to come back later. I did, and she was gone, and so was the typewriter. But there was a woman's things in a couple of the bureau drawers, a nightie and all that. And there was woman's things hangin' in the closet."

He looks at her again. "Do you make it a point to rummage through a guest's things when you do up a room?" he asks her.

She purses her lips. "It's my duty," she says primly. "We got to see if a guest's checked out or not. Sometimes a guest will try to check out without checking out, if you receive my meaning. I got to check on things like that. Anyway, she was still there again this morning. When I first come in, I heard her singing in the shower.

When I come back later, she was gone again, but her things was still there."

"I think you've got the wrong room," he says.

"Huh! Not me. Think I don't know my deluxe suites? If your friend's in seventeen-fourteen, he's got a girl there with him. So what? I say. So what if she looks young enough to be his daughter? It takes all types to make a world is what I say. So what about it, Mr. Tane? Care for a little companionship? Nothing wrong with a little companionship is what I say."

"No, I don't think so, Estelle," he says.

"Care to buy a girl a drink? But in your business I bet you get all you want for free."

"As a matter of fact, we don't," he says. "Look, Estelle—why don't you go up to the hospitality suite? I think you'll do better business up there."

"*Business*! Hey, just what the hell do you think I *am*?" she says, "I'm a self-respecting girl is what I am! Besides, I was just up there. The place is dead."

"Come back Friday night," he says. "There'll be plenty of action then, when this conference is over. The hospitality suite should be jumping for you then." He starts to rise.

"Hey, you givin' me the brush-off?" she says.

"That's right, Estelle," he says. He slides a ten-dollar bill across the bar in the direction of the bartender. "Good night, Estelle. Sweet dreams with whoever you wind up with." He steps off the stool.

"Snob!" she says. "Stuck-up snob! Think you're better than the next one. Think you're better than seventeen-fourteen and his teenage floozy. Or are you gay? Is that it?"

He leaves the bar without looking back at her.

"Gay! Gay!" she shouts after him. "Gay-faggot-gay!"

"Not having a good night, eh, Estelle?" the bartender says.

"Shuddup," she says. "Gimme a tequila sunrise."

"I can't believe this, Billy," Beryl Stokes is saying. "I can't believe that you actually remember me from the eighth and ninth grades, when I was Beryl Price. You were only thirteen, fourteen years *old*."

"I remember you vividly," he says. "You were considered one of the finest teachers at Horace Mann. You were—inspirational, actually."

"Really?" Beryl squeals. "And I was only a sub!"

"You've had a career, dear?" Georgette Van Degan says. "Oh, how I envy you. When I was growing up, I so wanted a career. But Daddy wouldn't hear of it. He said, 'No woman in this family has ever worked,' and so, after my debut, there was nothing left for me but Truck Van Degan." Mary passes hors d'oeuvres. "Oh, yum-yum-yum," Georgette says. "I'm going to try one of these yummy-looking little cheesy businesses."

"A sub?" he says.

"A substitute teacher. But you were my star pupil."

"That's why I remember you so vividly. We always used to hope that one of the regular teachers would get sick, so we could have you as a sub. Let's see, the regular teachers were—"

"Mrs. Espy and Miss McCracken."

"Of course." He beams proudly at her.

"Oh, Billy, you really do remember," Beryl says. "I can't believe it. And now you're so rich and famous. But I always knew you would be."

"And you haven't changed a bit," he says. "You're just as beautiful as ever."

"Oh, Billy. I am a few years older now."

"It doesn't show."

"Is that an Adolfo, dear?" Georgette asks her.

"Yes."

"I had to give up on Adolfo," she says. "I felt he was spreading himself too thin." She turns to Bill Luckman. "Mr. Luckman, I want you to mark the date of June seventeenth on your calendar. It's a Thursday. That's the night that Carol and I are having a coming-out party for Anne and my daughter, Linda. At the Piping Rock. We're going to insist that you be there." She turns to Anne. "Aren't you excited, dear, about the party?"

"Yes, but—"

"Now, Georgette—" Carol starts to interrupt.

"But I'm not sure I remember Linda from school."

"Nonsense, dear. You were the best of friends. Inseparable."

Carol Liebling clears her throat. "Georgette, I think that all this talk about a party is a little premature," she says. "I haven't had a chance to talk to my husband about all this. He's out of town this week, and—"

"Well, it's too late to back out now," Georgette says airily. "I've already ordered the invitations from Cartier."

"And you've set a date?"

"It's the only date that Peter can *do* it! Duchin, that is. He doesn't have another date available that month, and so we had to grab it. I talked to him yesterday, and he's all signed up. He wants twenty-five thousand for the evening, and that's a very special price for me, of course. Fifty percent on signature, and the balance on the evening of the performance. You can send me your check for your half whenever you get around to it."

"Georgette, I never agreed—"

"And Carol's husband's company is supplying all the liquor for the party," she says to Bill Luckman. "So you can see what an absolutely *marvelous* evening it's going to be. The best champagne, the best—"

"But, Georgette, I just said that *possibly*—"

"Are you trying to back out on that? Carol, you *promised*—"

"Perhaps he might be able to supply it at cost, but—"

Georgette Van Degan's eyes flash wide open. "At *cost*? You said it would be *free*!"

"I said I needed to discuss it with Noah," Carol says. "And I haven't had a chance to do that yet."

"Why? Why do you need to discuss it with him? Do you need to discuss every little minor thing with your husband? I certainly don't. In fact, I haven't really discussed it with Truck, either." She turns to Beryl. "Do *you* have to discuss every little minor thing with *your* husband, dear?" she asks her.

Looking flustered, Beryl says, "Well, perhaps not *every*—"

"Husbands should be kept out of things. Until all final plans are made."

"To me this isn't such a little minor thing, Georgette," Carol says. "You're talking about a very major party!"

"Well, this is a fine kettle of fish," Georgette says, tapping the toe of her Delman pump crossly on the parquet floor. "Trying to back out at this late stage of the game. After dates have been set, invitations have been ordered, and contracts have been signed. I'm at a loss for words, Carol. Well, you just can't back out now."

"I'm not backing out of anything," Carol says evenly. "Because I was never really *in* anything, you see." She rises. "Can I freshen your drink, Bill?"

He smiles and hands her his glass. Then, lighting a cigarette and letting out a thin stream of smoke with a soft hiss, he says, "By the way, where is Melody?"

"She's taken a job with a theater company," Carol says from the bar. "A new play that's trying out in New Haven."

"Really?" he says. "Well. How very odd."

"What's odd about it?" Anne asks him.

"Well," he says, "for one thing, there is no new play trying out in New Haven."

"Perhaps she said it was in rehearsal there," Carol says. "Anyway, that's where she is."

"That's even odder," he says. "Plays frequently try out in New Haven. But the Shubert Theatre is never used for rehearsals." He looks at Anne questioningly, but she merely lowers her eyes and studies the backs of her hands.

"Odd," Bill Luckman says again.

"Well, I must be running along," Georgette Van Degan says, gathering up the twin chains of her Chanel bag. "Just remember it's too late to try to wriggle out of this, sweetie," she says to Carol. "At least if you think you have a chance of getting my porcelains for your museum. Meanwhile, Roxy's promised to run another item about us in tomorrow's column."

"Just think, Billy," Beryl Stokes says, gazing at him adoringly. "You were my star pupil, And look at you now. . . ."

Bill Luckman glances at Georgette and rolls his eyes.

From Roxy Rhinelander's column:

Flash! Update! Seems that years and years ago, when yours truly wasn't even a twinkle in her daddy's eye (well, almost that long ago), the late Mr. and Mrs. Truxton Van Degan III made a big point out of moving out of their big spread at 1000 Park Avenue at *the very moment* when Mr. and Mrs. Jules Liebling were moving into the building. Seems that the Mayflower-descended Van Degans didn't think the Billionaire Booze Baron and his wife (the former Hannah Sachs) were quite up to snuff for that posh address. Too nouveau, maybe? Well, they *did* call Jules Liebling an ex-bootlegger, dontcha see, and he *did* have his picture snapped making nice to Al Capone. Anyway, the hatchet's been buried between the two Feuding Families at last with the coming-out bash **Georgette Van Degan** (Mrs. Truxton IV) and **Carol Liebling** (Mrs. Noah) are planning for their delectable deb daughters on June 17. Moral: Time heals all wounds, by the time the next generation rolls around, at least.

"What in the world is going on?" Pookie Satterthwaite is saying to Patsy Collingwood on the telephone. "How is Georgette managing to get so much ink over this nonsense? Do you think she's paying Roxy off?"

"Well, I ran into Roxy the other night, and it looked like she was wearing a new mink coat," Patsy says.

"Those old skins? Blackglama gave her that at least ten years ago for doing a 'What Becomes a Legend Most' ad."

"Weren't we nice enough to Roxy at Christmastime?"

"Well, *I* certainly was. I don't know about *you,* sweetie."

"I happen to have been *especially* nice to her at Christmas."

"Look at it this way, Patsy. Every bit of ink that's going to Carol Liebling is ink that could be going to you and me."

"Exactly. You, Georgette, and me—we're supposed to be the Big Three, aren't we? This town isn't big enough to make it a Big Four."

"But I think I've figured out what Roxy's doing, Patsy."

"What?"

"Every now and then she likes to throw in a new name. It makes her column more interesting, supposedly."

"Does that mean she's turning us into old names?"

"Not necessarily, sweetie."

"And Carol Liebling, of all people. She's nobody."

"Not as of this morning, sweetie. That's a good ten inches of column space she's got."

"Infuriating. I've got half a mind to tell Roxy exactly what I think."

"That's definitely not the way to do it, lovey. Don't antagonize Roxy. Roxy can be mean as pig shit. On the other hand, I think it would be smart if we were both a whole lot nicer to Carol Liebling."

"And drop Georgette?"

"Hmm." Pookie pauses. "Well, I've often said that if you gave Georgette enough rope, she'd hang herself," she says. "Let's lunch."

In the town house on Sutton Square, Ruth Liebling di Pascanelli is reading aloud to him. " 'And when Clarissa saw Jonas standing in the doorway, her heart stopped.' " She puts down the manuscript. "That's as far as I've gotten," she says.

"I don't know much about writing books," Ector says. "But I really like what you've written. I mean I think it's really good."

"Thank you, Ector."

"That Jonas character. I bet he's going to cause that Clarissa a lot of trouble—right?"

"Right."

"I figured. And, you know, it's a funny thing."

"What's a funny thing?"

"I don't know just how to say this," he says. "But in my business, I've taken out a lot of rich women. Rich men, too. And a lot of them's been older than me, like you. But you're different. I mean, most of them, all's they want is sex. But you don't. You don't want me for that at all. I mean, like you're a countess, you're rich, you're a movie star, you're an author, and yet all you seem to want is to have me around. And, I mean, like I always try to show the client a little affection. That's easy enough for me to do. I can fake that stuff easy. But with you it's like I don't have to fake that stuff. I mean, I—I mean the longer I stay here with you, the more I really like you. I like being with you."

"I'm glad you like being with me, Ector."

"You don't mind that I'm a hustler?"

"There are a lot worse things to be."

"I didn't always used to be, you know."

"I'm sure you weren't."

"It was a guy I met who got me into this. When I first came here from Abilene, looking for a job. Guy said I'd be good at it. Said there was money in it. Said I looked like I had talent. He took me on. And one thing just sort of led to another."

"I can understand that."

"But maybe now I'd like to sort of settle down. So what if—I guess what I'm trying to say is that I really like you a lot." He sits forward in his chair and gazes at her intently. "What if—what if you and me was to get married?" he says. "I'm serious. I like you a lot. I really do. I mean, I've met a lot of women. But I've never met a real lady, like you, before. Maybe I'm not saying it right. But I've never felt this way about anybody else before. I really never have."

"This letter was hand-delivered, madam," Albert, Hannah Liebling's majordomo, says to her, handing her the envelope.

"Thank you, Albert."

She carries the letter to her writing desk, fishes in a drawer for her reading glasses, opens the letter, and reads:

> *My dear Hannie,*
> *I don't know whether or not my name will mean anything to you at this point.*
> *I'd heard you married a man named Liebling. But I didn't know who he was until I happened to see the enclosed item in this morning's paper, which mentioned your maiden name and also included your address.*
> *I have . . .*

There is something about the handwriting that is familiar, from years and years ago. She turns the letter over, to the signature, and her hand flies quickly to the strand of pearls at her throat.

She sits down hard in front of the little desk.

PART TWO

———◦(◦)◦———

Grandmont, 1945

13

Deals

Oh, if you could have seen Grandmont! It was not the big turreted stone house itself that was so spectacular. It was the setting Jules Liebling chose for it—high on a hill overlooking a wide bend in the Hudson, with grassy terraces, separated by parterres, cascading down toward the river's edge. It was at its best by moonlight, with the light from the moon and stars reflected and refracted from the water's surface. The river is tidal at this point, and so its flow is forever shifting, first running north, and then, with a perceptible rippling, reversing its direction and flowing south—tidal and saline, so the smell of the river is a constant reminder of its connection to the sea, that the moon-driven Atlantic is ceaselessly directing the river this way and that, that the moon and the ocean are in charge of things here. An Atlantic storm is on the way if the seabirds fly inland and settle on the river.

To the north, from the west-facing verandas and terraces of Grandmont, the lights from the Tappan Zee Bridge glowed in a snaky curve, a double strand of diamonds. Just to the south, on the river's opposite shore, were the lights of the village of Sneden's Landing, tucked into the first drop in the Palisades. Before Hannah Liebling went to bed at night, she liked to lie in her chaise longue and look out at these lights, and the lights from the river traffic, from her bedroom windows. Around eleven o'clock the night excursion boat to Albany came twinkling into view, with the sounds of laughter and swing music pouring from its decks. And, periodically, there would be distant rattles and whistles from the trains of the New York Central's Albany Division as they made their way up and down the valley.

Hannah found all these night sounds and sights restful and reassuring.

He had not built Grandmont for her, however. He had made that quite clear from the beginning. He had built it for his son Cyril, after Cyril was born in 1934. Jules had ordered a huge playground built at Grandmont for his little son, with industrial-size slides and swings and seesaws and sandboxes, and a great deal else. For Cyril's third birthday Jules bought him a baby elephant, complete with a miniature howdah in which the child could ride. The elephant, whose name was Baba, was trained to kneel on command and accept a small passenger in the howdah, but Hannah was too fearful of the boy's falling to let him ride in it. The next year came a frisky zebra for a pet, and presently Grandmont contained a small, private zoo, where a bush baby became Cyril's favorite animal.

In 1939 their daughter, Ruth, was born, but Jules made it clear that the playground equipment and the animals were for Cyril's enjoyment only. But then, as we know, by 1945 Cyril had become a severe disappointment to his father. Soon the playground equipment was being allowed to go to rust and disrepair, and the menagerie was being disposed of—either sold or given away. "I want us to make another son," Jules said to Hannah.

And so they went through the ritual of trying. This wasn't a particularly easy period for Hannah, since she had been told she could bear no more children. "The uterus has become tipped," her doctor explained to her. "It will be a miracle if you are ever able to conceive again."

Still, she prayed for a miracle. And, lo and behold, the miracle happened, though not in the way she had wanted it to happen, and it happened in the moonlit garden at Grandmont.

The bush baby was the first to go. "Oh, please," Hannah begged him. "He loves that little creature so!"

"He must be punished," Jules said. "What better punishment than to take away a favorite pet?"

"But he's still just a little boy," she said. "Don't all little boys experiment with themselves that way? Didn't you, when you were that age, experiment with other boys your age—with sex—like that? I'm sure you did."

"Never!"

"That headmaster—that Mr. Litchfield—he overreacted to it, I think. St. Anselm's is such an old-fashioned school."

"He disgraced us. The whole school knows about it now. They've made that little nigger kid a hero. They've labeled my son a pervert. From the report that Litchfield sent out, there isn't another boarding school in New England that will take my son now. He'll have to go to public school, the way I did."

"But not the bush baby, Jules. Not his precious little Potto."

"His precious little Potto is already on his way to the Bronx Zoo."

"They've taken away Potto!" Cyril screamed, rushing into his aunt Bathy's room. "They've taken away Potto, and they won't tell me where he's gone!" Bathy Sachs took him, sobbing, into her arms.

"Now, that's not the way," she said, trying to comfort him. "You want to show your papa what a little man you are, don't you? This isn't the way to do that, is it? Dry your tears, keep a stiff upper lip, and show your papa what a brave little man you are. That's what he wants to see."

"I hate them!" he sobbed. "I hate them both!"

"There, there," she said. "Potto's in a nice new home, with lots of nice new little friends. Don't let your papa see you crying like this. Now just go downstairs and act grownup, and show your papa what a big, brave little man you are. Do that for me, Cyril."

"I want to kill him!"

"No, you don't. Your papa is angry at you now. But your papa is a good, kind man at heart, Cyril. He really is."

Oh, he was handsome enough, Hannah supposes, particularly when he was younger, as he was then. Women found him attractive. The Duchess of Windsor, when she came to visit Grandmont after the war, pronounced him "charming," and he could be charming. From the portrait in the dining room at 1000 Park, which was painted later, he looks a little stern when she gazes up at it from

the table. A little stern and sad, and the down-drooping
mustache doesn't help; nor does the Napoleonic pose
with his right hand inserted in his vest. He looks, more
than anything, disappointed. That is the expression in
his eyes. If Jules Liebling had a tragic flaw, it was that
he was too prone to disappointment. Perhaps it was because he was so used to everything going his way. He
couldn't understand why everything could not always go
his way. But no one's life goes exactly the way one wants
it to. Life takes no one's orders. And so her husband
died of disappointment.

"You really do remember me from Horace Mann,"
she says to him for perhaps the dozenth time. "I just
can't believe it, Billy."

"Of course I do." He is sprawled, naked, across her
bed, smoking a cigarette.

"I only subbed, maybe, ten or twelve days, at the
most, during the two years when you were there. And
yet you remember little old me."

"Little old you were a pretty memorable teacher. Plus
being the most beautiful teacher in the whole damn
school."

"*Really?*" She giggles. "Well, that wouldn't have been
hard to be—when I think of some of the others."

"You still are." His lips curl into a smile. "Beautiful,
that is." He runs a fingertip along the curve of her spine.

"Of course, I didn't have the money then that I have
now," she says. "That was before I married Frank." She
reaches over the side of the bed and picks up the pink
Adolfo that was dropped in a heap on the floor, and
arranges it, more tidily, across the seat of the slipper
chair beside the bed. "What was it we were reading in
that last English class I taught? Do you remember? Was
it—?"

"*Silas Marner?*"

"Yes! Yes, I actually think it was. I'm positive it was
Silas Marner. What a memory you have, Billy."

"You could even make a dud like *Silas Marner*
interesting."

She giggles again. "And you were my star pupil. I
could tell you were going to have a brilliant future even
then. But I shouldn't have let you seduce me, Billy. I

think I had a little bit too much to drink at Carol's party tonight."

"Aw, *c'mon*, teacher," he says. "We went out to the elevator together. You mentioned that you lived right downstairs, and had some old Horace Mann yearbooks I might like to look at. The old come-up-and-see-my-etchings routine. You wanted it as bad as I did. So don't give me the I-shouldn't-have-let-you-seduce-me bit, Beryl baby."

"Well—perhaps I did. But—but I guess it's because you've become such a celebrity. It seems like every time I turn on the television, there you are. I guess I sort of got carried away."

"What the hell? You wanted it, I wanted it. We both wanted it. So what the hell, teacher baby, what the hell?"

"But I'm just an ordinary little old New York house-wife. And you—"

"Me, I'm just an ordinary guy who likes to fuck," he says.

"It doesn't bother you, does it, that I'm—well, that I'm one or two years older than you?"

"Hell, no! You're not about to get all guilty on me, are you, teacher?"

She hesitates. "I guess not," she says at last. "But I'm the one who should be calling you 'teacher,' Billy dear. You've taught me things tonight that I never knew before, Billy."

He stubs out his cigarette. "Oh? What sort of things?"

"Feelings. Depths of feelings I never knew I was capable of before."

"Say, that's quite a compliment," he says.

"I mean it, Billy."

"You cheat on your husband much?"

She looks away. "Not *too* much," she says.

"Just now and then, huh?"

"Yes. Especially when—"

"Especially when he's out of town. Right?"

"Now, Billy," she says. "Don't imply that I'm a—you see, the thing is, Frank trusts me. I couldn't do this if he didn't trust me."

"Yeah, that's important. That he trusts you."

"The trouble with Frank is, he's stupid."

"Look," he says, rolling over on his side and propping himself on his left elbow. "Why don't you come right out and say so? You like a guy's hot cock pumping into your tight little pussy. And you don't get all that much from old Frank—right?"

"Well, after eleven—no, ten years . . ."

"You liked my cock, didn't you?"

"Oh, yes . . ."

"So why not come right out and say so?" He grabs her by the shoulder and kisses her a little roughly. "I believe in being honest, don't you? I believe in honesty."

"Oh, yes," she says. "Definitely. So do I. And you're one of the most honest men I've ever known."

He swings his long legs over the side of the bed. "Let me ask you something, while we're on the subject," he says.

"Okay. Ask me."

"Do you think Noah Liebling's getting it off with that Melody Richards? His daughter's friend?"

"Oh, no!" she gasps. "That couldn't possibly be. What makes you—?"

"She stays with them a lot, doesn't she?"

"Well, over school vacations, but—"

"Has for several years, right?"

"The last two, maybe three years. But—but what makes you think that anything could possibly be going on between Noah and Melody?"

"I dunno. Intuition, maybe. I'm a very intuitive sort of guy. I sized you up right, didn't I?"

"Oh, yes . . ."

"The other night, New Year's Eve, when I had dinner with them. There were little looks—little looks that passed between them, across the table. Intimate little looks. I'm very sensitive to that sort of thing, you know. As a writer I have to be."

"Well, I think you're being a little *overly* sensitive in this case, Billy. Noah is such a—well, such a straight arrow, I guess you'd call him. I know, because—"

"Because why?"

"Because—well, I guess I might as well tell you this, Billy. You see, Noah *is* a terribly attractive man. And a couple of years ago—I guess I'd had a little too much to drink—I made a little kind of a pass at Noah. It wasn't a serious pass. It was just a kidding sort of pass, I was just joking with him, really, just teasing him to see how he'd react. Anyway, he just sort of walked away from me and pretended nothing happened. That's how I know that Noah would never cheat on Carol."

"Any man who could resist you would have to have a lot of willpower," he says.

"That's what I mean!" she says, a little too quickly.

"So, where is Miss Melody now?"

"Didn't Carol say she's in New Haven? With some play that's trying out?"

"But there's no play doing tryouts in New Haven now. I know, because I go to school in New Haven. At least I go to classes when I feel like it."

"You're sure there's no play there?"

"Positive. The Shubert's down the street from where I live. It's empty."

"That does seem strange. Why would she lie?"

"Exactly. And she left the same day Noah did. Funny coincidence, don't you think?"

"No, not really. It just—"

"And why did she leave the building through the basement service door, out through the back alley?"

"She *did?*"

"I run a lot in this neighborhood. Monday afternoon I happened to be turning the corner from First Avenue into Fifty-third Street, and I saw Miss Melody coming out of the alley, hurrying, carrying a suitcase. She looked as though she was sneaking away. Escaping, didn't want to be seen. I stepped into a doorway so she wouldn't see me. But she practically ran to Fifty-second and flagged an eastbound taxi."

"Well, I can't explain that unless—oh, my God!"

He lights another cigarette. "Unless what?" he says.

"I just remembered something! I was talking to Frank on the phone Monday night, and he said he'd seen somebody who looked just like Melody in the lobby of that hotel they're staying at, in Atlantic City. But when he mentioned it to Noah, Noah got—well, got all sort of *squirrelly* about it. Do you think—?"

"Of course. It's obvious they're shacking up there together."

"Oh, my God! I've got to tell Carol! Carol is my best

friend! I've got to tell Carol *now*!'' She reaches for the phone.

"Now, wait a minute," he says, holding out his hand. "Let's think this thing through. Let's not go off half-cocked."

"But, my God, this is *awful*! The girl is—that girl is Anne's age—even younger!"

"That's right. It's what's called contributing—"

"To the delinquency of a *minor*! Oh, God . . . oh, God . . ."

"Male menopause. Male midlife crisis. It happens to a lot of men Noah's age. They can't help it. But that little girl knows what *she's* doing. I can tell that little tramp's been around the block more than once."

"Oh, and Carol is always going on about what a *sweet* child Melody is. And, all along, *this* has been going on. Poor Carol! I really think one of us has got to tell Carol about this *at once!*"

"No, wait," he says. "I think we've got to be a little more subtle about this. A little more—artistic."

"Before this goes any further?"

"Ideally, from an artistic standpoint, Carol should be the last person to find out about it. And she should find out about it from a totally unexpected source. Not from someone obvious, like you or me. Georgette Van Degan?"

"Georgette Van Degan? Why her? Why should we tell her? I hardly know her. I just met her for the first time this afternoon."

"This coming-out party she's planning for Anne and her daughter. This might make her change her mind about that."

"And ruin little Anne's coming-out party? That doesn't sound very nice, Billy."

He steeples his fingers. "I'm thinking of the big picture," he says. "The artistic picture. It's my creative juices working. I'm thinking of what will make the best *story*. Carol doesn't sound too keen on the whole coming-out party idea. If Georgette pulled out, that would give Carol an excuse to pull out, too. In the long run, you'd be doing Carol a big favor. I'm just thinking out loud. I admit it's not perfect, but it might be worth a try."

"But *I'm* thinking of giving Carol a chance to slap a

separate-maintenance suit on Noah Liebling so fast he won't know what hit him! That's the kind of favor *I'd* like to do for her. There's a lot of money there, you know. Not just him, perhaps, but his mother. Carol could come out of this a very rich woman."

He winks at her. "Think she'd split it with you?"

"Why, Billy, I never thought of that. Do you think I should ask her?"

"Only kidding," he says. "You see, the one I'm trying to nail is Melody. That little tramp needs to be knocked down a peg or two."

She giggles. "Or knocked *up*? *That* would teach Noah a lesson, wouldn't it?"

"No, she's too clever to let that happen."

"But the one I'd like to nail is *Noah*. One little peck on the cheek was all I gave him. And he pulled away from me as though I'd made a major pass. I was—*insulted*, is what I was!"

"Of course you were, Beryl baby."

"Carol should never have married Noah in the first place. Her mother told her so. She told me her mother had an absolute fit when she married Noah!"

"Her mother . . ."

"An absolute fit!"

He snaps his fingers. "Her mother's the one!"

"The one for what?"

"To tell Carol what's going on. Mother would say, 'I told you so.' Where is her mother?"

"I have no idea. Some nursing home. Carol doesn't like to talk about it."

He strokes his chin thoughtfully. "I might have a way—I might be able to engineer a way—of finding out. Yes. You see, it gives this little scandal we've uncovered a certain symmetry. Years go by, but in the end Mother has the last word. Mother knows best. Thank you, Beryl baby!"

She stares at the ceiling. "The more I think about it— one little peck on the cheek was all it was. And he re- acted as if—"

He rolls over on his side and drops his cigarette into a half-filled wineglass, where it goes out with a quick sizzle. "Speaking of little pecks," he says, "and little peckers, look what's happened to my little pecker. It suddenly got big again." He rolls onto his back, smiling at her and stroking himself. "Take a look at this. You ready for another little go-around, teacher?"

"Oh, Billy, do you really think we *should*? After what you've told me, it seems sort of—"

"Look at it this way. Why should those two be the only ones who are getting any?" He jumps to his feet and stands in front of her, displaying himself. "You like a little S and M?"

"Well, I don't know. I've never really—"

"Nothing too kinky. But I've got a nice pair of police-issue handcuffs."

She is giggling again. "You mean like—*Gerald's Game*?"

He laughs. "I wouldn't cuff you to the bedposts," he says. "Just hands behind your back. A lot of women really get off on domination-submission. Anyway, I didn't bring my cuffs. But maybe next time, okay? Meanwhile, I did bring this." His jacket lies across a chair, and he fishes in a pocket and produces an inhaler. "Ever try this, teacher?"

"What is it?"

"Just a li'l ole popper. Puts kind of a different spin on things." He unscrews the cap and places the inhaler first in one nostril, then the other. "Now you take a couple of good whiffs," he says, and hands her the inhaler.

She inhales, and falls quickly back across the bed. "Oh-oh-oh-oh-oh-oh!" she cries. "My star pupil!"

"Your star pupil is now your star muff-diving instructor," he says. "I'm going to do to you what Tarzan did to Jane—something he learned from the apes." And he flings himself on top of her.

"Oh-oh-oh-oh-oh-oh," Beryl says. "Oh, Billy-Billy-Billy. Oh, Billy, I love you so!"

"*Grrrrr!*" he says. "Your Billy has a big club. Get ready to go Greek!"

Now it is Thursday afternoon, and Hannah Liebling sits alone in the library of her apartment at 1000 Park Avenue. Once more she lifts his letter from her desk and reads it through again. What a strange, mysterious city New York is, she thinks. It is a city of hiding places.

Old lovers lie hidden from each other here for years, successful stowaways in their secret lairs. Her old friend Molly Bernbach once told her that she had spent ten years living in the same building as her ex-husband without realizing it, and when they finally met they didn't recognize each other. And here, all along, on West Eighth Street, less than a mile and a half away, has been living George Noville, Radioman First Class, when Hannah knew him, but now, from his letterhead, "Captain, U.S.N., Ret."

Once again, as she has been doing regularly for the past several hours, she picks up the receiver of the telephone to call him, and then quickly replaces it in its cradle in a panic. Why? What is she afraid of? It is not like Hannah Liebling to be terrified of placing a telephone call. Is she afraid that a woman's voice may answer? His letter does not say whether he ever married, or whether he has a wife living now. He merely says, "I have thought of you often, and fondly, over the years." That would not indicate a wife at the moment. And if a woman's voice answers, she could just hang up, though that seems even more cowardly. A woman's voice could belong to a maid or housekeeper. The thing to say is simply: "Is Captain Noville in?" So that is not what frightens her.

She knows exactly what it is. She is terrified of calling him because she is terrified of seeing him again. And she is terrified of seeing him again because she is terrified of seeing how he has changed, and of him seeing how she has changed. That is the only thing that frightens her.

Through the open doorway, across the entrance foyer, she can see the dining room, where her portrait hangs. When that was painted, Hannah was young and slender and pretty, and soft, and innocent, and poor. Now she is old, and heavy, and far from pretty, and hard, and tough, and rich. She can see the look of disappointment that will fall across his face. And her own look of disappointment will surely match his, because he is older than she is—eighty-eight now. No, eighty-nine. And she remembers too vividly the young sailor who put the gardenia between his teeth and danced a finger-snapping little jig on the sidewalk beneath her window. She thinks she could not bear to see that sailor now. She would proba-

bly burst into tears. And how many years has it been
since Hannah Liebling did that? More years than she
would care to count.

And, then, what would they have to say to each other?

"Hello, George."

"Hello, Hannah."

And then what after that? She picks up the receiver,
then puts it down again with a shaking hand.

She picks it up once more, but now it is Albert to the
rescue! Her majordomo has appeared at the door.

"Excuse me, madam," he says as she replaces the receiver. "Mrs. Noah Liebling is here to see you."

"Carol?" She is somewhat surprised, since it is unlike
Carol to drop by without telephoning first.

"Yes, madam."

"Please show her in, Albert," she says.

The two women exchange pecks on the cheek. "I tried
to call you, Nana," Carol says. "But your line's been
busy-busy-busy."

"Yes," Hannah says. "I've been on the phone much
of the afternoon."

"Anyway, I was at a museum meeting, so I just decided to walk over."

"Sit down, dear. Would you like a drink? A cup of
tea?"

"Nothing, thanks." She sits down in Hannah's visitor's
chair and carefully removes her gloves, finger by finger.
"Nana," she says, "I've gotten myself in a bit of a pickle.
I need your advice."

"I see," her mother-in-law says.

"That's not even quite true. I haven't gotten my*self*
into this pickle. Someone else has gotten me into it."

"I think I know," Hannah says. "I think I've been
reading about it in the newspapers. Something about a
coming-out party for Anne and this Van Degan girl."

Carol nods. "Nana, this Georgette Van Degan is like
a bulldozer! She came up with this idea, and suddenly
she was off and running with it! There doesn't seem to
be any way to stop her, and now things have gotten
completely out of hand. She keeps feeding these items
to Roxy Rhinelander!"

"We've never given coming-out parties for anyone in

this family, Carol. We've just never gone in for that sort of thing."

"I *know* that, Nana. And it certainly wasn't my idea. But my question to you is—"

"Old man Van Degan and his wife moved out of this building the same day my husband and I moved in. My husband spent the rest of his life trying to live down that insult, and now here it is again, all over the newspapers. Again."

"I remember you telling me about that, Nana, but I didn't realize it was the same family. But Georgette obviously—"

"Tell me something," Hannah interrupts. "Does Anne want this? This party?"

"Well, I think she thinks it would be a lot of fun. What girl that age wouldn't? Though I don't think she and Linda Van Degan were ever all that close. But—"

"It said in one of those stories that we had promised to supply free booze. Who promised that? You? Noah? It was certainly not I."

"*No*body promised that, Nana! That's Georgette Van Degan again. I promised nothing of the sort. And Noah doesn't even—"

"We *never* supply free booze. Not even for the worthiest of worthy causes. That's been company policy as long as we've been a company, Carol."

"I *may* have suggested that *perhaps* the company could provide the liquor at cost. But I promised her nothing."

"And we never supply liquor at cost, either. That's also a company policy."

"Well, I didn't know that," Carol says. "That's why I said 'perhaps.' But she's taken my 'perhaps' to mean—"

"What does Noah think about all this? I telephoned him on Monday, and couldn't get a straight answer out of him."

"You *did*? But Noah doesn't know a thing about any of this, Nana."

"He *doesn't*? You mean you and the Van Degan woman have been planning this—this spectacle, and you haven't even discussed it with your husband, who's going to be paying all the bills?"

Carol bites her lip. "Noah's been out of town all week,

as you know, while all this has been going on. And he's got so many other, much more important things on his mind. I didn't want to bother him with this. But now it's gotten completely out of hand."

"What things? What important things has he got on his mind?"

"Ballachulish-Fifteen? Don't you remember? He's making the presentation to the sales conference tomorrow afternoon."

"Oh, that," Hannah says.

Oh, that, Carol thinks. Noah has told her that it will cost the company between twenty and thirty million to launch and test-market a new label, and his mother is able to dismiss it with "Oh, that," Noah has devoted most of his time and energy to this for more than a year. He has agonized over it, spent sleepless nights over it. But now it is just "Oh, that."

Slowly, Hannah Liebling rises from her desk and begins moving about the room, fingering small objects as she goes—a crystal paperweight, an onyx obelisk. "The thing is," she says, "that this is all wrong from a public-relations standpoint. I've discussed this with my sister Bathy, and she agrees with me. For years, you know, Bathy was our director of advertising and public relations, and she was the best one we ever had. We both feel that the publicity your proposed party has already generated has been very bad for us. Any more publicity like this will only make it worse. You see, we've always tried to project an image of—what shall I call it? Probity. Responsibility. Respectability. Trustworthiness. 'Ingraham—the label you can trust.' That was one of our slogans. We showed a visual of the Leaning Tower of Pisa. The subliminal message was, 'You can trust the Leaning Tower of Pisa never to fall down,' The copy said, 'You can trust Ingraham never to let you down,' Bathy's famous Christmas ad. It stressed sobriety—responsibility, consideration for others. We've tried to avoid anything that would show us as frivolous, or extravagant, or show-offy. People think the Lieblings have too much money, anyway. And they think of it as dirty money, tainted money, money with the blood of bootleggers all over it. Anything we do in any public way that seems the least bit ostentatious, like the kind of party I've been reading about, simply reinforces this view in the public's mind, and that's not good for business. That's why we've tried to stay out of the society columns and the gossip columns. An article in *Fortune* or *Forbes* or *Business Week* we don't mind. But stories in Roxy Rhinelander's column are something else again. Reading things like that, the public, who are our customers, think, 'Well, what can you expect? Rich, vulgar Jews.' "

"I know exactly what you mean, Nana," Carol says. "That's why I came to see you today. To ask you how we can contain, or control, this situation."

"We? It seems to me that you've got yourself into this situation, Carol. It's up to you to get yourself out of it. Why not just tell this woman that you've changed your mind? Just tell the woman no."

"I can do that," Carol says quickly. "But there's another aspect to this that I'd like you to consider, Nana."

"Oh? And what is that, pray?"

"Truxton and Georgette Van Degan own an extremely important collection of Chinese and Japanese export porcelains. The collection was started by Mr. Van Degan's great-grandfather. His grandfather added to it enormously, and his father added even more. Right now it is one of the most important collections in the world, probably worth at least a hundred million dollars, but really priceless. The public has never seen any of it. Some of it is displayed in vitrines in the Van Degans' Fifth Avenue apartment, but most of it is in storage, gathering dust. It's such a shame—a princely collection."

"They've always been in the glass business. It stands to reason they'd collect porcelain. But what's that got to do with a coming-out party for a couple of silly *girls*?" She pronounces it *guh-uhls*.

"The museum would die to have the Van Degan collection. The museum's been after it for years, and even Mrs. Astor couldn't get them to part with it. Now, thanks to me, the Van Degans are thinking of offering at least part of it. Their lawyers are working on a gift proposal now. But there's a hitch. Mrs. Van Degan told me last night that if I didn't go along with this party, they might withdraw the gift."

"So she's blackmailing you into giving this party. No party, no porcelains."

"In a sense, yes. But there's more to it than that. For one thing, just think of how important this gift would be to the people of the city of New York, and to the museum-going public in general. And, for another, if I could be the person who got the Van Degan collection for the museum, it's almost certain that I'd be placed on the museum's board."

"You think so? That would feed your ego, I suppose."

Carol smiles. "I admit I'd be flattered to be put on the board," she says. "I've been working for the museum for nearly twenty years, after all. But I also think that if I were on the board, it would add a certain luster to the Liebling family image—the image you say you've been trying to cultivate for all these years."

Now Hannah Liebling is smiling, almost to herself, stroking the facets of the crystal paperweight with the tip of her right index finger. "Why, yes," she says softly. "Mrs. Noah Liebling, named to the board of directors of the Metropolitan Museum of Art."

"One of the country's most important cultural institutions."

Hannah chuckles. "It's something my husband would never have dared to dream of," she says. "If he could have lived to see that . . ."

"Mrs. Noah Liebling, wife of the president of Ingraham's."

Hannah throws her a quick look. "I'm still president," she says.

"I know. But someday . . ."

"Well, yes. I suppose. We'll see how things work out with this Bally-whatchamacallit business."

"Ballachulish."

"I can never remember that name. They're going to have to get a better name for it."

"They will," Carol says.

"But there's only one thing I can't figure out," Hannah says. "Why did the Van Degan woman pick *us*? Why did she pick *you*? Why didn't she pick one of her fancy friends from Roxy Rhinelander's column?"

"Probably because she and I have daughters the same age, who went to Brearley together."

"No, there must be more to it than that. There always is. Oh, I know what it is. Her husband's behind it."

"What do you mean?"

"The glass business. My husband would never buy from the Van Degans after what they did to us. But now the son's probably heard we're about to launch a new brand. There've been rumors in the street—there always are. Van Degan wants our bottling contract. It's as simple as that."

Carol feels her cheeks redden. "I suppose you have a point," she says. "I hadn't thought of that, frankly."

"That's business. In business there's always a tit for a tat, as my husband used to say."

"Then perhaps you should consider giving him that contract," she says. "In light of him giving the museum his collection. And my going on the board."

"It's worth thinking about, I admit," Hannah says. "Though Jules would be spinning in his grave."

Carol decides to press this point no further. "There's just one other thing," she says.

"What's that?"

"Noah."

"What about him?"

"When I tell him about this, as I'm going to have to when he gets home tomorrow night—flushed with triumph, I hope, after his presentation—he's not going to be very happy. I know exactly what he's going to say. He's going to say we can't afford this sort of thing."

"Why? Why would he say that?"

"The way Georgette is talking, Nana, this is going to be a very expensive party."

"How expensive?"

"I have no idea, but perhaps as much as two hundred thousand dollars. The orchestra alone is costing twenty-five thousand, and Georgette is talking about hiring a second band, a rock group in a separate tent."

"Well, money shouldn't be a problem for you, should it? Speaking of *princely* things, your husband gets paid what I'd consider a rather princely salary!"

"But we have a lot of expenses, Nana—Anne's tuition, my mother's care "

"Ah, yes. Your mother."

"Noah worries about money a lot."

"Really? How very strange!"

"And so what I was thinking, Nana," Carol says, hurrying along, "was that if you could tell him that you approve of this party, that you're in favor of it—"

"But I do not approve of it! I am not in favor of it. I think I should have made that quite clear by now."

"But if you could *say* you were, it would make Noah think about this a little differently."

"What you're saying, Carol, if I understand you correctly, is that what *I* say to your husband is more important than what *you* say to him."

"Yes. That's what I'm saying, Nana."

"Which is not the way things should be in a family, is it?"

"Perhaps not. But that's the way things are in this family, Nana. It's always been that way."

"I see," she says carefully. "And I also think, if I hear you correctly, that you're not just asking me to endorse this idea for an expensive party. You're also asking me to pay for it. Am I correct?"

Carol sits forward in her chair. "Yes," she says simply. "If you could do that, it would solve everything. Unless—"

"Unless what?"

"Unless you're ready to finally turn the company over to Noah."

"My dear young woman," her mother-in-law says, "I offered to turn the company over to Noah less than ten days ago. On New Year's Eve, at your house, in fact. I have offered to turn the company over to him repeatedly in the past—on one small condition. But he has repeatedly refused to accept that small condition."

"I know about that, Nana."

"Then perhaps if you could persuade him—"

"He'll never accept that condition, Nana."

"Why? Why not? His feelings about my sister are so irrational. They make no sense at all. He refuses to explain—"

"He feels he was betrayed by his aunt Bathy."

"Betrayed? How betrayed? What did my sister ever do to betray him?"

Carol bites her lip again. There is no point in pursuing this line of conversation, either. At this point she does not want to risk making her mother-in-law angry at her. She averts her eyes and says, "Noah's feelings about your sister are very personal ones. They're his feelings. Not mine. They have nothing to do with me."

"But they do now, don't they? They've become the only stumbling block. You see, my dear, there are a great many things about Bathy that you do not understand, and that Noah doesn't understand. There are things that only I know about, and they are things that matter deeply to this entire family. I could tell you things—but I won't, because I promised long ago that I would never tell another living soul, and if there's one thing I am, it's a woman of my word. Suffice to say that this family owes Bathy a great deal. She was treated very shabbily by this family years ago. She wasn't left a penny in my husband's will, and she should have been amply provided for. The family has a great debt to Bathy, and you will have to take my word for that. She has suffered a great loss because of us."

"What kind of debt?"

"The debt exists. That's all I'm going to say. I know it, and Bathy knows it, and she and I are the only ones who need to know. And she's been very patient about never demanding the reward she's due. Do you think you could convince your husband of that?"

"I doubt it," Carol says.

"Would you be willing to try?" She is smiling now. "After all, any grudge my son bears against my sister is a very old grudge. Surely it isn't a grudge worth bearing after all these years. Could you convince him of that? Could you convince him that any—injustice—which he may feel Bathy committed against him did not occur at all in the way he supposes it did? Could you convince him that he has nothing to forgive Bathy for—that, in fact, he has a great deal to thank her for? Could you at least convince him that it's time to let bygones be bygones? Could you convince him that what he doesn't know won't hurt him, and that what he *thinks* he knows is only a tiny fraction of the whole truth? If you could convince him of that—well, that would shed an entirely different light on things, wouldn't it? What do you say? Will you try to convince him?"

"I will try," Carol says. "But—"

"If you could do that, a great many old wrongs from the past would be set to rights."

"And, Nana, if you'll agree to go along with the party, I'll see to it that Georgette stops sending column items to Roxy Rhinelander."

"Roxy Rhinelander! I can remember when her name was Rose Ruttenberg!"

"I promise that any publicity this party gets will be more dignified, Nana. It will reflect more—what was your word? More probity."

"Now, wait a minute. I haven't agreed to anything yet. I'll agree to think about it. And you agree to try to get Noah to be kinder to Bathy. So do we have a deal on that?" She extends her hand. "As my husband used to say, doing business is just giving a tit for a tat."

"I'll try," Carol says again. "But it won't be easy."

"Good," Hannah says, and takes Carol's hand in hers. "Let's shake on it. My husband used to say that a man's handshake is worth more than his signature. I agree to think, you agree to try. And getting a Liebling—just think of it, the Booze Baron's daughter-in-law, no less!— on the Met's board of directors should be worth the effort, don't you think? And remember I warned you years ago that being a Liebling in this city was not going to be easy, Carol dear. I may not have told you everything I know about this family, but I've never lied to you."

At Mortimer's, Patsy Collingwood and Pookie Satterthwaite are in a lunchtime huddle over Perrier with lime at one of the thin tables. "Well, I've found out who Carol Liebling's supposedly best friend is," Patsy is saying. "She's somebody called Beryl Stokes, and she's supposed to be a real nitwit."

Pookie squeals, "*Beryl Stokes!* She lives at River House, too! And she is a nitwit. She and her husband are always voting for extra assessments. Everybody in the building hates her."

"Well, that doesn't mean you can't be nice to her. Why don't you have a little cocktail party for some of your River House neighbors? The Lieblings and this Stokes person. Including me, of course. And Roxy."

"Well," Pookie says hesitantly, stirring her drink with a red-lacquered fingertip, "my apartment isn't quite finished yet, you know. My furniture, which is all being hand-made in Morocco, hasn't arrived yet."

"I thought it was Majorca."

"No, Morocco."

"Well, have the party downstairs at the club."

"Well, actually," Pookie says, "Darius and I aren't members of the club."

"*Really?* I thought everybody at River House belonged to the River Club, lovey."

"They charge a little extra to belong. And, well, Darius and I—since we have the biggest apartment in the building—we just didn't feel we'd use the club that much."

"Well, do *some*thing, darling. After all, since you live at River House, you've got the inside track. I don't. And it seems like ages since you've done any entertaining, darling."

"Yes, I suppose you're right," Pookie says, but she doesn't sound convinced.

"Remember, every minute we waste is a minute that Carol Liebling and that rat Georgette will be gaining on us with the coming-out-party nonsense. The reason you and I haven't been getting any column mentions is because we haven't *done* anything. I wouldn't tell you this if you weren't my best friend."

14

Lightning

Grandmont is gone now, as you know—gone to a wrecker's ball and a developer's cupidity. A thousand little tract houses cover that lovely hillside now as part of a development called, regrettably, Morewealth Villas. Why is it that the grandest of American houses seem to fall to ruin first? Answer that riddle.

"After a war," Jules used to say, "real estate values always drop." Well, he was wrong about what happened after World War II. Soldiers, home from the war, and rich from GI loans, each wanted a little piece of suburbia, a square of lawn to mow, with a split-level house at its center with foundation plantings and a picture window and, framed in that window, the ultimate table lamp. And yet Jules Liebling hung on to Grandmont, even as he saw estates all around him being torn down and broken up into half-acre lots. After the war Grandmont became an anachronism. But then perhaps it always was.

On that particular early spring evening, it was unseasonably warm, and there was a full moon, and it reflected palely on the surface of the river below, and Hannah was out walking in the garden. The gardens of Grandmont had become her particular domain. She had supervised the design and planting of the parterres, and the beds of perennials that they contained, and now she oversaw their pruning and maintenance. As she usually did when she walked in the garden, she carried a small pair of pruning shears in one hand, and a basket over her arm to collect the cuttings, as she snipped off the occasional browned leaf, or blasted bud, or pulled the occasional weed the gardeners had missed, always paying particular attention to her dahlias, including the prize-winning white hybrid which she had developed herself, and which had been named the Hannah Sachs Liebling dahlia. Turning a corner on one of the graveled walks, she was startled to come upon a figure in dahlia white seated on a stone bench, and she let out a little cry. "Oh, it's you!" she said.

"Just me," Bathy said.

She sat down beside her on the bench. "Lovely night, isn't it?" she said.

"Yes." The night sky brightened briefly, then was dark again. "Lightning," Bathy said. "Is there going to be a storm?"

"Just heat lightning, I expect," Hannah said. "See?— there's no thunder." There was another small flash, followed by dark and silence.

"You were very quiet at dinner tonight," Hannah said.

"Was I? I'm sorry."

In fact, Hannah had noticed a change come over Bathy in recent weeks. She had become more quiet and withdrawn, not her usual bright and cheerful self. Hannah already had an inkling of what it might be, but she had waited for a moment to be alone with Bathy, like right now, and for Bathy to tell her what it was. "Is something on your mind, dear?" she asked her at last.

"Yes, there is," Bathy said. "Yes, I'm afraid there very much is."

"Something's troubling you."

"Yes. Oh, yes." She turned away from her. "Oh, Hannah, the most awful thing has happened!"

"Can you tell me what it is?"

"I don't even know how it happened. I don't think I wanted it to happen. It just—happened! It happened in Toronto, last month, when Jules and I went up to interview the new Canadian ad agency. We were celebrating the new contract, and we—"

"I see," Hannah said quietly. "I see. You made love."

"Will you ever forgive me, Hannah? He made me swear I'd never tell you, Hannah, but I had to tell you. I couldn't go on living here like this, knowing what I'd done to my own big sister, without—"

"Let's make one thing quite clear," Hannah said. "I'm never going to tell him that you told me, and you're never going to tell him that you told me, either. Let's make that solemn promise to each other right here and now."

"But what am I going to *do?* I mean, I love working for Ingraham and I—"

"What are you going to do? Nothing."

"But I can't stay here like this, Hannah, after what's happened. If Settie were still alive, I'd go to her, but—"

"Nonsense. I promised Mama on her deathbed that I'd always take care of you, and I always will. You belong right here with Jules and me."

"You mean—"

"This is not the end of the world, Bathy. Things like this have happened before in families. And they'll happen again, as long as there are men and women. But I'm not going to let you throw your life away, and your brilliant career, over what happened one night in Toronto."

"But, you see—it was—it's—oh, it's such a mess!"

"I see," Hannah said again. "I think you're trying to tell me you're in love with him."

"Yes. That's the worst part. I think I am."

"If you think you are, you are. Is he in love with you?"

She shook her head. "No," she said miserably. "I don't think Jules is in love with anybody, except—"

"Except himself? Don't say that. Jules is a very complicated man, with powerful needs. He needs love."

"I was going to say except his company. And you. If he didn't care for you, why would he make me promise never to tell you about this affair we've been having? If he didn't care for you, he'd offer to divorce you and marry me. But he'll never do that!"

"No, I suppose not."

"Because he cares so God damn much about what the God damn public thinks of the great Jules Liebling!"

"Now, Bathy, don't say that about him, either. I think it's more likely that he loves us both, but in different ways. I think that's possible, don't you? He needs us both."

"How? How does he need me?"

"I'll tell you how. He needs you because you're like the son he's always wanted, the son who'd take an interest in the business, ever since Cyril turned out to be a— disappointment to him. He needs you because you're brilliant at what you do. And now I think he also needs you for—the other thing."

"What other thing?"

"The physical side of marriage, as Mama used to call it. I'm afraid I've never been very good at that, with Jules. He still wants another son, and I've been trying to give him one. But it hasn't worked, and I think it's because he knows my heart isn't in it. But it's hard to pretend that one enjoys that sort of thing when—well, when one just doesn't."

Bathy looked at her. "Did you ever enjoy sex with Jules, Hannah?" she asked her.

"No, looking back, I suppose I really didn't."

"Ever? With any man?"

"Oh, yes. Long ago there was someone."

"What happened to him?"

"He was—inappropriate, or so Papa said. I don't want to talk about him, Bathy. It was a very unhappy time for me."

"And so you married Jules."

"He was the bird in the hand, as Mama put it. He was attractive. And very rich. And I didn't want to be a spinster. And he wanted to marry Marcus Sachs's daughter."

"For his precious respectability, I suppose!"

"That's what the family said at the time. But don't be too hard on him, Bathy. I think he also loved me. He's been a good husband!"

"You can say that even after your sister has just told you she's been sleeping with him?"

"Yes, I can say that. Jules is a good man, Bathy."

"But the sexual attraction was never there."

"Not really. I tried, though. I'm still trying, though it gets harder as the years go by. Sometimes I think that sort of attraction only happens once to a woman."

"Perhaps."

"And now it's happened to you."

She nodded. "I'd be lying if I said it hadn't," she said.

"And for the first time?"

"Oh, yes."

"A woman never forgets that first time, you know. It lives with her for the rest of her life."

"That wouldn't surprise me, Hannah."

There was a flicker of heat lightning in the sky, and the words floated into Hannah's mind: *Bathy, perhaps there's something I ought to tell you now.* . . . But she kept the words buried there, unspoken. Instead she said, "Bathy, this could be good for us both. For your career and—"

Bathy turned to her almost angrily. "Are you trying to say that I did this to try to build a fire under my *career?* Went to bed with the boss to try to get a promotion? Like a Joan Crawford movie? I'm not that stupid, Hannah. I know how to advance my career without that! I didn't set out to seduce him. And he didn't set out to seduce me. It just—happened."

"I know, I know," Hannah said soothingly. "I know how these things happen. They happen. I just meant that this is another reason why he needs you. You can satisfy him in that way. He needs us both. Perhaps we should both consider ourselves lucky. Perhaps this was inevitable."

"Lucky? Inevitable? Oh, Hannah, what strange words you use to describe this mess we're both in!"

"Why not? Where's the mess? Show me a mess. I don't see a mess. I see a solution to a lot of problems. Of course you're lucky. Jules is still a very attractive man. He needs you. You're seventeen years younger than I am. You're beautiful. You love him. I'm—well, I'm not so young, not so beautiful anymore, and child-bearing has certainly taken its toll on what was considered my best point, my figure. You can make him happier, and if he's happier, I'll be happier. We'll all be happier, as a family. Perhaps this is the best thing that could have happened to us, Bathy."

"You're saying we could—*share* him?"

"Why not? We've always been—well, closer than most sisters. Somehow, to me, this makes you seem even closer."

Bathy shivered. "I'm not sure I'm going to be able to do this, Hannah."

"Of course you can. You're a Sachs. Sachses take care of one another. Sachses can do anything. Sachses are geniuses. Descended from rabbis and scholars since the sixteenth century. Royal blood. Sachses are tough. We're not put together with flour-and-water paste."

"It won't be easy, Hannah."

"Mama used to say, 'Anything worth doing is worth working hard to do,' and Mama was only a Sachs by marriage, but it rubbed off. We'll both work, and we'll both work hard."

"How do we—begin?"

"Begin? We begin right now." She reached for her basket and her pruning shears, and rose to her feet. "Let's go find him. He's probably in the library now, having a brandy and a cigar, and probably feeling miserable with guilt—as miserable as you were when I found you sitting here. Let's make him happy, Bathy. I'll play the piano, and you can sing. He loves to hear you sing. Let's fuss over him the way he loves to be fussed over." She reached out and took Bathy's hand, but Bathy held back.

"But won't we both be just becoming—more of Jules's possessions?" she asked. "Like Mozart manuscripts?"

Hannah laughed. "We are already," she said. "And we're all in safekeeping here at Grandmont." She pulled the reluctant Bathy to her feet, and the two women started up the garden path together toward the lighted house. "We'll say we've been out strolling in the garden, looking at the heat lightning." She took Bathy's arm. "We'll act as though nothing at all has changed," she said.

"Even though everything has," Bathy said. "Even though nothing will ever be the same."

Suddenly Hannah stopped, gripping Bathy's arm. "I think perhaps there's something that I ought to tell you now," she said.

"What is it, Hannah?"

"No. Never mind. It's nothing," she said. They continued toward the house.

And later the sounds of singing and laughter could be heard from the open windows across the warm spring night, while in the moonlight the huge moon-white blooms of the Hannah Sachs Liebling dahlias nodded in the breeze.

*   *   *

If it hadn't been for that arrangement with Bathy,
Hannah thinks now, where would I be today? Who
knows? But certainly not in an apartment at 1000 Park
Avenue, with a voting majority of Ingraham's stock.
What wisdom I had then! she thinks. What tolerance.
What understanding. What forbearance. What sophisti-
cation, to propose an arrangement that was so mature,
so intelligent, so practical, so—*European!* A ménage à
trois that operated perfectly (well, almost perfectly) for
the next thirty years. How proud Mama would have
been of me—Mama, who loved intrigue, deceptions, secrets, plots. Of course, this is all baloney, she knows that
now. She acted to save her own skin, in order to have
her cake and eat it, too.

Why do you deceive yourself, lady? Why do you try
to lay at the feet of others the responsibility for what
you yourself did? Admit it now. You used Bathy, deliberately and heartlessly, to suit your own selfish purposes.
You simply went about setting up Bathy as your surrogate, your stand-in to do the dirty work you were too
cowardly to admit you didn't want to do yourself. You
hired a stunt girl to do the scenes that would have been
too rough on the star. You assigned Bathy to take your
falls for you. When you began to be afraid that your
husband would sense your indifference to his needs, and
would take a mistress anyway, you decided that Bathy
was the best choice for the job. She was the in-house
choice, the choice you could control because she was
already on the payroll. Pretty nasty thing to do, wasn't
it, grooming Bathy to be your husband's lover? But
that's what you did, old girl, old girl. And you did it
step by calculated step. Inevitable? That was not exactly
the precise word. Orchestrated would be a better one.
And the word for you? Procuress.

You were the one who planned the sleeping arrangements at Grandmont: your bedroom, sitting room, dressing room, and bath at one end of the long carpeted
upstairs hallway, Jules's at the other, and Bathy's quarters in between these two master suites. The nursery,
the children's rooms, and the servants' quarters were all
in a separate wing, approached by a separate staircase.
The three adults in the house were to be free to come

and go as they wished, in uninterrupted privacy, in that house and elsewhere:

"I have a business dinner in Washington next week, Hannah. Can you come with me?"

"Oh, Jules, you know how I dislike those things."

"But I need to entertain some congressmen, Hannah. I need a hostess."

"Then why not take Bathy? She's so amusing and decorative, and she knows so much more about the business than I do. And the experience would be wonderful for her, meeting all those senators. She'd be much better than I'd be at persuading them not to vote for more of their damned federal excise taxes. . . ."

"I have to be in San Francisco in October. Would you like to come?"

"October? No, no, Jules dear. In October I have to supervise the planting of the spring bulbs. If I'm not around, they'll get the colors of the tulips all wrong. But take Bathy with you. You know how much she gets out of these business trips of yours."

Et cetera, et cetera.

And soon it was, "I've asked Bathy to come along on the Canada trip with me. I hope you don't mind."

"Of course not, darling. It's an advertising meeting. Bathy belongs there."

At hotels they always registered separately, in separate bedrooms, often on different floors. On trains they traveled in separate compartments. On planes Jules flew first-class, and Bathy flew economy, all in the guise of probity, respectability. You could always count on Jules to be discreet, for the slightest whiff of scandal was what he dreaded most. Still, after that evening in the garden, Hannah knew the scandal was finally there, in place and running, and only Hannah held the key to that Pandora's box. Let Jules make one misstep, and Hannah would threaten to release all the ills of his world.

Piously, she had tried to tell herself, tried to convince herself, that she was really doing all this out of her consideration for Jules. This was all for Jules's happiness. He wanted, needed—so she tried to make herself believe—a younger woman's warm and passionate body, and so—out of the boundless generosity of her heart—

she had led Bathy to be sacrificed before the altar of
the great Jules Liebling.

This was all a lie, of course. It is interesting to see
how far human beings can go to deceive themselves
about their true motives. The truth was a little more
stark. Jules's happiness had nothing to do with it. The
fact was that she would stop at nothing to keep her
husband and his money, for Jules and his money provided the only toehold left in life for her. Without Jules
and his money, where would she go? Without Jules and
his money, who would she be? Cast adrift from Jules
and his money, where would she land? She had grown
far too accustomed to the things Jules and his money
could buy. She had grown far too accustomed to being
a rich man's wife. As she approached middle years, that
rich man's money had become the anchor to which the
ship of her life was secured. Hannah might have tried
to deny that to herself then, but she admits it now. As
her marriage entered its second decade, she had grown
increasingly fearful of losing that golden anchor.

Try to get rid of me, she would tell him, and I will
take Bathy with me, and then where will you be? She
is part of the package, part of the deal you made when
you bought me.

Try to marry Bathy, and I will spill the beans about
what has been going on, and you, Mr. Respectability,
will discover what a real Liebling family scandal is all
about. Try to mess with me, Mr. High-and-Mighty, Mr.
Probity, and the first person I'll go to will be someone
like Roxy Rhinelander, and smear your precious name
all over town.

And so, that moonlit night in the garden, Bathy's news
seemed to Hannah almost like a blessing, the answer to
a prayer. Now, if she could just produce another son for
Jules, the blessing would be complete. Her final obliga-
tion to her husband would be paid. The anchor of her
life would be set even more securely. She could never
become unmoored. With a son Jules would remain teth-
ered to her for the rest of his life, and she would be free
at last.

That night in her dressing room, as she sat before her
mirror creaming her face, preparing for bed, there was
a tap on her door. "Come in!" she called out airily. It

was Jules in his dressing gown, and as she looked up at his reflection in the mirror, his expression was serious, almost solemn, as though embarrassed by his mission. "Shall we try again tonight?" he said a little hoarsely. "To make another son?" "Of course, darling," she said with a bright laugh. "Why not?" Outside, the heat lightning flickered palely through the drawn window hangings. Why not, indeed? With the way her luck was running, this might be one of the last times she'd have to do it.

And yet when she remembers that night now, she recalls approaching the chore in a different spirit. This was what her mother had described as a woman's wifely duty to her husband, her cross to bear. But that night it didn't seem like that at all. Knowing that she now knew his and Bathy's secret gave her a certain sense of power. She no longer felt submissive. She was in control and, wonder of wonders, she'd even felt herself beginning to enjoy it a little. Is it possible that, in the middle of it, she actually cried out, "I love you, Jules"? It is possible. Life is filled with such conundrums.

And when Noah was born nine months later, she thought of this baby as a special gift from Bathy. Bathy owed this to her.

Owed? Yes, owed. Bathy owed everything to her, her whole life. But did she owe Bathy nothing in return? No, nothing, except, perhaps, the truth. . . .

"You must simply forget that Bathy is your daughter," her mother had said to her. "You must simply drive it from your mind. She is your *sister*. It has been made *official*."

"But couldn't I tell her—someday?"

"Never!"

"Why not, Mama?"

"Because if she ever knew, she would never be able to find a decent husband. No decent man would have her. She would die a spinster, the worst thing that can happen to a woman."

And so she had kept her promise, and now Bathy would die a spinster anyway.

"Just forget she's your daughter. Drive it from your mind. It will be the easiest thing in the world to do."

But of course it was not the easiest thing in the world

to do. It was impossible to do. There was no way she
could ever drive it from her mind, no way she could
simply forget it. It was there, in Hannah's mind, indelibly
imprinted, every waking moment of her days, and often
in her dreams at night. At times in the past she has
thought of telling Bathy in her will: "To my beloved
daughter Bathsheba Sachs, I bequeath . . ." But that
seemed too cowardly, to tell Bathy the truth from her
grave. Which was worse, clinging to a painful secret or
breaking a promise? It is another conundrum, all the
more difficult when the secret and the promise are the
same thing. And now, perhaps, it no longer matters. Too
much time has gone by. Too many opportunities have
been missed. It is too late. Still, Hannah reminds herself,
everything you did to Bathy years ago, every way you
used her, every lie you told her, she was—and is, and
always will be—at the bottom of things, your daughter.
Forget that. Drive that from your mind. But it's useless
even to try. Even helping Bathy and Jules become lovers
didn't help. It was supposed to help, but it didn't.

Hannah is thinking all these thoughts as she wanders
through the empty rooms of the vast apartment—empty
now, for her servants have the half day off. There is
Orion on the ceiling, chasing the Pleiades endlessly
across the heavens. There are the twin Steinways, the
golden harp, the Stradivarius quartet, the Mozart manuscripts. But of all the treasures money can buy, the greatest is power, and power comes from need. "The secret
of a successful business is making a product people
need," Jules used to say. "People need booze, and so I
sell it to 'em." She is in the entrance hallway now, where
the curving staircase used to lead up to the floor above,
where Cyril lives now, and where God only knows what
goes on. Next door, in the library, hangs the Sargent
portrait of her father. "Would you be proud of me,
Papa, for what I did?" she asks him now. "Or would you
be ashamed?" The answer is merely Papa's steady gaze.

What I did, she thinks, was to create a perfect circle
of dependency and need, with myself at the center of it.
Bathy needed me to keep her secret for her, and to keep
Jules, and to keep her job. Jules may have needed
Bathy, but I made sure he needed me more. Noah needs

me, and I've made sure he goes on needing me. Now Noah's wife needs me, and so does their daughter. Ruth needs me to protect her from herself, and Cyril needed me to protect him from his father, and he still needs me because he wants to inherit this apartment. The need for me goes on and on, I've made sure of that. *Oh, how we all need you, Nana Hannah!* their angry faces seem to scream at her. Is there anything more rewarding to a woman than seeing she is needed by every life she touches? Nothing. And is there anything more shameful than knowing the heavy prices she has made them all pay for needing her so?

Jules's portrait in the dining room frowns down on her now. She asks him, "Did you ever know how scheming I was? Did you ever know I was ready to blackmail you to keep you? Will you ever forgive me? At least I gave you Noah." Naturally, there is no reply.

But I didn't give you Noah as a gift to anyone but myself, did I? He was my insurance policy, my secret weapon, my hostage with a heavy ransom on his head. And there were worse injustices than that. As all these memories, trapped like hapless insects in the cobwebs of Hannah Liebling's mind, struggle to free themselves, she sees the inequities and contradictions. Hannah, who forsook her marriage, still got to keep the husband she didn't love. Bathy, who did love him, couldn't marry him, and never fell in love again. By rights Noah should have been Bathy's child, but Hannah got him. Hannah is rich, Bathy is poor. Bathy was told the biggest lie, and yet Bathy is the only one who really doesn't need Hannah anymore. Is that why she wants to bring Bathy back into the company? To make Bathy need her again? Because right now Bathy is the one who is free, while Hannah, who wanted freedom, remains enslaved, chained to the lies of the past.

Nice going, old girl, she tells herself. You did it all. And what have you got to show for it? Mozart manuscripts. And a heavy heart.

The telephone rings, and Hannah answers it.

"Hannah," he says, "it's George."

"George . . ."

"Your message was on my answering tape. I'd really like to see you again, Hannah. . . ."

*   *   *

In the apartment at River House, she lies sprawled across the bed, but even in this decidedly compromised position she looks up at him adoringly as he rebuttons himself into his shirt and trousers. "You're so wonderful for me, Billy," she is saying to him dreamily. "You've taught me so many different things."

"Oh?" he says, suddenly interested again. "What sort of things?"

"You've taught me to rethink my whole life," she says. "My needs, my priorities. My desires. I've decided to pay more attention to the *me* in me from now on. I'm not going to let other people walk all over me anymore. I'm tired of living my life for other people. I've decided to set out on a new course in life and discover my true self. And it's all thanks to you, Billy darling."

"Well, you're quite welcome, I'm sure," he says with a little bow.

"You've helped to unmask the real woman in me, Billy. I'm a whole woman now."

He grins down at her. "If a little bondage has done all that," he says, "maybe I'll leave you like this. Maybe I won't unlock the cuffs."

A brief look of fear crosses her face. "Now, Billy, don't tease me," she says. "Please don't tease me, darling. Unlock me now. I'm getting a cramp in my shoulder."

He has actually considered doing this, leaving her like that. It is an amusing picture: Beryl Stokes left naked in her bedroom, shackled, with her hands pinned behind her back in police-issue handcuffs. Could she dial 911 with her nose or with her toes? And how would she explain her unusual situation to the rescue squad when it arrived? With her hands pinned behind her, would she even be able to lift a telephone receiver from its cradle? With her teeth perhaps? She would probably be able to operate a doorknob, by backing into it. And he has the uproarious mental vision of Beryl creeping, naked, in the handcuffs, out into the elevator lobby, pushing a button and confronting one of River House's notoriously haughty elevator men. Or making her way to a next-door apartment and kicking—or knocking with her head—on a neighbor's door to be let in. And then trying to explain what had been going on. She certainly wouldn't dare tell the truth. And then a locksmith being called. The picture of all this is so hilarious that he laughs out loud.

"Now, darling, no more teasing. Unlock me now."

"Get down on your knees and beg," he says.

She slides sideways off the bed and kneels in front of him. "Please, darling," she says.

"Now give me a nice lick, and promise to be a good puppy dog."

She licks his trouser leg. "I promise to be a good puppy dog," she says.

He pats her head. "Nice doggie," he says. "Nice doggie. Say bow-wow-wow."

"Bow-wow-wow," Beryl says.

He fishes for the key in his trouser pocket and unlocks the handcuffs. After all, she could still be of some use to him.

She stands up, rubbing her wrists. "Oh, look," she says, "you've hurt your hand. Did that happen when we were—fooling around just now? I know we both got—a little rough."

"That happened several days ago. Slammed a car door on my hand."

"Ooh, poor baby. Look, it's still swollen." She reaches out and touches his hand. "Does it still hurt?"

"Hey, cut it out!" he says sharply, pulling his hand away from her. "Now look what you've done! You've made it start bleeding again, bitch!"

"Ooh, I'm so sorry, darling," she says.

He licks the blood from his palm. "I've gotta go," he says.

"Will you—will you be back, my darling?"

"I dunno."

"Oh, please, Billy."

"Well, maybe. When's your husband get home?"

"Tomorrow night. But not till quite late. Nine, ten o'clock, at the earliest."

"Well, we'll see."

"I'll be here alone all day, Billy."

"I said we'll see."

"Where do you stay in New York?"

"Yale Club."

"You could—spend the night here," she says hesitantly.

"Can't do that. Things to do."

"I'll call you in the morning, then," she says.

"No, don't call me. I'll call you. Or write me a letter."
She reaches for her robe. "I'll see you to the door,"
she says.

"No, I'll let myself out," he says, and he is gone.

But when he reaches the elevator lobby, he does not
push the elevator call button. Instead he heads quickly
down the hallway toward a lighted EXIT sign and the
service stairway. He is counting on two things. It is
Thursday afternoon, and Thursday afternoons in Manhattan are usually the maids' afternoons off. Also, he
knows that Tuesday and Thursday afternoons are when
Carol Liebling works as a volunteer for the museum. So
the first thing he is counting on is that the apartment
will be empty. He is also counting on the good possibility
that the service entrance, which opens into the kitchen—
the Lieblings' apartment has the same floor plan as the
Stokeses'—will be unlocked. He leaps up the metal staircase two steps at a time. With luck, good use will also
be found for his bleeding hand!

He tries the door. Unlocked. He opens it, and steps
quickly inside, and pauses, listening. Silence. There is a
penciled note to Carol on the kitchen table, a good sign.
The maid is out. The first room he checks is the maid's
room, just off the kitchen. He opens the door cautiously.
Empty. Then, moving fast and on tiptoe, he checks all
the other rooms, and is satisfied that he is alone in the
apartment. Now, still moving swiftly, he goes about his
other work.

He finds the thing he wants, in Carol's desk in the
library, almost immediately, but there is still much more
to do. He goes through the apartment, room by room,
starting from the back of the apartment and moving
toward the front, doing his work thoroughly, systemati-
cally. Order is of the essence here. Ah, Melody's room!

It takes him no more than fifteen minutes to complete
what he has to do. He then takes one last look around
to assure himself that his work is complete. Suddenly

the telephone rings, and he stops dead in his tracks. The phone rings twice, a third time, and a fourth. Then he hears a click as the answering machine picks up, and he listens as a woman's voice says, "Carol, darling, it's Georgette. Give me a tinkle, sweetie, as soon as you can. It's desperately important. Bye-eeee."

The sound of another human voice in the apartment has managed to spook him, and he rushes back through the rooms to the kitchen, lets himself out, remembering to push the button on the spring lock so the door will lock behind him, and runs down the stairs again to Beryl's floor. He presses the elevator call button, and is still out of breath when the car arrives.

"Taxi, sir?" the elevator man asks him.

He has regained his composure. "Yes, please," he says.

Riding back to River House in her own taxi, Carol is thinking: Is it really such a far-fetched idea—me, Carol Dugan Liebling, being invited to serve on the board of trustees of the Metropolitan Museum of Art? Me, Carol Dugan Liebling of Rumney Depot, New Hampshire, who always wanted to know, but never actually did meet, the glamorous McClaren sisters? Yes, it is far-fetched. It is utterly outrageous. And yet it is not impossible. Nothing is really impossible if you have a plan. And energy.

To serve on the board of trustees of the Met. There are only thirty-five members, and of course Carol knows who all of them are. Two have announced their plans to retire in June. They will need to be replaced. A third member, Brooke Astor, though still going strong, is already well past her ninetieth birthday.

To serve on the Met's board of trustees is nothing short of gaining the absolute apex of social, intellectual, and artistic position in the United States of America. Talk about cachet! There is absolutely nothing to equal it. To serve on the Met's board is to help preside over a combination of the Vatican, Versailles, the Sultan's Court, and the Cave of Ali Baba. It is to follow in the footsteps of people like Frederick W. Rhinelander, Henry Gordon Marquand, J. P. Morgan, Horace Havemeyer, and any number of Rockefellers. The public impression of the Met trustee is of a person of high and privileged rank, moving in a serene and elegant world of impeccable manners, one devoted to the encouragement of beauty and taste and the public weal. What would having a Liebling on the board do for the public's perception of Ingraham brands? Hannah had been quick to see it.

But it is an impossible notion. Carol had known this when she threw it out to Hannah, almost in desperation, as a bargaining chip. But now, as her taxi waits for a light on the street of dreams, Park Avenue, she thinks: Is it?

Being on the Met's board has always been about money, but it has been about Old Money, about money that has been aged and refined by time, like good whiskey, with all the rough, raw edges worn off the fortunes that were made by those early robber barons, who were never accused—what is Hannah's word?—of probity. The Lieblings' money is barely one generation old. Still, it is money, and there is quite a lot of it.

The taxi moves forward, and Carol asks herself: Do I want the cachet of trusteeship for myself? Oh, yes, she thinks. I'd be a liar if I tried to deny it. But I want it also for other reasons. I want it for Noah, and for Noah's family. And I want it because I want to see the Van Degan porcelains at the Met.

Georgette Van Degan has been trying to manipulate me, and I am not a woman who enjoys feeling herself being manipulated, particularly by another woman. She has come up with this notion of a party for the girls, which nobody else particularly wants, because her husband wants the contract to manufacture the bottles for Ingraham's new label. How much would that contract be worth to Truxton Van Degan? She has no idea, but she supposes it would be worth quite a bit—particularly if the label is a hit, since Ingraham purchases its bottles on a royalty based on sales—the greater the sales, the higher the royalty percentage. And what if Ingraham were to offer to purchase bottles for all its labels from Van Degan Glass? How much would that be worth to Mr. Truxton Van Degan? She will have to discuss all this with Hannah, of course.

I can be a manipulator, too, she thinks with a smile,

as her taxi turns left into Fifty-second Street and her plan forms in her mind. After all, as old Jules Liebling used to say, doing business is just a tit for a tat.

I'll tit if you'll tat, Georgette, she thinks.

15

Piss-assed Drunk

". . . And so now," he is saying, "before we all adjourn to the social room next door, to sample Mr. Angus Kelso's whiskey—*and* his fresh springwater—I just have one more announcement to make. Our company will award a prize of ten thousand dollars to the individual who can come up with the perfect name for this whiskey and this water. Obviously, we can't call it Ballachulish— nobody would know how to spell it, much less pronounce it. So we need the *perfect* name. This contest, incidentally, is open to anyone connected with our company, from the boys in the mail room on up, and husbands, wives, and even children over the age of eighteen can submit entries. All entries should be submitted by the first of March. Then, to keep on schedule, we'll need three months to work up an advertising and promotion campaign. Three more months to test-market, and then the plan is to introduce the label nationally right after Labor Day, in time for the holiday season. Thank you all . . . and now let's go next door and try some Ballachulish. I think you're going to like it."

Seated cross-legged on the sofa with the script in her lap, Melody claps her hands. "Perfect!" she cries. "Absolutely word perfect. You won't need the script. It'll go over so much better if it seems extemporaneous."

He winks at her. "I don't have your theatrical training," he says. "What if I get stage fright? Forget my lines?"

"You won't," she says. "But let's go through it one more time, from the top. Remember—look straight out at the audience."

"Okay. 'For me, it all began in the tiny Scottish . . .' " He presses the remote control for the slide projector, but just then there is a knock on the door. The two exchange quick looks, and Noah looks at his watch. It is nearly ten o'clock. "Who is it?" he calls out.

"It's me. Frank. Can I come in a minute?"

Melody whispers, "I'll hide in the bedroom. If he needs to use the bathroom, have him use the one off the kitchen."

"Hold on a sec," Noah calls back, and Melody tiptoes out of the room and silently closes the bedroom door behind her.

Noah goes to the door, which is on the chain, and opens it.

"I know you had your sign up, Do Not Disturb," Frank says. "But I gotta talk to you, Noah. Jeez, I gotta talk to somebody, Noah. Can I come in?"

"Sure, Frank." He turns off the slide projector. "Just going through my Ballachulish pitch for tomorrow afternoon."

"I need a drink," Frank says.

Noah studies his friend, who looks a little windblown. "My old man used to say that there's a difference between a man who says, 'I'd like a drink,' and a guy who says, 'I need a drink.' It looks like you might have had a few already, Frank."

"Okay, cut the sermons, buddy. I still need a drink."

"Ballachulish okay? I've got quite a lot on hand, as it happens."

"Whatever you got," Frank says.

"I'll join you," Noah says. He steps into the kitchen and fixes drinks for them both. When he returns to the sitting room, a glass in each hand, Frank is slumped on the sofa, staring at the opposite wall.

Noah hands him his drink. "Well, what's up, Frank?" he says. "You look a little—well, not quite in the pink."

"Lousy," he says. "Fuckin' lousy." He takes a deep swallow of his drink. "Yeah, this is good stuff. This is really good stuff. Be a hit, I can guarantee, buddy."

Noah sits in one of the club chairs across from him. "So? What's wrong, Frank?"

Frank Stokes stares at his shoes. "Jeez," he says, "you're not gonna believe this. I can hardly believe it myself. It's Beryl."

"Beryl? What's the matter with Beryl?"

"She called a coupla hours ago. She wants a divorce."

"Well!" Noah says, and for a moment that is all he can think of to say. Then he says, "That's a hell of a note. I mean, I thought you two were—well, pretty happy."

"That's what I thought, too," Frank says miserably. "I thought so, too. That's why this has hit me like—like a ton of bricks. Ton of bricks. But that's what she says she wants. A divorce."

"Any idea why, Frank?"

Frank looks up at him. "That's the thing," he says. "I don't. She says things like—like I just don't do it for her anymore. She says I've failed to recognize her needs. She says she needs to rediscover the child within her. Jeez, I thought she was trying to tell me she was pregnant, for God's sake, when she told me that! She says it means she needs to get back in touch with her real self. She says she needs to remake contact with her center, whatever the hell *that* means. She says she needs more personal space. How can she need more personal space than in an apartment at River House? She says she needs to vent."

"Sounds like she might be seeing some sort of shrink. Has she been?"

"Not that I know of! Wouldn't I know it if she were? Wouldn't I have been paying the bills for it?"

"Well, I just don't know, Frank," he says, sipping his drink.

"Anyway, she wants me to move out of River House. Wants me to be out by tomorrow night. She's gonna pack my things. Wants me out. Move to University Club. Someplace like that."

Noah takes another swallow of his drink. "Now, I'd be a little careful about that," he says. "At least until you've talked to a lawyer. Somewhere I read that in a divorce, if one party moves out on the other, it can be considered abandonment. She could claim ownership of the apartment, and that apartment is worth a hell of a lot of money, as I'm sure you know."

"Yeah. I know."

"So don't give in to her on that one, Frank. You and Beryl own that apartment jointly. You've got as much right to be there as she does, at the moment. So don't move out. Move to the guest room. At least until you've talked to a lawyer."

"But the thing is—why? Why does she want this? All of a sudden, like this. Why?"

"You still love her, Frank?"

"Hell—yes! Sure! Of course I still love her!" He rattles the ice cubes in his empty glass. "Mind if I have another?"

Noah stares at his own glass. "This stuff we're drinking is one-oh-five proof," he says. "So I'd take it a little easy, Frank. This is old Angus's private stock."

"Skip the lectures, Noah. Tonight I feel like getting good and drunk. Okay?"

"Okay." He rises to refill their glasses.

"You ask me, do I still love her," Frank says when he returns. "Christ, you never knew her, Noah. When I first met her, I mean. When I first met her, she was so sweet. So pretty. So innocent. A virgin, too. She taught school, you know. Grammar school kids. She was like a little grammar school kid herself. Naive." He wipes a tear from his eye. "You see, that's the thing, Noah. She thought I was big stuff. I mean, I had this great job. Making lots of money She was real—I mean, she was like real *impressed* with me. Maybe that's the thing. You think so, Noah?"

"I'm not quite sure I follow you," he says.

"I mean, maybe she wasn't cut out for this kind of life. People like you. Your family. Rich people. River House. I mean, maybe she should have stayed a little spinster grammar school teacher. She'd have been happier maybe. You think that's it?"

"Maybe." Noah nods absently. "Maybe."

"Or you think maybe there's maybe another guy?"

"I dunno," Noah says. "What do you think?"

"I dunno, either. But the thing is, Noah—did she ever mention anything to Carol? About some other guy. I mean, sometimes women tell each other these things. Carol ever mention anything to you?"

"No. But it's been a couple of days since I talked to Carol."

"I mean, I know that sometimes Beryl can be—well, a little bit flirtatious. With other guys."

"Yeah."

"You noticed that?"

"Yeah, I've noticed it."

"She ever try to come on to you?"

Noah says nothing, merely stares at the drink in his hand.

"You mean she did?"

"Yeah. Once. I didn't take it seriously. She'd had a few drinks."

"That's what I mean. There was never anything serious about it. It was just Beryl being flirtatious. Just Beryl being Beryl. So what do you think?"

"I think—" he begins, and breaks off. "A beryl is a semiprecious stone," he says.

"What do you mean by that?"

"Hell, I don't know what I meant by that. It just popped out."

"You mean you don't like Beryl?"

"I sure as hell don't like what she's doing to you right now," he says.

"But, Noah, this is serious business. She's packing my things. She's moving me out!"

"But I thought you weren't going to do that, Frank. At least until you've talked to a lawyer. She can't force you out of your house. There's no way she can—"

"Shit," he says. "I guess it doesn't matter. It's still a hell of a way for me to have to go home tomorrow night. All my things packed."

"I think you ought to call your lawyer first thing in the morning, Frank."

"Yeah." He wipes another tear from his eye. "Like a ton of bricks," he says.

The two men sit in silence for a while, nursing their drinks.

"Use your john," Frank says, rising a little unsteadily.

"Use the one off the kitchen," Noah says quickly.

He uses Frank's absence to fill his drink, a little darker this time. Somehow he feels things are spinning out of control. Bring it back, he tells himself. Bring it back under control.

"You ever cheat on her, Frank?" he asks as Frank comes back into the room.

"Never. I swear to God I've never cheated on her, Noah, not once in twelve years of marriage. Oh, I've thought about it, of course. I wouldn't be normal if I hadn't thought about it, I mean. And I've had opportunities. I wouldn't lie to you and say I haven't had opportunities, when it would've been a pretty easy thing to do. But I've never done it, Noah. I swear to God."

"Maybe it would be better if you had."

"What d'you mean by that?"

"Hell, I don't know what I mean by that. Maybe you'd feel better about what's happening now is what I mean. The present circumstances is what I mean."

The two sit down again and sip their drinks, and another silence falls.

"And no kids," Noah says at last.

"Never wanted any. She said she'd had enough of kids when she was a schoolteacher. Seen how tough they were to raise. In today's world. Kids get promiscuous real young these days."

"They do?"

"Oh, yeah."

Then Noah says, "So how does it make you feel, Frank? Knowing that you've never cheated on your wife. Does it make you feel—proud?"

"Yeah," he says. "Yeah, I guess it makes me feel proud of myself for having resisted the temptation."

"Lead us not into temptation. That's what the Christian prayer says."

"Right! So what about you, Noah? You ever cheated on Carol?"

"Let's have another drink," Noah says, rising to collect their glasses.

"Damned good scotch. You got a winner here, buddy. So answer me. You ever cheated on Carol? You've been married longer than I have."

"Yes," he says, pouring the whiskey, splashing a little on the countertop as he does so.

"You make it sound like it was kind of recent."

"Do I? I didn't mean to make it sound that way."

Frank smiles slightly. "Was it that Jackie from the Louisville office? She looked like she was trying to put the make on you at the kickoff cocktail party the other night."

Noah laughs softly. "No, it wasn't Jackie from Louisville," he says.

"But seriously, Noah. That's the thing about you, you see. I mean, you're a really nice-looking guy. Me? Well, hell, I know I'm no Robert Redford. Losing my hair. Gut's not as flat as it used to be. But you, you've kept yourself in great shape. So you've probably had a lot more opportunities than I have—not that I haven't had quite a few opportunities. Just last night, in fact. Hooker at the bar. And your family owns this company. That makes a difference, too, in the way women look at you."

"You think it does, Frank?"

"Hell, yes! That sort of thing turns women on. I've heard a lot of women say you turn them on. Why, I bet there's not a woman works for this company who wouldn't hop into the sack with you if you asked them to—including Edith, your secretary."

"Aw, Edith's an old maid."

"What's that got to do with it? I'm talking about the way women are when it comes to wanting to hop into the sack with the executive v.p., with the boss's mother. I mean son."

Noah studies his friend's worried, homely-handsome face. "Well, maybe," he says at last. "You know you're very loyal, Frank. That's a fine quality you have. You're a very loyal human being. Someday you're going to be executive v.p., Frank—you know that? Beryl is damned lucky to have you, if you ask me. And if she's really serious about this divorce business, she's throwing over a damned good thing. She's behaving like a goddamned fool, and you can tell her I said so."

"Maybe, but you see, this is what's thrown such a curve at me. Knowing I've never cheated on her and now finding out she's been cheating on me."

"But you don't *know* that, Frank," he says, handing him his drink. "You don't actually know that, do you?"

"What else could it be?"

"A lot of things. Sometimes women—women and men, too, I guess—just get tired of a relationship. The old fire just fizzles out. And when the flame dies—"

"Smoke gets in your eyes. That's from a song." He brushes his fingertips along the skin under his eyes once more.

"Maybe it's time to try courting her again. Have you thought about that?" But somehow his words sound loose and hollow and without conviction. "Hell, don't listen to me," he says. "I don't know what I'm talking about. Talk to a lawyer."

Frank shakes his head slowly back and forth. "She says her mind's made up," he says. "She says she wants no further discussion on the subject. Those were her exact words. No further discussion. I'm to move out of the apartment. That's it. Jeez!"

Noah sighs. "Well, it's a helluva note," he says. "It's a helluva note, all right." He takes another swallow of his drink and stares darkly into his glass again. The whiskey is not taking him where he wanted to go tonight. It is not being his friend. In the odd evening stillness of this anonymous hotel suite, with the garish anonymity of this Atlantic City hotel furniture, flocked-velvet wallpaper, swagged window valences trimmed with hundreds of fluffy, puffy little cherry-sized red nylon balls, with his old friend Frank sitting there, he is just not going where he wanted to go. Where was that? The old days. The memory of college conviviality, and what it was like to be young and drunk in the places where they all used to go to be young and drunk together—cobwebby places with dust and dim lights, with initials carved in tabletops with Swiss army knives, or traced on ceilings with candle smoke, places with beer labels pasted on windowpanes, places noisy with talk and the clatter of glassware and good times, and singing, places that smelled of beer and piss, and then the long walks home afterward past the lighted doorways of the dorms in winter, or the longer, wilder rides into the night with his friends on their bikes. And the easy sex, with your rolled-up pants to prop up her ass on the grass. Loretta, Lorena, Louella, Louisa, whoever you were. But all those places and people have eluded him tonight. Instead, he is filled now with an infinite sadness for both Frank and himself. Loretta-Lorena-Louella-Louisa was no more than seventeen years old at the time. And there is another seventeen-year-old girl waiting for him now beyond that bedroom door in this piss-elegant Atlantic City hotel suite. "Shit," he says. "They wanted the old man to give them free booze. That's all they wanted."

"Who? What're you talking about?"

"Fraternity brothers. Dear old Delta Chi Epsilon."

"I bet it's a younger guy," Frank says. "It's gotta be, don't you think? A guy with a full head of hair and a flat belly. Don't you think? That's what Beryl used to like. My flat belly."

"Hell, I don't know what to think," he says angrily.

"Don't bite my head off, buddy!" Frank says.

"Sorry. I'm getting piss-assed drunk, and all you can talk about is your flat belly."

"Ha-ha. I was piss-assed drunk when I got here, and now I'm more piss-assed drunk."

"So fix yourself another drink. We're both gonna get piss-assed drunk. To celebrate."

"Celebrate what?"

"Not the word I meant. I meant commiserate. With you for the loss of your flat belly, and with me for my fall from grace."

Frank stands up carefully, goes to the bar, and splashes more whiskey in his glass.

"There's more scotch in the cabinet under the sink. More in a storeroom downstairs. Lots and lots. Cases and cases. Plenty of scotch."

From the kitchen, Frank says, "You know you've been acting kind of funny these past few days. I guess you know you've been acting kind of funny."

"Funny? Funny how?"

"Sticking to yourself. Do Not Disturb signs on your door."

"Presentation. Been working on this goddamned presentation. For the goddamned meeting tomorrow afternoon."

"It's damned good stuff, I'll tell you that much."

"Yeah. Top me up while you're at it." He holds out his half-empty glass. "More's under the sink."

"So how many times you cheated on Carol? Lots of times?"

He shakes his head. "Uh-uh," he says.

"So how many times?"

"Once."

"You only cheated on Carol once? Just one time?"

"Just one girl. Woman. Girl."

"Carol find out about it?"

"Uh-uh."

"You're lucky. They usually do. Wives."

"You think so?"

"They notice little things. That's one reason I never cheated on Beryl. I knew she'd find out about it if I did. Beryl's smart."

"You saying Carol's not so smart?"

"Hell, no. I'm not bad-mouthing Carol. I'm crazy about Carol, you know that. But, you know, Beryl was a schoolteacher and all that."

"I thought she was just a teaching substitute."

"Yeah, but it takes a lot of higher education even to be a substitute." He hands Noah his glass. "Beryl's got an M.A."

"So does Carol!"

"Quit biting my head off! Boy, you're a bundle of nerves tonight, aren't you? You're as jumpy as a hen with ticks. All I said was you're lucky—"

"Forget it. It's the goddamned presentation tomorrow. And I'm taking my nerve medicine." He takes a swallow of his drink. "You ever been impotent, Frank?"

"No . . ."

"If you ever are, this stuff will cure it," he says.

"So how did you feel about cheating on Carol?"

"Feel?" he says. "Feel?" He is staring into his glass again.

"Yeah, besides feeling lucky she didn't find out about it."

"Frank," he says at last, "am I your best friend?"

"I think so."

"Are you my best friend, Frank?"

"I hope so."

"Okay. Remember the first day we got here, the girl who was sitting in the lobby you thought looked like—"

"Like that Melanie, your daughter's friend."

"Melody. Her name is Melody. Her mother heard a song. That was her."

"You mean—oh, *Jesus*!" He sinks back into the armchair. "Jeez, Noah—she's just a little girl!"

"That's right." I have betrayed myself, he thinks, and I have betrayed Carol, and now I have betrayed Melody. And why am I hoping that, behind that closed door, she is listening to all this? But I am. Listen to me, Melody. I'm speaking the truth.

"You brought her here to sales conference? But you know the rules—no wives, no—"

"Don't tell me about rules, Frank. I wrote the rules."

"Jeez. Then that Estelle was right!"

"Estelle? Who's Estelle?"

"That hooker I told you about. In the bar. She works here at the hotel as a maid. She said you had a young girl in your room. She said she walked in and saw a girl typing. She said she found a woman's things in the dresser drawers. She said the next day when she came in there was a girl singing in the shower. She said— Jesus, Noah, she's not still *here,* is she?"

Noah says nothing, merely stares at his glass.

"Jeez, Noah! Jeez! How did you get involved with her?"

"It doesn't matter how, does it? What matters is I did."

"Oh, Jeez, Noah!"

"That's why we're sitting here getting drunk. That's why I am, anyway."

"What you just told me has sobered me up. Jeez, Noah, what if the girl blabs? If the girl blabs, you could be in—"

"She won't blab."

"How can you be sure? If she does, her parents could—"

"She won't blab. But that makes me a real bastard, doesn't it? So let's drink to me being a real bastard."

"Jeez, Noah. What are you going to *do*?"

"Do? What is there to do? Except sit here and be a bastard and get drunk. The worst bastard is a drunk bastard, and so I guess you could say I'm the worst kind of bastard there is."

"Jeez, Noah. I don't know what to say. What if Carol finds out?"

Again he says nothing.

"Don't ever tell Carol, Noah. Carol would kill you! Don't ever tell anybody else about this, Noah."

"Still, I'm kind of glad I told you," he says.

"I'll never tell another living soul, Noah, I swear to God. I swear to God I'll never tell another living soul."

"I believe you, Frank. That's why I told you. I had to tell somebody. Had to get it off my chest. I knew you'd never tell another living soul. Because you're loyal. Loyalty is your middle name. Frank Loyalty Stokes, who's never cheated on his wife."

"Now, don't be sarcastic, Noah. I meant it. I am loyal."

"Sorry. Didn't mean it to sound that way. You are loyal. But me, I'm a full-fledged, licensed, card-carrying bastard. Of the first order. So let's drink to that."

"Listen, Noah, the first thing you've got to do is get yourself out of this mess. I mean, I'm sure she's a nice little piece of ass. She's a cute little trick. Nice tits, nice bod, but—"

"Please don't talk about her that way, Frank."

"But you gotta get yourself out of this mess, Noah. I mean, she's a *minor,* and—"

"What if I don't want to get out of it?" he says.

Frank stares at him. "You mean—?"

"What if I'm in love with her, Frank? What do I do about that? What if I'm thinking about chucking Carol, my job, my career with this company, my whole life and family, and just—"

"Jesus H. Christ, Noah. That's crazy talk! You don't mean that."

"Shit, I don't know what I mean," he says. "I don't know what I think. I don't know what I feel. If I'm in love with her, that means I'm also a crazy bastard on top of everything else, doesn't it? The only thing I know is I'm piss-assed drunk."

"I'm really worried about this, Noah," Frank says earnestly. "I'm really worried hearing you talk like this. It worries me seeing you like this. In all the years I've known you, I've never seen you like this before, letting something get to you like this. It scares me, Noah."

"Scares you. It scares me, too. But I'm glad, Frank."

"Glad about what?"

"Glad I told you, Frank. I'm drunk, but I'm glad I told you, anyway. I'm glad you're my best friend. It's good to have somebody to talk it over with. Especially you, Frank. You don't seem to be blaming me. Not particularly, anyway, and I'm glad of that, Frank. I'm grateful for that. Your loyalty."

"No, I don't blame you, old buddy," Frank says.

"Thanks. Let's drink to that. One more." He rattles the ice cubes in his empty glass.

But Frank does not stir from his chair. "She sure must be some hot little piece of ass, this girl," he whispers.

"*Don't*—" he begins. Then he says wearily, "Don't let's talk about this anymore. Let's just drink. Okay?"

But still Frank does not move. "And I thought I had problems," he says at last. "But jeez, you're in even a worse mess than I am, Noah. You're in a helluva worse mess." He strikes his forehead with the heel of his palm. "Oh, jeez, jeez, why'd I mention Estelle to Beryl?" His head inclines slightly to one side, and the tears stream freely from his eyes.

When he enters the bedroom, she is standing by the window, looking out. The curtains are parted, and the throbbing lights from the neon sign outside illuminate her profile in alternating colors: white, yellow, blue. "I heard what you said," she says without turning to look at him. "I didn't hear it all, but I heard most of it, and I didn't stand with my ear to the keyhole, either. It's true. A maid came into the room the other day while I was typing your script, even though the Don't Disturb sign was on the door. And I do sing in the shower."

He stares at her across the darkened room.

"You told him about us. You didn't have to. You promised not to. You broke your promise. You promised not to tell another living soul until you and I had figured out what we were going to do. You said it was to be our secret. Well, it's not our secret anymore." She sighs. "I'm disappointed with you, Noah."

"Jesus, Melody—I had to tell *some*body. Frank's my—"

"Your best friend. Yes, I heard that. Then what am I? I heard you say, 'What if I'm in love with her?' That's not quite the same as saying you're in love with me, is it? It's just 'What if?' I know what you're doing, Noah. You're looking for an escape hatch—a way out of this. I heard what you called this. You called it a mess."

"*He* said that, Melody!"

"But I didn't hear you disagree! I don't want a mess. I didn't come here to make a mess."

"What do you want, Melody?"

"I want a man I can love and believe in and respect—the kind of man I thought you were, Noah."

"I'm sorry, Melody—"

"*You're* sorry? I'm much sorrier than you are, Noah. That's how much you've let me down. I'm leaving tomorrow, Noah."

"Where are you going?"

"I don't know. Somewhere. I'll find somewhere to go. I obviously can't go back to River House."

"But Carol and I are supposed to be—"

"In charge of me?" She laughs harshly. "Nobody's in charge of me! I'm in charge of myself and always have been."

"Let me give you some money."

She laughs again. "Buy me off? I don't want your money. I have plenty of money—as much as I need."

"But you can't just—go. Not like this."

"Don't tell me what I can do and can't do. I want to stay and hear your presentation tomorrow. After all, it's as much mine now as it is yours. I'll sit somewhere in the lobby near the ballroom, where I can hear it. After it's over, I'll go."

"Melody, please. I think—I think I am in love with you."

"That's not enough! If you love me, you're going to have to prove it in some important way. Until you do, I'm leaving."

"I'll try . . . I'll try . . ."

"Then try! Try now." Her tone now is imperious.

"Too drunk," he says. "Can't think. But just don't go, Mellie. What if—"

"What if something awful happens to me? Then it will be your fault, won't it? You'll have to bear the guilt for whatever happens to me, won't you?" She shrugs. "It'll be *your* mess, not mine."

"Jesus, Melody, don't talk like that. Melody, just tell me what you want me to *do!*"

She turns and looks straight at him for the first time, the colored lights alternating across her face. "Do?" she says. "I'll tell you exactly what I want you to do. I want you to go home tomorrow night and tell Carol you don't love her. I want you to tell her that you never loved her. I want you to tell her that you love me, that I've

done things for you in four days that she's never done
for you in twenty years of marriage. I want you to tell
her that you want a divorce, and that you want to
marry me!"

With a sob he flings himself across the king-size bed.
"Oh, Jesus, Mellie," he says. "I just can't . . . I just can't
do that. . . ."

"Then you're not the man I thought you were," she
says.

"Jesus . . . Jesus . . . piss-assed drunk," he says.

"Come back to me when you've had time to grow
up!" she says.

In the apartment at River House, the telephone is
ringing, and Carol answers it somewhat distractedly. The
telephone has been ringing steadily all evening. Her
mother-in-law, who in telephone calls always dispenses
with such formalities as salutations and farewells, begins
speaking immediately in her distinctive voice with its
double-syllable vowel sounds. It is a voice, Hannah Liebling assumes, that anyone who even remotely knows
her will instantly recognize, and so she never troubles to
identify herself. "I know it's late to be calling you,
Carol," she says. "But I've been thinking all evening
about our conversation this afternoon. About the Met.
Do you really think that if you could get the Van Degans
to give them their collection, the Met would really put
you on their board? Would that really be enough to do
it? Because that would really be a wonderful honor for
us, Carol, for this family and this company. Nobody's
ever honored me like that. The biggest honor I ever got
was having a hybrid white dahlia named after me by the
Garden Clubs of America, and my husband never got
any honors at all. When he introduced Ingraham's Majestic Bourbon, he sent a case of the stuff to King
George the Sixth, but we never heard boo from Bucking-
ham Palace. The best thing we ever got was to get an
ex-king and his snooty duchess to come to dinner at
Grandmont. Oh, he got that honorary doctor of science
degree from that college, but that was because he gave
them a new hockey rink. But from a p.r. standpoint,
Carol, this would do wonders for us—Mrs. Noah Liebling on the board of trustees of the Metropolitan Mu-

seum. The prestige. The publicity. That's the kind of image we've always been after, and you just can't buy that sort of thing. But my question to you is, can you really pull it off? Can you *guarantee* this, Carol? If you can, it would be worth buying bottles from those anti-Semites, even if their bid is on the high side. After all, bottles are bottles, and we have to buy them somewhere."

"Nana, I really can't talk now," Carol says. "Something terrible has happened."

"What? What's happened?"

"The apartment's been burglarized."

There is a long silence. Then Hannah says, "The Sachs family silver. It's gone, of course. It belonged to my great-grandmother. By now it'll be all melted down."

"No, the silver wasn't taken. In fact—"

"Have you counted it?"

"Yes, yes. The fact is—"

"Have you called the police?"

"No, because the fact is that nothing really seems to be missing. I've called the building's security, of course. But the last thing this building wants to have is police cars lined up outside. And since nothing was taken—"

"Have you called Noah?"

"No. I don't want to worry him with this, Nana. He's got that big presentation tomorrow—remember?"

"Oh, that."

Oh, that. Again.

"And since nothing was really taken—that's the weird part. But the *mess,* Nana! You won't believe the incredible mess they made. Dresser drawers emptied out on the floor. Closets dumped. Beds pulled apart. My jewelry scattered all over my dressing table, but nothing missing, not even the ruby lavallière you gave me. Nobody can figure out what they were after. In fact, the only thing that seems to be missing from my desk is my address book."

"How did they get in?"

"Nobody can figure that out, either. The front door was locked on the chain. The service entrance was locked. Nobody came up to this floor today who didn't belong here. There's no sign of a break-in. That's what's so weird about it. There's nothing except this awful, un-believable mess everywhere."

"It's obviously an inside job," Hannah says. "It's that maid of yours. That Mary."

"But, Nana, Mary's been with me for seventeen years!"

"But they all have boyfriends, those people. The boy-friends are all on cocaine. They'll do anything for their boyfriends—anything their boyfriends ask them to."

"But Mary's happily married. Her husband works for the post office."

"That doesn't mean she doesn't have a boyfriend. They all do, and they're all on cocaine. This is New York City—remember? It was definitely Mary."

"The building wants to question both Edna and Mary tomorrow, but I'm not going to let them. After all, Mary's been with me for seventeen years, and Edna for twelve."

"Oh, it wouldn't be Edna. She's white."

"But why would somebody like Mary ransack my apartment to steal my address book? She knows where I keep it. If she wanted an address, she'd either ask me for it or just copy it out of my book."

"Well, I guess you have a point," Hannah says begrudgingly.

"Anyway, the security staff at River House isn't very happy with me at this point. One of them even went so far as to suggest that I'd made this godawful mess *my-self,* as part of some sort of insurance scam. Can you imagine that?"

"Dreadful! If nothing was taken, where's the scam?"

"Anyway, I've got to get this mess cleaned up before Noah comes home tomorrow night. I don't even want Edna or Mary to walk in and see this place looking like this tomorrow morning."

"Is Anne there to help you?"

"No, she left to spend the weekend with a friend—thank God! She'd be no help. I know where everything belongs, and she doesn't."

"Well, I guess you've got your work cut out for you, Carol."

"I'll call you about the other business tomorrow. I'm working on a little plan. But meanwhile this burglary thing has just been so strange—and scary. I suppose I can't really call it a burglary, since nothing was taken. It's more like some terrible invasion . . . like vandalism . . . like my home has been raped. If you could just see this place, Nana . . ." She continues like this for a moment or two longer before she realizes the line is dead. Hannah, as is her custom, has hung up. The conversation is over.

In the bedroom, she decides to tackle Noah's closet first. His suits, shirts, neckties, and belts have all been thrown in a heap on the closet floor. She picks up the articles one by one, replacing them on their wooden hangers in the order in which her tidy husband likes to keep them: business suits on one rack, sports jackets and slacks on another, business shirts on a lower shelf, sports shirts on the one above. Carefully, she tries to smooth out any wrinkles. Perhaps, she thinks, I won't even mention this awful invasion to Noah at all. It would only upset him. She lines up his suits on their racks according to color: dark blues, dark browns, lighter browns, grays. . . . It is an oddly satisfying work, creating order out of chaos. Performing this wifely chore, restoring her husband's closet to its original symmetry, is indeed a labor of love, and she finds herself falling in love with him all over again. She lifts his familiar things tenderly, one by one.

Now, toward the bottom of the pile, she comes upon a pale blue lacy garment that at first seems totally unfamiliar, a piece of lingerie. Lifting it, she sees it is a woman's nightie. She turns the label: Victoria's Secret. Now she remembers seeing Melody wearing this. As she lifts the nightie, out from its folds falls a pair of women's panties. She kneels to pick these up. These are neither hers nor Anne's, and once more she inspects the label: Victoria's Secret again. Kneeling there on the floor and turning these in her hands, she sees that they are stained with what appears to be fresh blood.

The doorbell rings with such unexpected stridency that she freezes with fear. The intruder has returned. She jumps to her feet and nearly falls forward into Noah's closet. It is after eleven o'clock, too late for any ordinary caller, and why wasn't the visitor announced from the lobby downstairs? For several moments she is too terrified to move.

But then, she thinks, it is probably just the building's security people again, with more questions, or more theories.

She drops the objects in her hands and goes to the door. Making sure it is on the chain, she opens the door a crack and peers out.

But she sees that it is just Mr. Nelson, Hannah Liebling's chauffeur, in his full daytime livery.

He tips his cap. "Mrs. Liebling thought you might be nervous, staying alone in your apartment tonight, after what happened," he says. "She thought you might like to borrow this."

Through the opening in the doorway, he passes her Hannah Liebling's Smith & Wesson .38-caliber automatic pistol with its bone handle. He offers it to her politely, with a little bow, handle first.

"Please be very careful with this, Mrs. Liebling," he says as she stares at the gun in her hand. "It's fully loaded. And if you need to use it, it's safest to fire from a crouched position."

16

Morning

William Luckman is enjoying a hearty breakfast at the Yale Club, slathering butter on one of the club's famous blueberry muffins, and rereading the letter that was in his box this morning. "My precious darling," it begins. "You asked me to write you a letter . . ."

I miss you desperately, my darling. I miss everything about you—your handsome face, your beautiful body, your rippling pectorals, our hours of lovemaking. Never in my life have I felt so completely dominated by a lover! So completely overcome and overpowered by a man. I never thought it was possible to have multiple orgasms, but you've opened up the true, basic woman in me. It is so different from poor Frank, who has never really been able to "turn me on." I'm still amazed that you remember me from the eighth grade, when you were still a bright, sweet-faced, rosy-cheeked kid, but already with such palpable promise. . . .

Bullshit, he thinks. The fact is, I don't remember you at all.

Since you left, I have been having the wildest thoughts about you, darling. I have been thinking of what it would be like if you and I were to run away together, to some secret place, where the two of us could spend hours and hours, days and nights, just making uninhibited love. I'm quite serious, my love. I feel nothing for Frank anymore, and would gladly leave him and run off with you, if you would just give me the tiniest of "green lights." . . .

Fat chance. Haggard old bitch.

*After you left, I had a long talk with Frank in A.C.,
and I finally "laid down the law" to him. Now I think
he knows exactly where I stand. But before that I found
out a little more about "the situation" down there. . . .*

Now she's getting to the good part, he thinks.

*It seems that Noah L. has been acting most peculiarly
down there! It seems that there's a "Do Not Disturb"
sign hung on his door most of the time, and he hasn't
been "socializing" with the other men the way he usually does. And then—this cinches it for us, darling—
Frank said one of the hotel maids told him Noah had
a girl in there—young, with long dark hair. Frank says
the maid is just trying to be a troublemaker, but we
know who that girl is, don't we, darling? It's got to be
Melody Richards, since we know she's not in New
Haven, where she said she was going to be. Just to
make sure, I phoned the Shubert Theatre, and you're
right. There's nothing playing there, and won't be until
March. Why would she lie unless she was going to A.C.
to "shack up" with Noah Liebling?*

*Darling, this whole thing worries me terribly, and I
think one of us should tell poor Carol what's going on.
After all, Melody is a minor. This is "contributing to
the delinquency," or whatever they call it. Carol could
get Noah on the same "rap" that Mia Farrow tried to
pin on Woody. . . .*

*Oh, my darling, I miss you so achingly, so longingly,
from the deep hunger for you in my groin to the roots
of my . . .*

And blah, blah, blah. The letter is signed, "Your devoted slave—B." Bill Luckman refolds the letter carefully and places it in the breast pocket of his Morty Sills
blazer. He takes a last, thoughtful bite of his buttered
blueberry muffin, places his napkin on the table, stands
up, and goes to one of the telephones in the entrance
lobby, snapping his fingers as he goes. She has turned
out to be a better slave than he had ever dared to
hope for!

*   *   *

THE WRONG KIND OF MONEY

And now he sits in Cyril Liebling's office at 1000 Park Avenue, opposite Cyril at the big carved walnut partners desk that Cyril bought from the auction of the William Randolph Hearst estate.

"I'm very flattered that you're interested in employing the services of our agency, Mr. Luckman," Cyril is saying. "But the fact is that I'm not sure there's very much more this agency can do to promote or publicize your book. Your book has had so much publicity already. You've done the eighteen-city tour. You've appeared on all the national talk shows. You've been written up in *Newsweek, Time, Vogue,* and *Vanity Fair.* There just aren't that many publicity outlets left."

"Yes, I suppose you're right," he says.

"We wouldn't want to lead you down the garden path," Cyril says. "And promise to get you and your book more exposure than they've already had. With a book there are only so many things you can do, and it seems to me you've already done them all."

"You have a very good point, Mr. Liebling," he says. "I just hadn't thought of that. It's just that I was so very impressed with you the night I met you at Noah and Carol's house."

"Well, thank you," Cyril says, lowering his eyes modestly. His tall frame is slouched in the big leather chair, and he picks up a pencil and twirls it between the thumb and forefinger of his left hand. "Now, with your next book, on the other hand—" he says.

"Yes?" Bill Luckman sits forward eagerly in his chair.

"When that's finished and ready for publication, we might be able to do something with that."

"Gosh, that would be wonderful, Mr. Liebling," he says.

"Something about the secret rich, I think you said? The secret rich and their secret scandals?"

"That's right!"

"It sounds interesting. So, as soon as you have that book in proof form, bring it around, and my staff and I will take a look at it. We'll see what we might be able to do."

"That would be wonderful, Mr. Liebling. I can tell it's going to be a wonderful experience working with you."

"Well, we'll see about that, won't we?" Cyril says with

a thin smile. "How long do you think that's going to be, Mr. Luckman?"

"Sixteen months—eighteen, max, I work fast."

"Good. When that's ready, give me a call."

Bill Luckman looks around the office. "How large a staff do you have, Mr. Liebling?" he asks.

"Oh, that varies," Cyril says with a wave of his hand.

"I understand your mother—Mrs. Jules Liebling, that is—lives in the apartment just below."

He studies the younger man's face. "That's correct," he says.

"Is she at home now?"

"No, I don't believe she is. I believe she's at her office in the Ingraham Building. Why do you ask?"

"It's just that—well, I know this is probably a very impertinent request. But if we're going to be working together, I'll ask it anyway. I've heard it's an absolutely fabulous apartment."

"It is."

"I don't suppose you could show it to me, could you?"

Cyril's expression grows thoughtful. "Well, I have a key, of course," he says. "But no, I think not. I don't think *Maman* would like that. *Maman*'s and my relationship is—somewhat uneven at this point. Perhaps some other time, when she's at home, I can arrange to have her show you the apartment herself."

"I'd love that," Bill Luckman says. "I found her to be a fascinating woman."

"Yes. Fascinating."

"Obviously a woman of many facets."

"Many facets. Yes." Cyril half rises from his chair. "Well, Mr. Luckman," he says, glancing at his watch, "if you have no further business with me, I do have some important client calls to make. I'll hear from you again when your new book is ready."

"There's just one more thing, Mr. Liebling," he says.

"Oh? What's that?"

"Under some rather odd circumstances, I've come into possession of a certain letter. It seems to pertain to members of your family. I had doubts about whether to show it to you or not. But since we're going to be working together, I think perhaps I should." He withdraws the letter from his jacket pocket and hands it across the partners desk to Cyril.

Cyril places a pair of pince-nez across his nose to read, one of several trademark affectations for which Cyril Liebling is reasonably famous. The two men sit in silence as Cyril reads.

"To whom is this letter addressed?" Cyril asks at last.

"I have absolutely no idea."

"Was there no envelope?"

"Not when it was given to me, no."

"May I ask how you came to be in possession of it?"

"Now, that was really strange," he says. "I was standing in front of Saks's window yesterday, on the Fiftieth Street side, looking at some golf shoes I was thinking of buying, and a woman—fortyish, I'd say, well dressed—approached me on the sidewalk, and said, 'Aren't you William Luckman?' I suppose she was one of my fans, who recognized me from one of my television appearances."

"Yes. I suppose so."

"And so I said I was, and she said, 'I read in Roxy Rhinelander's column that Noah and Carol Liebling had a dinner party for you. Here's something that sheds a little light on what your friends are up to,' and she handed me this letter. Then she disappeared."

"Curious. Very curious," Cyril says.

"I thought so. When I read it, I saw that it did contain references to members of your family. But I have no idea who the other people are. The letter is signed 'B.' But who would 'B' be? And who is Frank? And what does A.C. stand for?"

"Frank could be Frank Stokes, a business associate of my brother's. B could be Beryl, his wife. And A.C. could refer to Atlantic City, where my brother and Mr. Stokes are attending a sales meeting."

"Well, I've never heard of any of those people. And who is the other woman mentioned—Melody somebody?"

"Melody Richards. She is a college friend of my niece Anne's. You met her the other night at my brother's house, if you recall."

"Oh—the other young girl? I'm afraid I didn't pay that much attention to her, Mr. Liebling."

"Why was it my impression that Melody had invited you to the party?"

"Oh, no," he says, shaking his head. "I'd never met her before."

"Hmm," Cyril says. "Tell me, was the woman who gave you this letter shortish, on the plump side, with frosted hair?"

"No, she was a tall, quite attractive blonde."

"Then it wouldn't have been Beryl Stokes herself," Cyril says. "I would describe her as quite unattractive."

"But why would Beryl Stokes have given me a letter she'd written to some lover? That wouldn't make much sense."

"No, you're quite right. It wouldn't."

"My theory is that some man's wife, the wife of the man this letter was written to, discovered this letter in her husband's pocket when she was sending his suits to the cleaner's, or something like that. She passed the letter on to me, knowing I was a writer who's written on the subject of marital infidelity, hoping I'd publicize the letter to embarrass her husband. Of course, that's just a theory. That's just the writer in me, always trying to figure out motivations."

"Your theory is possible," Cyril says. "If a bit far-fetched." He taps the letter with a manicured fingertip. "We must consider the effect that this letter could have on my brother's marriage," he says, "as well as on the Stokes ménage. There are two families involved here, both of which could be irreparably damaged by the contents of this letter. The contents of this letter must be handled with kid gloves."

"That's why I decided to turn it over to you," Bill says. "I certainly don't want to get involved in this. I knew you'd know what to do."

"Yes. Well, thank you. May I keep this, then?"

"Absolutely. I have no use for it."

"This is the original? Not a photocopy?"

"As far as I know, sir."

"With the quality of photocopies these days, it's often impossible to tell. You've made no copies?"

"Of course not. Why would I do that, sir?"

"Of course, there's no reason in the world why I should believe you," Cyril says.

"I beg your pardon?"

"Never mind," Cyril says. "Tell me, Mr. Luckman, do your pectorals ripple?" He balances the letter between his fingertips.

"I beg your—"

"Never mind. Just being facetious." He rises to his full height behind the desk and removes the pince-nez. "Now I really must roll my calls," he says, "as they say on the Coast. It's been an interesting meeting." He extends his hand. "Good day, Mr. Luckman."

And now, since he really has nothing else to do, and since it is a fine mid-winter morning with the temperature in the forties, Cyril decides to take a walk. He selects a full-length lynx coat and a walking stick with a silver handle in the shape of a wolf's head. The walking stick is another of his famous trademark affectations. If he stays on Park Avenue, he thinks, a street with very little pedestrian traffic, he will be safe from animal rights activists with cans of spray paint and hatpins to jab into his elbows.

He strides downtown, swinging his stick, the lynx coat billowing behind him, a conspicuous figure on the New York scene.

At Saks, he spends some time studying the windows on the Fiftieth Street side of the store. Then, for good measure, he inspects the windows that address Fifth Avenue, as well as those on the Forty-ninth Street side. Then he steps inside the store. The men's shoe department is on the street floor.

"Yes, my good chap," he says to the clerk who steps forward to help him. "Yesterday I happened to see a good-looking pair of golf shoes in one of your Fiftieth Street windows. But I don't see them there today. Have you changed your window displays?"

"No, sir. Our window displays change once a week, usually on Wednesday or Thursday afternoons."

"Funny, but I distinctly remember those golf shoes."

"Actually, Saks doesn't carry a golf shoe, sir."

"Ah. Well, perhaps it was Lord and Taylor."

"Perhaps, sir," the clerk says.

Whistling and swinging his stick, Cyril heads uptown again. At a corner trash basket, he pauses, removes the

letter from his pocket, tears it into shreds, and drops the
pieces into the basket. Cyril Liebling may be guilty of
certain unspeakable vices, but being a litterbug is not
among them. He continues homeward, a spring in his
step and a song in his heart. Bathy is coming to lunch!

And now, not many blocks away, Carol Liebling is
meeting with the five-member Acquisitions Committee
of the Metropolitan Museum of Art. The meeting is
being held in Room 704 of the Yale Club, of which Mr.
Corydon McCurdy is a member, the room the club calls
its "Board Room." The committee members are poised
with pencils and yellow pads.

"I've had a long conversation with Mrs. Truxton Van
Degan," Carol is saying. "And I'm pleased to say that
the Van Degans have agreed to turn over their collection
of Chinese Export porcelains to the museum."

There are smiles around the room.

"The Van Degans' gift, however, is being made subject
to certain restrictions and conditions," she continues.

The smiles become more guarded, and Cory McCurdy
says, "Can you outline those for us, Carol?"

"To begin with, the Van Degans are ready to turn
over approximately half their collection now. The other
half is to be kept for Mrs. Van Degan's discretionary use
until her death, at which time Mrs. Van Degan agrees
to leave the museum the balance of the collection in
her will."

Corydon McCurdy clears his throat. "That sounds
very generous on the surface of it, Carol," he says. "But
tell me, what do the Van Degans mean by 'Mrs. Van
Degan's discretionary use'?"

"I think we have to bear in mind, Cory," Carol says,
"that Mrs. Van Degan is quite a few years younger than
her husband. In the normal course of things, Mr. Van
Degan can be expected to die first. I think the Van Degans want to set it up this way so that if, after her husband's death, Mrs. Van Degan decides to sell any pieces
from the remaining collection, she can be at liberty to
do so."

"I see," he says.

"But," Carol says, "I did get her to agree that before

she sells anything, she will first offer it to the museum to see whether the museum wants to purchase it."

"Fair enough, I guess," he says. "Of course, another purchaser might be able to offer her more than we could."

"True. But at least the museum would be in on the ground floor in any bidding. We'd get first crack at whatever it is. And it might not even be anything we'd want."

"From the Van Degan collection? From what I know of it, I'd like to get my hands on it *all.*" There is light laughter around the room. "Which brings me to my next question. You say they're willing to turn over half of the collection to the museum. Which half? Who decides?"

"Here I think the Van Degans are being very generous," Carol says. "They'd like us to go through the entire collection, and tag fifty percent of the items that we particularly want. In any dispute—that is, if there's a piece we particularly want and that the Van Degans particularly want to keep—they suggest that the matter be decided by cutting cards."

"Cutting cards?"

"Yes. Cutting a deck of cards. High card wins."

"Carol, this is the Metropolitan Museum of Art. This is not Las Vegas."

Carol feels her cheeks redden. "That was merely their suggestion," she says. "Any other form of lottery would do, I'm sure. Drawing straws. Whatever. I'm sure I don't need to remind you, Cory, that with even half of the Van Degans' collection, plus what we already own, we would have the most important collection of Chinese Export in the world."

"Hm," he says. "Drawing straws. Like children on a playground."

"Now, the next part gets a little tricky," she says, looking down at her notes and deciding to ignore his last remark. "This involves the porcelains the museum already owns. Mr. Van Degan would like to purchase the museum's entire collection in return for his gift."

"*What?*" he cries.

She looks across at him. "May I finish, Cory, please? I told you this is rather complicated. I told you there were certain conditions."

"He wants to purchase *our* porcelains? In exchange for his?"

"When you're finished, I'll go on," she says carefully. "Yes, he wants to purchase the museum's porcelains, at the price the museum paid for them when they were first acquired, which was back in the nineteen twenties. He will then give these pieces back to us, along with his pieces. All the pieces are then to be designated 'Gifts of Mr. and Mrs. Truxton Van Degan.' "

"Outrageous! I never heard of such a thing!"

"His reason is taxes. If he gives our pieces back to us along with his own pieces, appraised at today's current, real market values, he can take a tax deduction far in excess of the value of his gift. It's all perfectly legal. He's consulted his tax attorneys. In fact, as I understand it, this is their idea."

"Outrageous!" he says again.

"Finally, he wants the entire collection—those pieces that are currently ours, plus those that are currently his—to be exhibited together in a room to be designated Van Degan Hall."

"Outrageous. I'm sure the director will never stand for this."

"It's unusual, I'll admit," she says. "But considering the importance of the gift, isn't it worth exploring? As I say, it's perfectly legal."

"It may be legal," he says, "but it's certainly—shifty, to put it mildly. Tell me something, Carol. Is this a Van Degan deal? Or is it actually a Liebling deal?"

She gazes at him coolly. "What do you mean by that?" she asks him.

"I mean exactly what I say. This sounds like a Liebling-type deal to me."

"And what exactly is a Liebling-type deal, Cory?"

Corydon McCurdy's prominent jaw juts out even farther. "My father was Richard McCurdy," he says. "Does that name mean anything to you?"

"No. Should it?"

"Your father-in-law, Jules Liebling, stiffed my father on the price of an apartment he was selling at One thousand Park Avenue. That's what I call a Liebling-type deal. This deal smacks of that. Also, I find it hard to believe that a fine old New York family like the Van

Degans would ever come up with a deal like this one. It sounds more like one of those shifty, under-the-counter deals that I understand are so common in the liquor business. That's what I mean."

A sudden chill falls over the room. Mr. Corydon McCurdy has just made a comment that, in New York City, is considered both politically incorrect and politically unwise. But no one in the room says anything. Carol decides to steer her course directly into the iceberg. "Mr. McCurdy," she says, "you obviously bear some old grudge against my late father-in-law, whom I never knew, and who has been dead for more than twenty years. I don't think that grudge has any bearing on what we've been discussing, nor do I think it's appropriate to bring it up at this meeting."

There is a silence after this. Then Bernice Walton, one of the committee members, breaks it to say brightly, "Anyway, I think Carol deserves to be congratulated on having carried the negotiations with the Van Degans this far."

There is a polite round of applause.

Corydon McCurdy scowls. "Well, perhaps," he says. "I'll have to discuss all this with the director, of course. And with our own legal counsel."

And Carol leaves the meeting trying to conceal her fury.

"Well, I've found out this much about that Beryl Stokes," Pookie Satterthwaite says to Patsy Collingwood as they sit having coffee at the E.A.T. Café on Madison Avenue. "One of our doormen told me that William Luckman, who wrote that dirty book, has paid quite a few visits to Mrs. Stokes this week while her husband's been out of town. What do you make of *that*, sweetie?"

Patsy covers her mouth with her fingertips to conceal a yawn. "So what?" she says. "So she's having an affair. Everybody has affairs. I thought you were going to do something to get us included in the Lieblings' circle."

Pookie looks briefly crestfallen. Then she says, "The Lieblings' apartment was burglarized last night."

"Everybody gets burglarized. Did they get away with a lot of good stuff?"

"That's the funny thing about it. The burglars apparently didn't take a thing."

"How humiliating—to have a burglar who can't find anything worth taking. I suppose Roxy will do an item on it. More ink for Carol Liebling."

"Now, Patsy. That's the *last* thing River House needs—an item about a burglary. It was apparently an inside job. Everybody says it was her black maid. I know what's going to happen, though."

"What?"

"Noah Liebling's the president of our board. He's going to use this thing to try to slap another assessment on us for more security. But we're not going to let him."

"Well," Patsy says, "I've got to run. Consciousness-raising class." She signals the waiter for their check. "By the way, I got our last lunch at Mortimer's. Today's on you."

"Patsy, you did *not* get our last lunch. I did. I distinctly remember, sweetie."

"Pookie, I got our last *two* lunches, actually. Today is definitely on you."

"You did *not*, sweetie. I did. I can even show you the credit card receipt." She fumbles in her Chanel bag. "I know I've got it in here somewhere."

"Look, Pookie, you're getting off easy today. Two cups of coffee."

"But at three dollars a cup! Oh, all right." She hands the waiter a gold American Express card.

"Sorry, ma'am. We don't take credit cards for anything under twenty-five dollars."

"But I didn't bring any cash. . . ."

"Oh, for heaven's *sake*!" Patsy says, and she tosses a ten-dollar bill on the table. "Keep the change. Now I've really got to run. . . ."

On the thirtieth floor of the Ingraham Building, Miss Edith Ackerman is seated at her desk. But it is not her regular desk, and this is not her regular office, and that is part of the trouble.

Edith is Noah Liebling's secretary, and has been for the past nineteen years. This week, with her boss out of town, she was looking forward to catching up on her reading—she is three issues behind with her *McCall's*—

without much else to do besides fielding his telephone calls, taking his messages, forwarding the important calls, and faxing the important mail, to his numbers in Atlantic City. The earlier part of the week was just like that, routine.

But this morning, seated at her usual desk outside her boss's office, after finishing transcribing some letters for him and signing them for him "Dictated, but not signed," she had just reached into her shopping bag for the November *McCall's,* which announced a new and absolutely foolproof diet, when all hell broke loose.

It was Jonesy, Miss Hannah's private secretary, on the phone. "She's *here!*" Jonesy said with great urgency. "We need you here to help out!" And so Edith has been commandeered by the old lady. "Since you won't have much else to do today," was the way Jonesy put it.

"Commandeered" is the right word. This has happened before when her boss has been out of town, and Edith always resents it when it does. Miss Hannah does not come to the office on any regular basis. Sometimes weeks go by without her putting in an appearance, and some people might say this is a blessing. But to Edith this is the worst part about it. Miss Hannah's appearances are always sudden and unannounced, and when they occur the entire building is galvanized into looking busy and all hell breaks loose.

Edith loves working for Mr. Noah, as everyone calls him. Everyone in the company loves Mr. Noah. Edith herself, though she would never admit it to a soul, is secretly in love with Mr. Noah. Sometimes at night, alone in her bed with Kitty, her Siamese, on the pillow beside her, Edith has dreamt that she was being passionately embraced by Mr. Noah, and awakes from the dream feeling ashamed of herself. After all, Mr. Noah is really some sort of cousin of hers, though Edith is not certain how the cousinship works out. Her father, when he came from Poland as a boy in 1910, was told to look up "rich Cousin Jules in America." Work was found for him in the New Jersey bottling plant, and after she graduated from high school, work was found for his daughter Edith as well. And here she still is.

Like everyone else, Edith Ackerman feels sorry for Mr. Noah, always under Miss Hannah's thumb yet never complaining, always cheerful. Mr. Noah is a saint, always so nice to everyone.

Miss Hannah is something else again. Miss Hannah, of course, is no relative of Edith's at all. Miss Hannah is what Edith's father used to call "one of those high-and-mighty Deitsch." Everyone hates Miss Hannah. No, "hates" is not the right word. The word is terror. Everyone is terrified of Miss Hannah. She is called Miss Hannah, and whenever she decides to loom on the scene, it is "Miss Hannah wants this!" "Miss Hannah wants that!" As underlings scuttle about the building, carrying out her orders. She is Miss Hannah to her face, as in "Yes, Miss Hannah," "No, Miss Hannah," "Right away, Miss Hannah!" "Can do, Miss Hannah!" "I'll get those figures for you, Miss Hannah!" Behind her back Miss Hannah is "the old lady," or "the old bag," or "the old battle-ax," or the old less polite word beginning with b.

When she makes one of her appearances in the building, she arrives by private elevator and ascends nonstop to the thirtieth floor, where she is escorted to her corner office, where she sits in splendid isolation behind closed double doors, as she is sitting now, presumably. This morning her actual physical presence has not yet been revealed to Edith Ackerman. It is the kind of isolation reserved for kings and village idiots. No one would dare approach her directly unless summoned, and no one would think of initiating a conversation. The job of her executive secretary, Miss Jones—and, oh how Jonesy loves that title—is primarily to shield Miss Hannah from lesser mortals. Of course, as an executive secretary, Jonesy has her own secretary. Lately, in fact, Edith has noticed that Jonesy has begun billing herself on memos as "Executive Assistant to the President," an even grander form of address.

What Miss Hannah actually *does* when she visits the big corner office is something of a mystery to Edith. Because Miss Hannah's office has its own bathroom, once Miss Hannah is in there, she never needs to come out. That bathroom is a sacred place. Edith wonders if even Jonesy has ever seen it, though the building's cleaning crew places fresh soap and towels in that bathroom every night, whether anything has been used or not. There is a story, perhaps apocryphal, that a new girl was once caught by Miss Hannah using her bathroom. The girl was summarily fired, so the story goes. This is probably a fiction.

When Miss Hannah comes to the office, she hardly ever lunches out. Her lunch is sent in by messenger, a "21" Club hamburger, medium rare. If it is too rare or too well done, an alarm goes off. No, it is merely a buzzer, but everyone reacts as though a bomb had exploded in the basement, tearing about, rushing to telephones, frantically ordering the replacement burger. "This is Mrs. Hannah Liebling's office calling!"

But other than eat, what exactly does Miss Hannah *do* in there? Sometimes Edith has glimpsed Miss Hannah at her big desk poring over what appear to be long columns of figures. Proofs of Ingraham's ads are always brought to her for final approval and initialing. What else? Meanwhile, Edith Ackerman always knows exactly what she will be expected to do when summoned to "help out" in Miss Hannah's office. She will be asked to do all the little things that Jonesy and Jonesy's assistant don't like to do. When Miss Hannah's buzzer sounds, Edith will be expected to leap to her feet, seize a steno pad and pencil, and rush into Miss Hannah's room. Often the order will simply be "Open that window," or "Turn up the thermostat." Obviously, a woman in Miss Hannah's position cannot be expected to place her own telephone calls—though Mr. Noah has no problem doing this—and so the order could be "Get me Mr. So-and-so." And Edith will be expected to have memorized all the frequently called numbers so she will not have to take the time to look them up, or run them through the telephone's electronic memory bank.

Then there is the important matter of Miss Hannah's Venetian blinds. When she visits her office, Miss Hannah likes the morning sunlight from the east, and so the blinds must be tilted to catch that. But as the sun moves westward, it can shine in Miss Hannah's eyes, and so the blinds must be tilted the other way. Of course, since the sun moves north in spring and south in the fall, the offending sunlight falls upon Miss Hannah's eyes at a slightly different time each day. And so an elaborate chart has been worked out, listing the precise dates and times for the Tipping of the Blinds ceremony. This is performed daily, whether Miss Hannah is there or not. After all, who knows when she may suddenly appear? If the blinds are in the wrong position, there is hell to pay.

No matter what time Miss Hannah arrives, she always leaves the office at precisely five o'clock, and in a great hurry, as though she had a train to catch, which she does not. Mr. Nelson, her driver, is always waiting for her with the car outside the building's entrance, in a space especially designated "No Parking" just for her. As the hour for her departure approaches, another ritual must be observed. At four-thirty Edith will tap on her door and say, "Four-thirty, Miss Hannah." A nod. Then, fifteen minutes later, she will announce, "Four forty-five, Miss Hannah." After the second announcement, announcements are made at five-minute intervals. "Four-fifty, Miss Hannah . . . Four fifty-five, Miss Hannah." Why these reminders are necessary, Edith Ackerman hasn't the remotest idea. Miss Hannah wears a wristwatch. There is an electric clock on her desk, and another with chimes on the mantel over her fireplace. But the announcements must be made, or heads will roll. Can't the old battle-ax tell time?

With the five o'clock announcement, Miss Hannah will heave her large frame out of her chair and make her way to the coat closet. There Edith will stand waiting to help her into her coat, a heavy mink at this time of year. If it is raining, or looks as though it might, Edith will hand her an umbrella. Then she will hand her her reticule and gloves. Miss Hannah usually wears a hat to work, and because Miss Hannah's hands will now be full, Edith will help her on with the mink hat, securing it to the silver-blue hair with a hatpin. Edith has often thought of ramming that long hatpin right through Miss Hannah's eardrums. Last of all, if Miss Hannah was wearing them today, Edith will help her into her mink-trimmed boots, easing Miss Hannah's feet into them one at a time, while Miss Hannah leans on Edith's shoulder for support, then zipping them up.

Then, without a word of thanks for any of this, Miss Hannah will stride down the corridor toward her elevator, while employees clear a path for her, murmuring, "Good night, Miss Hannah . . . Good night, Miss Hannah. . . ."

Meanwhile, though very little seems to be happening inside Miss Hannah's office when she is there, Jonesy and her assistant always make it a point to be consumed with almost frantic industry—Jonesy clicking bossily about in her spike heels, issuing instructions in her reedy voice. When Miss Hannah is closeted in her inner sanctum, an atmosphere of perpetual harassment hangs over the outer office like a mushroom cloud. They are always frowning, those two, too harried and preoccupied to talk as, wearing earphones, they transcribe dictation tapes, place and receive urgent telephone calls, initial important documents and memoranda, and fling confidential pieces of paper from their In boxes into their Out boxes, simultaneously pressing buttons to summon bonded messengers. The urgency and energy of these two ladies is exhausting just to be around on days like this. So vital to the company is the work being done here today that Edith knows she will have a headache by the time she leaves for home tonight. On days like this, this office is run like a crisis center, a war room with an emergency a minute. Working for Mr. Noah is altogether different, sheer joy.

Edith Ackerman has been with Ingraham almost longer than anyone else, though not always as Mr. Noah's secretary, of course. Heavens, she can remember when Mr. Noah was just a little boy. The standing joke is that Edith has lasted with the company as long as she has because she knows where lots of corporate skeletons are buried. Edith does nothing to discourage this notion, but actually she knows of hardly any corporate skeletons at all. She has made it a point not to know of skeletons. She remembers old Mr. Jules, of course. Mr. Jules was something of a tyrant, too, but somehow that was all right. Mr. Jules was a man. In Edith's book, a male tyrant is acceptable, while a female tyrant is just a pain in the kazoo. She knows there's a double standard here, but that is what she believes. She has a right to what she thinks.

She remembers some troubled times for the company. She remembers a time, toward the end of the war, when there was almost a major scandal involving price fixing. But Edith is not even sure what price fixing means. She knows that liquor prices vary widely from state to state, and in some states from county to county, and in some towns from store to store. What Ingraham did was to figure their pricing backward from retail. The liquor store owner needed to make a fair margin of profit, and so did the wholesaler, and what was left over went to Ingraham. It seemed a fair enough arrangement to Edith. But there was a Louisville retailer who took the company to court, charging price fixing. She remembers how skillfully Mr. Jules handled it in the end.

He called two of his vice-presidents into his office. "Eddie and Charlie," he said, "somebody's going to have to sit for this. The Kentucky attorney general isn't going to let us off unless somebody sits. It's going to be one of you. Which one of you is it going to be?"

The two men eyed each other uneasily. "Flip a coin?" one of them said.

"Now, look at it this way," Mr. Jules said. "Charlie is thirty-nine, married, with three kids. The oldest enters Penn State in the fall. Eddie, you're twenty-seven, no wife, no kids."

"A fiancée," Eddie muttered, looking at his shoes.

"Which one of you do you think it should be?"

"I guess me," Eddie said at last.

Now that, Edith thinks, is the way to run a company. It was only, she was assured, a white-collar crime, which was like no crime at all. Eddie's sentence was only two years. His prison was more like a country club, and every week Mr. Jules sent him a box of homemade brownies. In nine months' time, with good behavior, Eddie was out, and back at work at Ingraham's with an increase in salary. There was no publicity. Would Miss Hannah ever be able to solve a problem as neatly as that? Edith thinks not.

Edith also remembers Miss Bathy. Now, *there* was a woman who was a delight to work for, as different from her older sister as night from day. If Miss Hannah is the Wicked Witch of the West, Miss Bathy was Glinda, the Good Witch. Everybody loved Miss Bathy. She was as pretty to look at as she was fun to be with, always a smile for everyone. Miss Bathy was considered to be the company's advertising genius. To Edith, Ingraham's advertising no longer has the special flair it had when Miss Bathy handled it.

Edith remembers the famous "Men of Eminence" campaign, for instance. In that series famous scientists, educators, authors, concert artists, doctors, captains of industry, and even a U.S. senator and a Supreme Court judge were persuaded to pose for photographs showing them enjoying a glass of V.S.O.P. The copy stressed that these distinguished gentlemen were not being paid for their endorsements. Instead, a contribution of one thousand dollars was being paid by Ingraham to their favorite charities, though Edith happens to know that, in the case of one college president, his favorite charity had been his son-in-law's bank account. Then there was Miss Bathy's "Gracious Living" series. In that one the message was that, by serving V.S.O.P., a host or hostess could greatly improve his or her social status. It was this series that had been the first in history to show a woman pouring, and even sipping, a cocktail. Everyone had quaked in fear over those ads, sure that there would be a public outcry over this, and that the government would step in and force them to cancel the campaign. But, as Miss Bathy predicted, nothing of the sort happened, though sales figures for the brand soared. Those Gracious Living ads, it was said at the time, changed American liquor advertising forevermore, as everyone in the industry scrambled to copy Ingraham.

Edith has heard all the rumors about there being a "relationship" between Miss Bathy and Mr. Jules. She doesn't believe a word of any of it. Whenever she saw Mr. Jules and Miss Bathy together, their relationship was all business, and nothing but. Miss Bathy also supplied another important service to the company. There were plenty of times when certain corporate skulls had to be cracked together. Mr. Jules and Miss Hannah handled this unpleasant work, and then Miss Bathy applied the bandages, the soothing poultices, the healing compresses of cotton gauze, the comforting words, the boxes of homemade brownies. After a dose of Miss Bathy's tender, loving care, the violent dressing-down from Mr. Jules—who often hurled heavy objects in the direction of people who brought him unwelcome news—never seemed quite so bad.

Mr. Noah fulfills that function now. Miss Bathy retired after Mr. Noah joined the company. Edith has heard it said that Mr. Noah and his aunt do not get on. What may have caused this, Edith does not know. It is none of her business, and she has never asked.

In addition to her job and Kitty, her Siamese, there is only one other light in the life of Edith Ackerman, and that is the woman she calls the Little Girl. The Little Girl is fifty-three years old now, but Edith has always called her that, though her given name is Tillie. The Little Girl is her niece, and Edith has had her since 1949, when she was eight, and Edith's brother was shot down in Korea, and the Little Girl's mother didn't want to keep her. The little girl is feebleminded. Oh, Edith knows this is not a term one is supposed to use anymore. Today she would probably be described as learning disabled, or intellectually challenged, but whatever you call it, the Little Girl's mental age is that of a five- or six-year-old.

She must be watched very carefully. During the day the Little Girl attends a special school for others like her, and at the end of the day, Edith picks her up and takes her home to her apartment in Kew Gardens, where the Little Girl has the spare bedroom. For the most part, she is sweet and gentle-natured. She plays endlessly with Kitty. But there are times when she wants to be sexually active, and then she must be restrained.

The Little Girl is also diabetic. Edith gives her her insulin injections, tests her urine, weighs her food, and supervises her exercise on the stair-climbing machine. But this morning she had some sort of seizure. Her bed was drenched with sweat, her neck was twisted at an awkward angle, she was making incomprehensible gurgling sounds in her throat, and she seemed in danger of slipping into a coma. Her blood-sugar count had shot up for some reason, and Edith quickly gave her a shot. After that she seemed to improve, but Edith decided not to send her to her school today. Instead, a neighbor had agreed to come in and take care of her. For all the worry she is, Edith loves the Little Girl very much, and frets about her night and day.

Now the buzzer sounds, and Edith Ackerman springs to her feet, seizes her steno pad and pencil, and rushes to the double doors.

"Yes, Miss Hannah?"

Miss Hannah sits crouched behind her big desk, many pieces of paper spread out in front of her. Without looking up, she says, "What time is it?"

Edith consults the clock on the mantel. "Ten-eighteen, Miss Hannah," she says.

"I want you to call my son in Atlantic City," she says. "He may be in a meeting, and if he is, don't bring him out. Just leave a message for him. Tell him I want to see him at my house tonight, first thing, when he gets back to New York."

"That may be quite late, Miss Hannah."

"It doesn't matter. I'll be up."

"He'll have luggage, Miss Hannah. He may want to drop that off at River House before—"

"No. I want to see him at One thousand Park *before* he goes home. I want to see him first *thing*, the minute he gets back to the city. My doorman can watch his luggage."

"Yes, Miss Hannah."

"Make sure he gets that message. It's very important."

"Yes, Miss Hannah."

Edith starts to withdraw.

"Oh, and one other thing," she says.

"Yes, Miss Hannah?"

"Phone my daughter-in-law and tell her I'd like her to join me for lunch."

"Yes, Miss Hannah. Will you be eating here at the office, Miss Hannah, or would you like me to call for a reservation?"

"We'll be lunching at my apartment. Twelve-thirty."

"Yes, Miss Hannah. By the way, Miss Hannah, that Mr. William Luckman called again."

"Keep telling him what I told you to tell him. That I am not available. I was not impressed with that young man. He spells trouble, if you ask me. I don't wish to speak with him."

"I understand, Miss Hannah."

Miss Hannah pushes her chair back from her big desk. "I'm ready to go home now," she says. "You can fetch my things."

"Yes, Miss Hannah."

While Miss Hannah leans heavily on Edith's shoulder, as Edith helps her into her mink-trimmed boots, Edith thinks: Praise the Lord. Miss Hannah is actually leaving the office early. Now perhaps she, too, can leave for home early, and check in on her Little Girl.

Miss Hannah straightens up. "Thank you, uh—uh—"

"It's Edith, Miss Hannah."

"Thank you, Edith."

That's another thing. For all the years Edith has worked for the company, Miss Hannah has never been able to remember her name.

17

Noon

"Mrs. Liebling? This is Joanne Satterthwaite calling. I live in Twenty-nine A."

"Oh, yes, Mrs. Satterthwaite," Carol says. "How are you?"

"I'm well. May I speak to Mr. Liebling, please?"

There is something in Mrs. Satterthwaite's tone, a certain undue formality, considering they are neighbors in the same building, that alerts Carol to the possibility that this may not be a friendly telephone call. "I'm sorry, but Noah's out of town today," she says. "He'll be back around—"

"Well, I might as well tell you," Pookie Satterthwaite says, "and you can relay it to your husband. There are a number of us—quite a few of us, in fact, here at River House—who are not at all happy with what's going on in this building."

"Oh?" Carol says. "What's the matter?"

"My husband, Darius, and I have decided to head up a protest committee."

"Oh? To protest what?"

"Your burglary."

"Well, please put me on your committee, too," Carol says smoothly. "I'm the one who's been most put out by it, even though nothing was—"

"It was obviously an inside job," Pookie says. "It was obviously one of your colored maids."

"I only have one maid," Carol says, "and Mary was visiting her son and daughter-in-law in Islip yesterday afternoon when it happened. So Mary had nothing to do with it."

"Well, as you know, most of us here at River House try not to employ colored. They're unreliable. They have relatives, and friends. They bring strangers into the building."

"Mary has been with me for seventeen years, Mrs. Satterthwaite," Carol says. "She is absolutely—"

"Obviously, we can't dictate who you want to hire and who you don't. But this situation is getting out of control, and our committee's purpose is to bring it under control. The main thing is—and I want you to make this quite clear to your husband—we are not going to let you use this inside-job burglary of yours as an excuse to slap another assessment on us for stepped-up security. And if that's what your husband's got on his mind to do, we are simply not going to stand for it, Mrs. Liebling."

"Since Noah doesn't even know about the burglary, I'm sure he has no such thing on his mind," Carol says.

"He will, though. We're all sure of that, because that would be just like him. One of our committee's purposes is to try to stop him before he tries to do it. I might as well tell you, Mrs. Liebling. There are a number of us here in the building who are not at all happy with the job your husband is doing as president of our board."

"I'm very sorry to hear that," Carol says.

"We have quite a number of other tenants on our side in this," Pookie says. "We've lined up the Taylors, the Vadricks, the Gerridges, the Sturtevants, the LeMosneys. We've got Monica McCluskey and Graham Grenfell. They're all behind us. And I don't need to remind you, Mrs. Liebling, that Darius and I own one of the largest apartments in the building. That gives us more voting shares than almost any other tenant. In fact, we think we've got enough votes to call for a reelection and throw your husband out as president."

"I think you ought to discuss this with my husband," Carol says. "He'll be home late tonight. I suggest you call him at his office Monday morning."

"And I suggest *you* tell him so *he'll* be prepared for what *we're* prepared to do, if he tries to pull anything!"

"Very well. Now, I really must hang up, Mrs. Satterthwaite. I've got—"

"And you can tell him we've got a plan."

"What sort of plan?"

"For security."

"Very well. I'll tell him."

"It's a three-part plan. First, every servant who works at River House will be required to be photographed, full-face and in profile, and to wear these on a photo-ID badge while working in the building. Second, each servant will be fingerprinted, and the fingerprints will be kept on file in the front office. They'll have all this done at their own expense, of course, so it won't cost any of us a penny. And third, if any servant is given a key to an apartment, these keys must be turned in to the front office before the servant leaves the building, and picked up when he comes back in again. This will prevent them from going out and having their keys copied, and handing them out to all their friends."

"I don't think you could get anybody to work in this building under conditions like that," Carol says.

"Well, if they want the privilege of serving families who live at River House, that's what they're going to have to do," she says.

"The privilege of serving people like *you*?"

"What do you mean by that crack? I've never understood how people like *you* got into this building in the first place. I thought there were supposed to be certain *standards* at River House."

"At least my apartment has *furniture*," Carol says.

There is a little pause. "Our furniture is all being hand-made in Manila," she says. "That takes time."

"Since nineteen eighty-four?"

"Wait a minute. You've never set foot in my apartment. How did you know we're still—waiting for a few pieces? Did your husband tell you that? That's tenant confidentiality. Your husband has violated tenant confidentiality! We can nail him with that one, when I tell my committee that. He'll be off this building's board so fast he won't know what hit him!"

"Oh, shut up!" Carol says.

"Kike!"

Carol slams the receiver down.

"It sounds like you really blew it, sweetie," Patsy says. "You'll never get anywhere with her now that you've picked a fight with her. And you won't get anywhere with that Stokes woman, either, if she's Carol's best friend."

"She started it! She made a crack about how my apartment is decorated. I wasn't supposed to take that lying down, was I? She's never been inside my apartment!"

"Hmm. Now that you mention it, neither has anybody else. It's funny, Pookie. In all the years I've known you, you've never once invited me over."

"It's not *finished* yet! As soon as it's finished, we're going to have a big party and invite everybody."

"Hmm. Well, if I were you, I'd get after that decorator of yours, whoever it is you're using."

"It's not his fault. It's Darius's. We can't seem to agree on a color scheme."

"Hmm. Well, it sounds as though you really blew it this time, sweetie. . . ."

"Carol? It's Roxy Rhinelander at the *News*. How are you, my darling?"

"Fine, Roxy. How are you?"

"Just wonderful, my darling. Say, a little bird tells me there's a big feud brewing over at River House. Anything in that for my column?"

"No, Roxy. There's no feud."

"You sure, my darling?"

"Absolutely."

"Something about security, I was told."

"Really? Who told you that, Roxy?"

"Confidential sources, my darling! Well, if anything breaks, you'll make sure I'm the first to know, won't you? Don't forget, I've given you *and* your daughter quite a lot of nice ink lately."

"There's no feud, Roxy."

Damn her, she thinks. She can see the column item now: "Carol Liebling hotly denies rumors of a big feud brewing over security at oh-so-exclusive River House. . . ." Could Pookie Satterthwaite be behind this? Noah will be furious.

"I'm quittin', Miss Liebling." Mary stands with her feet planted squarely in the doorway, her hands on her hips.

"Oh, *no*!" Carol cries. "What's the matter, Mary?"

"Girls downstairs in the laundry room. They be giving me fishy looks. They be saying I robbed your apartment. I ain't been robbing no apartments."

"Of course you haven't, Mary!"

"I'm quittin', Miss Liebling."

"Now, Mary, *please*. You've been with us so long. We get along so well. We need you, Mary. Don't do this just because of what some silly girls in the laundry room are saying!"

"They say we all got to have mug shots taken and wear badges to get in and out. They say we all got to be fingerprinted, like criminals, Miss Liebling! All account of me."

"Nonsense, Mary. You don't have to be fingerprinted because you haven't done anything wrong. Nobody can make you be fingerprinted."

"I'm quittin', Miss Liebling. I ain't workin' in this building no more."

"Look, Mary. When something happens in a building like what happened here yesterday afternoon, people get kind of—hysterical. They get crazy, and they say crazy things. When all this blows over—"

"Mr. Roger, in the front office. He even axed me if I done it."

"I spoke to Mr. Roger. I told him I knew you hadn't done it. I told him you couldn't possibly have done it. I told him you were out in Long Island yesterday, visiting your family."

"He axed me their name. Their address. Their telephone number. So he could check up on me, see if I was lyin' to him."

"Mr. Roger was just trying to do his job, Mary."

"They don't like colored here."

"Now, Mary, that's just not true. There are quite a few black people working here. There's Cecil, the porter. There's Hilton, the building's engineer. There's—"

"That don't matter. They don't like colored here. I known that all along."

"Listen, Mary. Mr. Liebling is coming home tonight, and I'm going to talk to him. I think it's high time you got a nice raise, and I'm sure he'll agree."

"No, ma'am. I'm quittin'."

"Oh, Mary, *please*! Don't do this to us. Now look what you've made me do. You've made me start to cry, damn it!"

"I'm sorry, Miss Liebling. I'm quittin'."

"Oh, hello, Mrs. Van Degan," Anne says, looking up from a stack of museum correspondence she is filing.

"You mentioned you were working here," Georgette says. "And I just happened to be in the museum to see the Diana Vreeland show, so I thought I'd just stop by and say hello. Is it a fascinating job?"

Anne smiles. "Well, I wouldn't call it fascinating, exactly," she says. "But every now and then an interesting letter comes through—though if I stop to read it, it slows up my filing, which is what I'm supposed to be doing. I call it a Catch-22 job."

"Catch-22?"

"If I'm going to get anything out of this job in terms of Bennington, I've got to learn something about how an art museum works. But if I try to learn how the museum works, I can't do the job properly."

Georgette Van Degan looks at her watch. "It's twelve-thirty," she says. "Have you had lunch?"

"Not yet, Mrs. Van Degan."

"Good. Let's have lunch. There are some things we need to discuss about the party. If I can use your phone, I'll call Le Cirque." Then she looks down at what Anne Liebling is wearing: faded jeans, a sweatshirt with the words GOTCHA COVERED emblazoned on the front, and a pair of bamboo chandelier earrings. "Well, let's not bother with Le Cirque," she says. "I live just across the street. I'll have my cook fix us something. Soup and a salad okay?"

"That would be lovely, Mrs. Van Degan," and she reaches for her down-filled parka, while Georgette Van Degan buttons herself into her fisher jacket.

"Aunt Carol, it's Becka Hower," the woman's voice says, and for a moment Carol has no idea who this is. Then she remembers Ruth's estranged daughter from California.

"Oh yes, Becka."

"Aunt Carol, I'm here at Mother's house, and things are in a terrible state. I just don't know what to do."

"What's wrong, Becka?"

"It's Mother. I've got to get back to California, but she won't let me go. She says she's been desperately lonely. She wants me to stay and live with her. I can't do that, Aunt Carol. But she says she'll kill herself if I leave! And she sounds as though she means it!"

"Now, Becka. Tell me exactly what's been happening."

"I came here to see her because she asked me to. And because I was curious. I never really knew her, and my father would never talk about her. But ever since I got here, there's been nothing but—craziness. Do you remember that young man, Ector, who she brought to your house on New Year's Eve?"

"Of course."

"Well, he's still *here,* for one thing. I think she's paying him to stay here. I don't know that for sure, but it doesn't seem like Ector has anyplace else to go. I don't know what their relationship is supposed to be. I don't think they're lovers, because she's given Ector his own room. Actually, Ector turns out to be rather sweet. He's done everything he possibly can to help. He's even offered to marry Mother, if that will help."

"Oh, dear . . ."

"I don't think she'd do anything as crazy as that, but I don't know. She reads to him. They watch old movies together. But whenever I try to slip out of the house, she says she needs me. She says she needs us both, for the companionship. She wants us to stay with her for the rest of her *life,* Aunt Carol. She's offered to pay me a lot of money if I'll spend the rest of my life with her, but I can't do that. And if I say I've got to go, she says she'll kill herself. And Ector—poor Ector—is caught in the middle of it. And then, two days ago, that Mr. Luckman came to call."

"Yes . . ."

"I think he must have said something to her that upset her. She started drinking—"

"Oh, dear," Carol says. "And she's been sober now for—what? Seven years?"

"You mean she's had a drinking problem before?"

"Oh, yes. But I thought—we all thought—"

"Well, she's been drinking steadily ever since. Oh, she'll pass out for a few hours, but then she'll wake up and call for us—for Ector and me—to join her. At all hours of the day and night."

"You don't drink with her, I hope."

"Oh, no. She just wants us to listen to her, and to listen to the most awful—garbage, Aunt Carol. She blames her father for all her troubles. She says her father destroyed her first marriage. She says her father destroyed her second marriage, too, to the only man she really loved—Giulio, who was the count. She says it was her father's fault that Giulio committed suicide, because her father wouldn't pay Giulio the alimony he wanted, and that she'd promised him in a prenuptial agreement. Wouldn't pay because she was underage when she signed it and lied about her age on the marriage certificate."

"I'm afraid I've heard all these stories before, Becka," Carol says with a sigh.

"And Ector—poor Ector—Ector is some kind of saint, really—says we should listen to her. He says I owe it to my mother to listen to her stories. He says he wishes he'd listened to his mother when she was alive. In a funny way, I think Ector is actually in love with Mother. But I'm not sure how much more of this I can take. Yesterday she came up with a really bizarre idea. She said she'd decided to *adopt* Ector. She said she'd even called a lawyer to draw up the necessary papers. Ector says he's willing to go along with this, since he has no real family of his own. But, nice as Ector is, I really don't think Mother ought to get involved that way with a man like that—do you?"

"No, I don't," Carol says. "I think that's a really bad idea."

"But, you see, I'm such a stranger in this family—such an outsider, really—that I don't really feel I'm in a position to say things like that to her. I mean, she's my mother, but she's also a person I hardly know at all. But she says she always wanted two children, a daughter and a son. She told us that after she divorced Giulio, she discovered she was pregnant with his child. The pregnancy was aborted, but the fetus was male. She says that it's as if Ector was sent to her by his escort service to replace her baby boy. I mean—craziness! But how can I tell my mother she's crazy?"

"It's the drinking," Carol says. "Whenever she drank, she used to get very—grandiose."

"How rich is she, Aunt Carol?"

"She has a trust fund, from which she gets an income. I really don't know how much that income is, but I imagine it's—considerable."

"She has enough to be able to afford to fly off on these crazy tangents, then. But this morning she had an even crazier suggestion. She wants Ector and *me* to get married! She says we should get married, and then we could live with her and take care of her for the rest of her life. I honestly think Ector would go along with this. Of course, I told him it was out of the question. All I want to do is get out of here!"

"Where is she right now?"

"Passed out in her bedroom. That's why I took this opportunity to call you."

"Maybe you should take this opportunity to get out of there, Becka. Make your escape."

"But she says she'll kill herself if I leave. Ector thinks she's serious. Do you think she is?"

Carol hesitates. "Well, yes," she says at last. "She might be."

"She's threatened suicide before?"

"Yes."

"Tried it?"

"Once. No, twice, that I know about."

"So you see, Ector is right! I can't leave my mother, Aunt Carol, if she might try to hurt herself. Even though I hardly know her, I can't leave if she might try something like that. After all, she is my mother."

"Yes. Yes, I suppose you're right."

"But I have a life of my own on the West Coast. I can't just stay here *forever*. Aunt Carol, do you suppose if you came over, you could talk to her? I know she likes you."

"Not if she's been drinking, I can't. It wouldn't do any good. You've got to catch her when she's sober. That's the only way."

"Perhaps—when she wakes up?"

"I have a twelve-thirty lunch. Then I have to drive to Connecticut. I'm having some problems with my own mother, at her nursing home. They telephoned this morning and asked me to come up."

"What about my Grandmother Liebling? Would she be able to help?"

"That," Carol says firmly, "I would not recommend. Ruth's relationship with her mother has always been very fragile, to say the least. As you may have noticed at dinner at my house the other night. Bringing Hannah in on this could only make matters worse."

"Is there anyone *else*? Does Mother have any *friends*? Is there anybody who—"

"Tell you what," Carol says. "My husband's been away all week, but he'll be home tonight, though it probably won't be until quite late. He's always been able to handle his sister better than anyone else. In fact, he's always been able to handle everybody in this family better than anyone else. I'll speak to him about this when he gets home and see what he suggests."

"Well, perhaps," Becka says doubtfully. "But I think Mother's a little angry at your husband right now."

"Angry at Noah? Why?"

"She didn't say. But the other night she called him a—well, never mind what she called him."

"That was probably just the drink talking. Noah will know how to handle it. If you can stick it out for a few more days, Becka, I'm sure Noah will come up with something."

"Well . . . all right," she says.

"And in the meantime, if you can catch your mother in a sober moment, ask her to describe the twelve steps in her program. Ask her to recite the little Serenity Prayer. And ask her for the name of her sponsor in A.A., if she has one, and try to get her to call that person."

"You have a beautiful apartment, Mrs. Van Degan," Anne is saying.

"Thank you, dear." Georgette Van Degan unbuttons her fisher jacket. "Here, let me hang up your coat."

Anne steps to the stairwell that curves upward from

the entrance foyer, and looks up at two blood-red vases, each of which stands in a recessed niche of its own in the stairwell, lighted by hidden spots. "Oh, look!" she says. "Lang Yao *sang-de-boeuf.* Late seventeenth century?"

"I see you know a thing or two about porcelains, dear," Georgette says.

"My mother," Anne says. "It's something of a hobby of hers. She has books and books on the subject."

"It's very rare to find a pair," Georgette says. "In fact, these two are the only pair in existence, as far as we know. I had my architect create those niches just for them."

"Beautiful," Anne says, and steps up the stairs for a closer look.

"Don't touch them!" Georgette says a little sharply.

"Oh, I wouldn't dream of it, Mrs. Van Degan."

"I don't even let my maids dust them. I do that myself."

"They're signed, of course."

"Of course. And by the same potter, which makes them so rare. Now, shall we see what friend cook has fixed for our lunch?" She leads the way down the long gallery, where more porcelains are displayed in vitrines and lighted cases, toward the dining room. "The collection was started by my husband's grandfather," she says.

"These pieces should be in a museum, Mrs. Van Degan. Look—that's a Sung bowl, isn't it?"

"Yes. Tenth century. Nine-sixty A.D., actually. Some of this may end up in a museum, if your mother plays her cards right."

"Nine-sixty! The very beginning of the Sung period. Just think, that bowl is over a thousand years old. . . ."

"Uh-huh. Sit down, dear. Oh, yum-yum. She's fixed her famous watercress soup. Now, let's talk about our party, dear," she says, picking up her spoon. "It's not going to be just the party of the year, or even the party of the decade. I'm talking up this party as the party of the *century,* since the twentieth century is beginning to wind down. Roxy Rhinelander has agreed to give us a double spread in the *News,* with lots of photographs, of course, and so we've got to make sure we give a party that won't let Roxy down. Now, I realize, dear, that you haven't done as much entertaining as I have, and so there's one thing you need to remember. It doesn't matter what you serve for food. It doesn't matter who does the music. It doesn't matter what you do with flowers, with the decor, with the waiters' uniforms, or anything else. What matters is the *guest list*. Everything else can be the best, the most expensive you can buy, but if you don't have an important guest list, you're dead in the water. So that's what we've got to make sure we have— an absolutely drop-dead guest list. People who are *now*. People who are on the cutting edge. People who people are talking about—like your friend Bill Luckman, for instance. People who are *today*. We can't afford to have any of yesterday's people. To get a guest list like that, one has to be absolutely ruthless. One has to slash, slash, slash. To get a guest list like the one we want, friendships have nothing to do with it. That's what I want to talk with you about today."

"Sure," Anne says, lifting her spoon from the array of silver.

"Your friend Melody Roberts."

"Richards," Anne says. "She's my best friend."

"Yes. Well, she's our first casualty, I'm afraid. She winds up on the cutting-room floor."

"But I couldn't have a party without Melody, Mrs. Van Degan!"

"Well, you're going to have to. As I said, friendships just can't count in something as important as this."

"But Melody's my *room*mate, Mrs. Van Degan. She's my roommate and my *muse!* She'd be terribly hurt if I didn't ask her."

"Then she'll just have to be hurt," Georgette says, reaching for a thin round of Melba toast. "She just won't *do,* dear. I've done a little research on her family. Her people are nobody. It's not just that they don't have any *money,* and she probably couldn't afford the right kind of dress to begin with. Her people have no style. Her father has some sort of minor job with the State Department. I looked him up in both *Who's Who* and the *Social Register,* and he isn't in either, so you see they can't be anybody. They have no social value, and no publicity

value, and we want a drop-dead guest list. And then, of
course, there's the fact that your friend is having an affair with your father. . . ."

She drops her spoon in her saucer. "With my *father*?"

"Which makes her a rather—well, *inappropriate* guest
at our party, don't you think? I mean, people would
giggle. People would laugh at us, and that's the last thing
we want, isn't it?"

"You're saying Melody is having an affair with *my*
father?"

Georgette looks at her from across the table, her
soup spoon poised in midair. "You mean you didn't
know?" she says. "Oh, dear, I thought surely you
knew. Everybody else does. She's with him right now
in Atlantic City, in fact. I gather it's been going on for
some time."

"My father would *never*—"

"Now, you mustn't blame your father, dear. All men
do this when they reach your father's age. It's called
male midlife crisis, or something like that. My husband
went through it years ago. He wanted a younger woman,
and that was yours truly. But I held out for this," and
she taps and twirls the big diamond solitaire on her ring
finger, which has several more diamond guard rings surrounding it. "Forty carats," she says. "And we're not
talking West Forty-seventh Street, honey. We're talking
Van Cleef and Arpels."

"Mrs. Van Degan, I just can't believe this." Tears are
welling in her eyes. "It just can't—it just can't be true."

"What can't be true? Oh, you mean about your father
and your friend? Well, it's the truth, so you can see why
we simply can*not* invite her, can't you? Your darling
friend Bill Luckman is the one who told me, when I
called him to make sure he saves the party date, and
thank God he did! He wanted to spare us the embarrassment of including her on the list. He says she's just
a smart little cookie who knows the ropes, and who'd
probably go to bed with anything in pants, particularly
if he was rich. Why, Bill Luckman told me that she even
tried to put the make on *him*—can you *imagine*? So you
can see what kind of a friend she is of yours—a girl
who's not only shacking up with your father, but also

making a pass at your new best beau! So, if you want to blame somebody, you mustn't blame your poor father. Blame her. Why, honey, you've hardly touched your soup!"

"I think—I think I'm going to be sick," Anne says.

18

Hannah's Way

The newly installed automatic elevators at 1000 Park Avenue have turned out to be something of a mixed blessing to the tenants of the co-op. Yes, they are faster. And, as the members of the building's board pointed out at the meeting, by eliminating six full-time and three part-time elevator men—a vanishing breed to begin with—the building should have been able to trim its payroll considerably.

But then the building's three full-time and two part-time doormen complained, and their union backed them up, that they deserved higher wages, since now the major responsibility for the building's security rested with them. Also, the doormen pointed out, if a single on-duty doorman happened to be out in the street, trying to flag a cab for a tenant, it would be possible for anyone to walk into the building from the street unchallenged, and then into the elevators and up into the apartments. The doormen demanded backup men in the entrance lobby. And so in the end, with this new personnel, and with the cost of the new elevator cabs factored in, everybody's maintenance charges went up anyway.

Now two women, one older, and one younger, enter the south elevator car together, press the buttons for their respective floors, and the elevator doors slide closed. The elevator starts upward smoothly enough, but suddenly there is a little jerk, and a little bump, and the car stops abruptly. Both women press their buttons again, and when nothing happens they look at each other.

"Where are we?"

"Somewhere between nine and ten, I think."

"These are brand-new elevators."

"Yes, I know."

"There should be an alarm button."

The younger woman finds it and presses it. But no alarm sounds, and the elevator remains at a standstill. Both women laugh nervously.

"Is there a telephone in that little box on the panel there?"

The older woman opens it and lifts the receiver, jiggling the hook up and down. "It doesn't seem to be working, does it?"

"Well!"

"Well!"

"Maybe there's been a power outage, do you think?"

"But the lights are still on."

"You're right."

"Well."

"Well."

"Here we are."

"I'm sure someone will notice this sooner or later, won't they?"

"Oh, I'm sure. And I'm sure there's plenty of oxygen in here for us. Isn't there?"

"Oh, I'm sure. These things are ventilated, aren't they?"

"I'm sure they are. I wonder where the ventilation comes from, though."

They laugh nervously again. "The main thing is not to panic."

"Absolutely."

"Do you live in this building?"

"No."

"Neither do I."

"Should we try—screaming, or something?"

"I don't know. That might use up too much oxygen. Because, frankly, I don't see where any ventilation could be coming from, do you?"

"No."

"So. Let's just stay put until someone notices that this elevator's out of order."

"Yes."

There are little benches in the corners of the car, and each woman takes a seat on one of these daintily padded triangles.

Silence.

Then the younger woman says, "Since we may be here for a while, we might as well introduce ourselves. I'm—"

"As it happens, I know who you are," the older woman says. "You're Carol Liebling. My name is Bathsheba Sachs."

"Oh," Carol says.

"I'm on my way up to have lunch with Cyril."

"And I'm on my way up to have lunch with Hannah."

"What an odd place for us to finally meet," Bathy says.

"There's not much we can do about it, is there?" Carol says.

"No."

There is a little silence, and then Carol says, "Of course, I've heard a lot about you, Miss Sachs."

"I'm sure. And not all of it good, I'm also sure."

"Yes, I must admit that's true."

"And please call me Bathy. Everybody does. Or Aunt Bathy. We don't have to be friends, but it wouldn't hurt us to be friendly, would it?"

"No. I quite agree."

"I know how Noah resents me, and I know perfectly well why. And I imagine you do, too."

"Yes, I do, Bathy. Noah told me all about it years ago. You sent him a Christmas card. He tore it up."

"I was his father's mistress. For quite a few years. One morning he arrived at Grandmont from college unexpectedly—he'd been booted out, in fact, after that motorcycling escapade—and he came into a room where he found his father and me in—well, let's just say he found us in a situation that would have been difficult to misinterpret. He never spoke to me again."

"I know. Noah told me all that."

"I'm sorry he feels that way. I was always very fond of Noah. But there's nothing I can do about it now. One can't undo one's past."

"No, but you see the thing is, Bathy, that Hannah has no idea why he feels the way he does about you. He doesn't feel up to telling her, and I certainly don't think it's my place to tell her."

Bathy's eyebrows go up. "*Really?*" she says. "Hannah told you that? That she has no *idea* why Noah resents me?"

"None whatsoever. She'd give anything to know."

Bathy laughs. "My dear, I'm afraid my big sister has misled you. She knows perfectly well why. I told her all about the incident on the afternoon of the day it happened. We haven't discussed it since, of course. There's been no need to. But she knows perfectly well why Noah feels the way he does about me."

"But—then why does she keep insisting that Noah tell her what's troubling him?"

"My dear, that's just Hannah's way. She insists that everyone she deals with lay his cards flat out on the table, face up. Even when she knows the answer, she wants to hear it from the horse's mouth. Remember, I've known her a lot longer than you have. My big sister knows *every*thing. But she's the kind of woman who'll demand an explanation even when she already knows perfectly well what the explanation is. She's the kind of woman who'll buzz for her secretary to ask what time it is even when there's a big clock facing her on the opposite wall."

"How very interesting," Carol says.

"That's Hannah for you. She knew all about Jules and my affair from the very beginning. She even encouraged it. In fact, I sometimes think she actually helped initiate it, putting us together all the time. She was certainly all for it."

"Really?"

"Oh, absolutely. Hannah and I had a deal."

"A deal . . ."

"And yet—and yet I really loved old Jules," she says. "That was something I couldn't deal with. Can anyone deal with love?"

"She's told Noah that she won't turn over his stock to him unless he agrees to take you back into the company."

Bathy laughs again and slaps her knee with her gloved hand. "Oh, dear," she says. "Oh, dear, dear me! Is she still on that tired old subject? She knows better than that. I wouldn't go back to work for that company if everybody in the family got down on their hands and knees and begged me!"

"You *wouldn't?*"

"*Never!*"

"But Hannah says—"

"It's just not the same company it was when I worked for it—when Jules was still alive. It was *fun* then. There was a wonderful raffishness about the liquor business in those days. We flew by the seat of our pants. We were always looking over our shoulder to see if the sheriff was coming around the corner. It was almost as though what we were doing was still against the law, and some of it probably was. We never knew when the government might decide to crack down on us with more rules and regulations. That made it exciting. But today Ingraham is just another giant corporation. The fun's gone out of it."

"But Hannah keeps insisting that Noah has to bring you back."

"Well, that's Hannah for you. She knows I won't come back. But she's got the idea that I need more money. I may not be as rich as the Lieblings, but I've got all the money I need, and all the money I want. I had a wonderful career in the company, but I'm happy to be retired."

"I find this all very interesting," Carol says. "Because if you refuse to come back to Ingraham, that could mean that Noah will *never* get his stock."

"So it's a Mexican standoff, is it? Well, that's just like Hannah, too—this kind of arm wrestling. To see who'll give in first. She's good at that. Of course, you know the real reason she wants me back, don't you?"

"No, I'm afraid I really don't."

"When she steps down, she wants someone she can trust to be there to keep an eye on Noah—to make sure he doesn't jump ship."

"Jump ship? Why would he do that?"

"It's something he used to talk about. Not threaten, exactly, but he used to talk about it. Hasn't he ever mentioned Aesop to you?"

"Yes, as a matter of fact he did—just the other night. Something about an alternative plan."

"So, you see? That's what worries Hannah—that once he gets his shares of stock, he'll go off and establish the Aesop thing."

"But what exactly is the Aesop thing?"

"Then, you don't know?"

"No."

"Well, you'd better get Noah to explain that to you. It's a little complicated and visionary and—to me, at least—a little bit pie-in-the-sky. But I told Hannah that if she wants me to go back to work at the mill just to make sure Noah stays on the straight and narrow, she's got the wrong woman. But I suggested that you might be useful to her in that capacity."

"I see," Carol says thoughtfully. "I wonder if that's why she wanted to have lunch with me today."

"Could be," Bathy says. "When Hannah asks someone to lunch, you can be sure she's got something on her mind."

"Interesting," Carol says again. "Because if I can be useful to her, then she can be useful to me. A tit for a tat."

Bathy laughs heartily. "That was one of Jules's favorite expressions. A tit for a tat. I haven't heard anyone say that in years!"

"You know, I'm really awfully glad we had this meeting, Bathy," Carol says. "You've made a lot of things clear to me that weren't clear before. And you've given me several good ideas."

"Good. I'm glad. And do you know something? I really think we could be friends, don't you?" She extends her hand, and Carol takes it.

"I think so, too," she says.

"I mean we might as well be, since we may both be about to die of starvation in a stalled elevator."

"Or of suffocation. Have you noticed the air in here getting to seem a little—close?"

Bathy touches her forehead. "Well, now that you mention it—yes."

"But we mustn't panic."

"No. But we might try prayer—"

And with that word, as though a deus ex machina has been summoned, the elevator rattles to life. There is a downward lurch, followed by an upward jolt, and both women clutch the seats of their little corner benches and eye each other with alarm. Then the elevator continues smoothly upward.

"Well!"

"Well!"

Carol gets off first, at Hannah's floor. "Good-bye, Bathy," she says. "Let's get together again."

"I'd like that," Bathy says. "Good luck with Hannah," and she gives her a little wave before the doors close, and she continues on to the floor above.

And now Carol sits in Hannah's dining room with its walls covered in pale blue watered silk. "I'm a little worried about Noah," Hannah is saying. "Our meeting at your house the other night did not go well. He even used vulgar language with me, which isn't like him. Do you think launching this new label has been putting too much of a strain on him?"

"Let's not talk about Noah for a minute, Nana," Carol says. "Let's talk about the Van Degans and their museum gift."

"Well, as a matter of fact, I was going over the figures for Van Degan Glass at the office just this morning. My spies got them for me. Carol, that company really is in terrible shape."

"Good," she says.

"Good? Why?"

"It's good for our side, Nana. It gives us more bargaining power."

"Even if we gave them the contract to manufacture bottles for all our labels, I don't know if that would get them out of the hole they're in."

"Could we do that, Nana?"

"Could we do what?"

"Offer them a contract to manufacture for all our labels?"

"Well, I suppose we *could*, but—" She glances nervously at the portrait of Jules Liebling at the end of the room. "Goodness, I hope he isn't listening to us talk like this. He'd be spinning in his grave. Except he isn't in any grave. He's in that yellow jar on the sideboard over there."

"Here's what I'm thinking, Nana," she says. "You liked the idea of my becoming a trustee of the Met, didn't you?"

"Oh, yes, of course. It would be wonderful. If you really think you could pull it off."

"Let me tell you how it could be done, Nana," Carol says, and Hannah puts down her salad fork, listening.

"Let's suppose," Carol begins, "that we were to tell Van Degan Glass that we're considering offering them a contract to manufacture bottles for all Ingraham products. That would be a nice little piece of new business for Van Degan, wouldn't it?"

"Absolutely. We're the biggest distillers in the country."

"In the millions?"

"In the millions."

"The high millions?"

"I should think so, yes."

"Right now the Van Degans are willing to turn over roughly half of their collection to the museum, with a few little bells and whistles attached to the gift which their lawyers have tacked on for their clients' tax benefits. But if we were to offer them a contract like that, I think I could persuade the Van Degans to donate even more—perhaps seventy-five percent of it, even ninety percent. Don't you?"

"I see your line of thinking," Hannah says. "No collection, no contract."

"That's right. Squeaky wheels get oiled. And from what you tell me, the wheels at Mr. Van Degan's company are particularly squeaky right at the moment."

"Indeed they are."

"And, as a nonnegotiable condition to their gift, I will have Mr. Van Degan insist—"

"That you be placed on the Met's board."

"That's right. No trusteeship for me, no collection for the Met. A tit for a tat."

"Will the Van Degans buy this?"

"I don't see why they wouldn't. It makes no difference to them whether I go on the board or not. And they'll get wonderful publicity from it—the great philanthropists and all that. They'll get a big hunk of new business from us. And they'll get a big tax deduction, which, if their lawyers are smart enough, they can probably spread out across several years. And for us—"

"A Liebling on the Met's board!"

"It's a deal from which everyone will profit."

"What about the museum? Will they accept that condition?"

"We'll have to wait and see, won't we? But considering the importance of the gift, I rather think they will."

Hannah studies her daughter-in-law appraisingly across the table, her eyelids half closed. "You know," she says at last, "I'm seeing a side of you today, Carol, that I've never seen before. It's a side I never knew existed. You really like to *hondel,* don't you."

Carol smiles. "I've enjoyed planning this one," she says. "And I've even carried my thoughts a little further. If Ingraham can get its toe as firmly into Van Degan's door as this deal would do, is there any reason why, at some point, we wouldn't be in a nice position to take over Van Degan Glass?"

"That was something my husband often talked about—owning his own glassworks. Not having to rely on outside suppliers and gambling on price fluctuations in the marketplace."

"It would seem to make good business sense, Nana."

Now it is Hannah who is smiling. "That would show those Van Degans, wouldn't it?" she says. "If we took over their company. Moving out the day we moved in!"

"Well, yes," Carol says. "I did think of that, too."

"And so," Hannah says, "what's the next step? Are you prepared to follow through on all this?"

"Absolutely," Carol says. "All I need is your approval."

"I think it's better if you handle the Van Degans. You know them. I've never met them. If I called them, they'd think I was trying to pull some sort of fast one. They know I hate 'em. In fact, don't mention my name at all. Tell them this is Noah's idea."

"All I need is a green light from you, Nana."

Hannah nods. "You just got it," she says.

Carol pushes aside her plate, realizing that in her excitement she has hardly touched her cheese soufflé. "If you'd like, I can telephone Truck Van Degan at his office right now," she says.

"Go for it!" Hannah says.

Carol jumps from the table and walks quickly out through the hall to the telephone room, leaving Hannah alone at the table, toying absently with her food.

Carol is not gone long. "Well, the ball is now in play," she says a little breathlessly. "I talked to Mr. Van Degan. He said, 'I understand the terms of your proposal completely.' He's going to call the chairman of the Acquisitions Committee."

"And that person is—?"

"A man named Corydon McCurdy. A man who, for personal reasons, I'd very much like to see put in his place."

"We bought this apartment from some people named McCurdy."

"Yes, I know. This is their son."

"Snobs. Like the Van Degans."

"I think I know how to handle him. I've got a few cards up my sleeve that I haven't told you about."

A footman appears at the door. "*Pêche flambée au Cognac,*" he announces.

"Skip it," Hannah says with a wave of her hand. "We don't want dessert. So," she says as the footman departs, "what happens next?"

"Next?" Carol says. "Well, having just set in motion what I'm trying to do for you and your company, I'm going to ask you to do something for me, Nana."

"Oh?" she says suspiciously. "What's that?"

"Give Noah his stock. Turn over the company to him, and without insisting that Bathy has to be part of the deal. Bathy doesn't want to go back to work for Ingraham anyway."

"Perhaps not. But there might be ways I'd have of forcing her to."

"Somehow," Carol says, "Bathy doesn't strike me as the kind of woman who can be forced to do anything she doesn't want to do."

"You've talked to Bathy?"

"Yes, I have."

"Well, I still have a little problem with Noah. I told you he used vulgar language—"

"Your problem with Noah is that you've waited too long to give him the top job. I can promise you something else, Nana, if you give it to him now."

"What's that? What can you promise me?"

"I can promise you that if you give him the job, you'll never hear another word about Aesop."

"Oh? Is he still talking about that?"

"Very much so. More than ever before. You see, Nana, Noah's Aesop idea is an idea that was born out of frustration. Frustration has nourished the idea in his mind. And his frustration is frustration with *you*, Nana. He feels he's just spinning his wheels with the company now. He feels as though he's treading water, getting nowhere. And as each day goes by, he gets more and more frustrated. And the more frustrated he gets, the more he thinks about some sort of escape hatch—like Aesop. But if you give him the job, Nana, I can promise you he'll never give another serious thought to Aesop."

"You can promise me that?"

"Yes, I can. Another tit for another tat."

"He's told you that?"

"He's as much as told me," she says quickly.

"As much as told you isn't quite the same as told," she says. "But it's always been such a totally im*prac*tical idea—Aesop."

"Yes, and in his heart of hearts I know he knows that. And yet, as things stand now—"

"Well, let me think about it," Hannah says.

"Don't think about it too long, Nana. If you think about it too long, I can promise you something else—something neither of us wants at all. You'll see him walk out of his office at the Ingraham Building and never come back. He'll devote the rest of his life to the Aesop project, and there won't be anything you or I can do about it. You know how stubborn Noah is. I'm warning you, Nana—things have reached that crucial a stage. He's about to explode with frustration, and when that happens any usefulness he might have for you or the company, now or in the future, will come to a screeching halt. It will end with a loud and resounding bang. You say he used vulgar language? That's just the beginning, the tip of the iceberg!"

"Goodness, you almost make it sound as though he might—well, never mind."

"I'm saying there's no telling what he might do. Remember—you may be his mother, but I'm his wife. I hear the voice on the pillow at night. I watch him tossing and turning in the next bed, fighting to get some sleep—"

Hannah shivers. "Well, I told you I'd think about it. I promise you I'll think hard. That's all I'll promise you for now."

"Thank you, Nana."

"Meanwhile, you haven't said boo about the party for Anne and the Van Degan girl. Just where does that stand?"

Carol shrugs. "That's neither here nor there as far as I'm concerned," she says. "You disapproved of the idea. I was never really in favor of it. Noah and I haven't discussed it, and I'm not even sure Mr. Van Degan knows about it. Georgette implied that he didn't. I'm tabling any party plans for the time being. Don't forget, we're calling the shots with the Van Degans now."

"Yes, but if my Little Bird really wants this party so badly, then perhaps—"

"But I really think what we've just been talking about is more important than any coming-out party. Don't you agree? More important to you as well as to me?"

"Yes. Yes, I agree."

Carol glances at her watch. "I've really got to run," she says. "I've got to drive up to Connecticut and see my mother. They're having some sort of problem with her there."

"Just one more thing," Hannah says. "That Mr. Luckman has been calling me at my office."

"Oh? What's he want?"

"I don't know. I've refused to take his calls. I didn't like that young man. I didn't like all that talk about money and scandal at your dinner table. Talk about controlling people. He may have written a book about education, but he didn't seem to know much about the subject. He'd never heard of my father, the famous Dr. Marcus Sachs. That young man spells trouble, if you ask me."

"You think so, Nana?"

"It's a feeling in my bones. I'm not going to talk to him, and I suggest that you not talk to him, either. We don't need any more trouble in this family. Lord knows, we've had enough trouble. But remember, if there's trouble, what my father used to say. He'd say, 'If there's trouble, rise above it. Let it wash around your ankles. Stand tall, young woman. Stand tall.' That's what he used to say to Settie and me."

"Good advice," Carol says. They both rise from the table.

"And you know something?" Hannah says. "I'm beginning to think you could run this company as well as the next one."

Carol smiles. "The power behind the throne?" she says. "Isn't that what you were for a long time, Nana?"

"Yes, I suppose I was. And think of it—if Ingraham could take over Van Degan Glass! Wouldn't Jules be pleased? A tit for a tat, he'd say. Moving out on the very day we moved in!" As she leaves the blue dining room, she touches the Ming Yellow urn with the tip of her index finger. Almost lovingly, Carol thinks.

And now, back at River House to change quickly into a sweater and jeans for her drive to the country, Carol finds a message on her answering machine: "Mrs. Liebling," a secretary's voice says, "please call Mr. Corydon McCurdy at your earliest convenience. It's quite urgent."

Still smiling, she places the call.

"Mrs. Liebling," he says, and she notices immediately that they are no longer on a first-name basis.

"Yes, Mr. McCurdy."

"I've had a conversation with Mr. Van Degan."

"Yes, I thought you might have."

"And I've also spoken to the director of the museum. Quite frankly, he prefers the Van Degans' first offer to the present one, Mrs. Liebling."

"But the Van Degans are now offering to give the museum everything in their collection with the exception of the pieces they have displayed in their Fifth Avenue apartment. That's close to ninety percent of the collection, and it seemed greedy to ask them to denude their apartment."

"But this new proposal contains some unacceptable provisions."

"The trusteeship, you mean?"

"Frankly, Mrs. Liebling, that provision was so completely outrageous—so totally out of the question, and so absurd—that I didn't even mention it to the director. He would have laughed me out of his office."

"But, Mr. McCurdy," she says carefully, "you seem to be forgetting how the museum operates. It's not the director who tells the board of trustees what to do. It's the other way around. The director is just a hired employee, selected by the board. The board selects its own membership."

"Mrs. Liebling, you're not suggesting—"

"That you go to the board of trustees? Of course I am. Who else would you go to? The director has no say whatever about who goes on the board. I would have thought you knew that."

"Mrs. Liebling, that is something I flatly refuse to do."

"But isn't that your job? I'd have thought so, with a gift the size and importance of this one, and since it involves a trusteeship."

"This is simply too outrageous!"

"Are you saying that you, a mere committee chairman, are taking it upon yourself to turn down this gift?"

"I can't, but—"

"I should tell you," she says, "that it is quite within my power to have Mr. Van Degan withdraw his gift offer altogether. In the meantime, the Nelson Gallery in Kansas City is eager to have those porcelains to add to their Oriental collection. The Kimball in Fort Worth is also eager. It's a shame not to have the collection stay in New York. But you heard Mr. Van Degan's offer. It's this or nothing."

"You're trying to blackmail the museum!"

"So I suggest you go to the trustees. And I suggest you do so rather quickly. It would be unwise, and also rude, to let the Van Degan offer dangle in front of you for too long a time."

"So it's just another Liebling deal," he says. "Just another shady, crooked Liebling deal. Like father, like daughter-in-law."

"Why, thank you, Mr. McCurdy!" she says. "Coming from someone like you, I take that as quite a compliment."

"This is another Liebling swindle!"

And Carol Dugan Liebling hangs up the telephone without saying good-bye.

And Carol has no sooner replaced the receiver in its cradle than she hears a key turn in the front door, hears the door open, then close. Anne walks rapidly past the library door, in her blue parka, her shoulders hunched under her backpack. "Anne?" Carol calls out to her. "Annie?" But Anne does not answer her, and continues down the hall toward her room where, again, Carol hears the door open, then close. She stands up and goes down the hall to Anne's room, and taps on the door. "Annie? May I come in?"

When there is no immediate reply, Carol opens the door. Anne is sprawled face forward on her bed, still in her parka. "Anne? Are you all right?" she asks her.

Speaking into the bedclothes, Anne says, "I'm okay."

"I thought you were going to spend the weekend at Susie Carpenter's."

"I changed my mind."

"You're home from work awfully early, aren't you?"

"I quit the job."

"Anne—you didn't! I got that job for you."

"I know."

"But what about your winter work program? What about Bennington?"

"I'm not going back to Bennington."

"Oh, Anne. Of course you are."

"Uh-uh."

She sits on the corner of Anne's bed and rubs her daughter's shoulders. "Anne—what's the matter?"

Anne turns her face to the wall. "I told you, Mother. Nothing. I just don't want to talk right now."

She strokes her daughter's fine blond hair. "Listen, darling," she says. "I've got to drive up to Connecticut and see Granny Dugan. They're having some sort of problem with her, and I've got to see if I can straighten it out. I've really got to leave right now. But I'll be back by dinnertime, and we can talk then—okay?"

"Okay," Anne says to the wall.

"Good-bye, darling," she says.

In the front hall, she puts on her shearling driving coat, collects her purse and gloves, checks to make sure she has her keys, and starts toward the front door. Now the telephone rings again, and Carol hesitates, thinking she will let the machine pick it up.

The telephone rings three times. Then she hears a woman's voice say, "Yes, this is Mr. Truxton Van Degan's office calling for Mrs. Liebling. Will you please give Mr. Van Degan a call at your earliest opportunity? The number is—"

Carol rushes for the phone and picks it up. "This is Mrs. Liebling," she says.

"Please hold for Mr. Van Degan," the woman says.

"Carol? Truck Van Degan."

"Yes, Truck," she says easily, noticing how quickly they are using first names, though they have never actually met.

"Have you heard from Cory McCurdy?"

"As a matter of fact, I have," she says. "And I think Mr. McCurdy is going to be a bit of a problem."

"Cory McCurdy is an asshole. I've known him since he was a kid. His old man, Dick McCurdy, was a faggot, and I think Cory's one, too. Don't worry. I can handle Cory McCurdy."

"Well, that's good to know," Carol says.

"Barbara McCurdy was in the middle of divorcing Dick McCurdy when Dick McCurdy died. Fishy death. Supposed to be suicide, but they never found the weapon. Afterward, Barbara insisted on getting the divorce anyway. Posthumously. Cory McCurdy's original name was Richard McCurdy, Junior. After the old man died, his mother had his name changed to Corydon, after her father. I could tell you a few other things about the McCurdys, but I won't bore you."

"Well!" Carol says, unable to think of anything else to say.

"So leave little Dickie boy to me. That's what we used to call him, Dickie boy. But anyway, that's not why I called you, Carol. I was thinking about our conversation earlier this afternoon. And I was thinking, Carol—if there's one thing that'd make me happier than selling my bottles to Ingraham, it'd be selling Ingraham my whole damn company."

"Really?"

"I mean it. The plastics bastards are killing us. Everything is plastics nowadays. But you guys will always bottle your product in *glass*—right?"

"Plastics have been tried," she says. "But spirits bottled in plastic just can't retain the same flavor."

"That's what I hear. Like Coke in cans. Doesn't taste

the same. So what do you think? Do you think a deal like that could be in the cards? It could be a sweetheart of a deal for both of us, Carol."

"Yes," she says. "I think a deal like that could definitely be in the cards."

"Hell, I'm thinking of retiring, anyway. The only thing is—what about the old lady? Will old lady Liebling go along with it?"

"Yes," she says again. "I think the old lady will definitely go along with it."

"When your husband gets back, we should all have a meeting. But remember, Carol—not a word to the press about this. If the press got word that my company's for sale, the whole deal could come unstuck."

"Not a word. I promise."

"Good. And I suppose we should have some kind of earnest money up front, just between you and me."

"Earnest money?"

"Yes, because I see you as pivotal to any deal we make, Carol. I think we're going to need your help with any deal we make, in terms of what you want—uh—in terms of the museum, and all that. You know what I mean."

"I'm not sure I quite under—"

"I'm not thinking money, exactly. I'm thinking of just a little something, just between you and me, that would just ensure that you and I are on the same team, and after the same thing. I think you receive my meaning, Carol. Now, I happen to have a couple of old Chinese vases—"

"Vases?"

"Yeah, they're called Young Louie, or some damn thing."

"Lang Yao. *Sang-de-boeuf.*"

"Something like that. They're supposed to be pretty good. I'm going to give them to you, just to clinch this part of the deal, at this particular preliminary stage. It'll just be between you and me."

"You'd give those to *me?*"

"Whaddya think? It'll help me know I've got your full support in this, Carol. I need you. You need me."

A tit for a tat. "But what about—"

"What about what?"

"Georgette."

"Don't worry about Georgette. I can handle her. Don't worry your pretty head about her. I'll get those red vases over to you. But just remember that this is all totally, strictly between you and me. . . ."

And now—*at last*! feeling light-headed from the crowded events of the day—she is off, speeding up the Merritt Parkway into Connecticut behind the wheel of her little bottle-green Mercedes 450 SEL sports coupe. She loves her little bottle-green car. She loves its gleaming French walnut dashboard, with all its little dials and buttons and knobs and switches, some of which she has never fathomed the meaning of, nor does she care. They wink and blink at her, registering miles per hour, oil pressure, revolutions per minute. She loves her little car's sweet-smelling beigey leather interior and bucket seats, her seat that cuddles her fanny like a catcher's mitt. In her car she is completely cushioned from the outside world, isolated, protected, and safe. She is glad she resisted Noah's suggestion that she have a telephone installed in it. If she had, it would probably be ringing now. If she had, this would no longer be her little car— five years old, 40,000 miles, oil changed every 2,500, and not a scratch or nick or even the tiniest pit mark on its shiny, bottle-green finish. A telephone would mean she would have to share her car with other people. In her car she is the Green Hornet, the Masked Avenger.

She has always enjoyed exceeding the speed limit by a bit—five, six, even ten miles faster than the posted signs decreed. And she has always loved the Merritt Parkway, its gentle, hilly curves, its wide, landscaped center strip, the sudden vistas, the graceful bridges that arch across the highway, no two alike, the side roads with their quaint, Revolutionary names. She presses the Search button on her car's radio, hoping to find some pretty Broadway show tunes, or something from the fifties, when she was young. Something soothing and sweet.

". . . Shelling today of thousands by Serbian nationalists . . . President Clinton insisted he had nothing to hide . . . The jury in the trial of Lorena Bobbitt for severing her husband's . . . The unidentified teenager who has accused Michael Jackson of . . . '*Bad, bad Leroy*

Brown' . . . And when Jesus saw their faith, he said unto the sick of the palsy . . . *'Hey, Poppa, I'm a be-boppa'*—" She switches off the radio.

"Your mother's in a very bad way today, Mrs. Liebling," Sister Margaret Mary said to her on the telephone this morning. "We're thinking it may be time to move her to another level of care."

"What's she been doing, Sister?"

"Talking constantly of sin and redemption."

"But isn't that what she always talks about?"

"Yes, but *shouting*, Mrs. Liebling. Screaming, really. Waving her hands in the air."

"Oh, dear."

"And you know she doesn't sedate well, Mrs. Liebling. In the dining room this morning she had to be restrained."

"But she's had these episodes before."

"Not quite with such *force*. There was a fax message for her this morning."

"A fax?"

"Naturally, we didn't read it. But it's possible its contents may have been what set her off."

"Who would be sending her a fax, Sister?"

"We have no idea, but we do think you should come up to see her. Your visits always seem to have a calming effect on her."

"Well, they certainly don't have a calming effect on *me*," Carol said.

Now there was a genuine note of reproach in Sister Margaret Mary's voice. "We've noticed it's been a long time since you've visited your mother, Mrs. Liebling," she said.

"Very well. I've got an important museum meeting this morning, and then a lunch I can't get out of. But I'll drive up this afternoon. Can you give me your address again, Sister? I seem to have lost my address book. . . ."

And, right now, Noah would be finishing his lunch and getting ready to make his presentation in Atlantic City. And tonight, when he is home again and they are sitting in their cozy library at River House, having perhaps a nightcap together before going to bed, where they will perhaps make love, and perhaps with a nice fire going in the fireplace, he will tell her how it all went this afternoon, and she is sure it will have gone well. And then he will ask her, "And how was your week, darling?"

"Oh, nothing out of the ordinary. Mother had another violent spell today. Mary quit. Joanne Satterthwaite in 29-A is organizing a committee to have you thrown out as president of the building. Anne's quit her job, and announced she isn't going back to Bennington, even though her tuition's paid for the full year. Cory McCurdy was insulting to me at a museum meeting because of something your father did to his father years ago. Roxy Rhinelander called, and she'll probably have an item in her column in the *News* tomorrow morning about a feud that's supposedly going on in our building, and that seems to have you and me at the center of it. Your sister's drinking again and threatening suicide. I got into a bit of a *mano a mano* with your mother over lunch, and then into another *mano a mano* with Cory McCurdy after that. Told a few lies, a few exaggerations, made up some stuff, tried to throw my weight around. Got called kike and swindler all in the same day. Met your notorious Aunt Bathy, who actually seems rather nice. Nearly suffocated in a stalled elevator. Oh, and I almost forgot—our apartment was broken into, though nothing was taken except my address book. But when I was cleaning up afterward, I found some pieces of what looked like Melody's underwear in the bottom of your closet, which perhaps we need to talk about? There was blood on it. I'm *sure* there's a simple explanation! And, let's see, what else? Oh, yes. Edna says the dishwasher's acting up again. She says we need a new one. And the good news is? Well, there really isn't any, except for some vague promises and a lot of things left up in the air. Welcome home, my darling!"

She turns off the parkway at the exit marked Bullethole Road, and for the next three miles the little bottle-green sports coupe is forced to proceed more slowly, along winding country roads, and Carol has a sudden, wild craving for a cigarette.

It has been nearly twenty years since she smoked her last cigarette. She gave up cigarettes, on her doctor's advice, when she discovered she was pregnant with Anne. Before that she smoked rather a lot. She has experienced these nicotine cravings before. They come at odd, irrational moments, without warning, and for no apparent reason at all. In her dreams she will often discover herself enjoying a Kent. It is an addiction, she supposes, that will always be with her. This time the craving is almost overpowering. Her heart pounds, and her vision blurs. She even furiously slaps the pockets of her shearling coat to see whether, by some crazy chance, a half-filled packet of Kents has been left there from her smoking days, which is absurd, she knows, because she did not even own this coat then.

Now the little car turns off the road into a gravel lane lined high with rhododendrons, their dark leaves curled tightly in cigar shapes against the winter cold. This lane continues for a half a mile or so, until it reaches a high stone wall that can be entered only through a pair of heavy, wrought-iron gates. Beside the gates, a discreet bronze plaque reads: GREENSPRING HILLS. PRIVATE.

She stops the car outside the gates, lowers her window, presses the enunciator button, and announces herself.

Slowly the gates swing open, the way they used to do for her at Grandmont.

19

Afternoon

At first she didn't recognize him at all. It was a totally
unfamiliar face—an old man, slightly bent, rather formally dressed in a dark suit, white shirt with a starched
collar, and a blue-and-white-striped necktie with a wide
knot, a black pearl stickpin in the knot, leaning on a
cane. What pleased her most was his full head of white
hair. She thinks she would not have been able to bear
it if he had lost his hair.

"Come in, George," she said.

"I don't really need this," he said, holding up the
cane. "I carry it as insurance. The sidewalks outside are
icy in places."

She led him into the drawing room of the apartment,
the most formal of her rooms, a room always reserved
for special occasions.

"You have a beautiful apartment, Hannah."

"Thank you. It—suffices."

And now, sitting opposite him in one of a pair of
Louis XIV chairs, the mirror of memory has cleared.
The years have dropped away, and his face has resumed
its familiar contours, the same slightly off-center smile.
It is as though he hasn't changed or aged at all, and she
wonders if the same miracle of transformation has taken
place in his mind as well as he looks at her.

As though echoing her thoughts, he says, "You
haven't changed a bit, Hannah."

"Oh, Lord love you for a liar," she says with a laugh.
"Of course I've changed. And so have you. Though not
all that much, in fact. No, you haven't changed a bit,
either."

They sit in silence for a moment or two. "Would you
like a drink?" she asks at last. "Some tea perhaps?"

"No, thanks. Nothing," he says, and there is another silence.

"Well!" she says finally. "Here we are."

"This is going to be difficult for us, isn't it?" he says. "So much time's gone by. There's so much to talk about, and yet—"

"And yet so little."

"Yes."

"Did you marry, George?"

"Yes. Twice, in fact. I've buried two wives. That's not an expression I like much, but that's what they say. I've buried two wives."

"Children?"

"No, never any children. Sometimes I've regretted that, now that I live alone. You?"

"Three. No, four, actually."

"Ah."

"One of them was yours."

He smiles faintly. "I often wondered about that. That thought often crossed my mind, particularly when your letters stopped coming. But I was so far away, and there was nothing I could do."

"Of course there wasn't. She was a beautiful baby girl."

"And I'm sure you were a wonderful mother, Hannah."

"No, as a matter of fact, I wasn't. I wasn't at all. My mother took me to Germany to have the baby. She was raised as my baby sister. Nobody ever knew, not even my father. Especially not him."

"I see," he says.

"Do you? You see, it was such a different era, George. That German-Jewish crowd I grew up in. So proud. My father's family—all those distinguished rabbis and scholars in his family tree. And the women in those days. So strict and prim and proper. They wore long, high-collared dresses, and pearls—pearls, even for canoe trips and picnics in the Adirondacks! Everything had to be *just* so. It would have destroyed my father if he'd known what happened to me. I would have disgraced the whole family. I'd have been an outcast. The whole family would've been outcasts. I'd have disgraced the family name."

"I understand," he says.

"It's all so different today. Today nobody would bat an eyelash at what you and I did, or what happened to me. Today it would just be ho-hum. My granddaughter, Anne, who's eighteen—she says she's never going to get married. She says she's just going to have a long string of lovers! Of course, I think she says things like that just to tease me, but she says them just the same."

"It just wasn't in the stars for you and me, was it, Hannah?"

"No, it wasn't. But your daughter grew up to be a very beautiful woman, George. Very beautiful, and very bright, and very talented. She worked for my husband's company for a number of years. She even got to be rather famous. *Advertising Age,* which is a trade paper, once voted her Advertising Woman of the Year! You and I can be very proud of that, George. She—" She breaks off suddenly. "Would you like to meet her, George? I could arrange that."

"I don't know," he says. "What do you think?"

"It's up to you, George. I could—"

"But then you'd have to explain to her who I am, wouldn't you?"

"Yes, I suppose so, but—"

"Which could be difficult."

"Yes. Perhaps."

"So I think—no. It's a little late for me to start becoming a father at my age, Hannah."

"Let me at least show you some pictures of her." She rises and fetches a leather-bound photo album from a small table, and hands it to him.

He sits with the album unopened on his lap.

"Open it. It's full of—"

"No, I think I'd rather keep the picture I have of her in my mind's eye," he says. "But let me show you something." He reaches into his inside breast pocket and withdraws a small book. "I've always kept a journal," he says. "This one is from the year you and I met." He opens it to a page and shows her a small, dried, brown, and papery flower that has been pressed between the pages.

"My gardenia," she says, and suddenly she is tremendously touched and moved, and tears well in her eyes. "It was for my father, but you stopped and picked it up."

"It's been around the world many times, that little flower."

"You picked it up, and put it between your teeth like a gypsy, and danced a little jig."

"If you look closely, I think you'll find the teeth marks are still there. But I think I might have a little trouble now, dancing the jig."

"And then you left your cap."

"And you kept it for me."

"And you kept my flower." She stares down at it, and all at once the dried petals become white and fresh again, and, yes, she can see fresh teeth marks on the stem. She closes the little book carefully and hands it back to him, and he replaces it in his inside breast pocket. "George—do you remember—do you remember the sound you said the snoring sailors made from the bunks below you on your ship?"

He smiles at her. *"Manush, manush.* A lot of time's gone by, Hannie, and a lot has happened to both of us. But I have wonderful memories, my dear, wonderful pictures in my mind's eye." He reaches for his cane and rises, a little stiffly, from his chair to go.

She also rises. "George—will you come back again? Will you come back often? So we can talk some more, and remember more things?"

"Of course," he says, and smiles at her again, but something in the way he says this tells her that he will not come back again. They stand there, in her formal French drawing room, full of Louis XIV, a lifetime of collecting, and they are both suddenly a little hesitant and awkward. It is as though they have taken separate paths and met at the end of a peninsula, and all the ground behind them has washed away. He lowers his head and kisses her lightly on the forehead. "Good-bye, dear heart," he says.

The introductory applause dies down as Noah approaches the podium, and as he turns to face his audience of Ingraham people, the house lights dim, though a small spot remains on Noah's face. Behind him the big screen lights up. "For me," he begins, "it all began in

the tiny Scottish village of Ballachulish." He presses a
small button on the podium, and, *click,* the first image
fills the screen. "Population three hundred and sixteen,
not far from the entrance to the Firth of Lorne. It was
in the early spring of 1992, and the air was crisp and
fresh and new. What was I doing in this little town, so
small and remote that it doesn't appear on most maps,
a town that reminded me a little bit—"

Softly, at first, the overture from *Brigadoon* comes up
from the pair of speakers on the stage. The song is "The
Heather on the Hill." *Look at your audience,* he hears
her say. *Catch their eyes.*

Noah looks out across the sea of upturned and politely
expectant faces that fills the darkened ballroom—faces
he wishes he would one day learn to attach to names
without the help of name tags—and, beyond the faces,
to the pair of glass doors that leads into the lobby, and
sees a young girl with long dark hair sitting in a club
chair. A small blue suitcase sits beside her on the floor.
Her knees are pressed tightly together, and her eyes are
closed. Her lips are moving, and he realizes that she has
memorized the script, too, and is following it with him.
Suddenly he thinks he should forget the script and rush
out to her, telling her not to go without him, telling her
they'll work something out. Come with me, go with me,
I don't care where. Surely we are not the only man and
woman in the world to whom this sort of thing has happened. There are many more of us out there. We are
not alone. But of course he does not do this.

"—of Brigadoon."

As he speaks, the music rises briefly, then fades,
then disappears.

"Your mother's in the east sitting room, Mrs. Liebling," Sister Margaret Mary says. "And she's alone, so
you might want to have your visit with her there? You
can close the doors, if you like, for privacy."

"Thank you, Sister." She starts down the long, wide
corridor toward the sitting room.

The rooms of Greenspring Hills have been decorated
in the exuberant style of the late Dorothy Draper when
she was in her cabbage-rose period. The colors used are
all warm and vibrant, yellows, hot pinks, oranges and

lime greens, citrus colors that, supposedly, are designed to convey an atmosphere that is cheery and upbeat. Cabbage roses appear in persimmon on the wallpaper, and in lemony yellow on the polished chintz used to cover chairs and to create balloon-type window hangings. All the floral prints are oversize, and all the rooms are deeply carpeted in soft pastels, and all this use of fabrics gives Greenspring Hills a hushed quality, in which all sounds of distress are muted, if not silenced altogether. Here a scream would not carry far. Actually, these echoes of Dorothy Draper are not entirely accidental. Greenspring Hills was decorated by Carleton Varney, who was Mrs. Draper's handpicked successor.

Carol finds her mother seated in one corner of a plump pink and green chintz-covered sofa, her rosary beads in her hands. She is dressed, as usual, very simply, in brown slacks and a beige blouse, though Carol notices that the blouse is food-stained in the front. She reminds herself to speak to Sister about that before she leaves. She likes her mother to look tidy. Her mother was always a small woman, but today, sitting in that big sofa, alone in that big happy-colored room, she looks even smaller, her gray hair hanging to her shoulders straight, uncurled. Her mother does not look up when she enters the room, but continues fingering her beads.

"Hello, Mother," she says, sitting down beside her on the sofa.

"I'm making a very special novena," she says. "And I'm making it for you."

"Oh, that's nice, Mother," Carol says.

"The Blessed Virgin is weeping for you today, and also for me."

"I'm sorry to hear that, Mother."

"There have been sins committed, and for these there must be atonement. There must be redemption."

"Of course. Are you happy here, Mother?"

"Happy? Oh, I'm as happy here as I'll be anywhere, until I'm gathered into the arms of Our Lord Jesus."

"Sister Margaret Mary said there was a little problem in the dining room this morning."

"Sister Margaret Mary is a liar!"

"Oh? I thought you liked Sister Margaret Mary, Mother."

"She's a liar! And don't call me Mother! There is only one Mother, the Holy Mother of the Universe! She's with us now."

Carol reaches out and gently touches her mother's hand. "Mama, then. When I was little, I called you Mama."

"Don't interrupt me. Let me finish my beads."

And so they sit in silence while her mother mutters the words under her breath. "Hail, Mary, full of grace. . . . Our Father . . ."

At last she finishes, and her hands fall to her lap, though she still holds the beads. "Let us pray," she says. "Get down on your knees, Carol, and we will pray for forgiveness."

"I don't want to pray just yet," she says. "First, I want to talk about what happened in the dining room this morning."

"The angels spoke to me this morning."

"Yes—that's what I meant. What did the angels say to you, Mama? Sister Margaret Mary said—"

"Don't believe what *she* says! She's not the messenger of the Lord. I am!"

"Of course, Mama. So tell me what the angels said to you."

"That a sin has been committed. A mortal sin."

"Tell me what that was, Mama."

"The angels came into the dining room to tell me."

"And what did they say?"

"That there has been lechery, and there has been sin, and that you and I are to be punished for it."

"I see," Carol says, feeling helpless. Like so many of her conversations with her mother, this one is just spinning in circles, going nowhere. "Well," she says, "you mustn't let these messages upset you. Because when you get upset, it upsets everybody else who lives here. Isn't there a little pill you're supposed to take when you feel upset? A little yellow pill?"

"Pills are worldly things. This was Divine Word."

"But you see what I'm saying, Mama, is that when you inflict your upset on other people—well, that's not very Christian, is it? Remember, 'Do unto others—' "

"Don't talk to me about what's Christian! You married the Christ-killer. You're the apostate."

"Now, Mama, you know I don't like it when you talk this way."

"It's true! You know what Father Timmons said when you married a man of the people who crucified and killed Our Lord, the only begotten son of God and our Holy Mother. He said no good would come of it, and no good has. And now you're being punished for it—punished by your Christ-killer's lechery and unfaithfulness, by his treachery and betrayal. But I—I sat back and let you do it. I let you be delivered into the hands of Satan. You have your punishment now. But the Blessed Virgin hasn't decided yet what my punishment will be. That's why I'm making this novena."

Carol sighs. "Sister Margaret Mary said you received a fax this morning. Who was that from, Mama?"

"Fax? I don't know what you're talking about."

"One of those letters that comes over the telephone lines."

"There was a letter, yes."

"Who was it from, Mama?"

"The Blessed Virgin."

"I know the Blessed Virgin often speaks to you, Mama. But I didn't know she wrote you letters."

"Nonsense. She writes to me all the time."

"And I didn't know she had a fax machine."

"I don't know what you're talking about."

"What did the letter say, Mama?"

"It is Holy Writ. It was signed B, for Blessed Virgin."

"But what did the letter *say?*"

"The truth. The truth about you and the Christ-killer you married. And his young whore."

"Do you still have the letter, Mama?"

"Yes. I should probably burn it, since it's Holy Writ. I should burn it, and let the smoke rise up to heaven and join our Holy Mother and her heavenly angels who sent it to me."

"May I see the letter, Mama?"

"No! It is Holy Writ. It was not meant for the eyes of an apostatc."

"But if it concerns me, I'm sure the Blessed Virgin intended you to share the letter with me."

Her mother eyes her narrowly. "You think so?" she says.

"Oh, I'm quite sure of it, Mama," Carol says. "That would be the Christian thing, wouldn't it—to share?"

"To convince you of your sin, and your apostasy? Do you think that's what she wants?"

"Of course that's what she wants, Mama. It's quite obvious that's what she wants. How else would she convince me of my sin?"

"But she doesn't exactly say that in her letter."

"But remember Saint Augustine, Mama. He said, 'God always writes straight, but sometimes in crooked lines.' "

"That's true. At least you remember some of the things Father Timmons taught you."

"I remember everything he taught me. Is the letter upstairs in your room, Mama?"

"No, I have it here." Slowly she reaches inside her soiled blouse and withdraws the letter, and hands it to Carol.

". . . and now let's go next door and try some Balla-chulish," he says. "I think you're going to like it."

The lights in the room come up again, and the applause begins.

"Maybe you'd better hold your applause until after you've tasted Mr. Kelso's brew," he says, and there is laughter. "And now, before I leave the microphone, I have just one favor to ask of all of you before we all start partying in earnest. I'd like to conduct a blind taste test. As you enter the party room next door, each of you will be given two ballots. On the table on your left, in numbered plastic glasses, will be samples of Angus Kelso's whiskey along with samples of fourteen other premium single malts. I'd like you to taste each of these, and rank each on a scale of one to ten—based on the usual three criteria: taste, nose, and color. On the table on your right will be samples of the water from Mr. Kelso's caves, along with nine other premium bottled non-carbonated waters. I'd like you to do the same with these. When the results are tallied, then maybe we'll have something to celebrate."

There is more applause, and people begin rising from their seats.

Noah looks out across his audience to the double glass

doors that lead to the lobby. The girl and her suitcase
are gone.

And now the wrap-up cocktail party is in full swing.
The results of the taste test were even better than Noah
had dared hope for, with Angus Kelso's scotch coming
out the easy winner, and with eighty percent of the vot-
ers voting it their favorite. The test of the bottled waters
was almost as encouraging; sixty-five percent chose
Kelso's as their favorite. Now Noah moves around the
room, shaking hands, accepting backslaps and congratulations, using his old trick of looking a man straight in
the eye and at his name tag at the same time.

"Hey, Phil . . . Yo, Paul . . . How're you doing,
Harry? . . . Hey, Dave—your wife have the baby yet?"

"Little boy."

"Congratulations, buddy."

"Great presentation, Noah. Really great . . ."

"I got a great name for it, Noah—Highland Fling!"

"Not bad. Write 'em all down, send 'em all in. Ten
thousand to the winner . . ."

"What about Heather Hill?"

"Too close to Heaven Hill? But send 'em all in. Ten
thousand—"

"We're gonna knock the competition on its ass,
Noah."

"That's my intention, buddy."

Someone named Peter corners him. "Listen, I've got
a terrific marketing idea for this, Noah," he says. "We
should market the booze and the bottled water *under
the same name*! We can't advertise the booze on network
TV, but we can advertise the *water*. So the water pro-
motes the booze—get it? Hell, we can even advertise
the water in the Girl Scouts' magazine!"

"Believe it or not, that's exactly my thinking, Pete.
It's like what they say, great minds—"

Peter looks crestfallen. "Anyway, it's a million-dollar
idea," he says.

Noah finds Frank Stokes standing alone at the bar,
nursing a drink. "C'mon, Frank," he says. "It's not like
it's the end of the world. Nothing's like it's the end of
the world."

"That's what it's like for me," Frank says. "Like it's the end of the world."

With tongues loosened by liquor, the noise level in the room rises, and in certain sections the party becomes almost raucous, as waiters circulate with trays of drinks and others with trays of hors d'oeuvres.

"Anybody want to get laid tonight? There's this girl called Estelle . . ."

"Didja hear the one about the rabbi who got stranded on a desert island?"

"I won eight hundred bucks at roulette last night. Whaddaya think of that?"

"And it was quite a few years before he was rescued, you see, and by the time they rescued him he'd—"

"Roulette? Shit, that's a sissy game. I'm hitting the craps table one more time before I head home."

". . . built a hospital, a yeshiva school, a community center, and two synagogues."

"This Estelle gives great head, man."

"So they said to him, we can understand you building the hospital, the yeshiva school, and the community center. But why *two* synagogues?"

"Hell, you can't get AIDS from a girl giving you head!"

"And the rabbi said, 'The other one I wouldn't set foot in!' "

"You *can*?"

Noah moves, smiling, shaking hands, through all of this. Before he is finished, before he can leave the party and go home, it is essential that he greet every single person in this crowded, noisy room. "Hey, Dex . . . Yo, Wally . . . Hi, there, Eddie . . ."

"Telephone call for you, Mr. Liebling," a waiter says. "You can take it in that little room over there. Quieter . . ."

It is Edith Ackerman. "Mr. Noah," she says, "I just wanted to make sure you got my message—that Miss Hannah wants to see you at her house before you go home tonight. As soon as you get to New York, no matter how late it is. She says it's very important."

"Yes, Edith, I did get that message. Thanks."

"Oh, Mr. Noah!" There is a sob in her voice.

"What's the matter, Edith?"

"Oh, Mr. Noah—the most awful thing has happened.'

"What is it, Edith?"

"The Little Girl is dead!"

"Dead?" He carries the phone with him to a chair and sits down. "Now tell me," he says. "Tell me exactly what happened, Edith."

"This morning she had some sort of seizure. Her blood sugar was up. I gave her an injection, and she seemed better, but I didn't think she should go to her school today, and so I had my neighbor come in, and—"

"Oh, you're talking about your *niece*," he says. "Oh, thank God . . ."

"What?"

He bridges his left hand over his eyes, as though to shield them from the light, though the light is behind him. "I just meant . . . it must seem like such a release for you, Edith. She's been such a burden to you, Edith, such a care . . . all these years, and . . ."

"But still, Mr. Noah," she sobs. "But still. She was all I had. . . ."

You did this, Carol is thinking. You did this, yes, you did. And I hurt. I hurt here, and here. And also here. Oh, you bastard. You hurt me so much I no longer know where I'm going, or even where I've been, you bastard whom I hate. And also love. Because hating someone you love is the worst kind of hate there is. She adjusts the sun visor on her little green car.

Did you think I never had opportunities to do to you what you've done to me? Did you think Johnny Pearlstein never tried to put his hand inside my dress that night after we all went to see *Born Free,* and you were taking the sitter home, and I just pushed his hand away? Or were you doing the same thing to the sitter? How many chances to hurt you this way have I turned down? Dozens, you bastard, and even more than that, if I were to count all the times on my fingers. And just the other night, when Beryl and Bill Luckman and Georgette came up for drinks, did Bill Luckman—or did he not—whisper to me, "I find you very attractive"? And did I not just smile and go on passing the cheese and crackers? I could have hurt you like this dozens and dozens and dozens of times. But did I?

And speaking of Beryl, she's obviously been getting her jollies while Frank is out of town. In fact, she's probably been getting them from Bill Luckman. She was all over him like a tent that night. Yearbooks. I heard her tell him she had some old school yearbooks. "Come up and see my yearbooks." Sure, that's what she did. Took him up to her place after she left my place and screwed him. I could have done the same, you bastard. At least he's an adult. In fact, he's probably the one she wrote that letter to, though how it got faxed to Mama at Greenspring Hills I'll never know. Did you think I could be someone like Beryl, as dumb as she is?

How long has this been going on, you bastard? How long has Melody been spending her vacations with us? Three years? Four? As long as that? And right under my nose, under my own roof. That's the worst part. That's what hurts the most, because it makes me feel so stupid, stupider than Beryl Stokes, and that's pretty stupid. You think I'm stupid. No one ever called me stupid before. Four years of college in three, and a Phi Beta Kappa key even so. "No wives at sales conference, that's the rule," you told me. But what about teenage girlfriends? That was the question I was too stupid to ask, you bastard, my love I love to hate, my hate I hate to love. The line between the two is so thin that it's nothing but a tiny, blurry squiggle now. *Oh, I could kill you for what you've done to me, Noah, kill you for what you've killed in me, I really could.*

Where am I?

It is the sun, the sun in her eyes that is blinding her, altering familiar landmarks on the highway ahead of her, making everything she sees float strangely out of focus. In the sun's glare the landscape along the parkway, instead of gathering alongside her as she drives, seems to slide away from her on all sides and disappear. She has forgotten how far south the sun moves in mid-winter, and now, driving back to New York, as the sun sinks toward the horizon against a clear sky, it is directly in her eyes. She tries adjusting the visor again, which does not help, and she has left her sunglasses at home. She has always kept her little green car spotlessly clean and polished, but perhaps she has picked up some road dust on the trip, and this is helping the direct sunlight to shatter her vision so. Or perhaps her windshield is simply too clean, and its very cleanness is refracting the sun's light in her eyes too brilliantly.

Still, she drives the way she has always liked to drive, a little over the speed limit. Perhaps, she thinks, she has always gone at everything a little too fast. Perhaps that is the trouble. Perhaps she had wanted to leave the little town of Rumney Depot, New Hampshire, too fast, to leave the world of her Christ-obsessed mother and the ever present Father Timmons, who, her mother used to remind her, was the closest thing to a real father she would ever have. Perhaps she had wanted to leave that world so fast that she had left it before she ever understood it. Then she had put herself through college too fast, accelerating, squeezing four years' worth of study into three. Then she had gotten her master's degree in psychology too fast, in one year instead of two. Then she had speeded into marriage with Noah, whom she had met—fast—on a blind date, and fallen in love with too fast. Noah had told her he liked speed, too, speed and danger. They had run off and been married at City Hall without telling anyone, courting danger, courting disaster, and it was this marriage, Father Timmons had insisted to this day, that drove her mother over the edge, though there had been plenty of alarming signals before that. "When she heard you'd done that, she simply snapped," he said to her. "Snapped like a bough in the wind. It was a terrible thing you did, Carol. Now your mother is a broken reed." Then, with her accelerator pedal pressed to the floor, she sped into motherhood. *What was I trying to prove? And to whom was I trying to prove whatever it was?*

But I was in love.

One falls in love because one falls in love. That's all there is to it. It's as simple as that. There's no other explanation. And probably one really falls in love no more than once, and that is probably a lucky thing. Once is enough, and more than once would probably be unbearable. The rest of the time one is just waiting to be in love, or wanting to be in love, or trying to be in love, or thinking about being in love, or pretending to be in love, which is always fruitless and pointless in the end. Oh, yes. Sometimes at night, pretending to be asleep, I

will hear sounds—soft, secretive sounds—from the bed
next to mine, and I know that he is making love to
himself. When it first happened, long ago, I was bewil-
dered. Then I was hurt, then I was angry. Where were
his thoughts when he did this? Were they with some
other lover, someone he found more fulfilling than me?
Why was I not invited, not even permitted, to share
these secret moments with him? I would lie very still in
the other bed, keeping my own breathing soft and slow
and regular, pretending to sleep, until he finished. Then
I would hear him sleeping.

But then, long ago, I decided that these private, secret
moments of his were all a part of sharing my life with
him, a part of being in love with him and, of course, this
discovery only made me love him more. Loving is more
than fucking. Fucking is more like dancing, a pleasant
way to pass some leisure time. Loving is not a pleasant
pastime, no holiday in Capri. Love is rugged and thick
with tangled underbrush and sudden, unexpected pitfalls
and barriers between lovers, barricades that announce
NO TRESPASSING BEYOND THIS POINT, and this was the
worst part, the loneliest part of being in love, the whole
trouble with loving at all, why love is not for the fool-
hardy, or even for the wise and brave. Love is for those
willing to be left out. They might tell you that love is
sharing, but sharing means sacrifice, as every child learns
when he is being taught to share. The bigger the sacrifice, the more it hurts. And so when those times come
when sharing is no longer endurable, men and women
in love fight back with secrets. That was the crux of it,
that was the real trouble with it. When one is in love,
one is always in love alone.

And so—what to do now? Can I forgive him? That
would be the Christian way. The Christian prayer tells
us to forgive those who trespass against us. I wonder
what Hannah would say. "Forget it," I can hear Hannah's Old New York vowels saying. "Don't be ab*suh-
uhd*. Get on with your life, woman. *Shuh-uh*-ly this isn't
the worst thing that's ever happened to any woman in
the *wuh-uhld*. This isn't the *fuhst* time this has ever happened to a woman, and it *cuh*-tainly won't be the last."
But what kind of a life do I have to get on with, Hannah? Tell me that. And yet . . . and yet. After all, all he

did was fuck her. You must remember this, a kiss is just a kiss, a fuck is just a fuck. Fucking isn't loving. But I've already said that. And yet he wouldn't have fucked her if he really loved me, and so here I am again, right back where I started, talking in circles, getting nowhere.

And so now Carol is speeding blindly down the Henry Hudson Parkway with the sun in her eyes, courting an accident, but suddenly the thought of an accident is not without a certain appeal, a certain almost piquancy. Aren't there moments in every human life when the idea of self-destruction floats into the racing mind, beckoning with sirenish allure, holding out its gentle hand and offering a solution to everything? A temptingly fast solution? That was the best thing about it: it would be so fast.

Now her thoughts are measured and spaced out, and seem to be coming to her in slow motion. She is passing through the Riverdale section of the Bronx, and ahead of her is the Spuyten Duyvil Bridge to Manhattan. On her left is Baker Field, where she used to go to watch college football games. Below her, on her left, winds the Harlem River. On her right is the Hudson, looking deceptively wide and calm, and that narrow gap of water where the angry tides from the Harlem River boil into the larger river through a steep and narrow rock-strewn gap, some two hundred feet below. The railings of the Spuyten Duyvil Bridge do not look particularly substantial. One quick turn of her wheel, and her car would go flying through those railings, and it would be over, fast. She tries it, turns the wheel, and watches her car head for the railing. But when she feels her right foot fly to the pedal of the power brakes she knows she does not really want to die.

She sees the crash, everything, although she really cannot see it from her driver's seat. She sees her right front fender crumple against the railing, sees the right headlight shatter in a shower of glass. But now the car is at a standstill, its right wheel up on the concrete curb of the railing, the motor idling.

She puts the gearshift into park, and gets out to inspect the damage. The fender is caved in, but well away from the wheel, so the car will steer. The front bumper

is twisted, but secure. The right headlight is gone, but
at least a half an hour of daylight remains before she
will need it. No fluids are dripping from under the hood,
so the radiator is not cracked. The car will get her home.
Perhaps there is something to be said, after all, for driving an expensive car. This being New York, of course,
no one stops to help her, though motorists in both directions slow down for a better look at the accident.

The impact threw her chest against the steering wheel,
and she struggles to get her breath back, feeling a little
nauseated. But she gets back into the car and backs it
off the curb, into the roadway, where it lands with a
small bump and another scrape of the fender. Only then
does she see, in her rearview mirror, the spinning orange
light of a police car pulled up behind her, and a lanky
young officer walking toward her. She rolls down her
window.

"You all right, little lady?" he asks her.

"Yes, Officer. I'm fine, thanks."

"What happened?"

"The sun was in my eyes."

He looks up at the upper roadway of the bridge above
them, which throws where they are now into deep
shadow. "No sun under here," he says.

"I'm afraid I just wasn't concentrating on the road,"
she says.

"That's not a good thing to be doing when you're
driving a car, little lady—not concentrating on the road."

"I guess my thoughts were—elsewhere, Officer."

"It's also not good to have your thoughts elsewhere
when you're behind the wheel of a vehicle, little lady."

"I know. I'm sorry."

"Think you might have fallen asleep at the wheel, little lady?"

"No, and—look, that's the third time you've called me
that, Officer. I do have a name. Do you want to see my
license and registration?"

"That won't be necessary, ma'am."

"That's better," she says. She looks up at his face. He
is surely no more than twenty-four or twenty-five. She
wonders: Is he going to ask me to get out of my car and
into his while he writes out a ticket? She has heard lurid
stories about policemen who stop single women, rape

them at gunpoint, and then stuff them into the trunks of their cars.

"Where're you coming from?" he asks her. "Maybe from a cocktail party? Maybe had a couple of drinks?"

"No, but I wish I had."

He squints at her. "What do you mean by that?"

"Because that would have given me a good excuse for what I did. Want me to get out of the car and try to walk a straight line?"

"No, that won't be necessary, ma'am."

"It's funny. My husband's in the liquor business, and when you're in the liquor business you hardly ever think about drinking. Half the time I forget to stock the bar in my own house. My maid has to remind me."

"Oh, you've got a maid?" He smiles. "It figures, with a car like this."

"I used to have a maid. She quit this morning." She studies his uniform, which strikes her as an unusual combination of styles and periods. His gray Stetson calls to mind the hats J.R. Ewing wore in *Dallas*. His blue double-breasted jacket and wide belt could have belonged to a Union cavalry officer in the Civil War, while his gray jodhpurs and black boots seem to have been borrowed from a polo player, though she doubts those long legs have ever been astride a horse. His skin is smooth and clean-shaven, though his beard is dark. He has a strong jawline and kind, dark eyes with heavy lashes. If he turns out to be a rapist, she thinks, I could do a lot worse. In fact, his face reminds her of someone she knows. She knows who it is: Noah, when he was younger.

"I've been following you for about the last five miles," he says. "You were going a little fast—five, six miles over the speed limit. But I don't like to ticket anybody for as small a violation as that. You were driving just fine, but then suddenly you swerved and hit the railing here."

"I know. My mind was on something else."

"Where did you say you're coming from?"

"I don't think I did say, Officer. It's a place in Connecticut called Greenspring Hills. I don't know why they call it that. It's not green, there isn't any spring, and there aren't any hills to speak of."

"Oh, sure. I know that place. The funny farm. You an inmate there?"

"No, but my mother is. Yes, I guess you could say my mother's funny. She's funny that way. That's a song, isn't it? And incidentally, they don't call them inmates. They call them residents. Or guests. And it's not called the funny farm. It's called an inn." Why is she chattering with him like this, as though he were an old friend? "I got some bad news there this afternoon," she says. "That's why I wasn't concentrating on my driving the way I should have been."

"Bad news about your mom? I'm sorry to hear that. I lost my own mom just a month ago, so I know how you feel."

"I'm so sorry, Officer."

"Only forty-two. Too young. Cancer." He walks around to the front of her car, looks at the collapsed fender, and checks the bridge railing. Then he returns to her window. "No damage done to the railing," he says. "I'd have to ticket you if there'd been any damage done to that. Just some of your green paint scraped off. But it's going to cost you a few nickels to have that front end of yours repaired."

"A few nickels . . ."

"It's a shame, too. Nice car like that. Tell me something—did you have your seat belt fastened?"

"No, as a matter of fact, I didn't."

"I could ticket you for that, too." His face is very serious, frowning. "But the fact is, I didn't actually *see* you driving without your seat belt. The first time I saw you, you'd already gotten out of the car. So I couldn't stand up in front of a judge and swear I saw you driving without a seat belt, could I?"

"No, I guess you couldn't, Officer."

"You got far to go, ma'am?"

"East Side of Manhattan." Yes, she guesses that's where she's going. At the moment, at least, there seems to be nowhere else to go.

"Well, you'd better get on your way. You'd better get home before dark. It's dangerous driving around at night with only one headlight. Would you like me to escort you home, ma'am?"

"Oh, no, thanks. That's very kind of you. But I'm fine now."

"Anything else I can do?"

"No, thanks—unless—"

"Unless what, ma'am?"

"You don't happen to have a cigarette, do you?" she asks him.

"Sure," he says, and reaches in the side pocket of his Union cavalry jacket. "Marlboro okay?"

"Anything!" she says with a little laugh.

He shakes one loose from his pack, offers it to her, and lights it for her with a match, and she sees the gold wedding band on his ring finger. Somewhere, she thinks, there is a very lucky woman.

"Thank you," she says. "And thank you for letting me off without a ticket, Officer. You've really been very kind. I think, more than anything, what I needed was just somebody to talk to. I think that's why I had the accident. I need somebody to talk to."

"Don't mention it, ma'am. Now, you just drive carefully—hear? And fasten that seat belt."

"I will. I promise."

He gives her a snappy little salute, touching the brim of his cowboy hat with the tip of his index finger.

"Good-bye, Marlboro Man," she says with a smile as she rolls her window back up again.

She watches him in her rearview mirror as he walks back to his car. Then she buckles her seat belt, starts up her car again, and continues on across the bridge, the lighted cigarette clenched tightly between two fingers of her gloved hand.

20

Night

A letter from Jules Liebling to his son Noah, dated June 12, 1974, about six months before Jules died:

Dear Sonny,

The trouble with the booze business is there's not a damn thing to it. It's got no glamour. It's got no class. Any damn fool could make a few million bucks doing what I've done for a living, and don't let anybody tell you different. Now the wine business is something else again. "Vintners," as they call themselves, are very lah-di-dah. Those snobs out in the Napa and Sonoma valleys go off riding to the hounds. If I tried riding to the hounds, they'd laugh me off the horse. Don't ask me why the hell this is. Making wine and making booze involves pretty much the same damn process. Boil the water out of your wine, and you'll get brandy. The only difference between selling wine and selling hooch is that the hooch makes more money.

If you get a kick out of making money, as I've always done, you'll get a kick out of this business. If you don't, better find yourself some other line of work, like be a college professor.

You'll hear some people talk about the "distilled spirits industry" as if it was some sacred thing that's been around for centuries. That's bullshit. It hasn't. The motion picture industry is older, and so, almost, is television. Both those industries are complicated. Ours isn't. I can tell you everything you need to know about booze in about two pages.

Until the present century there was no booze industry as such. People made booze, of course, but it was strictly a home operation. The guy with a still in his cellar or backyard made his hooch and peddled it to his neighbors. Then somebody got the idea that booze should be taxed. Taxation created the industry because you needed volume production and national distribution in order to fight the Feds. Taxation also created two new booze-related professions: moonshining and smuggling. The booze maker had a choice: either go along with the revenuers, or hide from 'em. I chose the former course because it seemed a hell of a lot easier.

But these new professions probably account for the fact that, in the public mind, people in our business are still considered to be crooks or lowlifes, or else ex-crooks and ex-lowlifes. Well, a lot of 'em damn well are.

Years ago, your ma asked me, "When are the nice people in New York going to accept us! When are even the nice Jewish people in New York going to accept us?" (Her folks were supposed to be some of those people.) My answer was: "When there's a cold day in hell—though they'll always accept our money." She's more cynical now. She's maybe even more cynical than I am, and I'm pretty damn cynical.

Any kid with a chemistry set can make booze. Just put some water in a boiler and bring it to a boil. Meanwhile, set out your hogsheads. Add some corn meal and water to your boiling water, and mix it with an iron paddle called a mashing oar. This is called soaking the corn. Add more boiling water and keep on stirring. This is called scalding the corn. Next, add rye and stir some more. This is called mashing in the rye, and at this point the whole mixture is called the mash. It looks like hell; and stinks.

Next, cool the mash off by adding cold water. Then add yeast, and the mixture is now ready to work, or ferment. At this point your mixture is called stuff, or beer. When the fermentation is over, the mixture is said to be ripe, or ready to be put into the still. Your stuff gets poured into a trough leading to a condenser, and the condenser is charged—meaning you light a fire under it. Keep stirring, while the still is being pasted—its joints stopped up with paste to keep steam from escaping. As soon as the mixture boils, the liquor that runs off is called the singlings, also called swill or pot ale.

Charge up another condenser, called the doubling

still, *and repeat the process. Then repeat again, and
keep repeating until your booze has reached the proof
you want. Aging in barrels reduces bite. But a lot of
people like their whiskey raw.*

*So there you have it, sonny—all the secrets and mys-
teries of our industry.*

*My greatest achievement in this business was getting
John F. Kennedy elected president of the United States.
I suppose you wonder how I accomplished that.*

*Well, it started back in '24 or '25, when old Joe Ken-
nedy was just getting started in the business. He didn't
have the experience that some of my other customers
had, and he was always looking for shortcuts and trying
to cut corners. Joe was a very impatient man. I've never
known a man so impatient to make money, and that
impatience of his made him a lot of enemies. He came
to me one day complaining that a lot of my shipments
weren't making it to his men who were stationed to
receive them along the South Shore.*

*I said to him, "Joe, I've got a suggestion for you.
Ever hear of a corduroy road?"*

"No," he said. "What's that?"

*I explained to him that a corduroy road is a road
made out of a bunch of logs lashed together with heavy
rope or cable. It's a device used by the military to provide the wheels of heavy vehicles with traction when
they need to get through muddy terrain.*

*You see, there were only so many places along the
South Shore where you could back a truck down from
the highway to the water's edge, and load up the shipments of cases that came across the lake by boat at
night. What the revenuers and hijackers—and a lot of
the revenuers were hijackers as well—had learned to
look for was the marks of tire treads in the mud. They'd
station themselves in these places and lie in wait at
night, waiting for the trucks and boats to come in and
transfer the shipments.*

*I said to Joe, "Make yourself a few corduroy roads,
but make 'em reversible. Sod one side of your road
with grass and weeds. By day, your road will look just
like a grassy stretch. Then, at night, when a shipment's
due in, flip your road over and back your trucks down*

*from the highway. It'll make your transfers a lot faster,
too, and easier.*

Well, old Joe took my suggestion, and he had no
more problems. The money started rolling in. So you
see—if I hadn't helped old Joe Kennedy make his fortune, he wouldn't have been able to buy his son a seat
in the House, then in the Senate, and finally the presidency of the United States. But did old Joe ever thank
me for what I did for him and his family? Never! Your
mother and I weren't even invited to the White House
for his son's inauguration!

I'm only telling you all this because, if you decide to
stay in this business—and I hope you will, because I
want it to be all yours one day—I want you to do so
with your eyes wide open, under no illusions that what
you do will get you the Nobel prize. Just give Uncle
Sam his share, and you'll stay out of jail. I did. That's
the only piece of advice I have for you, after more than
half a century in booze. Your loving old—

Pop

P.S. Better burn this letter. If it fell into the wrong
hands, I could be crucified. And I sometimes think I've
been crucified in this life enough already.

But he didn't burn the letter. It was one of the few
letters he had ever received from his father.

And now he sits in the visitor's chair in his mother's
library at 1000 Park Avenue, waiting for her. It is after
eleven o'clock at night, and the big apartment seems
even bigger, and strangely empty and silent, with all the
servants either in bed or gone for the night—too big
for one old woman. He hears her slippered footsteps
approaching down the long gallery, and her footsteps
sound heavy and slow.

She comes into the room, wearing a pink wool dressing gown over a white nightie, her hair in rollers, and
the rollers secured in a pink chiffon scarf tied in a big
bow, the whole getup suggesting a large pink rabbit. He
stands up. "I hope I didn't get you out of bed, Ma,"
he says.

"No, no. I was watching Jay Leno. He isn't very funny,

or maybe I'm missing something. I told your secretary to ask you to come by no matter how late it was. Sit down, Noah."

He sits again in the visitor's chair, though she remains standing. "He was so unfunny that I was able to write an entire press release while he was doing his monologue."

"Press release?"

"I'll get to that in a minute. Meanwhile, my spies tell me you did very well with your pitch for the Balla-whatchmacallit."

"Spies? I didn't know you had spies, Ma."

She winks at him. "Of course I have spies," she says. "Did you think your old ma could run a business this size without spies? I have spies in every corner, spies at every meeting. Your father always had spies. You'll need spies, too, when you take over. I also heard you changed my president's message a little."

"I did a little editing, yes."

She waves her hand. "Doesn't matter. Nobody really listens to those damn things, anyway. They're just a formality. But I hear your Ballachulish pitch went really well. And it won the blind taste test, too."

"You've finally got it right, Ma—Ballachulish. Yes, I think it went well."

"Good. Get the salesmen excited. That's the first big step. Get the salesmen excited, and they'll get the whole-salers excited. Get the wholesalers excited, and they'll get the retailers excited. All this is important to do before you buy a line of advertising. But that's not what I really want to talk to you about, Noah."

"Oh? And what's that?"

She sits down opposite him. "Bathy," she says.

He sits back in his chair and crosses his legs. "I see," he says. "Bathy again. I think we've been down this road once or twice before, Ma."

She holds up her hand. "Not this road we haven't, Noah," she says. "Not this particular road. To begin with, I know why you've always resented Bathy so."

"Oh?" he says.

"To put it bluntly, you once walked into a bedroom at Grandmont unannounced, and found Bathy and your father in what is sometimes called a compromising position. Correct?"

"Hell, yes! You're damn right I did."

She sighs. "You've always been so secretive, Noah," she says. "You keep things to yourself too much. Why didn't you tell me about this a long time ago? I've given you every opportunity. Why didn't you share your feelings about this with me at the time? We could have discussed it, like the two grown-ups we're supposed to be."

"*Discussed* it? What the hell are you talking about?"

"I mean, you should have told me about it at the time. It wasn't my place to bring it up with you. But if you'd just told me what you saw, I could have given you a very simple explanation."

He stares at her in disbelief. "Ma—are you and I talking about the same *event*? I'm talking about walking into the old man's bedroom and find him fucking your sister. That's what I'm talking about! And later he lied to me. He told me I hadn't seen what I thought I saw. But I know damn well what I saw. He was terrified that I'd tell you about it."

"Was he? I doubt it. I'm sure he knew that I was well aware of what was going on, after all those years, though your father and I never discussed it. There was never really any need to. There are too many things to discuss in a marriage that are necessary. There just isn't time to discuss unnecessary things. But I suppose it might have been a little upsetting to you, finding out like that. I'll admit that."

"*Upsetting*? I was disgusted—disgusted with both of them. Just totally disgusted. Sick to my stomach. I ran back down the hall to my room and threw up."

"Poor Bathy was terribly embarrassed by the incident. What woman wouldn't be? Barged in on like that!"

He shakes his head. "So you knew about this all along."

"Of course. But you should never barge into a person's bedroom without knocking first. It's bad manners. A person who does that gets to see what he deserves to see. Besides, you were supposed to be away at college. I was in New York. Your father and Bathy thought they had the house to themselves. I often arranged that sort of thing for them. It was all part of the arrangement we had together."

"An arrangement," he says dully. "I knew ours was a screwed-up family, but I didn't know we were that screwed up. You *tolerated* that? You're pitiful, Ma. You're really pitiful."

"Pitiful?" she says sharply. "I am *not* pitiful. Triumphant is more the word. I won the battle. Bathy was your father's mistress. I was fully aware of it. I approved of it. I endorsed it. It had been going on for a long time—since before you were born, in fact. It was an agreement we had, Bathy and I, and it worked out to the benefit of all concerned. *All*. Including you."

"Endorsed it," he says.

"All but put my John Hancock on it! It started out as a simple experiment at first. We didn't know whether it would work or not. But your father needed me for certain things, and he needed Bathy for certain other things. He needed us both, and we both needed him, and Bathy and I also needed each other. She and I said, very well, let's try it. Let's see if it works. And, as it turned out, it worked very well."

"A ménage à trois," he says.

"No, it wasn't that at all. A ménage à trois, as I understand it, is three people involved in a three-way sexual relationship. Ours wasn't that at all. It was more like a blueprint for living and working happily together. It was an arrangement that made your father happy, and made me happy, and made Bathy happy. I won't go so far as to say that Bathy saved my marriage. But she certainly helped make my marriage happier than it had ever been before, and happier than it ever could have been without her. If you'd understood this, you could have spared yourself a lot of anger, and tearing around the countryside on your motorcycle, mad at the world."

He looks at her. "That wasn't why I tore around the countryside on my motorcycle," he says. "It was because I enjoyed the feeling of power."

"Well, anyway, now you know the story. And stop and think. If it hadn't been for Bathy, none of you children would have any of the things you have today. There would have been a divorce, and then what would have become of me? I had no one else besides your father— and Bathy. I can even say that if it hadn't been for Bathy, you probably wouldn't even be standing in this room today. We owe everything to Bathy. So you've no right to feel betrayed. Bathy is the one who was betrayed."

"Betrayed? How?"

"I got to keep my husband. She didn't. I got to have his children. She didn't. I inherited this company. She got no Ingraham stock at all."

"I guess the old man just got tired of her in the end," he says.

"No! That's not true. You made him make a choice. You gave him an ultimatum. You said you'd never work for Ingraham as long as Bathy worked here, too. You cost Bathy her job, so you owe Bathy a lot, too. It was either you or her, you said, and he simply loved you more, needed you more, wanted a son to carry on the business more than he wanted anything else. When he explained this to Bathy, she understood because she loved him, and because she loved you, too. But even after she retired, and even after she no longer lived with us, she remained a powerful part of your father's life. In fact, a strange thing happened during those last years of his life. The three of us became even closer. The sexual attachment—well, that simmered down, of course, as those things always do, as the years went by. But something even more powerful appeared in its place—a love, an incredible sense of *closeness* that's hard to describe, except that it seemed as though the three of us had one *soul.* It was a wonderful free feeling, now that sex was no longer a part of it, and yet at the same time we seemed to have become almost unbearably dependent on one another. We were bound together by an invisible cord of love, and of memories, too, and of things there was no longer any need to talk about. Just things we *knew* and had shared in the past. Yes, I think he knew that I knew about him and Bathy. But there was no longer any need for blame, or forgiveness, or anything like that. It was peacefulness. It was understanding. It was happiness. And happiness—I'm convinced of it— is the bird in the hand." She touches her eyelids, first one, then the other, with the sleeve of her pink dressing gown.

"And yet when he died, he left her without a penny."

"He was always so obsessed with—appearances. Pro-

bity. Respectability. The things he was hoping to get,
but didn't, by marrying me. 'Ingraham—the label you
can trust.' The Leaning Tower of Pisa. 'You can trust
the Leaning Tower of Pisa never to fall down.' Bathy
and I always tried to help him project that image, for
whatever it was worth, to try to make the public forget
what everybody knew—that he was an ex-bartender with
no education, who took over a Canadian gin mill when
its owner couldn't pay his own bar bill, a man who
helped Al Capone get his start and whom Mr. Capone
wanted to reward by being Cyril's godfather. There was
so much in your father's life that he wanted to hide, and
Bathy was just part of it. To your father, leaving Bathy
money in his will would have been like admitting publicly that he had another woman, and that the other
woman was his own wife's—baby sister. When he was
dying, at Grandmont, Dr. Arnstein was with him, and I
was waiting in the music room, and Dr. Arnstein came
downstairs and said to me, 'I don't think he has much
longer, Hannah,' and so I went up to be with him. And
when I saw him, I said to the nurse, 'Please send for
Miss Sachs.'

"And when Bathy got there from the Tarrytown Inn,
where she was staying, we both gestured to the nurse
that we'd like to be alone with him for a little while.
And we both sat, on either side of his bed, Bathy holding
his left hand and I holding his right. I think we both
felt that invisible cord of love I mentioned. And then,
suddenly, in one of those lucid moments that often occur
to a person just before he dies—and I know this because
I've seen more people die than you have, Noah—he
opened his eyes, and looked at me, and said, 'I want
you to go out and buy something pretty for yourself,
Hannah. Something really pretty.' And then he turned
to Bathy and said the same thing.

"'We will,' we said.

"Then he said, 'It wasn't all that bad, was it?'

"And we said, 'No, Jules, it wasn't all that bad at all.'

"And then he turned to me and said, 'Hannah, will
you be sure to fix everything?'

"I wasn't sure what he meant, but I said, 'I will.'

"And then he closed his eyes, and the rales began,
and then he died. We sat with him for another half hour

or so, still holding his hands, feeling them grow cold, and then I got up and went to fetch Dr. Arnstein and the nurse.

"And later, after we'd had the will read to us—which came as something of a shock to us—I decided I knew what he meant by 'fixing everything.' He meant fixing everything with Bathy and with you. Between the two of you."

She clears her throat. "Anyway, you asked about my press release," she says. "I've got it all written, and I'll have Jonesy type it up and fax it out to the financial media on Monday morning. I've kept it quite short and sweet. It simply announces that, effective immediately, I am resigning as president and CEO of Ingraham and appointing you as my successor. I am also turning over to you my voting shares of Ingraham stock, according to the provisions of your father's will. You see why I wanted you to stop by here no matter how late it was. I wanted you to have the weekend to prepare to move into my old office. The company's all yours now."

"Yes," he says quietly, not moving in his chair. But why, after waiting for this to come about for all these years, does he suddenly feel let down now that it has finally happened? Is it that thing about answered prayers? Or is it because he sees his vision of Aesop receding before his eyes? So much time has gone by. That vision has already begun to seem flimsy and elusive. Even when he explained it to Melody, he wondered if his heart was really any longer in it. And even Melody—with all the rosy idealism that supposedly goes with youth—did not seem enormously impressed with it. Perhaps it was always, as his mother said when he first described it to her years ago, "just a cockamamie notion, another harebrained save-the-world scheme." Perhaps he said good-bye to it, saw it evaporate in smoke, in their hotel room in Atlantic City. Now reality looms. Now he is wedded to Ingraham forever. The future is at last secure. Carol will be very happy. We will have to celebrate this This, he thinks, is the first day of the rest of my life. Still, there was once a bright bird there. But it had flown away.

"I just have a couple of favors to ask you," his mother says.

"Ah. Conditions," he says, still sitting there in her visitor's chair.

"Not conditions!" she says sharply. "Favors. Not even favors. Suggestions. My press release will stay the same whether you decide to follow my suggestions or not."

"Okay, shoot," he says. "What are they, Ma?"

"I'd like to *suggest* that you invite Bathy to be on Ingraham's board. I'm not asking you to find her a position in the company. She wouldn't go back to work for Ingraham if you had one for her. But to be invited to join the board—I think she'd be touched, Noah. It would show her—"

"That I forgive her?"

"*No!* Not that you forgive her! You have nothing to forgive her for. If you want to forgive someone, forgive *me*. But it would let Bathy know that at last you understand everything."

"Okay, Ma. What else?"

"When you're ready to market Ballachulish, give the contract for producing the bottles to Van Degan Glass."

"*What?*" he says. "I thought there was a blood feud between us and the Van Degans. I thought there was an ironclad rule that we never did business with Van Degan."

She sighs. "It was all so long ago," she says. "And another generation. Everyone connected with it is dead now—except for me. And fifty years seems too long a time to bear a grudge."

"Well, now you're finally talking some sense," he says. "I never had any quarrel with Van Degan Glass. As far as I'm concerned, they're a fine old company."

"Then lift the boycott."

"With pleasure! The damn boycott never made any sense to me, anyway."

"And," she says, "if we—or, I should say, *you*—lift the boycott for Ballachulish, what would you think of giving Van Degan a contract to manufacture all our labels?"

"*All?*"

"All."

"Wow," he says with a soft whistle. "What would Pop say to that one?"

"Pop is deader than a mackerel. Pop is in that yellow jar in the dining room. Pop isn't going to say boo."

"Well, I'd certainly have no objection to that," he says.

"You see," she says, "I've been thinking. It may have been just a coincidence that the Van Degans moved out of the building the same day we moved in. Perhaps your father was being too sensitive to take it so personally."

"Could be. I wasn't even born when it happened."

"Their company's bottom line doesn't look at all good at the moment. Our business will help them a lot, of course. And I noticed at this afternoon's closing their stock hit a new low. So I was also thinking, maybe before we ink in any deal with them, it might be a good idea if we snapped up some of their stock—on the q.t., naturally. What do you think?"

"Ah," he says with a smile, "I'm beginning to get the picture, Ma."

"And if we had some Van Degan stock, it would give us a toe in the door in case we decided to take over the company."

"So. You have a plan. A takeover."

"Actually, it's Carol's plan."

"Carol?"

"Carol's working on a plan which—if it works out—would do wonders for us, Noah."

"Tell me about Carol's plan."

"I'll let Carol tell you about it. But wouldn't it be nice if we had our own glass-manufacturing division? It would save us a bundle."

"Yes, it surely would."

"And there's another reason why I want us to make nice to the Van Degans. Mrs. Van Degan wants to have a joint coming-out party for her daughter and Anne. The girls were apparently good friends at Brearley. At first, as you know, I was very much against the idea. Carol thinks it's a little silly, too, and she's worried that it's going to be terribly expensive. But I've changed my mind. And I've also decided I'd like to pay for this party—Anne's share of it, that is. I want to do this for two reasons. First, I want to do it for Anne, since it's something she wants. But I also want to do it for public-relations reasons. A party this size is bound to get a lot of publicity. If the brand-new CEO of Ingraham were tossing this sort of bash for his daughter, it might look—well, a little bit extravagant and show-offy. But if it were being given by her dear old octogenarian granny—old granny who's retired from the company and hasn't much else to do—it would look, well, rather *sweet,* wouldn't it?" She gives him her sweetest smile.

"I see your point," he says. "And sweet thou ever wert, Ma."

"Don't get smart," she says. "I'm just trying to be practical. So what do you think of the idea?"

He is smiling, too. "I think it's very—sweet," he says.

"Of course, I'm really doing it for Anne. But being nice to the Van Degans wouldn't hurt when you and Mr. Van Degan sit down at the bargaining table and start hammering out a contract, would it?"

"Sweet," he says again. "You've thought of everything, haven't you?"

"Yes. Including even offering to pay for a little more than half of the party if that would sweeten the deal for them. Like providing free liquor. In any deal, every little bargaining chip helps, I find."

"Yes," he says.

"Carol doesn't like Mrs. Van Degan much. But I think I can deal with her, don't you?"

"Yes, Ma," he says. "I think you can."

"I've even picked out the dress I'm going to wear. Amy Vanderbilt says the grandmother of a debutante should wear blue."

"Sweet," he says again.

"But of course, if I'm going to be one of the hostesses of this party, there are certain people I'm going to want to invite."

"Of course."

"One of them is Bathy."

"Bathy, Bathy, Bathy," he says, rubbing his eyes. "Whenever we talk, Ma, we always somehow manage to circle back to Bathy."

"There's a reason," she says.

"What is it?"

She sits forward in her chair. "Noah, there's something important you ought to know about Bathy."

"Oh?"

"Years ago there was a young man in my life who went on to become briefly rather a celebrity. His name was Radioman First Class George Noville. . . ."

In the apartment at River House, the telephone rings, and Carol picks it up. "Hello?"

"Mrs., uh, Liebling?" a woman's voice says, in what used to be called a boarding-school stammer. "It's, uh, Brooke Astor. I apologize for calling you so late in the evening, but I've just come from a long trustees' meeting at the museum, and I have some, uh, important news for you."

"Yes, Mrs. Astor," Carol says.

"To begin with, we're thrilled with the way you've negotiated with Mr. and Mrs. Van Degan to persuade them to offer their porcelain collection to the museum. This will be one of the most important collections the museum has been offered in years—not since the, uh, Lehman collection, in fact."

"I'm glad I was able to help," Carol says.

"Help? It seems to me you did it all. We've been sending out polite feelers to the Van Degans since the nineteen eighties, and you've pulled it off in a matter of days. You're quite an, uh, amazing woman, Mrs. Liebling."

"Why, thank you."

"And we'd like to do something to—uh—express our tremendous gratitude to you, Mrs. Liebling. There's a vacancy coming up on our board of trustees in June, and we'd like to invite you to fill it."

"Why, thank you, Mrs. Astor," she says quietly. "That's a very—a very great honor."

Now the other woman's voice becomes more intimate and conversational. "Of course we were all made aware of the terms you laid out in order for us to receive this gift. And I'm sure you won't be surprised to learn that there was a certain amount of opposition to those terms."

"I'm not surprised, no," Carol says.

"Didn't think you would be. A certain amount of opposition is—uh—putting it mildly. There was a *hell* of a lot of opposition. That's why our meeting ran so late. I'm sure you can understand."

"Yes, I can."

"There was actual *shouting*. For a while, I actually thought a fistfight might break out in our lovely boardroom between two of the—uh—so-called gentlemen on our little board. This is not particularly unusual, I should add. Our meetings can get pretty down and dirty, and I've learned to shout with the best of them. But, in the end, the board was split down the middle on the matter. And, as a member of the—uh—female minority, I'm happy to say I had the swing vote. I had the last shout. I voted to accept your terms. Do you want to know why?"

"Yes. I'd love to know why."

"There's a certain mystique about being a trustee of the Metropolitan Museum. We're supposed to be these rarified human beings, with these glittering social veneers. We cultivate that image, of course. But we're just like anybody else—capable of greed, jealousy, ambition, and rage when somebody else seems to be stepping on our toes or trying to push us around. It can be like a jungle, serving on our board—man on man, and man against woman. You need the nerves of a gunslinger and the muscle of a ward boss. You need the heart of a gambler, and the, uh, *cojones* of a drug czar. You need to be tough, and you need to know how to fight. Most of all, you need to be a wheeler-dealer. I've thought of myself as a wheeler-dealer all my life, fighting my way in what's still essentially a man's world. I admired the way you set out your terms. My hat is off to you, Mrs. Liebling. Congratulations on being an even tougher wheeler-dealer than I am."

"Thank you, Mrs. Astor," Carol says.

"I like your style. Perhaps one day soon you and your husband can come to my house for lunch. I'd like to meet you both."

"Thank you. I'd love that."

"And I should also tell you that at our next meeting, I'm going to propose that we find someone a bit more, uh, uh, diplomatic to head our Acquisitions Committee than Mr. Corydon McCurdy. . . ."

Carol moves slowly to the bar and, after a moment's hesitation, carefully fixes herself a tall drink. She thinks:

I am dreaming, and this is a dream. But I'm not dreaming. This is no dream.

In the mirror above the bar, she studies her reflection. She lifts her glass in a little toast.

Well, now what do you think of that? she asks him. *Just what do you think of that? Twenty years ago I sat in your mother's blue silk dining room and listened to her tell me that the Lieblings would always be pariahs in this town. And I told her that I was going to change all that. And I just did it. So what do you think of that, you bastard? What do you think of that?*

"So you've used Bathy very well, haven't you, Ma?" he is saying to her now. "You've gotten a lot of mileage out of her over the years."

"What's that supposed to mean?" she says.

"You knew all along why I felt the way I did about her. But you pretended you had no idea."

Her lips are pressed together in a pout. "I wanted to hear it from you," she says. "I wanted to hear your explanation. In your own words."

"And because you knew I wouldn't—"

"I like things out in the open. No beating around the bush. That's the way I like to do business."

"No, I don't think that's quite it, Ma. Because you knew I wouldn't give you any explanation, in my own words, you kept me feeling I owed you one. As long as I owed you one, you had an excuse to keep trying to push Bathy down my throat—insisting that I offer her a job that you knew all along she wouldn't take. And because you knew I wouldn't have Bathy pushed down my throat, you had an excuse to keep me where you wanted me. You could have told me all this ten, fifteen years ago. But you preferred to keep me standing on my tiptoes, waiting to be kissed—waiting till you were damned good and ready to give me the old smackeroo."

She looks briefly away from him. "Well, perhaps you're right," she says. "Nobody's perfect." Then she rises to her feet and faces him, smiling brightly. "But now you've got your smackeroo," she says. "So it doesn't matter, does it? It was worth the wait. All good things are worth waiting for."

"Are they?"

"It was worth it for me," she says. "For the pleasure it's been for me to work with you for all these years. And now you may kiss me good night. It's been a long time since you've kissed your poor old mother good night, Noah. It's been years and years. Now I'd like you to do it. Kiss me good night."

He rises from the visitor's chair and steps to her. He bends and starts to kiss her on the cheek, but she offers him her lips instead. "Ma, you are a bitch to end all bitches," Noah says.

"Now run along home and tell Carol the good news," she says.

James, the night doorman at River House, steps to the taxi with his big umbrella open—a light rain mixed with snow has begun to fall—and opens the door for Noah. " 'Evening, Mr. Liebling," he says, tipping his cap with his free hand.

"Good evening, James." They each take a suitcase.

James escorts Noah up the front walk past the crack in the pavement where Caroline Taylor, on seventeen, claimed she caught her heel and nearly broke an ankle, and into the black marble entrance lobby. "Mr. Liebling, before you go up, could I have a word with you?" James says.

"Sure," Noah says, putting down his suitcase.

"This is really none of my business, sir," James says. "And I probably shouldn't be mentioning this at all. But then I thought perhaps I should."

"What is it, James?"

"Mrs. Liebling had a little accident with her car this afternoon, sir."

"Is she all right?"

"Oh, she's fine. It was just a fender bender, really. But I can tell she's pretty upset about it, sir. And I thought—you coming home from a long trip, and all— she might not want to tell you about it right away, for fear you'd be angry with her and all. You know how women are."

"Yes," he says. "I know how women are."

"So, sir, if you find her in a kind of funny mood when you get home, kind of edgy and upset, that'll be the reason, sir."

"I'll try to be understanding. I'm glad you told me, James."

"But please don't tell her I told you about this, sir. That would seem like I'm telling tales on her and all, and that ain't my way, Mr. Liebling."

"No. I won't mention we've had this conversation, James."

"Thanks, sir. It's just that, man to man, I ought to tell you that if you find your wife in a funny mood, that's the reason. You know, there's times when I come home and find my wife in a funny mood, and it's days and days before I can get her to tell me what's buggin' her. Women can get that way, 'specially if they've done something they feel a little guilty for. Like crashing a car."

"I know, James."

"And you know how much Mrs. Liebling loves that little car!"

"I know."

"Well, good night, sir."

"Good night, James."

He steps into the waiting elevator.

"Getting to be a nasty night out there, Mr. Liebling," the elevator man says.

"Sure is," he says. He has momentarily forgotten this night operator's name.

Somehow, at this late hour—it is well past midnight—he assumed that Carol would be in bed and asleep when he got home. But when he lets himself into the apartment, he sees that there is a light burning in the library. He calls out, "Hi, honey—I'm home!" But there is no reply.

He removes his overcoat and scarf, and hangs them in the hall closet. He places his two suitcases in the closet, to be unpacked in the morning, and closes the closet door. Then he starts down the hallway toward the library, and pauses at the door.

She is sitting, with her back to him, in one of the wing chairs. Only the top of her head, and her hands, are visible, and on her left wrist is her gold charm bracelet. He has added a gold charm to this bracelet on their wedding anniversaries for each of the twenty-one years they have been married: first a gold monkey, with moving arms and legs, and tiny emeralds for eyes; next a gold bell, with a sapphire clapper. And so on. In this hand he sees she is holding a drink.

This irritates him somehow. It has always irritated him when, on rare occasions, he has come home from the office to find that Carol has started their cocktail hour without him. His father, though he never professed to take the liquor business seriously, had some very old-fashioned, even puritanical, theories about drinking. "Watch out for the man who drinks alone," he used to say. "The man who drinks alone has a problem, and is already probably in serious trouble. Drinking is meant to be a social pastime, and social means with other people, with one's friends or one's own sort. The person who drinks alone is dangerous, to himself and to other people."

Then he notices that in her right hand Carol is holding a lighted cigarette. This surprises him. He can remember when Carol quit smoking, cold turkey, when she discovered she was pregnant with Anne. He remembers how proud of her he was for the ease with which she seemed to handle it. "It's harder for a smoker to give up tobacco than it is for an alcoholic to give up booze," his father used to say. Noah quit smoking when Carol did. He decides not to comment on either of these unusual circumstances. She has, after all, smashed up her green Mercedes, the little car she was proud to say had never received a scratch or a nick in the five years she'd owned it. He steps into the room. "Hello, darling," he says, and kisses her on the top of her head.

"Hello, Mr. Aesop," she says. "Got any good fables to tell me?"

He moves to the bar, rattles some ice cubes in a glass, and pours himself a drink. "The Ballachulish presentation went very well, if I do say so myself," he says. "The salesmen seemed to like it. That's always a good first sign."

"Good," she says.

He carries his drink across the room and sits down opposite her. "Well, cheers!" he says, and lifts his glass.

"Cheers," she says, neither moving nor looking at him.

"Sorry to be so late," he says. "But the cocktail party went on a little longer than I'd planned, and my mother wanted to see me before I came home."

"I see," she says, and takes another sip of her drink, and another drag on her cigarette.

"She had some rather remarkable things to tell me," he says.

"Did she." She says it as a statement, not a question.

"Want to hear what they were?"

"No," she says. "Not particularly. Not now, anyway."

"Okay," he says pleasantly. "So—how was your week?"

"Routine," she says.

"I see . . ." They sit in silence for a moment or two. Then, still trying to be cheerful, he says, "Say, I've been thinking, Carol. Now that sales conference is out of the way, maybe you and I should take a little trip. To the Caribbean perhaps. Or maybe Hawaii. Some place that's warm. Any place that's out of this rotten January New York weather. What do you think?"

"Feeling guilty?" she says.

"Guilty?"

"That sounds like a guilty person talking."

"Why should I feel guilty?"

"For not paying enough attention to me?"

"Yes, perhaps that's it," he says. "I've spent so damn much time on this Ballachulish business these last few months. So how about it? Just a week, perhaps. Ten days. Maybe a cruise."

"Perhaps," she says. "Perhaps not. I don't care." She stubs out her cigarette in the ashtray on the table beside her, and immediately lights another. The ashtray, he sees, contains the remnants, the filter tips, of many other cigarettes.

"Started to smoke again, I see," he says.

"Yes."

"Well!" There is another silence. Then he says, "I understand Anne wants to have a coming-out party with the Van Degan girl. That should be fun for her."

"I don't know," she says. "I don't think Anne wants to do that anymore."

"I see," he says. "Well, that's too bad. It sounded like a fun idea." He sets his drink on the coffee table. "Hey," he says, "what's this?" He touches the bone handle of the automatic pistol lying on the table. "Where'd this come from?"

"It's your mother's. She sent it over. She thought I might be nervous here alone."

"Alone? Where's Mary?"

"She quit this morning."

"Quit? Why?"

"For reasons too numerous to mention," she says. "For reasons I don't wish to go into here."

"I see," he says. He stands up to refill his drink. "Can I touch you up?"

"No, thanks. I'm fine." She stares into her half-filled glass.

From the bar he says, "I don't like the idea of guns lying around the house."

"Don't you? I do," she says.

He returns with his fresh drink and sits down again. "Look," he says, "you seem a little preoccupied tonight. A little uncommunicative. Is something on your mind?"

"A lot of things are on my mind. I do have a mind, you know. And if a person has a mind, there's usually something on it. I'm not as stupid as you think I am."

"Now, Carol. I don't think you're stupid."

"You think I'm as stupid as Beryl Stokes?"

"Carol. What a thing to say."

"I'm not stupid."

"I've got some real good news to tell you, honey," he says. "If you'd like to hear it."

"No," she says, and blows out a thin stream of smoke, "Don't want to hear my good news?"

"No!" she says again. "I'd rather hear a fable. Mr. Aesop's fables always had a moral at the end. What's yours?"

"That's the second time you've mentioned Aesop," he says, "What are you talking about, Carol?"

"More of your lies maybe?"

He is growing impatient with her. "Listen," he says, "if this is because you smashed up your car, forget about it. If it can be fixed, we'll have it fixed. If it can't be fixed, I'll buy you a new one. I know you love that car, but it's only a *car*, for chrissakes, and—"

"Shut up!" she says. "It's not because I smashed up my car. It's because you smashed up my life!"

"What are you talking about?" But, with a sense of dread, he feels he is beginning to know what she is talking about.

"Carol—" he begins.

"Is your moral 'Don't screw teenage girls'? Or is it don't screw teenage girls unless you're pretty sure you won't get caught?"

"Carol—"

"You see, I'm getting more and more like your mother. I want to get everything out on the table. All the facts. From the horse's mouth. So there's only one thing I want to hear from you! Have you been having an affair with Melody?"

He takes a quick swallow of his drink, looks briefly at the floor, then up at her. "Yes," he says. "I'm glad you found out about it, Carol, because I would have had to tell you about it sooner or later."

"Sooner or later!" She jumps to her feet.

"I don't know how it happened, Carol, but it did. I'm sorry, Carol."

"Sorry!" she cries. "Is that all you can say—you're sorry? Are you in love with her, Noah?"

"No, I don't think so!"

"You don't *think* so!"

"I love you, Carol!"

She turns away from him, tears in her eyes, and her voice is bitter. "I don't understand you, Noah," she says. "I don't understand you at all. I won't even ask you how you could do such a thing to me—to me, after all the things I've tried to do for you and your family, you repay me with this! I won't even ask how you could do such a thing to Anne. I want to know how you could do such a thing to *yourself*! Or are you just like your father—a philandering bum who always had to have another woman on the side?"

"Now, wait a minute, Carol—"

"How long has this been going on? Under my roof!"

"It just happened this week, Carol. She followed me to Atlantic City, and—"

"And one thing just led to another? Liar! Then what was her underwear doing in the bottom of your closet?"

"*What*? Carol, I swear to God—"

"With blood on it! What did you do—rape her first?"

"My God, Carol! I swear to you. It was she who—"

"The other night the toilet seat was up in my bathroom! You never use my bathroom! Did you have to use my bathroom because she was using yours?"

"Carol—"

"My sleeping pills were stolen! Did she take them? Or did you have to knock her out with pills in order to fuck her?"

"Carol, Carol—"

"I've heard you jacking off in the next bed! Was that who you've been thinking about? *Her*?"

"Carol, Carol—please listen to me. I love you, Carol,"

"*Love*! And after everything I've been working on, everything I've been trying to do for you this week. Everything I've done—and it's come to this!" She flings herself into a chair with a sob.

"Listen, Carol. My mother told me you've been working on some sort of plan. Tell me what it is—"

"It doesn't matter now. Nothing matters now. I wish I'd driven off the bridge this afternoon."

"Please listen to me, Carol. It's late. You're tired. We're both tired. You've had a few drinks. Let's go to bed and talk this all over in the morning, when we're—"

"No! I'm never going to sleep in the same room—under the same roof—with you again! Mother was right. Father Timmons was right. I never should have married you, you bastard!"

"Carol, it was just this week. I swear I don't know how it happened. I know it shouldn't have happened, but it did, and it's over. I swear to you it's over." He reaches out for her.

"Don't touch me!" She recoils sharply from him in the chair.

"I love you, Carol!"

"*Melody*! I think I could have accepted it if it had been any other woman. Or even any other *man!* But *Melody*—whom we'd taken into our house as our friend, our guest, a member of the family almost—a girl we'd agreed to be surrogate parents for, people her parents trusted, Anne's college roommate, for God's sake, Noah! That I can never accept!"

"So it's true!" Both of them turn now, and Anne is standing in the doorway in her nightgown, wakened by the sound of their angry voices. "So it's all true," she says again. She takes one step into the room. "You filth!" she says to Noah. "You filthy piece of shit! You filthy asshole!"

Carol jumps to her feet and, doing so, overturns the pie-crust table on its folding legs, the table holding her highball glass and ashtray. What's left of her drink spills, and her glass rolls across the carpet, spewing ice cubes, and many cigarette butts scatter across the floor. The small pillow on her chair, with its needlepoint legend, THANK YOU FOR NOT SMOKING, also rolls to the floor. "Get back to bed, Anne," Carol says. "This is between your father and me."

Anne takes another step into the room. "No, it's not between you and him. It's between me and him! Filthy piece of shit!"

"Shut up!" Carol says. "Don't you dare talk to your father that way! Get back to bed. You're the one who brought that piece of trash into this house to begin with! It's all your fault, you know!"

"Filthy piece of shit!" Anne says again, her voice rising, and raising her hand in a fist as though to strike him.

"I said shut up! Your father is the most wonderful man in the world!"

From the chair where he sits, her father says, "Go ahead and hit me, Annie, if it makes you feel any better."

She turns away from him and glares at her mother. "I think you're both filthy, stinking pieces of shit!" she says. "You're both filthy assholes!"

"Is everything all right?" A fourth voice is heard in the room, and the three others turn and see Melody standing in the doorway, still holding the keys with which she let herself into the apartment.

"What are you doing here?" Carol screams at her.

"I had to pick up a few things. It's so late. I didn't think anybody would still be up. But then I heard voices, and—"

"Get out of here!"

She turns to Noah with a look of utter calm on her face. "So you told her," she says. "I hoped you would.

I'm glad you did." She turns to Carol. "So now you know," she says. "Noah and I are in love. It's as simple as that. There's nothing more to say."

"I said get out of here!"

"I really think you'd better go, Mellie," Noah says.

"No, I belong here with you, Noah, to help you get through this."

"Please, Mellie—"

"I knew it wouldn't be easy, darling."

"Mellie, *please!*"

"Did you tell her everything, Noah? Did you tell her everything you told me?" She turns to Carol again. "Noah loves me, Carol. He never really loved you, Carol—ever."

"I never said that, Mellie. Now please—"

"Did you tell her that you want a divorce? That you want to marry me?"

"No, because—because I love Carol, Melody."

"Did you tell her how I've been able to do things for you that she could never do? Did you tell her what I did for you in Atlantic City? Did you tell her how I rewrote your script? Tell her now, Noah. I want to hear you tell her."

"Later, Mellie—not now. Now, please, just go!"

"Later?" Carol screams. "This is all news that I'm to be told *later?*"

"We've got to stop telling them these lies, Noah," Melody says. "We've got to tell them the whole truth now." And she steps quickly toward him and kisses him full on the mouth.

He pulls away from her. "Stop this, Mellie," he whispers.

With a little cry Carol springs to the coffee table and picks up the pistol, and now Noah is on his feet as well. "What the hell do you think you're doing, Carol?" he shouts. "Put that damn thing down!"

"I'm going to kill myself, that's what I'm going to do! I was going to kill myself this afternoon, but a policeman stopped me. I never want to see any of you again!"

Noah lunges for her and grabs her right arm. "Drop it!" he shouts, trying to pull her arm down, and they wrestle briefly, silently, for the gun. *"Stop this, for God's sake!"*

"Mother!" Anne screams.

"Let her do it, Noah," Melody says calmly. "It would solve everything."

The first shot, a flat crack, hits the window, and there is a noisy shatter of glass falling into the entrance courtyard below, as the curtains billow outward into the night storm, and the second shot—and it was the kick of the gun, the defense would contend, that triggered the second shot—strikes Noah just below the left ear.

Looking startled, he staggers backward, his hand clasped to his throat. Then his knees buckle, and he falls to the floor.

On the rear wheel of his bike, hunched against the handlebars and the wind, he is headed at full speed toward the fallen log, leaps over it, and plunges forward into the darkness.

Carol drops the gun, and it lands on the carpet with a soft thud. She flings herself to her knees on the floor beside him and cradles his head in her arms. "Oh, Noah!" she sobs. "I love you, Noah! Don't die!"

"You've killed him!" Melody cries, and she stoops to reach for the gun.

But Anne is too quick for her, and she, too, drops to her knees and picks up the small, bone-handled pistol. She points it blindly at Melody. "You did all this!" she sobs, and a third shot rings out, and the devastation is complete.

Already, through the broken window, the sounds of police sirens can be heard shrilling upward from the street below.

PART THREE

———◆———

Grandmont, 1994

21

Some Final Words

". . . according to police, appeared to have occurred after a long night of heavy drinking. It is the first time a violent crime has taken place at exclusive River House, arguably New York's most fashionable residential address."

Georgette Van Degan switches off the television set from the remote. "Well, we're off the hook, darling," she says to her husband. "We won't have to give that silly coming-out party, and we'll get to keep the porcelain collection."

The telephone rings, and she reaches for it. "Oh, yes, Roxy," she says, "how are you, my precious love? . . . Oh, no, no, *no*, my darling. There never *was* going to be any coming-out party, certainly not with that lush Carol Liebling. . . . Frankly, I didn't tell you because I know how upset you journalists get when you print something that isn't accurate. . . . And it wasn't your fault, my darling. I think you got that item from Jacques, the captain at Le Cirque. . . . I *thought* so. But he often gets things wrong. It's the language barrier, you see. . . . Yes, we did have lunch, but it was to discuss an entirely different matter. I don't really remember what it was. . . . Well, you can print a correction if you *want* to, darling. But at this point I'd really rather not have my name associated with that murderess. . . . Thanks, lovey, I appreciate that. Bye-e-e-e-e."

Her husband turns to her. "You know, you really are a god-damned fool, Georgette," he says. "You really are a stupid god-damned fool."

"Why? What's wrong? We're off the hook! Thank God!"

"Without Carol we'll never get the Ingraham business.

We'll never get shit from them as long as the old lady is running things!"

"Well, don't look at me as though I had anything to do with what's happened, Truck!"

"And the museum gift—that gift is designed to save me millions in taxes! Well, the gift offer still stands."

"But you said yourself you weren't sure they'd accept your terms."

"They will. They will, believe me, when they've had a chance to think about it. The museum isn't being run by Mother Teresa. You stupid fool. I was a fool to think I could take a slut like you out of the bean fields of Indiana and turn you into a lady."

"And *you're* the *gentleman?* All I've got is your first three wives' word on how you beat up on them. But I've had *my* bruises photographed. In color! And those photographs are all in a safe at my lawyer's office—so don't try to mess around with me!"

"Bitch!" And suddenly he pitches forward in his chair, clutching his shirt.

"What's the matter?"

His fingers paw his chest, and the color has drained from his face. "Heart," he whispers. "Pain . . . hurting . . . call nine-one-one . . . call nine-one-one . . . please . . ."

In all his years in the restaurant business, Glenn Bernbaum of Mortimer's has never put together a luncheon party the size of this one in such a hurry—twenty-six women, meaning nine four-tops have had to be pushed together, taking up more than half the main dining room. And Patsy Collingwood has indicated that she would have invited many more if her invitations hadn't had to go out at the last minute, right after hearing this morning's news. But her guests are all important women, all important customers, and so, for Mr. Bernbaum, all this hasty rearranging of the room has been worth the effort.

Patsy's guests are:

Marietta Spinola, Bitsy Walcock, Cinnamon La Farge, Bettina Musgrove, the Countess Grazzi, the Ballinger twins, Hermine McGovern, Pookie Satterthwaite, Corliss Thrue, Gloria Tunbridge, old Mrs. Nion Farwell (with the harelip), Cissie Warburton, Consuelo Custin, Lady Eve Cotterford, Chubby Corscadden, Roxy Rhinelander, Gussie Swinburne, Melissa Hart-Turnbull, Cherry de Rothschild, Ernestine Kolowrat, Flossie Bunce, Edwina Lahniers, Babs Goulandris, and Hyacinth Lafoon. Rarely have so many prominent New York society women been gathered at the same table. The *News* has sent a photographer to record the event.

And now Patsy and Mr. Bernbaum are setting out the place cards, tackling the arduous chore of *placement.*

"I don't see a card here for Georgette," Mr. Bernbaum says.

"Georgette? Georgette who?"

"Van Degan."

"Oh, *her.* Her husband's business is going down the tubes, and he's given away all their porcelains to save on taxes—and those porcelains were supposed to be her insurance when he dies, because he doesn't have any. She's become one of yesterday's people, I'm afraid. Now, if I could only have gotten Carol Liebling to come, that would have been the coup of all time! But she's in jail."

They return to the place cards. "Do you think Cissie Warburton can be trusted to behave herself next to Belinda Ballinger?" she asks him.

And now, after the usual disputes about who has been seated where, and after—as inevitably happens—the guests have rearranged the seating to suit themselves, they are all seated. Drink orders have been taken—mostly for chablis or Perrier with lime, with only old Mrs. Farwell insisting on her customary double bullshot—and Patsy Collingwood taps her water glass with her teaspoon. "Girls!" she says. "Girls! It's Topic A, and I want to hear everyone's favorite theory, one by one!"

"Pookie should go first. After all, it happened in her building."

"Well," Pookie begins, "all I know is what I heard from James, the night doorman. . . ."

Two white-coated orderlies carry Truxton Van Degan on a stretcher down the curving staircase of the Van Degans' Fifth Avenue apartment. Right behind them is a paramedic holding a gold plastic cup over Truxton Van

Degan's nose and mouth, and following him is a second
paramedic carrying a bottle of oxygen. Georgette Van
Degan supervises the operation from the top of the
stairs.

"Remember—no heroic life-sustaining measures," she
calls down to the men on the steps below. "My husband
has a living will. He requests no heroic life-sustaining
measures." Then she suddenly screams, *"For Christ's
sake, watch out!"* One of the paramedics has jogged one
of the pair of red Chinese vases with his elbow, and it
rocks slightly on its carved ebony base in its lighted
niche in the stairwell. "That's Lang Yao *sang-de-boeuf*!
Those vases are priceless! I won't even let my maids
touch them with a feather duster!"

The four men from the life squad give her an odd
look before continuing slowly down the stairwell with
their burden.

There were times, when he was in a jokey mood, when
Jules Liebling referred to Bathsheba Sachs as "Miss Fix-
It" for her ability to smooth over some of the rougher
moments that occasionally arose in the distilled spirits
industry. She was certainly Miss Fix-It during the trial.

The name Kaminsky, for example, is not uncommon
in New York, but when Bathy Sachs learned that the
case had been assigned to Judge Ida Kaminsky, she did
a little research. She discovered that Judge Kaminsky's
father, who had also been a judge, was indeed the same
Judge Saul Kaminsky who, back in the free-for-all days
of Prohibition, had acquired a certain indebtedness to
the Liebling family. There was no need to remind Judge
Ida Kaminsky of this fact. She knew.

Given these circumstances, Bathy had no trouble persuading the family that the defendant should waive her
right to a jury trial, and to allow the judge to reach a
just and fair verdict on her own.

A defendant who is clearly innocent, Bathy reminded
them, should never risk having her fate decided by a
jury, who will always be asked to wrestle with the knotty
problem of "reasonable doubt."

The New York County prosecutor, who was running
for reelection in November, seemed determined at first

to make this a major case, assuming that the amount of publicity the case would receive would keep his name and face in the newspapers and on television screens for some time. But when Judge Kaminsky chose the smallest courtroom on Foley Square for her hearing, with its limited space for press and spectators, and with television and other cameras banned, the prosecutor began to find himself frustrated at every turn. Still, he insisted that Carol should stand trial for something called "depraved-indifference murder," a charge not often heard in courtrooms. Judge Kaminsky, however, ruled that until she had reached her verdict, the word *homicide* would be substituted for murder.

With his stern prosecutorial eyes glaring at the defendant, the prosecutor kept repeating the obvious: Carol's fingerprints were on the lethal weapon; there were powder burns on her right hand. And since Carol had an alcohol level in her bloodstream of .10 at the time of her arrest, he asserted that the shootings occurred in "a wild, mad, drunken rage."

The lawyer Bathy had chosen for Carol's defense was a young man named Justin Baar. Quiet, polite, soft-spoken, and almost shy-seeming in Judge Kaminsky's presence, Mr. Baar had had little previous courtroom experience, and this, Bathy decided, would work to the defense's advantage. Because Mr. Baar refused to respond to the prosecutor's thundering oratory with much more than a raised eyebrow, the prosecutor's performance was robbed of the drama he clearly wanted. The prosecutor obviously wanted a courtroom battle, but there can be no battle when the opponent refuses to fight back. Each verbal climax on the part of the prosecution was followed by anticlimax on the part of the defense. And this tactic—as Bathy had hoped—made the proceedings in Judge Kaminsky's chambers seem decidedly unnewsworthy to the media.

There was, of course, one tricky problem. Immediately following her arrest, Carol had videotaped and signed a full confession. She and only she, she swore, had held the gun. Naturally, she did this to protect Anne, but this confession would be a major stumbling block for her defense. Mr. Baar, meanwhile, was growing tired of hearing his client described as "blind, stinking, out-of-her-mind drunk." A .10 alcohol level in the bloodstream, Mr. Baar pointed out to Bathy, is actually minimal for intoxication; it pained him to hear his client portrayed as no better than a Bowery bum. But Bathy had an interesting suggestion. "If Carol was blind, stinking, out-of-her-mind drunk when she pulled the trigger," Bathy said, "she must obviously have been blind, stinking, out-of-her-mind drunk ten minutes later when she taped her confession. Why would anyone believe a confession from a person in that condition?" Thus was the prosecutor's own rhetoric thrown back at him.

Anne was the final witness called in her mother's defense. And it was there that Bathy was able to execute her most brilliant move. Mr. Baar had succeeded in persuading Judge Kaminsky that because of Anne's age, she would testify as Jane Doe and not as Anne Liebling. But then—in a most unusual move, and over the most vociferous objections of the county prosecutor—he requested that Anne's testimony be heard on a Saturday morning. In no one's memory had a Manhattan courtroom been open on a Saturday; it was unheard of, the prosecutor bellowed. But in his customary shy and gentle way, Mr. Baar said, "We're only requesting this, sir, so that the young woman's studies at college will be disrupted as little as possible. Surely, this young woman's life has suffered terrible disruptions already. This testimony is going to be painful enough for her as it is. Surely you don't want her to suffer more pain and distress by having to be conspicuously absent on a school day—a day, incidentally, when she is scheduled to take an important examination for which she has been studying long and hard. We have struggled in this courtroom to preserve this young girl's anonymity and privacy, and to keep her out of the public spotlight. Please show a little human kindness, sir, by not forcing her to interrupt her valuable education. As a father yourself, wouldn't you ask the same consideration for your own teenage daughter, sir?"

Judge Kaminsky agreed, and announced that her court would go into special session on Saturday morning to hear Anne's testimony.

From her years in public relations Bathsheba Sachs knew that, except for extraordinary, fast-breaking news stories, men and women in the media never willingly go to work on weekends. Neither, as a rule, do county prosecutors, and this one was forced to cancel an important golf date.

And so, gently guided by Mr. Baar, Anne Liebling offered her tearful, truthful testimony. The prosecutor, clearly in a foul mood, declined to cross-examine her. Judge Kaminsky then declared the proceedings closed, and announced that she would deliver her verdict on Monday morning.

That Saturday, in fact, was yesterday. Now it is Sunday morning, and Bathsheba Sachs has just awakened from a vivid and disturbing dream. In it she was back at Grandmont again, that great castle Jules built of granite and French buhrstone high on a hill overlooking the Hudson. In her dream she approached the house as they all used to approach it in Jules's Pierce-Arrow, up the long, curving drive with its rhododendron hedges until the house itself appeared, its turrets and its battlements and crenels, designed in no particular style except what one critic rather waspishly described as Middle European Post Office. The house not only dominated the landscape. It loomed over it. Every window in the house was lighted in Bathy's dream, as though to welcome her home.

The wide green lawns swept down to the riparian wall, which obscured the New York Central's tracks from view. Mr. Vanderbilt's railroad had tried to ruin the Hudson's eastern shore, but it had not succeeded at Grandmont, where only the river itself was visible. The river is nearly a mile wide at this point and still tidal; the Indians called it the River That Flows Two Ways. Across the river, on its west bank, twinkled the lights of the village of Sneden's Landing, tucked against the shoreline in the first drop in the Palisades, and to the north the mercury lights of the Tappan Zee Bridge glowed like a chain of garnets.

Up the river steamed the night boat to Albany, and there was laughter and music from her decks. Outside slept the animals in the family's private zoo—a llama named Llewellyn, a tame zebra called Honey, a baby elephant named Baba au Rhum, and Cyril's beloved Potto, the bush baby.

But suddenly into the peaceful dream came the voices—voices from the village, and even from the corridors of the Ingraham Building itself—whispering voices: "Isn't it a scandal? His wife's own sister! How does his wife put up with it, do you suppose? She *must* know. She must be some kind of saint. It's been going on for years. How she must suffer . . . and yet she never lets on . . . but then, what can you expect from people like that? . . . With Jules Liebling's background . . . a bootlegger . . . He had people killed . . . ."

Bathy had learned to ignore such talk, to shrug it off, to laugh it off, because she knew that the truth was much different from what people thought it was, and that if people had known what the real truth was, the scandal would have been much greater. So why, in her dream, had these voices still not lost their power to hurt her?

Then, in the dream, a carousel of images appeared across her sleeping consciousness like color slides projected on a screen. *Click.* There was little Noah in a blue and white sailor suit and white cap, dressed that way by Hannah perhaps because she was remembering the young seaman who had been the one true love of her life. *Click.* There was Hannah herself, looking strong and purposeful in the garden with her pruning shears and a wicker basket over her arm. *Click.* There was Cyril, trying to make his father love him, holding out his arms to Bathy, asking for her to comfort him for some punishment he'd been given for some misdeed he'd committed in his father's eyes. *Click.* There was Cyril's little sister, Ruth, lively and pretty in those days, dreaming of becoming a movie star, much to her father's dismay. *Click.* There was the children's aunt Settie Kahn, who was killed by a swan, looking wan and stooped and bitter. Settie was always dropping by Grandmont on some excuse or other, mostly to get away from her husband, Bathy always supposed. After Settie died, Hannah reinvented Settie as some ethereal and beautiful creature, "too good to live," as Hannah used to say, one of Dr. Marcus Sachs's Three Graces—Settie, Hannah, and Bathy. But to Bathy, Settie was always a troublemaker who carried tales, some true, some false, between members of the family. Settie was always jealous of Hannah because Hannah had married a man much richer than Leo Kahn, and because Hannah had had children while Settie was barren. At the same time, Settie treated Jules in a haughty and condescending way, often referring to him behind his back—though she'd never have dared to do so to his face—as "the Polack."

Whenever Bathy thinks of Settie, she doesn't think of her stoop. She thinks of her sneer. The sneer was in her dream.

Click. Then, at last, came a picture of Jules himself, looking stern and disapproving and disappointed and disgusted, and other words beginning with the letter d. And in her dream his mouth suddenly flew wide open, as if he was about to roar, and she strained to listen to what he was about to shout out to her. It seemed to be some sort of accusation, that he was trying to say she hadn't forgiven him enough, though the words didn't seem to come. Then she knew that the letter d was important, that the word began with the letter d, and that the word was *do*. "Didn't I *do* enough for you?" she cried out to him. "Didn't any of us *do* enough for you?" The cry woke her up, trembling, and frightened and in a cold sweat. Because Bathy Sachs almost never has dreams like that—dreams that begin in tranquility and light, and end in terror and disorder. A word that begins with d.

And now she lies in her bed on this sunny Sunday morning, and her thoughts are filled with him. Why?

He never told her that he loved her. She thought she knew why. It was because to have done so would have been an act of betrayal to Hannah. If that was the case, she admired that in him. For the same reason she never told him that she loved him. It was as though they had a silent pact, always to leave those words unspoken. For Hannah's sake.

The most romantic thing he ever said to her was when he once said, "You're one person I can always count on. Miss Fix-It." Not *the* one person. Just one person. One thing he could always count on her to do was to forgive him. She did, even though they never made love again after that morning at Grandmont when Noah burst in on them together.

His greatest disappointment, of course, was Cyril. He never really got over that. A famous psychiatrist named Dr. Edmund Bergler once told Cyril that his problems with homosexuality stemmed from his hatred of his father. Dr. Bergler recommended that Cyril buy a gymnastic punching bag, pin a picture of his father to it, and "work out his rage" there. This always struck Bathy as an absurd notion. Cyril didn't hate his father. To be sure, he didn't always see eye to eye with him. Indeed, there was a long and painful period when Cyril did not see his father at all. Cyril didn't always see eye to eye with his mother, either, for Hannah has always been a woman who wanted to have her cake and eat it, too, and who has usually managed to do so. Hannah has always been a woman whom it is difficult to feel close to. And Hannah certainly did not handle the Cyril situation well. Though Hannah would never admit it, there were a number of situations that Hannah did not handle well. But Bathy thinks—playing devil's advocate—when Jules was alive it was difficult for anyone else to handle *any* situation! It wasn't until after Jules's death that Hannah began to come into her own. She proved herself to be a woman of many talents. But being a mother was never one of them.

Dr. Bergler also suggested that Cyril hated Noah. Not so, Bathy thinks. True, Cyril was often jealous of Noah, because he became so clearly his father's favorite. But Noah was too kind and sweet to hate. Cyril loved Noah. He loved his parents. He loved them all unbearably, for isn't love that is not returned the most powerful, cruel love there is? Bathy thinks so.

The kidnapping episode has always struck her as a case in point. It was certainly a bungled enterprise from the outset. It was originally the brainchild of Joey Fernandez, a youth with whom Cyril made an unfortunate acquaintanceship. Ruth had recently eloped with the Brazilian named Antonio Fernandez-Just, and there was much published about this in the press, due to the wide discrepancy in the couple's ages. The similarity of the names—they were obviously not related—caught the eye of Pal Joey. Also in the press was the notation that Sr. Fernandez-Just was the heir to a copper fortune estimated at 2.5 million dollars, but that this was "little more than lunch money to Jules Liebling, the billionaire booze baron." With Joey, Cyril had tried to conceal the fact that his father was rich. But now the cat was out of the bag, so to speak.

Joey Fernandez's rationale was this: "If your sister can latch on to two-point-five million dollars just by marrying some spic, why don't you deserve the same amount? And my brother and I are two spics who'll help you get it." And so the kidnapping plot was hatched. Since Cyril's cooperation was essential to the endeavor, the plan was for Cyril to receive half the ransom money, while the other half was to be divided between the brothers. Cyril went along with the scheme, as he explained to Bathy later, for two reasons. For one, he had made the mistake of falling quite madly in love with Joey Fernandez. But even more important, he was curious to see whether his father, into whose disfavor he had increasingly fallen, would actually pay that much money for his life. Was Cyril's life worth that much to Jules? Cyril felt he had to know. Was Cyril worth Jules's lunch money?

Of course, the answer to that question will never be known, since the money, when it was delivered—with the exception of a few hundred-dollar bills placed on the tops of the packets as decoys—consisted of cut-up newspaper stuffed into garbage bags by Jules, Hannah, Kevin Shaughnessy, and Bathy.

Of course, the whole scheme was badly botched from the beginning. But as Bathy once suggested to Jules, "I wonder whether Cyril didn't really want it to be botched—perhaps unconsciously. Unconsciously, he really wanted the plot to fail. He didn't really want to extort money from you. He just wanted to see how much you loved him."

"Bullshit" was Jules's reply.

Today, Cyril strikes most people as a very silly man. But, Bathy thinks, what most people don't realize about Cyril is that his silliness is calculated. Silliness is his defense, his only remaining weapon against the world, his mask. Behind the mask lurks a shy and sensitive and deeply hurt man whom Bathy has always cared for very much.

*   *   *

Well, Bathy thinks, now at least the trial is over. Another hurdle in their lives has been crossed, more or less successfully. There were at least three bad moments in it, to be sure. One occurred when a particularly dogged reporter for one of the New York tabloids, who kept trying to inflate the case into some sort of sensation, quoted the author William Luckman as saying that Carol's mother was a patient at a sanitarium called Greenspring Hills, and that Carol's family had "a long history of mental illness." Luckman hinted that he might have more to say about the Liebling family later on. This story prompted a small-town parish priest in New Hampshire, claiming to be an old friend of Carol's family, to call a press conference. In it he declared that he had predicted that Noah's and Carol's marriage would end disastrously, and added that Noah and Carol had never really been married "in the eyes of God." These linked stories made Bathy very apprehensive.

But this publicity was quickly deflected by, of all people, Yale University. Weary of the bad press their institution was receiving as a result of William Luckman's best-selling book, *Blighted Elms,* the university reluctantly instituted lawsuits for criminal libel against both Luckman and his publisher—fully aware that such an action, if it came to a trial, could only generate more publicity, and sales, for Luckman and his book.

But the gods were kind to Yale, as they often are. If Mr. Luckman had consulted with Cyril at the time, he might have received sounder advice. But, on his own, Luckman decided to act as his own counsel in the case. He figured there would be a public-relations advantage if he were depicted as a struggling young writer being legally harassed by a big, cold university. But in his initial deposition he was unprepared for the plaintiff's five-man legal team that faced him in the offices of Cravath, Swain & Moore that day. "Where are your notes?" they demanded. "Do you have copies of taped interviews? What is your basis for these allegations?" After six hours of brutal grilling, Mr. Luckman finally caved in and admitted that the assertions in his book were unsupported by evidence, and were without basis in fact. Thus satisfied, Yale gratefully dropped its suit and settled for a public apology from the publisher.

The gods were less kind to William Luckman. Less than happy with these various turns of events, his publishers promptly canceled their contract for his next book. Discredited as a news source, Mr. Luckman left town under something of a cloud.

What Bathy most feared was that Noah's and Melody's names might be romantically linked in the press. This almost happened in a "blind" item in Roxy Rhinelander's column, but as usual, Roxy got things a little wrong:

> *Cherchez la femme,* as they say in France. Was a recent society slaying the result of a love triangle? Could be. They say it could entail a Certain Somebody's Best Friend. But isn't it always? F'rinstance, two best friends were planning a joint coming-out party. Then those plans went pffft. How come? Could it entail a prominent glass manufacturer whose company is going pffft?

Bathy also worried that Beryl might turn out to be a loose cannon in the case, and might come forward to say that she had evidence to prove that Noah and Melody had been having an affair. But as it turned out, Beryl Stokes had more pressing matters on her mind, which had nothing to do with the disappearance of Bill Luckman from her life.

At her insistence, Frank Stokes moved out of the River House apartment and took a small room at the Athletic Club. But he also took Noah's advice and hired a lawyer. As a result, it was discovered that Noah had been wrong about one thing. Frank and Beryl did not own the apartment jointly. All their co-op's shares were in Frank's name only. A prenuptial separate-property agreement also turned up. And so, at his lawyer's suggestion, Frank Stokes put the apartment up for sale.

The first Beryl learned of this was when the building's agent telephoned her to ask if that afternoon would be a convenient time for him to show the unit to a prospective buyer. In a panic Beryl called Frank and begged him to come home. After demurring for a few weeks, Frank finally agreed.

And so the Stokeses' marriage continues on its uneven, unsteady course.

But now, Bathy thinks, all this is behind them, thank
God. And this morning, after that unsettling dream,
Bathy had a sudden urge to get out of the city for a few
hours, to get in her car and drive up to Tarrytown to
see what had actually become of Grandmont.

She expected to find a suburban sprawl of pretentious
houses, each priced to sell for more than Jules had paid
for all of Grandmont to begin with. But what she saw
when she drove through the old wrought-iron gates—
now emblazoned with a large sign that read MORE-
WEALTH VILLAS—LUXURY HOMES AND ESTATES—MODELS
OPEN—was something else. The sprawl was there, all
right, but it seemed to exist in pockets. Clusters of Tudor
and Georgian houses were set apart by wide and empty
spaces, with LOTS FOR SALE signs decorating them, as
though the developer of Morewealth Villas had aban-
doned his grand scheme halfway through completion.
Here and there an empty lot triumphantly proclaimed
itself SOLD!!! Still, the vacant lots looked like the landscape of the moon.

Probably this was because all the trees were gone. The
tall rhododendron and privet hedges, the boxwood parterres, the clumps of dogwood and the old live oaks and
copper beeches that once covered the hillside had all
been cut down, though their stumps had not been removed. The honeysuckle-covered riparian wall had been
taken down, perhaps to improve the view, but a spring
rain had left a mudslide at the foot of the hill that ran
down to the exposed railroad tracks. The only sight that
remained unchanged against this treeless terrain was the
curve of the wide river below, where the sight of a few
sailboats on the river provided the only suggestions of
humanity.

Gazing at this barren, rocky scene as she drove along,
she had the unpleasant feeling that she was attending
her own funeral. The streets—some built up, others
empty—were narrow and winding, and she noticed that
they had all been given the names of French wines:
Montrachet Place, Chardonnay Court, Sauterne Cres-
cent, Cabernet Lane, and so on. Had this been done

in tribute to the late Billionaire Booze Baron, Bathy wondered. Probably not, she decided. More likely it was just a part of the developer's fancy. But it might have amused Jules.

Then, turning a corner, she suddenly came upon a big Lincoln Town Car parked alongside the road. At the wheel sat Hannah's driver, Mr. Nelson, in his cap and uniform, but the passenger seats were empty. She drove along a little farther, and then she saw her, standing alone in the middle of an empty building lot, dressed in black, looking—from that distance—small and frail and all at once old. Bathy pulled her car over, stopped it, got out, and walked across the weedy, gravelly stubble to where she stood. "What in the world are you doing here?" she asked her.

She didn't seem particularly surprised to see her. "I thought I could find where my dahlia beds used to be," she said. "But it's no use. Everything's changed. Do you remember the big white hybrid I developed and the Garden Clubs named after me?"

"Of course I do."

"I had a whole bed of them planted somewhere around here. But everything's been bulldozed under."

There was a large, flat piece of stone projecting upward from the ground where they were standing now. It looked familiar, and then Bathy recognized it as a piece of one of the stone garden benches that used to be scattered throughout the garden. There were a great many of these benches, all alike, and so it couldn't possibly have been the same stone these two sat on that night in the heat lightning fifty years ago. But it might have been. "Let's sit here for a minute," Bathy suggested.

Hannah lowered her frame carefully to the stone, one buttock preceding the other as she sat. If she recognized the stone, she said nothing.

"You didn't drive all the way up here just to find your dahlia beds," Bathy said.

"I had some upsetting news this morning. Ruth called me. She's going to marry that dreadful young man. That Ector."

"Let her, Hannah."

"I just smell more trouble brewing for the family. I just smell it."

"Let her go, Hannah. Release her. Let them all go."

"Oh, I've made some mistakes in the past. I know that. Terrible mistakes I'm not proud of."

"We've all done that."

"And I thought perhaps if I came back here—"

"That you might succeed in turning back the clock? That's what I thought, too. But we can't do that, can we?"

"No."

"Each time we try turning back the clock, it just ticks a little further forward. All we can do is keep putting one foot down after the other, as Jules used to say."

"I made one decision this morning. I'm going to undivide the apartment and give the whole thing to Cyril. I don't need all that room. I'll find a smaller place."

"That's a good decision, Hannah. That will make Cyril very happy."

"Yes, I'm rather proud of that decision. Sometimes I make decisions that I'm proud of. Have you ever been proud of me, Bathy?"

"Oh, yes."

"When? When were you proudest of me?"

"Well, for the way you kept our secret, for one thing."

"But I don't think I kept it very well. I'm sure there were some people who suspected you and Jules. I know there were."

"Oh, yes."

"But at least we both stood tall. We Sachses do that."

"Yes."

"We never bowed our heads in shame!"

"No."

"So perhaps there was no need to have it be a secret in the first place. Perhaps it was a lousy secret."

"Perhaps all secrets are lousy secrets, Hannah."

"Yes. That may be true." She hesitated. Then she said, "There's another secret perhaps I ought to tell you, Bathy. It's such an old secret. I've kept it for so long."

She held up her hand. "Please don't," she said.

"Why not?"

"Because I don't want to know any more secrets."

"Oh," she said, looking at first disappointed, and then almost relieved. "All right," she said, and nodded.

She and Bathy had come to the edge of this precipice

once before. Bathy could have told her that she already knew what this secret was, and that in some intuitive, almost primitive way she felt she had always known it. As a little girl, there were those searching, guilty looks she sometimes noticed passing between Hannah and the woman they both called Mama, and the sorrowful looks she sometimes caught in Hannah's eyes when Hannah looked at her, and which she pretended not to notice. Bathy began to wonder if somehow she was different and, if she was different, whether there was something wrong with her. But when she looked at herself in the mirror, she could see that there was nothing wrong with her, and, if anything, that she looked a lot like Hannah. So if there was something wrong with her, was there also something wrong with Hannah? She used to puzzle about this. But then she decided that if there was something wrong with both her and Hannah, at least they had each other's company, and their differentness, to share. They weren't alone.

And then there were the passport pictures. Every few years as she was growing up, there were new passport pictures to be taken, and when the date for the photo session approached, there was great tension in the air. "Next Wednesday at three o'clock sharp, you must be ready to have your new passport pictures taken," Hannah would say to her, and the date would be circled in red on the calendar page. She used to wonder about this. She wasn't going anywhere, and none of her friends at school seemed to have this worry about passport pictures and passport-renewal applications needing to be submitted on time. Gradually, though, she began to piece things together. The passport pictures were important to both Hannah and her. They were in this conspiracy, whatever it was, together. The passport pictures were to prove who she was, or who she wasn't.

Then, when she was about fourteen, dear Aunt Settie Kahn blurted it all out to her. She'd come to call at Grandmont, as she often did, and her visits were always like Yom Klppur, the Day of Atonement. Settie criticized Bathy, she criticized Hannah, she criticized Jules and Cyril and Ruth and Noah, she criticized the household servants and the gardening staff, who were all people Bathy loved. Bathy hated Big Sister Settie, as she was known to her, even more than the Liebling children hated her.

That morning, for some reason, Bathy put her hair up in pigtails. And Settie suddenly turned to her and said, "You look stupid in pigtails, Bathsheba. You look like a Polish peasant." "Polish" was the worst word in her battery of insults. And Bathy, who must have been feeling a little fresh that day, stuck out her tongue at her and said, "I don't give a pig's rear end whether or not you like my pigtails, Settie!"

Her eyes got all narrow and squinty, and she said, "You're illegitimate, you know. You're what's called a bastard baby. Hannah's not your sister. She's your mother. Your father was a radio repairman who came to the house to fix the radio. Nobody knows what became of him. Hannah was a fornicator who brought disgrace on the family. The disgrace was you. Before she died, you know, our mama, God rest her soul, tried to foist you off on me because I was the oldest and the most responsible. But I wouldn't have you. I wouldn't have you in the same house with decent, proper children."

Settie spewed out all the horrid things she could think of to say to her and came to the end of her repertoire quite out of breath and red in the face. Bathy knew that she expected Bathy to run sobbing out of the room, but she wasn't going to give her that satisfaction. Bathy simply looked at her and said, "You don't have *any* children. Maybe it's because your fronts are so big no man wants to stick his thing in you!" She raised her hand as if to strike her, but Bathy ducked and ran off. She was so happy to learn that she had not been foisted off on Settie that she wanted to whoop for joy that she had wound up with Hannah, where she belonged. Nothing really worried her after that. She knew who she was, and was happy where she was.

And if she told Hannah now what Settie had said to her that day, she knew what Hannah would say: "Settie said *that*? My beautiful swan said *that*?" It was best to say nothing to Hannah.

"Your beautiful swan had a mean and nasty streak," she would have to tell her. And what would be accomplished by that?

And after that it didn't take too much research to find out about George Noville—there was a little packet of old letters that Hannah sometimes took out to read. And she even found his name in the Manhattan telephone book, and considered calling him up and introducing herself. Wisely, she had resisted that brief impulse. There was no need to open up old wounds.

And now, sitting on the remains of a stone bench in the ruins of Grandmont, with their respective stories still untold, Bathy suddenly felt incredibly close to Hannah, and somehow she felt that a similar surge of feeling assailed Hannah just then. It was a signal and, obeying it, Bathy quickly reached out and covered Hannah's hand with hers. "We've always been close, Hannah. As close as two women can ever be," she said.

There was a quick sob. "Oh, Bathy!" she said. "Look at us. Two old women. What a waste it's been . . . what a waste . . . all those years . . . where was love . . . ?"

"It wasn't a waste," she said firmly. "Unless all of life is a waste." She put her arm around her shoulders. "You are a Sachs," she said. "I'm a Sachs. That's enough. It's enough for me. Isn't it enough for you?"

"*No!* Sometimes it just isn't."

"Stand tall, woman! Stand tall! Remember the Tower of Pisa. It may lean a little. But it'll never fall down."

She quickly dried her eyes. "You're right," she said. "But there's something I must tell you. I did a terrible thing—an awful thing—a thing I'm still ashamed of. Right after the—the accident, and after they arrested Carol and took her away and put her in that awful place—Riker's Island—I went to see her there. I was so angry with her. Things were going so well, you see—everything was working out, everything was settled—for the company, for everybody. And then she had to go and reach for that gun—the gun I'd given her to protect herself! She told the police she was going to shoot herself, and the others were all struggling with her to get the gun away from her, and that was when it—happened. And all our plans went down the drain. And I was so angry with her that I thought to myself—Well, if she wants to kill herself, I'll help her do it! I was in a rage! Dr. Arnstein gave me the prescription, enough to do it, he assured me. He didn't ask me any questions. He just made me promise to take the druggist's label off the bottle because it would have his name on it. But I did more than that. I emptied the pills into a handkerchief, threw the bottle into the incinerator, tied my hankie in a knot, and put the knotted hankie into my reticule. My plan was to press the knotted hankie into her palm when we shook hands good-bye, and say to her, 'If you really want to kill yourself, Carol, here's a painless way to do it. Under the circumstances, I think that would be best for all concerned.' Can you understand my feelings, Bathy—right after it happened? Can you understand why I'd plan to do a thing like that?"

"Yes. I think I can."

"But then, when they led her out into that room where you can talk, she took my hand, and practically the first words she said to me were, 'Nana, I think you know I didn't *mean* to have that bullet hit Noah. But I wouldn't be telling you the truth if I didn't tell you that there was a moment—oh, just a tiny, fleeting fragment of a moment while we were struggling for the gun— when I actually *wanted* to kill him for what he'd done.' I thought that was very brave of her to say that to me. I thought it was a very courageous thing for her to say— don't you agree?"

"Yes, it was. Very courageous."

"She was standing tall when she said that. And I understood what she meant. I think I'd feel the same way myself in a similar circumstance. You see, she was trying to tell me that she really loved Noah very much. You have to love a person very much to feel such violent emotion when you discover he's betrayed you. If you don't love a person—well, then you don't feel much of anything at all, I guess, except relief, as I did when—but never mind."

"Yes," Bathy said.

"And so the pills and the hankie stayed in my reticule. And I suddenly thought—this was all *Melody*'s fault! If she hadn't come back to the apartment that night, none of this would have happened! Why did she come back?"

"Melody said she wanted to be an actress. Sometimes I think actors aren't real people. They're chameleons— always throwing themselves into roles. Looking for scripts with parts in them to play."

"I think she realized that Noah would never leave Carol and run off with her. She knew she'd lost Noah. And so she wanted to make the loss as unpleasant for Noah as possible. I'm sure that's it. And she certainly succeeded, didn't she?"

"She wanted a confrontation scene for the second act. Actors should learn never to try to write their own lines."

"And so now the company will be Noah's. But it's not the way I wanted it to be. Not the way I planned it."

"Why not, Hannah?"

"I wanted Noah and Carol to run the company together—almost like a team. Carol's got good business sense. And Noah's always seemed to need—"

"A strong woman behind him?"

"Yes!"

"Like you, Hannah?"

"Yes! Or you. But now, without Carol, I can see Noah going flying off, like a kite without a tail. His *Aesop* thing, and—"

"Why do you say he'll be without Carol, Hannah?"

"How could they possibly stay together after this? He hurt her terribly. No woman would stay with a husband who's done that to her—with another woman, and so much younger."

"You did," Bathy said quietly.

She looked momentarily flustered. "Yes, but—but that was different. That was family, and—"

"Isn't this? You see, I think Noah and Carol still love each other. You said it yourself. If she hadn't loved him so much, she wouldn't have reached for the gun. You said yourself that Noah would never have left Carol for Melody."

"You mean you really think that if Carol's acquitted— and after Anne's testimony yesterday, I'm certain she will be—you really think the two of them can patch things up?"

"Look at it this way. Maybe it's not just a question of patching things up. Right now Noah has an ugly scar across his left cheek to show for this. Perhaps that will fade in time. Later, he can claim it was a forceps scar. Or a dueling scar, if he wants to be romantic. But remember, Carol also has a scar—a deeper scar perhaps, and perhaps one that won't go away so quickly. Maybe, in a way, the score is even between them now. Maybe those scars will complement each other, compensate for each other. Maybe those scars will remind them both of how much they owe each other. A tit for a tat."

Hannah still looked dubious. "Well, I hope you're right," she said.

"All we can do is wait and see. But there's one thing I can tell you. I'm not supposed to tell anyone because it's—well, maybe it's a little bit unethical, but I can tell you. Ida Kaminsky called me yesterday. She's reached her verdict."

"*What is it?*"

"That it was an accidental homicide. Carol will be released tomorrow morning. It will be ruled a tragic accident."

"And my—my little *buh-uhd?*"

"One year's probation. Reckless endangerment. Reckless use of a firearm. Something like that. It won't affect her at school. Nobody up there will even need to know about it."

"Well, I suppose that's fair. Anne certainly was— reckless."

"But she wasn't reckless on the stand, was she? I thought she was very poised and clear about exactly what happened. When she said that she snatched the gun from Melody because she was afraid Melody might use it against her mother, that was all the judge needed to hear."

Hannah hesitated. "Of course, I was terrified that something might come up about Noah's—relationship— with that girl."

"But that line of questioning was never pursued, was it?"

"I don't suppose you had anything to do with that, Bathy. *Did* you?"

But Bathy's smile committed her to nothing. "Let's just say it's over, Hannah," she said.

"But why didn't Ida hand down her verdict yesterday? Why is she making Carol spend two more nights in that awful place?"

"It's part of our strategy to keep this out of the press as much as possible. No one from the media was in the courtroom when Anne testified yesterday, so no one in the media knows there's a verdict to be announced tomorrow. With luck, nobody from the media will be in court tomorrow, either. By Wednesday it'll be old news. And in a few weeks the whole thing will be forgotten. Or so we're hoping."

"I see. Miss Fix-It."

"I've tried to do my best," she said. "And Ida's turned out to be a good friend."

"Those Kaminskys always were *nice.*" Suddenly she slapped her thigh. "Wait a minute!" she cried. "I've just had a great idea! What if I made it a condition?"

"Made what a condition?"

"That I won't turn over the company to Noah unless he and Carol promise me that they'll stay together! Promise—*in writing!*"

"Oh, Hannah," Bathy said. "Would you really do a thing like that? And go back on the promise you've already made to him?"

Hannah's shoulders sagged. "Well, maybe you're right. Maybe that isn't such a good idea."

Bathy said nothing. There were times, Bathy had learned over the years, when it was best to let Hannah have the last word. Dealing with Hannah, she'd often found, was a little like playing a game of checkers with a small child, where the trick was learning how to lose quickly.

Hannah stood up abruptly. "Well, I've had it with this place," she said. "Let's get out of here."

Bathy also rose, and the two women started walking slowly together back toward Hannah's car. "Let Noah and Carol work their way through this by themselves," Bathy said. "The way you and Jules did."

"We did that with your help!"

"I'm glad it helped. That's why I decided to become Jules's mistress, because I thought it might help." Bathy circled her mother's waist with her right arm.

Hannah stopped short. In the middle of that barren, vacant, lunar-seeming landscape of unsold building lots where they all used to live, Hannah turned and stared at her. "Wait a minute," she said. "You say *you* decided? I thought *I* decided that!"

Bathy smiled. "Of course, that's what I hoped you'd

think. It made it easier at the time, if it seemed like your decision."

"*Your* decision? You say it was *your* idea?"

"I knew your marriage was in trouble. The whole family was in trouble. I thought if I became Jules's mistress, it might help things. And it did, for quite a few years, didn't it?"

"You mean you weren't in love with Jules?"

"Oh, no. Never. And he was never in love with me. I respected him and he respected me, and I think he needed me in a certain way. But that was all. That was why, after Noah walked in on us that morning, making our—well, making our loveless love—and it was clear that the situation wasn't helping anything anymore—it was so easy for us to stop."

Hannah continued to stare at her. "And all these years," she said, "I thought Jules was the love of your life!"

"You are the love of my life," she said.

Hannah's eyes quickly withdrew, as though she had not heard that last comment. Suddenly she raised a gloved fingertip and pointed past an uneven row of tree stumps. "Look," she said. "I think that's where they were. My dahlia beds."

Bathy's eyes followed in the direction of the pointed finger. "You know something? I think you're absolutely right," she said. "Look, I think I can still see outlines of the little path that ran between the beds. We should have put up a sign along that path and named it Hannah's Way."

22

1995

From the *New York Times:*

Gift of Rare Porcelains
Comes to Met Museum

An anonymous gift of a pair of rare Chinese porcelain vases has been received by the Metropolitan Museum of Art, and was unveiled today.

"We are absolutely thrilled," said Marcia Winburn, the Met's Curator of Decorative Arts, explaining that the vases are from the early K'ang Hsi period (1662–1722), and are in a color known as Lang Yao red, or *sang-de-boeuf* (oxblood). "I hesitate to use the word unique," Ms. Winburn said. "But I am forced to when describing these pieces."

Ms. Winburn was reluctant to put a dollar value on the gift because, she said, no matched examples of pieces like these have ever come on the market. Asked to guess their value, she would only say, "In the high seven figures, if not even higher."

The vases were originally a part of the extensive porcelain collection of the late Truxton Van Degan, a glass manufacturer. And how the vases came to the Museum is as much a mystery as the identity of their present donor.

Originally, Mr. Van Degan's widow reported to police that the vases had been stolen from the couple's Fifth Avenue apartment. Mrs. Van Degan accused members of the life squad who had transferred her husband to St. Luke's hospital after the first of a series of heart attacks which eventually proved fatal.

While assisting her husband, Mrs. Van Degan claimed, the life squad team "had reason to suspect the worth" of the vases, and had managed to spirit the objects into their ambulance while she herself was "totally distraught with concern" over her husband's condition. An insurance investigation was instituted to look into her claim, which was vigorously denied by the life squad team.

But Mr. Van Degan's attorney, Stanley Kornblau, immediately stepped forward and explained that he had personally removed the pieces from the apartment, at the specific bidding of Mr. Van Degan, who had summoned the lawyer to his hospital bedside.

Mr. Kornblau produced signed documents attesting to these instructions, in which he was directed to turn the precious objects over to an unnamed third party. It is this third party, presumably, who is the anonymous donor of the two pieces to the museum.

The reason why it is so rare—indeed, unheard of—to find an identical signed pair of vases such as these, Ms. Winburn pointed out, is that, "According to the Taoist philosophy of the 16th and 17th centuries, the potters believed that one of each pair should be destroyed in order to preserve the immortality of the original design." Therefore, how this pair managed to survive at all is still another mystery.

"Mr. Van Degan had a truly princely collection of Oriental porcelains," Ms. Winburn told The Times. "But these two pieces were definitely the collection's crown jewels."

A Foretaste of More to Come?

The late Mr. Van Degan was president and CEO of Van Degan Glass, now a wholly owned subsidiary of the Ingraham Corporation. And the current gift may prove to be just a foretaste of more that may come to the museum.

In his final will and testament, also executed from his hospital bed in the presence of Mr. Kornblau and other members of his firm, Mr. Van Degan bequeathed his entire porcelain collection to the museum. But this will is currently being contested by Mr. Van Degan's heirs, who include his widow and two sons by former marriages. These three have also instituted lawsuits against each other. Mrs. Van Degan, a onetime Manhattan socialite, is said to be living in seclusion somewhere in the Midwest, and could not be reached for comment. Repeated telephone calls to the Van Degan sons were not returned.

Mr. Van Degan died just hours after executing his will. But, Mr. Kornblau told The Times, "Though he was obviously in considerable pain, Truxton Van Degan was completely lucid when he dictated the final terms of his will. He knew exactly what he was doing, and was very specific about how he wished things left. With the exception of the special designation of that one pair of vases, everything else in the collection was to go to the Metropolitan."

"But," Ms. Winburn said, "with the will in litigation, and with everybody suing everybody else, it may be years before the Van Degan estate is settled—if ever. In the meantime, we don't even dare keep our fingers crossed about the outcome. We are definitely not counting our chickens now. We're just grateful to have received as much as we have."

As for the anonymous donor of the vases, Ms. Winburn said, "We have no idea who it might have been, and since this was clearly the donor's desire, we have no intention of trying to find out.

"In fact, we rather enjoy not knowing the donor's identity. The ceramicist who created these magnificent pieces believed that longevity and even immortality, in both art and life, can be attained through spiritual, and even magical means. In these beautifully preserved objects, it would seem that this belief has been sustained."

"It's a lovely story," he says to her now, putting down the newspaper. "You handled it beautifully."

"Thanks," Carol says. She consults her watch. "But we've really got to be going, Noah. We mustn't keep these people waiting."

He sighs. "No, I suppose not." He stands up slowly. "I guess you know how much I'm dreading this."

"I know. So let's just go and get it over with."

At first it was very hard for him to reconcile the appearance of Melody's parents with her descriptions of them. Paul Richards was a short, slightly built man in his early fifties, with a receding hairline and graying at the temples, and a small mustache. Where was the tall, well-muscled bronzed Adonis that Melody had described? He looked more like what he was—a scholar and translator or, as his letterhead proclaimed him, a foreign affairs officer.

His wife, to Noah, seemed almost incredibly chic. Celeste Richards, slightly taller than her husband, wore a navy Chanel suit with paler blue piping at the collar and cuffs. Her long, dark bangs were parted precisely at the center of her forehead to reveal a perfect oval face and wide, dark eyes.

Noah had not wanted to have this meeting. But we must," Carol said. "They're coming to New York to take her home. We've got to see them after they've come all this way. After all, she was our houseguest. We were supposed to be taking care of her. We were supposed to be—"

"Her surrogate parents."

"Yes."

"At least that's the way we advertised ourselves," he said.

"Yes."

And so then the question became: Where would be the best place to have this meeting? It did not seem quite right, Carol pointed out, to invite Mr. and Mrs. Richards to River House, where it had all happened, even though the apartment was now for sale. To meet them at a restaurant, or in a hotel lobby, or even at a private club, seemed inappropriate as well. Finally Carol had a suggestion. "They have these small, private rooms at Frank Campbell's," she pointed out. "They're more like little sitting rooms, for smaller services, or for families to wait in, before going into the main chapel. Let's see if I can arrange to get us one of those. They're really very pretty, very quiet, very private. . . ."

"I'll see that you have one of what we call our slumber rooms," the man at Campbell's told her.

"Just a small room. There'll only be the four of us. And we won't need it for much more than an hour."

"I know exactly what you want, Mrs. Liebling."

*   *   *

And so that is where the four are sitting now. That morning Carol thought to have two small arrangements of white summer flowers sent over for this room. The people from Campbell's placed them on two Chippendale side tables. In its hermetic stillness, the room smells of lilies and tea roses and a single lighted Rigaud candle.

The afternoon uniform of Campbell's staff—dark flannel trousers and dark blue single-breasted blazers—made them look more like English university dons than mortuary attendants. And after ushering them into this room, the Campbell's man excused himself briefly, and then returned with a small walnut box with a bronze plaque bearing Melody's name and dates. He placed this on a low table in front of the sofa where her parents sat. "We wish her a safe journey home," he said softly. Then he quietly withdrew, closing the door behind him.

Now Melody's mother reaches out and touches the box. Her father does the same, and their fingertips meet, then withdraw.

Carol is the first to speak. "We're both just so terribly sorry," she says. "There's really not much else either of us can say." Without looking at Noah, she says, "We were both terribly fond of Melody. Anne has always been—well, a little flighty and impulsive and high-strung. We liked Melody so much because she seemed to be such a stabilizing influence. We're going to miss her very much. That's just about all I can say."

Celeste Richards says, "Perhaps the way to think of this is as *Kami no Michi,* as the Japanese say. The way of the gods. And in Japan we say, *yao-yorodzu-no-kami.* There are eight hundred myriad deities."

"You speak Japanese?"

"Oh, yes. I teach English three mornings a week at a Japanese school. It's a fascinating culture. Having lived as long as I have in the Far East, I don't think I could ever live anywhere else. Even here, in New York, where I was born, everything seems strange now. Neither Paul nor I can wait to get home."

Noah says, turning to Paul Richards, "I understand you have regular meetings with the emperor at the imperial palace."

Paul Richards looks briefly confused. "No," he says.

"In fact, I don't think there's anybody on the embassy staff, including the ambassador, who's actually met the emperor. Most Japanese have never laid eyes on the emperor and empress. It's not like England. The Japanese royal family almost never appears in public. They're very cloistered. It's part of their mystique."

"I see," Noah says.

"Still, that's part of the excitement of living in that culture," Celeste Richards says. "Unfortunately, our daughter never felt that way. She couldn't wait to come to America. You see, it's been quite a few years since Paul and I have felt really close to our daughter."

"We used to be close," her husband says. "But then, when she was eleven or twelve—"

"She changed."

"It was as though she suddenly grew up too fast. Became an adult too fast."

"She became—so ambitious."

"One minute she was a little girl. And the next minute she was—this ambitious young woman. Almost a stranger to us."

"Or so it seemed," his wife says.

"She was determined to go to school in America."

"And you were opposed?" Noah says.

"Oh, no. We wanted her to choose her own life."

"She told me how she applied for the full scholarship at Ethel Walker," Noah says.

"Scholarship? No, there was no scholarship," Celeste Richards says. "She wanted to go to Ethel Walker because she'd heard it was fashionable. The same thing with Bennington. She wanted to go to school with rich people."

"So ambitious," her husband says again.

"I thought she mentioned—a scholarship," Noah says.

"Perhaps she meant that the State Department paid for her transportation," Paul Richards says. "They often do that for children who want to go to school in America."

"It was a toss-up between Walker and Farmington," his wife says. "We'd applied to both for her. She chose Walker."

"So ambitious."

"To become a great actress, I suppose," Carol says.

"Well, perhaps that was part of it," Melody's mother says. "She wanted success. Fame. Money. Power. All those things. She became a stranger to us. We tried. She was never deprived."

There is a little silence, and the Rigaud candle on the table between them flickers, sputters. Paul Richards sighs. "Still," he says, "it's tough to lose your only child."

Noah studies his fingers. "I thought she mentioned an older sister. Cassie?"

"No, there was only Missy."

"Missy?"

"We named her Melissa. But she complained that there were three other Melissas at her school. So she started calling herself Melody."

"Again, that was when she was eleven or twelve," Paul Richards says.

"I guess she thought the name Melody sounded more—"

"More suitable to the stage?" Carol suggests.

"Well. It was the name she chose for America," Celeste Richards says. "More dramatic perhaps. More unusual. More memorable."

Noah says, "Was there ever a boy named—" But he leaves the question unfinished.

"No, there was only Missy. And we were a very close-knit little family, until she suddenly became so—"

"Ambitious," her husband says. He presses the thumb and forefinger of his left hand against his eyelids.

"Yes," his wife agrees. "She wanted the sun, the moon, the stars, everything. Nothing was ever good enough for her."

Noah turns to Paul. Clearing his throat, he says, "She told me about how you and she used to go scuba diving together."

Celeste Richards laughs softly. "She may have done some scuba diving, but certainly never with Paul. Paul's terrified of the water."

Paul Richards looks sheepish. "I've never learned to swim," he says. "That can be a bit of an embarrassment when you live in a small island nation. I get teased about it."

There is another silence, and then Celeste Richards

rises, smoothing the front of her skirt with the palm of her hand. "I want to take home just one of these," she says. "May I?" And she plucks one small white rosebud from one of the pair of flower arrangements, and drops it into her Chanel bag.

Outside on the street again, Carol says, "Well, we got through that. If we got through that, we can probably get through anything."

"Do you think so?"

"I think so. I hope so. What do you think?"

"I hope so, too. I'm going to try."

"I'm going to try, too. I'm going to try very hard, Noah."

"Thank you, Madame Museum Trustee."

"And thank you, Mr. President and CEO." She tucks one hand into the crook of his elbow. With the other she shades her eyes from the sun. "It's such a pretty day," she says. "Shall we walk back home? After all, sometimes it's just a question of putting one foot after the other, as your father used to say. We can't promise what's going to happen to us, can we? But in the meantime—"

"In the meantime we can walk," he says.

And so the clock ticks on, and our story comes to no real end here. Daylight fades into dusk, and night brightens into dawn, as the days pass, and the years rise up swiftly and speed on, and the earth spins on its axis and makes its endless circlings of the sun. The past moves relentlessly forward with us at the same speed and leaves us in its shadow, never moving away, but never quite catching up, and men and women circle each other, reach out, touch hands, draw apart, make love, and draw apart again. And in these tireless circles, we wonder why we care. All we know is that we do care.

Yes, that's enough.